2027.

The date made him suck air through his teeth.

He pushed the door open. Outside, it was cool and dark, a few men and women on the sidewalks bundled up against the chill, walking purposefully, the way people did in this residential neighborhood. There was no one loitering and no bus.

His mobile phone was in his pocket where he kept it during the day to trade baby calls with Nancy. He entered the number.

"Hello, Mr. Piper." The voice was upbeat, borderline jocular.

"Who is this?" Will asked protectively.

"It's Henry Spence. From the motor home. Thanks for returning my message so promptly."

"What do you want?"

"I want to talk to you."

"About what?"

"2027 and other topics."

"I don't think that's a good idea." Will was fast-walking to the corner to see if he could spot the bus.

"I hate to be clichéd, Mr. Piper, but this is urgent, a life-and-death matter."

"Whose death?"

"Mine. I have ten days to live. Please grant a soon-to-be-dead man's wish and speak to me."

By Glenn Cooper

BOOK OF SOULS
SECRET OF THE SEVENTH SON

GLENN COOPER

BOOK OF SOULS

HARPER

An Imprint of HarperCollins*Publishers*

This is a work of fiction. Names, characters, places, and incidents are products of the author's imagination or are used fictitiously and are not to be construed as real. Any resemblance to actual events, locales, organizations, or persons, living or dead, is entirely coincidental.

HARPER

An Imprint of HarperCollins*Publishers*
10 East 53rd Street
New York, New York 10022-5299

Copyright © 2010 by Glenn Cooper
ISBN 978-0-06-172180-9

First Harper paperback printing: April 2010

HarperCollins ® and Harper ® are registered trademarks of Harper-Collins Publishers.

Printed in the United States of America

Visit Harper paperbacks on the World Wide Web at
www.harpercollins.com

10 9 8 7 6 5 4 3 2 1

Acknowledgments

My continued thanks to Steve Kasdin. Without his "divine intervention," *Secret of the Seventh Son* and *Book of Souls* might not have come to fruition. Also thanks to my first reader, Gunilla Lacoche, for her insightful comments, and to my terrific editor at Harper, Lyssa Keusch, and to the entire publishing team at HarperCollins. And, as always, thanks to Tessa and Shane for propping me up on the home front.

PROLOGUE

After thirty-odd years in the rare-books business, Toby Parfitt found that the only time he could reliably and deliciously muster a frisson of excitement was the moment when he would delicately stick his hands into a packing crate fresh from the loading dock.

The intake-and-catalogue room of Pierce & Whyte Auctions was in the basement, deeply insulated from the rumbling traffic of London's Kensington High Street. Toby was content to be in the silence of this comfortable old workroom, with its smooth oak tables, swan-neck lamps, and nicely padded stools. The only noise was the pleasant rustling of handfuls of shredded packing paper as he scooped them out and binned them, then, disconcertingly, asthmatic breathing and a thin-chested wheeze intruded.

He looked up at the blemished face of Peter Nieve and grudgingly acknowledged him with a perfunctory bob of his head. The pleasure of discovery would, alas, be tainted. He couldn't tell the youth to bugger off, could he?

"I was told the lot from Cantwell Hall was in," Nieve said.

"Yes. I've just opened the first crate."

"All fourteen arrived, I hope."

"Why don't you have a count to make sure?"

"Will do, Toby."

The informality was a killer. Toby! No Mr. Parfitt. No sir. Not even Alistair. Toby, the name his friends used. Times had certainly changed—for the worse—but he couldn't summon the strength to buck the tide. If a second-year associate felt empowered to call the Director of Antiquarian Books, Toby, then he would stoically bear it. Qualified help was hard to find, and young Nieve, with his solid second in Art History from Manchester, was the best that £20,000 could buy nowadays. At least the young man was able to find a clean shirt and a tie every day, though his collars were too generous for his scrawny neck, making his head look like it was stuck onto his torso with a dowel.

Toby ground his molars at the deliberate and childlike counting-out-loud to fourteen. "All here."

"I'm so glad."

"Martin said you'd be pleased with the haul."

Toby rarely made house calls anymore. He left them to Martin Stein, his Deputy Director. In truth, he loathed the countryside and had to be dragged, kicking and screaming, out of town. On occasion, a client would have some real gems, and Pierce & Whyte would try to wheedle itself in to snatch business away from Christie's or Sotheby's. "Believe me," he assured his Managing Director, "if I get wind of a Second Folio or a good Brontë or Walter Raleigh out there in the provinces, I will descend on it at warp speed, even if it's in Shropshire." From what he was led to understand, Cantwell had a trove of fair to middling material, but Stein had indeed told him he would enjoy the diversity of the consignment.

Lord Cantwell was typical of their clientele, an elderly anachronism struggling to maintain his crumbling country estate by periodically selling off bits of furniture, paintings, books, and silver to keep the taxman at bay and the pile from falling down. The old boy sent his really good pieces to one of the major houses, but Pierce & Whyte's reputation for books, maps, and autographs put it in leading position to land this slice of Cantwell's business.

Toby reached his hand into the inside pocket of his form-fitted Chester Barrie suit and extracted his thin white-cotton specimen gloves. Decades earlier, his boss had steered him to his Savile Row tailor, and, ever since, he had clothed himself in the best fabrics he could afford. Clothes mattered, and so did grooming. His bristling moustache was always perfectly trimmed, and visits to his barber every Tuesday lunchtime kept his gray-tinged hair unfailingly neat.

He slid on the gloves like a surgeon and hovered over the first exposed binding. "Right. Let's see what we have."

The top row of spines revealed a matched set. He plucked out the first book. "Ah! All six volumes of Freeman's *History of the Norman Conquest of England*—1877–1879, if I recall." He opened the cloth cover to the title page. "Excellent! First edition. Is it a matched set?"

"All firsts, Toby."

"Good, good. They should go for six hundred to eight hundred. You often get mixed sets, you know."

He laid out all six books carefully, taking note of their condition before diving back into the crate. "Here's something a bit older." It was a fine old Latin Bible, Antwerp, 1653, with a rich, worn, calf binding and gilt ridges on the spine. "This is nice," he cooed. "I'd say one fifty to two hundred."

He was less enthusiastic about the next several volumes, some later editions of Ruskin and Fielding in dodgy condition, but he grew quite excited at Fraser's *Journal of a Tour Through Part of the Snowy Range of the Himala*

Mountains, and to the Source of the Rivers Jumna and Ganges, 1820, a pristine first. "I haven't seen one of these in this state for years! Marvelous! Three thousand, easily. My spirits are lifting. Tell me, there wouldn't be any incunabula in the collection?" From the perplexed expression on the youth's face, Toby knew he was tapping a dry hole. "Incunabula? European printed books? Pre-1501? Ring a bell?" The young man was clearly stung by Toby's irritability, and he flushed in embarrassment. "Oh, right. Sorry. No incunabula whatsoever. There *was* something on the oldish side, but it was handwritten." He pointed helpfully into the crate. "There it is. His granddaughter wasn't keen on parting with it."

"Whose granddaughter?"

"Lord Cantwell. She had an unbelievable body."

"We don't, as a habit, make reference to our client's bodies," Toby said sternly, reaching for the broad spine of the book.

It was remarkably heavy; he needed two hands to drag it out securely and lay it on the table.

Even before he opened it, he felt his pulse race and the moisture dissipate from his mouth. There was something about this large, dense book that spoke loudly to his instincts. The bindings were smooth old calf leather, mottled, the color of good milk chocolate. It had a faintly fruited smell, redolent of ancient mold and damp. The dimensions were prodigious, eighteen inches long, twelve inches wide, and a good five inches thick: a couple of thousand pages, to be sure. As to weight, he imagined hoisting a two-kilo bag of sugar. This was much heavier. The only markings were on the spine, a large simple hand-tooled engraving, incised deeply into the leather: 1527.

He was surprised, in a detached way, to see his right hand trembling when he reached out to lift the cover. The spine was supple from use. No creaking. There was a plain, unadorned, creamy endpaper glued onto the hide. There was no frontispiece, no title page. The first page of the book, the color of butter, roughly uneven to the touch, began without exposition, racing into a closely spaced handwritten scrawl. Quill and black ink. Columns and rows. At least a hundred names and dates. He blinked in a large amount of visual information before turning the page. And another. And another. He skipped to the middle. Checked several pages toward the end. Then the last page. He tried to do a quick mental calculation, but because there was no pagination, he was only guessing—there must have been well over a hundred thousand listed names from front to back.

"Remarkable," he whispered.

"Martin didn't know what to make of it. Thought it was some sort of town registry. He said you might have some ideas."

"I've got lots of them. Unfortunately, they don't hang together. Look at the pages." He lifted one clear of the others. This isn't paper, you know. It's vellum, very-high-quality stuff. I can't be sure, but I think it's uterine vellum, the crème de la crème. Unborn-calf skin, soaked, limed, scudded, and stretched. Typically used in the finest illuminated manuscripts, not a bloody town registry."

He flipped pages, making comments and pointing here and there with his gloved forefinger. "It's a chronicle of births and deaths. Look at this one: Nicholas Amcotts 13 1 1527 Natus. Seems to announce that a Nicholas Amcotts was born on the thirteenth of January 1527. Straightforward enough. But look at the next one. Same date, Mors, a death, but these are Chinese characters. And the next one, another death, Kaetherlin Banwartz, surely a Germanic name, and this one here. If I'm not mistaken, this is in Arabic."

In a minute, he had found Greek, Portuguese, Italian, French, Spanish, and English names, and multiple foreign words in Cyrillic, Hebrew, Swahili, Greek, Chinese. There were some languages he could only guess at. He muttered something about African dialects.

He pressed his gloved fingertips together in contemplation. "What kind of town has this population diversity, not to mention this population density in 1527? And what about this vellum? And this rather primitive binding? The impression here is something quite a bit older than sixteenth-century. It's got a decidedly medieval feel to it."

"But it's dated 1527."

"Well, yes. Duly noted. Still, that is my impression, and I do not discount my gut feelings, nor should you. I think we will have to obtain the views of academic colleagues."

"What's it worth?"

"I've no idea. Whatever it is, it's a specialty item, a curiosity, quite unique. Collectors like uniqueness. Let's not worry too much about value at this stage. I think we will do well by this piece." He carefully carried the book to the far end of the table and put it on its own spot away from the others, a pride of place. "Let's sort through the rest of the Cantwell material, shall we? You'll be busy entering the lot into the computer. And when you're done, I want you to turn every page in every book to look for letters, autographs, stamps, et cetera. We don't want to give our customers freebies, do we?"

In the evening, with young Nieve long gone, Toby returned to the basement. He passed quickly by the whole of the Cantwell collection, which was laid out on three long tables. For the moment, those volumes held no more interest to him than a load of old *Hello!* magazines. He went straight for the book that had occupied his thoughts all day and slowly laid his ungloved hands on its smooth leather. In the future, he would insist that at that moment he felt some kind of physical connection with the inanimate object, a sentiment unbefitting a man with no inclination to this kind of drivel.

"What are you?" he asked out loud. He made doubly sure he was alone since he imagined that talking to books might be career-limiting at Pierce & Whyte. "Why don't you tell me your secrets?"

Will Piper was never much for crying babies, especially his own. He had a vague recollection of crying-baby number one a quarter of a century earlier. In those days he was a young deputy sheriff in Florida, pulling the worst shifts. By the time he got home in the morning, his infant daughter was already up-and-at-'em, doing her happy-baby routine. When he and his wife did spend a night together, and Laura cried out, he'd whine himself, then drift back to sleep before Melanie had the bottle out of the warmer. He didn't do diapers. He didn't do feedings. He didn't do crying. And he was gone for good before Laura's second birthday.

But that was two marriages and one lifetime ago, and he was a changed man, or so he told himself. He'd allowed himself to be molded into something of a twenty-first-century metrosexual New York father with all the trappings of the station. If, in the past, he could attend crime scenes and prod at decomposing flesh, he could change a diaper. If he could conduct an interview through the sobs of a victim's mother, he could deal with crying.

It didn't mean he had to like it.

There had been a succession of new phases in his life, and he was a month into the newest, an amalgam of retirement and unfiltered fatherhood. It had been only sixteen months from the day he abruptly retired from the FBI to the day Nancy abruptly returned to work after maternity leave. And now, for at least brief stretches of time, he was left on his own with his son, Phillip Weston Piper. Their budget didn't allow for more than thirty hours per week of nanny time, so for a few hours a day he had to fly solo.

As lifestyle changes went, this was fairly dramatic. For much of his twenty years at the FBI, he'd been a top-of-the-heap profiler, one of the most accomplished serial-killer hunters of his era. If it hadn't been for what he charitably called his personal peccadilloes, he might have gone out large, with accolades and a nice postretirement gig as a criminal-justice consultant.

But his weaknesses for booze and women and his stubborn lack of ambition torpedoed his career and fatefully led him to the infamous Doomsday case. To the world, the case was still unsolved, but he knew better. He'd broken it, and it had broken him in return.

Its legacy was forced early retirement, a negotiated cover-up, and reams of confidentiality agreements. He got out with his life—barely.

On the bright side, fate also led him to Nancy, his young Doomsday partner, and she had given him his first son, a six-month-old, who sensed the rift when Nancy closed the apartment door closed behind her and had started to work his diaphragm.

Mercifully, Phillip Weston Piper's high-pitched squall was squelched by rocking, but it abruptly resumed when Will put him back in his crib. Will hoped beyond hope that little Phillip would burn himself out and slowly backed out of the bedroom. He put the living-room TV onto cable news and tweaked the volume to harmonically modulate the nails-on-chalkboard squeal of his offspring.

Even though he was chronically sleep-deprived, Will's head was awfully clear these days, thanks to his self-imposed separation from his pal, Johnnie Walker. He kept the ceremonial last half-gallon bottle of Black Label, three-quarters full, in the cabinet under the TV. He wasn't going to be the kind of ex-drunk who had to purge the place of alcohol. He visited with the bottle sometimes, winked at it, sparred with it, had a little chat with it. He taunted it more than it taunted him. He didn't do AA or "talk to someone." He didn't even stop drinking! He had a couple of beers or a generous glass of wine fairly regularly, and he even got buzzed on an empty stomach. He simply prohibited himself from touching the nectar—smoky, beautiful, amber—his love, his nemesis. He didn't care what the textbooks said about addicts and abstinence. He was his own man, and he had promised himself and his new bride that he wouldn't do the falling-down-drunk thing again.

He sat on the sofa with his large hands lying dumbly on his bare thighs. He was set to go, kitted out in jogging shorts, T-shirt, and sneakers. The nanny was late again. He felt trapped, claustrophobic. He was spending way too much time in this little parquet-floored prison cell. Despite best intentions, something was going to have to give. He was trying to do the right thing and honor his commitments and all that, but every day he grew more restless. New York had always irritated him. Now it was overtly nauseating.

The buzzer saved him from darkness. A minute later, the nanny-troll, as he called her (not to her face), arrived, launching into an attack on public transport rather than an apology. Leonora Monica Nepomuceno, a four-foot-ten-inch Filipina, threw her carrier bag on the kitchenette counter, then went right for the crying baby, pressing his tense little body against her incongruously large breasts. The woman, who he guessed was in her fifties, was so physically unattractive that when Will and Nancy first learned her nickname, Moonflower, they laughed themselves to exhaustion. "Ay, ay," she crooned to the boy, "your auntie Leonora is here. You can stop your crying now."

"I'm going for a run," Will announced through a scowl.

"Go for a long one, Mister Will," Moonflower advised.

A daily run had become part of Will's postretirement routine, a component of his new-man ethos. He was leaner and stronger than he had been in years, only ten pounds heavier than his football-playing weight at Harvard. He was on the brink of fifty, but he was looking younger thanks to his no-scotch diet. He was big and athletic, with a strong jaw, boyishly thick tawny hair, and crazy blue eyes, and clad in nylon jogging shorts, he turned women's heads, even young ones'. Nancy still wasn't used to that.

On the sidewalk, he realized the Indian summer was over, and it was going to be uncomfortably chilly. While he stretched his calves and Achilles tendons against a signpost, he thought about shooting back upstairs for a warm-up suit.

Then he saw the bus on the other side of East 23rd Street. It started up and belched some diesel exhaust.

Will had spent the better part of twenty years following and observing. He knew how to make himself inconspicuous. The guy in the bus didn't, or didn't care. He had noticed the rig the previous evening, driving slowly past his building at maybe five miles per hour, jamming traffic, provoking a chorus of honks. It was hard to miss, a top-of-the-line Beaver, a big royal blue forty-three-footer with slides, splashed out in gray and crimson swooshes. He had thought to himself, who the hell takes a half-a-million-dollar motor home into lower Manhattan and drives around slow, looking for an address? If he found it, where was he going to park the thing? But it was the license plate that rang bells.

Nevada. Nevada!

Now it looked like the guy had indeed found adequate parking the night before, across the street just to the east of Will's building, an impressive feat, to be sure. Will's heart started to beat at jogging speed even though he was still stationary. He had stopped looking over his shoulder months ago.

Apparently, that was a mistake. Gimme a break, he thought. *Nevada plates.*

Still, this didn't have their signature. The watchers weren't going to come at him in a half-baked-Winnebago battle-wagon. If they ever decided to pluck him off the streets, he'd never see it coming. They were pros, for Christ's sake.

It was a two-way street, and the bus was pointed west. All Will had to do was run east toward the river, make a few quick turns, and the bus would never catch up. But then he wouldn't know if he was the object of somebody's exercise, and he didn't like not knowing. So he ran west. Slowly. Making it easy for the guy.

The bus slid out of its space and followed along. Will picked up the pace, partly to see how the bus responded, partly to get warm. He got to the intersection of 3rd Avenue and jogged in place, waiting for the light. The bus was a hundred feet behind, stacked up by a line of taxis. He shielded his eyes from the sun. Through the windshield he made out at least two men. The driver had a beard.

On the go again, he ran through the intersection and weaved through the sparse pedestrian sidewalk traffic. Over his shoulder, he saw the bus was still following west along 23rd, but that wasn't much of a test. That came at Lexington, where he took a left and ran south. Sure enough, the bus turned too.

Getting warmer, Will thought, getting warmer.

His destination was Gramercy Park, a leafy rectangular enclave a few blocks downtown. Its perimeter streets were all one-ways. If he was still being tailed, he'd have a bit of fun.

Lexington dead-ended at 21st Street at the park, where 21st ran one way west. Will ran east, along the outside of the park fence. The bus had to follow the traffic pattern in the opposite direction.

Will started doing clockwise laps around the park's perimeter, each lap taking only a couple of minutes. Will could see that the bus driver was struggling with the tight left turns, nearly clipping parked cars at the corners.

There wasn't anything remotely funny about being followed, but Will couldn't help being amused every time the giant motor home passed him on its counterclockwise circuit. With each encounter, he got a better look at his pursuers. They failed to strike fear in his heart, but you never knew. These clowns definitely weren't watchers. But there were other sorts of problem children out there. He'd put a lot of killers in jail. Killers had families. Vengeance was a family affair.

The driver was an older fellow, with longish hair and a full beard the color of fireplace ash. His fleshy face and ballooned-out shoulders suggested a heavy man. The man in the shotgun seat was tall and thin, also on the senior side, with wide-open eyes that furtively engaged Will sidelong. The driver stiffly refused to make eye contact altogether, as if he actually believed they hadn't been made.

On his third circuit, Will spotted two NYPD cops on walking patrol on 20th Street. Gramercy Park was an exclusive neighborhood; it was the only private park in Manhattan.

The residents of the surrounding buildings had their own keys to the wrought-iron gates, and the police were visible around there, prowling for muggers and creeps. Will pulled up, breathing heavily. "Officers. That bus over there. I saw it stop. The driver was hassling a little girl. I think he was trying to get her inside."

The cops listened, deadpan. His flat Southern drawl played havoc with his credibility. He got a lot of those out-of-town looks in New York. "You sure about that?"

"I'm cx-FBI."

Will watched for a short while only. The cops stood smack in the middle of the street and halted the bus with hand waving. Will didn't stick around. He was curious, sure, but he wanted to get over to the river for his usual circuit. Besides, he had a feeling he'd see these geezers again.

To be on the safe side, when he got back home, he'd take his gun out of the dresser and oil it up.

Will was grateful he had chores and obligations to occupy himself. In the early afternoon, he made the rounds to the grocer, the butcher, and the wine merchant without a single sighting of the big blue bus. He slowly and methodically chopped the vegetables, ground the spices, and browned the meat, filling the postage-stamp kitchenette and the whole apartment with Piper's trademark chili smoke. It was the only dish that was foolproof in his hands, dinner-party safe.

Phillip was napping when Nancy came home. Will shushed her then gave her a first-year-of-marriage hug, the kind where the hands wander.

"When did Moonflower leave?"

"An hour ago. He's been asleep."

"I missed him so much." She tried to pull away. "I want to see him!"

"What about me?"

"He's numero uno. You're numero dos."

He followed her into the bedroom and watched as she bent over the crib and kicked off her shoes. He'd noticed this before, but it really struck him at that moment: she had developed a serenity, a mature womanly beauty that, frankly, had snuck up on him. He impishly reminded her regularly that when they were first thrown together on the Doomsday case, she hadn't exactly make him woozy with desire. She was on the plump side at the time, in the throes of freshman syndrome—new job, high stress, bad habits, and the like. Candidly, Will was always more of a lingerie-model sort of a guy. As an adolescent high-school football star, he had been imprinted with the body image of cheerleaders the way a duckling is imprinted by a mother duck. All his life, he saw a great body, he tried to follow it.

Truth be told, he never thought about Nancy in a romantic way until a crash diet turned her into more of an hourglass. So I'm shallow, he would have admitted if anyone called him on it. But early on, looks weren't the only impediment to romance. He also had to introduce her to cynicism. At first, her fresh-out-of-the-academy gung ho, eager-to-please personality sickened him, like a stomach virus. But he was a good and patient teacher, and under his tutelage she learned to question authority, play loose with the bureaucracy, and generally sail close to the rocks.

One day, bogged down by the impossibility of the Doomsday case, he realized that this woman was doing it for him, punching all her buttons. She had gotten really pretty. He came to find her smallness sexy, the way he could envelop her in his arms and legs, almost making her disappear. He liked the silky texture of her brown hair, the way she blushed all the way down to her breastbone, her giggle when they made love. She was smart and sassy. Her encyclopedic knowledge of art and culture was intriguing, even to a man whose idea of culture was a Spider-Man movie. To top it off, he even liked her parents.

He was ready to fall in love.

Then Area 51 and the Library entered his consciousness and sealed the deal. It made him think about his life, about settling down.

Nancy handled the pregnancy like a champ, eating healthy, exercising every day, almost right up to delivery. Postpartum, she quickly shed pounds and got herself back to fighting form. She was hell-bent on maintaining her physique and erasing motherhood as a career issue. She knew the Bureau couldn't openly discriminate against her, but she wanted to make certain she wouldn't be treated, even subtly, like a second-class citizen, flailing ineffectively in the musky testosterone pool of striving young men.

The end result of all this physical and emotional flux was a maturation of mind and body. She returned to work stronger and more confident, emotionally like marble, solid and cool. As she would inform her friends, husband and infant were both behaving, and all was good.

To hear Nancy tell it, falling in love with Will had been utterly predictable. His hunky, dangerous bad-boyishness was as alluring as a bug zapper to a moth and just as deadly. But Nancy was not going to let herself be incinerated. She was too tough and savvy. She had gotten comfortable with the age difference—seventeen years—but not the attitude difference. She could happily deal with the naughtiness. But she refused to permanently hook up with a Wrecking Ball, the sobriquet Will's daughter, Laura, had bestowed on him in honor of years of destroyed marriages and relationships.

She didn't know or much care if his heavy drinking was a cause or an effect, but it was toxic, and he had to promise it would stop. He had to promise to be faithful. He had to promise to let her develop her career. He had to promise to let them stay in New York at least until she could get a transfer to someplace that floated both their boats. He didn't have to promise to be a good father; she had a sense that wasn't going to be a problem.

Then she accepted his marriage proposal, her fingers crossed.

While Nancy napped with the baby, Will finished the dinner prep and celebrated with a small Merlot to wet his whistle. The rice was steaming, the table was set and right on time, his daughter and son-in-law arrived.

Laura was just beginning to show, all beaming and radiant. She looked like a willowy free spirit, a latter-day hippie in a gauzy dress and thigh-high boots. In truth, he thought, she looked a lot like her mother a generation ago. Greg was in town covering a story for the *Washington Post*. There was a hotel room on the company's nickel, and Laura was tagging along for a break from her second novel. Her first, *The Wrecking Ball,* loosely based on her parents' divorce, was selling modestly to good reviews.

For Will, the book still stung, and as a kicker, whenever he looked at his copy, proudly displayed on an end table, he couldn't help thinking about its role in cracking the Doomsday case. He'd shake his head and get a faraway look in his eyes, and Nancy would know where his mind was straying.

Will picked up on Greg's moodiness before he was over the threshold and shoved a glass of wine into his paw. "Cheer up," Will told him, as soon as Laura and Nancy slipped into the bedroom for some baby time. "If I can do it, you can do it."

"I'm fine."

He didn't look fine. Greg always had a lean and hungry look, caved-in cheeks, angular nose, sharply dimpled chin, the kind of face that cast shadows on itself. It didn't look like he ever ran a comb through his hair. Will always thought he was a caricature of a beat reporter, caffeined-up and sleep-deprived, taking himself way too seriously. Still, he was a good guy. When Laura got pregnant, he stepped up to the plate and married her, no questions, no drama. Two Piper weddings in one year. Two babies.

The men sat. Will asked what he was working on. Greg monotoned about some forum on climate change he was covering, and both of them got bored quickly. Greg was in early-career doldrums. He hadn't found a big story yet, one he could latch onto to change his oblique trajectory. Will was well aware of this when Greg finally asked, "So Will, last time I checked, nothing ever materialized on the Doomsday case."

"Nope. Nothing."

"Never got solved."

"Nope. Never."

"The killings just stopped."

"Yep. They did."

"Don't you find that unusual?"

He shrugged. "I've been out of it for over a year."

"You never told me what happened. Why they took you off the case. Why they had a warrant out for you. How it all got resolved."

"You're right. I never did." He got up. "If I don't stir that rice, we're going to need chisels." He left Greg behind in the living room to glumly finish his wine.

Over dinner, Laura was ebullient. Her hormones were in fine fettle, stoked by holding Phillip in her arms and imagining her own. She ladled heaping spoonfuls of chili into her mouth and in between was gabby. "How's Dad doing with retirement?"

"He's lost momentum," Nancy observed.

"I'm sitting right here. Why don't you ask me?"

"Okay, Dad, how're you doing with retirement."

"I've lost momentum."

"See?" Nancy laughed. "He was doing so well."

"How many museums and concerts can a man stand?"

"What kind of man?" Nancy asked.

"A real one who wants to go fishing."

Nancy was exasperated. "Then go to Florida! Go fishing in the Gulf for a week! We'll get the nanny to do more hours."

"What if they want you to do overtime?"

"They've got me on identity theft, Will. I'm just online all day. There's no chance of overtime till they put me back on real cases."

Will changed the subject, petulant. "I want to go every day, whenever I want."

She stopped smiling. "You just want us to move."

Laura kicked Greg under the table, his cue. "Do you miss it, Will?" he asked.

"Miss what?"

"Working. The FBI."

"Hell no. I miss fishing."

He cleared his throat. "Have you ever thought about writing a book?"

"About what?"

"About all your serial killers," then off Will's piercing stare, he quickly added, "except Doomsday!"

"Why would I want to revisit that crap?"

"They were infamous cases, popular history. People are fascinated."

"History! I think it's sordid crap. Besides, I can't write."

"Ghost it. Your daughter writes. I write. We think it'll sell."

Will got angry. If he'd been drunk, he would have exploded, but the new Will just frowned and deliberately shook his head. "You guys need to make your own way. I'm not a meal ticket."

Nancy slapped his arm. "Will!"

"That's not what Greg was saying, Dad!"

"No?" The apartment buzzer went off. Will pushed himself out of his chair and hit the intercom button hard with irritation. "Hello?" There was no response. "Hello?" The buzzer went off again. And again. "What the hell."

Will angrily rode the elevator down to the lobby and peered at the empty vestibule. Before he could jump onto the street for a look-about, he saw a business card stuck at eye level onto the lobby door with a piece of tape.

THE 2027 CLUB. HENRY SPENCE, PRESIDENT. And a phone number with a 702 area code. Las Vegas. There was a handwritten note in small block letters: Mr. Piper, Please call me immediately.

2027.

The date made him suck air through his teeth.

He pushed the door open. Outside, it was cool and dark, a few men and women on the sidewalks bundled up against the chill, walking purposefully, the way people did in this residential neighborhood. There was no one loitering and no bus.

His mobile phone was in his pocket, where he kept it during the day to trade baby calls with Nancy. He entered the number.

"Hello, Mr. Piper." The voice was upbeat, borderline jocular.

"Who is this?" Will asked.

"It's Henry Spence. From the motor home. Thanks for returning my message so promptly."

"What do you want?"

"I want to talk to you."

"About what?"

"About 2027 and other topics."

"I don't think that's a good idea." Will was fast-walking to the corner to see if he could spot the bus.

"I hate to be clichéd, Mr. Piper, but this is urgent, a life-and-death matter."

"Whose death?"

"Mine. I have ten days to live. Please grant a soon-to-be-dead man's wish and speak to me."

Will waited until his daughter had left, the dishes were done, and his wife and son were asleep before he slipped out of the apartment to rendezvous with the man on the bus.

He zipped his bomber jacket to his throat, stuffed his hands into his jeans for warmth, and paced back and forth, second-guessing the wisdom of humoring this Henry Spence fellow. Out of an abundance of caution, he had slung his holster over his shoulder and was getting reacquainted with the weight of steel over his heart. The sidewalk was empty and dark, and despite scattered traffic, he felt alone and vulnerable. A sudden siren from an ambulance navigating toward Bellevue Hospital startled him and he could feel the butt of the gun tight against his jacket lining, heaving with his accelerated breathing.

Just as he was about to bag the whole thing, the bus arrived and slowed to a halt, its air brakes sighing. The passenger door opened with an hydraulic whoosh, and Will found himself staring at a bushy face high in the driver's seat.

"Good evening, Mr. Piper," the driver called down.

There was a shadow of activity from the rear.

"That's just Kenyon. He's harmless. Come on board."

Will climbed up, stood next to the passenger seat, and

tried to get a snapshot of the situation. It was a habit from the old days. He liked to swoop onto a new crime scene and suck it all in like a giant vacuum cleaner, trying to see everything at once.

There were two men, the heavyset driver and a beanpole bracing himself against the kitchen counter midway up the rig. The driver, who seemed to be in his sixties, had the physique of a man who could fill a Santa suit without padding. He had a generous beard the color of squirrel fur, which spilled onto a Pendleton shirt and lay inanimate between a set of brown suspenders. He had a full head of gray-white hair, long enough for a ponytail, but he allowed it to flow over his collar. His skin tone was blotchy and slapped-cheek, his eyes tired and cloudy. But crinkle lines radiating from his eyes suggested a bygone sprightliness.

Then there were his appliances. Pale green plastic tubes wrapped around his neck and plunged into his nostrils through prongs. The tubing snaked down his side and plugged into an ivory white box, which was softly chugging at his feet. The man was on oxygen.

The other fellow, Kenyon, was also in his sixties. He was mostly skin and bones wrapped in a buttoned-up sweater. He was tall, awkward in posture, conservative in manner, clean-cut with crisply parted hair, jaw-jutting intensity, and the unapologetic eyes of a military man or a missionary or, a fervent believer in—something.

The inside of the bus was pure recreational-vehicle eye candy, a box car of rolling opulence, black-marble tiles, polished maple-burl cabinets, white and black upholstery, flat-paneled video screens, cool recessed lighting. At the rear was a master suite, the bed unmade. There were dirty dishes in the sink and the lingering smell of onions and sausages in the cabin. The place looked lived-in, a road trip in progress. There were maps, books, and magazines on the dining-room table, shoes and slippers and balls of socks on the floor, baseball caps and jackets strewn on chairs.

Will's instant take was that he wasn't in danger. He could safely play this out for a while to see where it went.

A car honked. Then another.

"Have a seat," Spence said. His elocution was rounded and earnest. "New Yorkers aren't the most patient folks." Will obliged and sat on the passenger seat as Spence shut the door and lurched forward. At the risk of toppling, the tall man folded himself onto the sofa.

"Where are we going?" Will asked.

"I'm going to drive around in some sort of geometric pattern. You can't imagine the complexities of parking this behemoth in New York."

"It's been extremely challenging," the other man added. "My name is Alf Kenyon. We are very pleased to meet you, sir, even though you almost got us arrested this morning."

While he didn't feel threatened, Will wasn't feeling comfortable either. "What's this about?" he asked sharply.

Spence slowed and braked at the red light. "We share an interest in Area 51, Mr. Piper. That's what this is about."

Will kept his voice even. "Can't say I've ever been there."

"Well, it's not much to look at—aboveground at least," Spence said. "Belowground is another story."

But Will wasn't going to take the bait. "Is that right?" The light changed, and Spence headed uptown. "How's the mileage on this thing?"

"Is that what you're curious about, Mr. Piper? The mileage?"

Will worked his neck muscles to keep both men safely

in view. "Look, fellows, I don't have a clue what you know about me or what you think you know. Let's just say for the record that I don't know jack shit about Area 51. My guess is you're lucky if you get five miles per gallon, so I can save you some money by getting off here and walking home."

Kenyon was quick to respond. "We're sure you've signed confidentiality agreements. We've also signed them. We're as vulnerable as you. We have families too. We know what they're capable of. That puts us on equal footing."

Spence chimed in. "We'll be in each other's hands. I don't have much time. Please help us."

The traffic on Broadway was light. Will liked being high up, observing the city from a throne chair. He was detached from New York; he wanted no part of it anymore. He imagined commandeering the bus, tossing these men out on their ears, swinging back to pick up Nancy and his son and driving south until the sparkling aquamarine waters of the Gulf of Mexico filled the giant windshield. "What is it you think I can do for you?"

Spence answered, "We want to know the significance of 2027. We want to understand what's so special about February 9. We want to know what happens on February 10. We think you also want to know these things."

"You must want to know!" Kenyon added emphatically.

Of course he did. He thought about it every time he watched his son sleeping in his crib, every time he made love to his wife. The horizon. It wasn't so far away, was it? Less than seventeen years. In a blink, it would be there. He'd be there too. He was BTH, beyond the horizon.

"Your card said The 2027 Club. How do you get into that club?"

"You're already in it."

"That's funny, I don't recall getting my membership in the mail."

"Everyone who knows about the Library is a member. De facto."

Will was clenching his jaw hard enough to ache. "All right. Enough. Why don't you tell me who you are?"

Over the next hour Will lost track of their route. He was vaguely aware of moving through Times Square, Columbus Circle, passing the dark, sprawling Natural History Museum, looping through Central Park a few times, the wide tires of the bus sending showers of brittle leaves shooting through the night air. He was listening so hard the city almost disappeared.

At Princeton, Henry Spence had been a prodigy among prodigies, a teenager with an advanced case of precociousness. It was the early sixties, the Cold War in full bloom, and unlike many of his peers who applied their intellectual horsepower to the natural sciences, Henry immersed himself in foreign languages and politics. He mastered Mandarin and Japanese and had serviceable skills in Russian. He minored in international relations, and given his conservative Philadelphia Main Line roots, his earnestness and rectitude, he practically wore a flashing "recruit me" sign on his back, beckoning the local CIA man. The professor of Soviet Studies rubbed his hands in anticipation every time he saw the crew-cut young man smoking at the Ivy Club, his pale, intelligent face stuck in a book.

To this day, Spence remained the youngest recruit in CIA

history and some of the old-timers still talked about this genius kid, prancing around Langley with his giant ego and enormous analytical powers. It was probably inevitable that in time, he would be approached by a nondescript man in a suit, pressing an unlikely business card into his hand bearing the insignia of the US Navy. Spence, of course, wanted to know what the navy wanted with him, and what he was told set his life on its current arc.

Will recalled the same puzzlement the day Mark Shackleton told him Area 51 was a naval operation. The military had its traditions, some of them stubbornly silly, and this was one of them.

As Will had learned, in 1947, President Truman tapped one of his most trusted aides, James Forrestal, to commission a new, ultrasecret military base at Groom Lake, Nevada, in a remote desert parcel bordering Yucca Flats. Carrying the cartographic designation, Nevada Test Site—51, the base came to be called Area 51 for short.

The Brits had found something extraordinarily troubling at an archaeological excavation on the Isle of Wight on the grounds of an ancient monastery, Vectis Abbey. They had opened their Pandora's box a crack, then slammed it shut when they realized what they'd stepped into. Clement Atlee, the Prime Minister, recruited Winston Churchill to be the go-between with Truman to persuade the American President to take the trove of material off their hands, lest the postwar reconstruction of Britain be sidetracked by this monumental distraction.

Project Vectis was born.

Forrestal happened to be Secretary of the Navy when he got the assignment, and the project stuck to the Navy Department like paste, qualifying Area 51 as the driest, most landlocked naval base on the planet. The Project Vectis Working

Group, personally chaired by Truman, hit upon an ingenious idea to shroud the Area 51 site in disinformation, a ruse that was still working after sixty years. They capitalized on the country's mania about UFO sightings, orchestrated a staged little drama at Roswell, New Mexico, then spread the rumor that a brand-new base in Nevada might have something to do with alien spacecraft and the like. Area 51 got on with its real mission, the gullible public none the wiser.

The Secretary of the Navy in every administration was, by practice, the Pentagon's point man on all matters related to the base and one of a small handful of officials who had the slightest idea what all the clandestine fuss was about. Recruiting Henry Spence from the rival CIA was considered enough of a coup that Spence was ushered into the Secretary's office for a meet and greet shortly after he signed on. The jaw-dropping truth of his new assignment was so fresh that he stumbled through the meeting with little subsequent recollection of its substance.

Will listened intently as Spence described his first day in the Nevada desert, deep underground in the Truman Building, the main Area 51 complex. As a newbie, he was solemnly taken by his supervisor down to the Vault level and, flanked by humorless, armed guards, the watchers, led into the vast, quiet, chilled space, a high-tech cathedral of sorts, where he first laid eyes on seven hundred thousand ancient books.

The most singular and peculiar library on the planet.

"Mr. Spence, here is your data," his supervisor had declared with a theatrical arm wave. "Few men are given the privilege. We're expecting great things from you."

And Spence began his new life.

Area 51 had found more than a talent—the organization had found a zealot. Every single day that he descended un-

derground, for the better part of thirty years, Spence luxu-
riated in the privilege his old boss had described and the
heady entitlement of being plugged into the most rarefied,
secret institution in the world. His linguistic and analytical
skills served him well, and in a few short years he was in
charge of the China desk. Later, he would become the Director of Asian Affairs and would close out his career as the
most decorated analyst in the history of the lab.

In the seventies, he pioneered a comprehensive approach
to obtaining person-specific data utilizing available, albeit
primitive, Chinese databases and rudimentary census reports, combined with a vast network of human intelligence
he developed in cooperation with the CIA. Maoist purges
and population dislocations often forced him to rely on statistical models, but his greatest coup early on was his prediction in 1974 of the July 28, 1976 natural disaster in northeast
China, in the mining town of Tangshan, which killed
255,000 people. As soon as the earthquake struck, President
Ford was in a position to offer premobilized disaster support to Premier Hua Guofeng, solidifying the post-Nixonian
US-China thaw.

It was a heady time for Spence. He described, with morbid
pride, the excitement he had felt when the first reports
reached Nevada of the deadly earthquake, and when he saw
the odd look on Will's face, he added, "I mean, it wasn't as if
I'd *caused* the damned thing. I just *predicted* it."

In his youth, Spence was a cocky, good-looker who en-
joyed life as a single man in boomtown Vegas. But ultimately, blue-blooded WASP that he was, a fish out of water
in a new-money, grasping town, he gravitated to birds of a
feather. At his country club, he met Martha, a wealthy developer's daughter, and the two of them married and had
children, all of them now accomplished adults. He was a

grandfather, but sadly, Martha passed had away from breast cancer before the first grandchild was born. "I never looked up her date," Spence insisted. "Probably could have gotten away with it, but I didn't."

He left the lab when he hit the mandatory retirement age, shortly after 9/11. He probably would have stayed longer if they'd let him; it was his life. He had a voracious interest in Area 51 business and liked to insert himself into hot topics, even if they were off the Asia beat. During the summer of 2001, with retirement looming, he made a point to have lunch every day with folks from the US department, trading theories and predictions on the events that would soon kill three thousand people at the World Trade Center.

When he retired, he was physiologically old but extremely wealthy thanks to his wife's family fortune. Her death took a heavy toll on his constitution, and his lifelong two-pack-a-day habit gave him worsening asthmatic emphysema. Steroids and a weakness for rich food made him fat. In time, he'd be scooter- and oxygen-dependent. His dual retirement passions, he confessed, were his grandchildren and the 2027 Club. This bus, dubbed the grandpamobile, was his ticket to mobility and his far-flung family.

Spence finished, and, on cue, Alf Kenyon leapt into his own story without giving Will a chance to interrupt. Will felt like he was being played. These guys were opening their kimonos to soften him up for something. He didn't like it, but he was curious enough to go along.

Kenyon was the son of Presbyterian ministers from Michigan. He grew up in Guatemala but was sent stateside for college. At Berkeley, he became fired up by the Vietnam War protest scene and mixed Latin-American studies with a growing sense of radicalism. Upon graduation, he ventured to Nicaragua to help peasants press land claims against the Somoza government.

By the early seventies, the Sandinista rebels were starting to get some traction in the countryside, mobilizing antigovernment opposition. Kenyon was a strong sympathizer. His work in the central highlands, however, attracted the unwelcome attention of progovernment militias, and, one day, he was surprised to be visited in his village by a cherubic young American named Tony who was about his age. Tony mysteriously knew an awfully lot about him and offered some unsolicited, friendly advice on keeping a low profile. Kenyon was on the naïve side but worldly enough to recognize Tony as an agency man.

The two young men were chalk and cheese, polar opposites politically and culturally, and Kenyon angrily sent him away. But when Tony returned a week later, Kenyon admitted to Will that he was happy to see him again, and brightly blurted out, "I don't think either of us really knew we were gay!" Will assumed the Tony story had a broader purpose than a disclosure of the man's sexual identity, so he let Kenyon ramble on in his slow, precise way.

Despite their political differences, the men became friends, two lonely Americans on their opposing missions in the hostile rain forest, one Catholic, one Protestant, both devout. Kenyon came to understand that a different CIA man would have probably thrown him to the wolves, but Tony showed genuine concern about his safety and even tipped him off to a militia sweep.

Then, with Christmas 1972 approaching, Kenyon made plans to spend a week in Managua. Tony came to visit, and begged, "Yes, begged me!" he said, not to go to the capital. Kenyon refused to listen until Tony told him something that would change his life.

"There will be a disaster in Managua on December 23," he said. "Thousands will die. Please don't go."

"Do you know what happened on that day, Mr. Piper?"

Will shook his head.

"The great Nicaraguan earthquake. Over ten thousand killed, three-quarters of all buildings destroyed. He wouldn't say how he knew, but he scared me silly, and I didn't go. Afterward, when we became, shall I say, closer, he told me he had no idea how our government knew what was coming, but the prediction was in the system, and he understood it was as good as gold. Needless to say, I was intrigued."

Tony was eventually transferred to another assignment, and Kenyon would leave Nicaragua when full-blown civil war broke out. He returned to the States to get a Ph.D. at Michigan. Apparently Tony had put Kenyon's name into the system, and Area 51 recruiters got wind of it because they were on the lookout for a Latin-American specialist. One fine day he was visited at his Ann Arbor apartment by a navy man who startled him by asking if he'd like to know how the government knew about the Managua quake.

He most certainly did. The hook was set.

He joined Area 51 a few years after Spence and was put to work on the Latin-American desk. He and Spence, both cerebral types who loved to talk politics, gravitated to each other and quickly became commuting buddies on the daily shuttle flights between Las Vegas and Groom Lake. Over the years, the Spence clan, for all intents and purposes, adopted the single man and hosted him at holidays and family occasions. When Martha died, Kenyon was Spence's rock.

They retired on the same day in 2001. At the EG&G shuttle lounge at McCarran Airport on their last return flight, the men hugged each other and got misty-eyed. Spence stayed at his country-club estate in Las Vegas, Kenyon moved to Phoenix to be near his only family, a sister. The men stayed close, bonded by their shared experiences and the 2027 Club.

Kenyon stopped talking. Will expected Spence to pick up the stream again but he too was silent.

Then, Kenyon asked, "Could I ask if you're a religious man, Mr. Piper?"

"You can ask, but I don't see it as your business."

The man looked hurt. Will realized the two of them had been sharing their personal lives in hopes of getting him to open up to them. "No, I'm not very religious."

Kenyon leaned forward. "Neither is Henry. I find it remarkable that anyone who knows about the library isn't."

"To each, his own," Spence said. "We've had this discussion a thousand times. Alf is in the camp that the Library proves that God exists."

"There's no other explanation."

"I don't want to relitigate the matter just now," Spence said wearily.

"The thing that always tickled me," Kenyon said, "is that I was born into the perfect religion. As a Presbyterian I was hardwired to incorporate the Library into my spiritual life."

"The man is still acting out the Protestant Reformation," Spence joked.

Will knew where he was going. Over the last year, he'd thought about these things himself. "Predestination."

"Precisely!" Kenyon exclaimed. "I was a Calvinist before I had a concrete justification for being one. Let's just say the Library turned me into a High Calvinist. Very doctrinaire."

"And very opinionated," his friend added.

"I've spent my retirement becoming an ordained minister. I'm also writing a biography of John Calvin, trying to figure out how he had the genius to get his theology so right.

Frankly, if it weren't for Henry's passing, I'd be happy as a clam. Everything makes sense to me, which is a nice place to be."

"Tell me about the 2027 Club," Will said.

Spence hesitated at the wheel as a light turned green. He had to decide whether to swing through the park again. "As I'm sure you know, the last book of the Library ends on the ninth of February, 2027. Everyone with no recorded date of death is BTH, beyond the horizon. Everyone who's ever worked at the Library has endlessly speculated why the books ended and who was responsible for them in the first place. Was the work of these savants or monks or fortune-tellers or extraterrestrials—yes, Alf, my explanation is as good as yours—was it interrupted by external factors like war, disease, natural disaster? Or is there a more sinister explanation that maybe the people of earth ought to know about. As far as any of us are aware, there was never much of an official effort to understand the significance of the horizon, as it's called. The Pentagon's always too focused on mining the data and generating intelligence findings. There's a lot of badness in the cards, megadisasters in the not-so-distant future that our folks are obsessing over. Something big is looming in Latin America, truth be told. Maybe as 2027 gets closer, it's going to occur to these ge-niuses in Washington that we really ought to know what the hell is going to happen the day after. But let me tell you, Mr. Piper, one's curiosity about the horizon doesn't cease with retirement. The 2027 Club was formed in the 1950s by some ex–Area 51 types as part retirement social club, part amateur sleuthing group. It's all very sub rosa, violates our retirement agreements and all that, but you can't stamp out human nature. We're curious as hell, and the only folks we can talk to are ex-employees. Plus it gives us a chance to get together and drink adult beverages."

The long soliloquy winded him. Will watched his chest heave.

"So what's the answer?" Will asked.

"The answer is . . ." Spence paused for dramatics, "we don't know!" He let out a belly laugh. "That's why we're driving around Manhattan trying to romance you."

"I don't think I can help you."

"We think you can," Kenyon said.

"Look," Spence added, "we know all about the Doomsday case and Mark Shackleton. We knew the guy, not well, mind you, but if someone was going to go off the reservation, it was going to be someone like Shackleton, a grade-A loser, if you ask me. You had some kind of connection to him beforehand, no?"

"He was my college roommate. For a year. What's your source of information on me?"

"The Club. We're networked like crazy. We know that Shackleton smuggled out the US database all the way to the horizon. We know that he set up a smoke screen by inventing a serial-killing spree in New York."

Kenyon sadly shook his head and interrupted. "I still can't believe the rank cruelty of sending people postcards with their date of death!"

Spence continued, "We know his real purpose was base: to make money from a life-insurance scheme! We know you exposed him. We know he was critically wounded by the watchers. We know you were allowed to retire from the FBI and presumably live an unfettered life. Therefore, Mr. Piper, we strongly suspect, virtually to the point of certainty, that you have unique leverage over the authorities."

"What would that be?"

"You must have a copy of the database."

Momentarily, Will was back in Los Angeles, fleeing from the watchers, in the backseat of a taxi, urgently downloading Shackleton's database from his laptop onto a memory stick. Shackleton: rotting away like a vegetable in some godforsaken back ward.

"Not going to confirm or deny."

"There's more to tell," Kenyon said. "Go on, Henry, tell him everything."

"Back in the midnineties, I got friendly with one of the watchers, a man named Dane Bentley, to the point that he did me the ultimate Area 51 favor. I was insatiably curious. The only people with access to what I wanted to know were the people tasked with making sure we had no access! The watchers, as you know, are a grim lot, but this fellow, Dane, had enough humanity to break the rules for a friend. He looked up my date of death. October 21, 2010. At the time it seemed very, very far away. Kind of creeps up on you."

"I'm sorry."

"Thank you. I appreciate that." He waited until the next red light before asking, "Did you look yourself up?"

Will didn't see the point in playing possum any longer. "I did. Given the circumstances, I felt I had to. I'm BTH."

"That's good," Kenyon said. "We're relieved to hear that, aren't we, Henry?"

"Yes we are."

"I never wanted to know my date," Kenyon said. "Preferred to leave it squarely in God's hands."

"Here's the thing," Spence said energetically, banging his hands against the steering wheel. "I have ten days to learn the truth. I can't postpone the inevitable, but goddamn it, I want to know before I die!"

"I can't see any way I can help you. I really can't."

"Show him, Alf," Spence demanded. "Show him what we found a week ago."

Kenyon opened a folder and took out a few pages, a printout from a Web site. He handed them to Will. It was an online catalogue from Pierce & Whyte Auctions, an antiquarian bookseller in London, announcing an auction on October 15, 2010, the day after tomorrow. There were multiple color photographs of Lot Number 113, a thick old book with the date 1527 tooled onto the spine. He studied the images and the detailed description of the item that followed. Will skimmed the text, but the gist of it seemed to be that although it was a unique item, the auction house didn't know what it was. The indicated price range was £2,000 to £3,000.

"Is it what I think it is?" Will asked.

Spence nodded. "It was a well-known piece of trivia around the shop that one volume of the Library was missing. A book from 1527. With under two weeks to live, I discover the son of a bitch has surfaced at an auction! I've got to have it! The damned thing's been floating out there for six centuries! The one missing book out of hundreds of thousands. Why did it get separated from the others? Where's it been? Did anyone know what it was? Christ, it may tell us more than every other book sitting in the Vault in Groom Lake. I don't want to get ahead of myself, but for all we know, it could be the key to finding out what the heck 2027 is all about! I've got a feeling, Mr. Piper, a strong feeling. And by Hades, before I die I've got to find out!"

"What does this have to do with me?"

"We want you to go to England tomorrow to buy the book for us at auction. I'm too sick to fly, and Alf here, the stubborn bastard, refuses to leave my side. I've got you booked in first class, coming back on Friday night. Nice hotel suite too at Claridge's."

Will gave him a black look, started to reply, but Spence interrupted.

"Before you answer, I want you to know that I want something else that's even more important to me. I want to see the database. I know my own DOD, but I never looked up any of the people who matter to me. For all I know, that fucker, Malcolm Frazier, may Alf's God strike him dead tomorrow, is onto us. Maybe it's not my rotten lungs that are going to get me in ten days. Maybe it's Frazier's goons. I refuse to shuffle off this mortal coil without knowing if my children and grandchildren are BTH. I want to know if they're safe. I'm desperate to know! You do these things for me, Mr. Piper, get the book and give me the database, and I'll make you rich."

Will was shaking his head before the man even finished. "I'm not going to England tomorrow," Will said flatly. "I can't leave my wife and son on short notice. And I'm not touching the database. It's my insurance policy. I'm not going to risk my family's safety to satisfy your curiosity. I'm sorry, but it's not going to happen, even though the rich part sounds pretty good."

"Take your wife too. And your son. I'll pay for everything."

"She can't get off work just like that. Forget about it." He imagined how Nancy would react, and it wouldn't be pretty. "Make a right onto Fifth Avenue and take me home."

Spence got agitated and started to shout and sputter. Will had to cooperate! The clock was ticking! Couldn't he see that he was desperate!

The man began to cough severely and wheeze to the

degree that Will thought he might lose control and crash into parked cars.

"Henry, calm down!" Kenyon implored. "Stop talking. Let me handle this."

Spence was speechless by then anyway. He dipped his mottled head and signaled Kenyon to take over.

"Okay, Mr. Piper. We can't force you to do something against your will. I thought you might not be inclined to get involved. We'll bid on the book by telephone. At a minimum, allow us to have a courier hand-deliver it to your apartment on Friday night, where we'll take possession. In the interim, do us the courtesy of considering the rest of Henry's generous offer. He doesn't need the entire database, just DODs for fewer than a dozen people. Please, sleep on it."

Will nodded and remained silent the rest of the way downtown, concentrating on Spence's wheezing and the hiss of oxygen flowing through his nasal prongs.

At that moment, Malcolm Frazier awoke with a start and a scowl, uncharacteristically disoriented. The credits were rolling on the in-flight movie, and the elderly woman in the middle seat was tapping his granite shoulder to get past him to the lavs. The coach seats on the American flight were not configured for his large, muscular body and his right leg was pressure-numb. He rose and shook out the pins and needles and cursed his superiors for not springing for business class.

There was nothing about this assignment he liked. Sending the head of security at Area 51 on a mission to buy a book at auction seemed ludicrous. Even this book. Why couldn't they have sent a lab toad? He would have gladly dispatched one of his watchers to babysit. But no. The Pentagon wanted *him*. Unfortunately, he knew why.

The Caracas Event.

It was T minus thirty days and counting.

One of those seminal Area 51 predictions was bearing down on them, but this one was different. They weren't in their usual reactive, defensive mode. They were going to capitalize on the data, go on the offense. The Pentagon was geared up. The Joint Chiefs were in perpetual session. The Vice President was personally chairing a task force. The full heft of the US government was pushing hard on this. It was the worst possible time for the one missing book to surface. Secrecy was always the top priority at Groom Lake, but no one wanted to be talking about a possible security breech with a month to go until Operation Helping Hand.

Helping Hand!

What Pentagon spin doctor came up with that?

If the missing book wound up in some egghead's hands, who knew what kinds of questions might be asked, what kinds of facts might surface?

So Frazier understood why he got the assignment. Still, he didn't have to like it.

The pilot announced they were approaching the coast of Ireland and would land at Heathrow in two hours. At his feet was an empty leather case, specially sized and padded for the job. He was already counting the hours until he was back in Nevada, the priceless 1527 book sitting heavy and snug inside his government-issued shoulder bag.

The auction room at Pierce & Whyte was off the main hall on the ground floor of the Georgian mansion. Bidders signed in at a reception desk and entered a fine old room with fawn-colored hardwood floors, a high, plastered ceiling, and one entire wall lined with bookcases that required a ladder to reach the top shelves. The auction room faced the High Street, and with the drapes pulled back, yellow shafts of sunlight intersected with neat rows of brown wooden chairs making a chessboard pattern. There was space for seventy to eighty patrons, and on this fine bright Friday morning, the room was filling up briskly.

Malcolm Frazier had arrived early, anxious to get on with it. After registering with a pert girl who cheerfully ignored his surliness, he entered the empty room and sat down in the first row, directly in front of the auctioneer's podium, where he absently twirled his paddle between a meaty thumb and forefinger. As more people arrived, it became increasingly apparent that Frazier was not the typical antiquarian book buyer. His fellow bidders didn't look like they could bench-press four hundred pounds or swim underwater a hundred yards or kill a man with one weaponless hand. But Frazier was decidedly more nervous than his nearsighted, flabby brethren, since he had never attended an auction and was only vaguely aware of the protocol.

He checked the catalogue and found Lot 113 deep in the brochure. If this was the order of the day, he was afraid he'd have a long, agonizing sit. His posture was erect and stiff, his feet planted heavily beside his shoulder bag, a big block of a man with a face with more angles than curves. In the second row, the chair behind him stayed empty because he blotted out the view to the podium.

He had learned about the auction from a Pentagon e-mail flashed to his encrypted BlackBerry. He had been pushing a shopping cart at a suburban Las Vegas supermarket at the time, dutifully following his wife through the dairy section. The chime that went off on the device was the high-priority one, an insistent whoop that made his mouth go dry in a Pavlovian way. Nothing good ever followed this particular alert tone.

A long-forgotten Defense Intelligence filter that scanned all electronic media for the keywords "1527" and "book" had been triggered, and a low-level analyst at the DIA forwarded the finding up the line, curious but clueless why anyone in military intelligence would give a hoot over a Web-site listing of an old book coming to auction.

But to the cognoscenti at Area 51, this was a bombshell. The one missing volume. The needle in a haystack, found. Where had the book been all these years? What was its chain of possession? Did anyone know what it was? Could anyone figure it out? Was there anything special about this particular volume that could compromise the lab's mission? Meetings were held. Plans were drawn. Paperwork was pushed up the line. Funds were allocated and wired. Operation Helping Hand was looming, and Frazier was personally chosen by the Pentagon for the job.

With the room near capacity, the auctioneers arrived and took their positions. Toby Parfitt, impeccably turned out, approached the podium and began adjusting the microphone and his auction implements. To his left, Martin Stein and two other senior members of the books department seated themselves at a draped table. Each dialed into a telephonic connection for off-site bidders and, with receivers pressed against ears, placidly awaited the start of the proceedings.

Peter Nieve, Toby's junior assistant, positioned himself to his master's right, a fidgeting dogsbody at the ready. Nieve made sure he was closer to his boss than the new lad, Adam Cottle, who had joined the department only a fortnight earlier. Cottle was a dull-eyed blond in his twenties with short hair and sausage fingers, by looks more of a butcher boy than a book dealer. Apparently his father knew the Managing Director, and Toby was told to take him on, even though he didn't need the extra help, and Cottle lacked a university degree or, indeed, any relevant experience.

Nieve had been merciless to the fellow. He finally had someone lower on the pecking order, and he delegated his most mundane and humiliating chores to the colorless young man, who would quietly nod and get on with the task like a subservient oaf.

Toby surveyed the audience, nodding curtly to the regulars. There were a few new faces, none more imposing than the large, muscular gentleman seated in front of him, oddly out of place.

"Ladies and gentlemen, the appointed hour has arrived. I am Toby Parfitt, your auctioneer, and I am pleased to welcome you to Pierce & Whyte's autumn auction of select antiquarian books and manuscripts, representing a diverse selection of high-quality literary collectables. Among the many featured offerings today is a veritable treasure trove of material from the collection of Lord Cantwell's country house in Warwickshire. I would like to inform you, we are also accepting telephonic bids. Our staff is at the ready to assist you with any inquiries. So without further ado, let us begin."

A rear door opened, and a pretty female assistant with white gloves entered with the first lot, demurely holding it out in front of her bosom.

Toby acknowledged her, and began, "Lot 1 is a very nice copy of John Ruskin's *The Unity of Art,* a lecture delivered at the Annual Meeting of the Manchester School of Art in 1859, published at Oxford in 1870. The copy is lightly browned in its original wrappers and would make a worthy acquisition for Ruskin aficionados and art historians alike. I would entertain starting bids of £100."

Frazier grunted and steeled himself for an ordeal.

In New York City, it was five hours earlier, two hours before the sun would crack the chilly gloom over the East River. Spence and Kenyon had awoken early at their nighttime domicile, a Wal-Mart parking lot in Valley Stream, Long Island. In the bus's kitchen, they made coffee and bacon and eggs, then hit the road to beat the rush hour into lower Manhattan. It was four thirty when they arrived at Will's door. He was waiting at the curb, shivering from the cold but steaming from an early-morning argument.

It hadn't been a great idea to argue with his wife while she was breast-feeding. He figured that out halfway through their contretemps. There was something mean-spirited about raising his voice and drowning out his son's gurgling and sucking, not to mention wiping Nancy's usual look of maternal serenity off her face. On the other hand, he'd made a promise to help Spence, and he argued that at least he hadn't agreed to haul off to England. Nancy was hardly placated. For her, Doomsday was in the past, and the Library was best forgotten. She understood the danger of black groups like the watchers. She was all about the present and the future. She had a baby she loved and a husband she cherished. Life was pretty good right now, but it could turn on a dime. She told him not to play with fire.

Will was nothing if not stubborn. He had grabbed his jacket, stormed out of the apartment, then immediately started feeling rotten. But he refused to turn tail and apologize. The give-and-take of married life was a concept he understood intellectually, but it wasn't ingrained, and might never be for all he knew. He mumbled something to himself about being pussy-whipped and hit the elevator down button hard, like he was trying to poke someone's eye out.

As soon as he boarded the bus, Will admitted, "Good thing we're not doing this in my place."

"In the doghouse, Mr. Piper?" Spence asked.

"Just call me Will from now on, okay?" he answered moodily. "You got coffee?" He slouched on the sofa.

Kenyon poured while Spence touched GET DIRECTIONS on his GPS unit and pulled away from the curb. Their destination was the Queens Mall, where Will figured they could park the bus without much hassle.

When they arrived, it was still dark, and the mall was several hours from opening. The parking lot was wide open and Spence parked at the periphery. His cell phone had five bars, so they wouldn't have to worry about signal quality.

"It's 10:00 A.M. in London. I'll dial in," Spence said, getting up and wheeling his oxygen box.

He placed the cell phone on the kitchen table on speaker mode, and the three of them sat around it while he punched in the international number. An operator connected them into the auction, and an officious voice answered, "Martin Stein here of Pierce & Whyte. With whom am I speaking?"

"This is Henry Spence calling from the United States. Hear me okay?"

"Yes, Mr. Spence, loud and clear. We've been expecting your call. If you could indicate which lots you intend to bid on, it would be most useful."

"Just one, Lot 113."

"I see. Well, I think we might not get to that item until well into the second hour."

"I've got my phone plugged in and I've paid my wireless bill, so we'll be okay on this end."

In London, Frazier was fighting jet lag and boredom, but he was too disciplined and stoical to grimace, yawn, or squirm like a normal person. The old books kept marching past in one dull stream of cardboard, leather, paper, and ink. Histories, novels, travelogues, poetry, ornithology, works of science, mathematics, engineering. He seemed to be the only uninterested party. His compatriots were in a lather, bidding furiously against one another, each with a characteristic style. Some would flamboyantly wave their paddles. Others would raise them almost imperceptibly. The real hard-core regulars had facial expressions that were recognized by the staff as indications—a sharp nod, a twitch of the cheek, a raised brow. There was some serious disposable income in this town, Frazier thought, as bids on books he wouldn't shove under a short table leg, rose into the thousands of pounds.

In New York, dawn had come, and daylight filled the bus. Every so often, Stein came onto the line with a progress report. They were getting closer. Will was getting impatient.

He'd promised he'd be back before Nancy had to leave for work, and the clock was spinning. Spence's body was noisy. He was wheezing, coughing, puffing on an inhaler, and whispering curses.

When Lot 112 came up, Frazier's mind cleared, a surge of adrenaline goosing his respiratory rate. It was a large, old volume and at first he mistook it for his target. Toby sang the praises of the book, pronouncing its title fluently in Latin. "Lot 112 is a very fine copy of the anatomy book by Raymond de Vieussens, *Neurographia Universalis, Hoc Est, Omnium Corporis, Humani Nervorum,* published in 1670 in Frankfurt by G. W. Kuhn. There are twenty-nine engraved plates on contemporary vellum, some short tears, but otherwise a remarkable copy of an historic medical treatise. I will start the bidding at £1,000."

The bidding was brisk, with multiple interested parties. A dealer at the rear, a heavyset man with an ascot who had been particularly keen all morning on scientific offerings, led the way, aggressively bumping the price by hundred-pound increments. When the dust settled, he had it at £2300.

Martin Stein came on the line, and announced, "Mr. Spence, we have reached Lot 113. Please stand by."

"Okay, gentlemen, this is it," Spence said. Will looked anxiously at his watch. There was still time to get home and avoid a big domestic dustup.

Frazier locked his eyes on the book the instant it was brought into the auction room. Even from a distance, he was certain. It was one of them. He'd spent two decades in and around the Library and there was no mistaking it. The time had come. He'd spent the morning watching the action and had learned the mechanics of bidding. Let's get ready to rumble, he thought, psyching himself.

Toby spoke about the book wistfully, as if sorry to see it go. "Lot 113 is a rather unique item, a hand-inscribed journal, dated 1527, beautifully bound in calf hide, over a thousand pages of finest-quality vellum. There is, perhaps, an endpaper that has been replaced at some distant point. The book appears to be an extensive ledger of births and deaths, possessing an international flair, with multiple European and oriental languages represented. The volume has been in the family collection of Lord Cantwell perhaps since the sixteenth century, but its provenance cannot be otherwise ascertained. We have consulted with academic colleagues at Oxford and Cambridge, and there is no consensus as to its origin or purpose. It remains, if I may say, an enigma wrapped in mystery, but it is an outstanding curiosity piece which I now offer at a starting bid of £2,000."

Frazier raised his paddle so obviously it almost made Toby jump. It was the first significant physical movement the large man had made in almost two hours.

"Thank you," Toby said, "may I hear £2500?"

From their tinny speaker, Will heard Stein offering 2500, and Spence said, "Yes, that's fine."

Stein nodded to Toby who said, "There is a telephone bidder at 2500, may I hear 3,000?"

Frazier shifted uncomfortably. He'd hoped there wouldn't be any competition. He raised his paddle.

"I have 3,000, looking for 3500," then a quick "Thank you," as he pointed to the rear. Frazier turned to see the heavy man with the ascot nodding. "Now looking for 4,000," Toby said quickly.

Stein relayed the bid. "This is horseshit," Spence whispered to his companions. "I bid 5,000."

"I have 5,000 here," Stein called out to the podium.

"Very well, then," Toby continued smoothly. "Do we have a bid for 6,000?"

Frazier felt a spasm of anxiety. He had plenty of dry powder, but he wanted this to be a cakewalk. He raised his paddle again.

"I have 6,000, may I hear 7,000?"

The man in the ascot shook his head, and Toby turned to the phone desk. Stein was speaking, then listening, then speaking again until he announced rather grandly, "I have £10,000!"

"Let me take the liberty of asking for £12,000," Toby said boldly.

Frazier swore under his breath and lifted his hand.

Spence's palms were moist. Will watched him rub them on his shirt. "I don't have time to play games," he said.

"It's your money," Will observed, sipping his coffee.

"I'm jacking this up to 20,000, Mr. Stein."

The announcement set the room buzzing. Frazier blinked in disbelief. He felt for the bulge of his cell phone in his pants pocket, but it was premature to reach for it. He still had plenty of room.

Toby's moustache moved upward ever so slightly as his lip curled in obvious excitement. "Well, then, shall we say 30,000?"

Frazier didn't hesitate. Of course he was in.

After several moments, the response came from the telephone desk. Stein announced, in a daze, "The bid has been raised to £50,000!"

The murmuring from the audience crescendoed. Stein and Toby looked at each other in disbelief, but Toby was able to maintain his indomitable composure, and simply said, "I have 50,000, may I ask for 60,000?" He beckoned

Peter Nieve to his side and whispered for the lad to fetch the Managing Director.

Frazier could feel his heart pounding in his barrel chest. He was authorized to go up to $200,000, about £125,000 which his masters had assumed would be an absurdly ample cushion given the upper estimate of £3,000. There wasn't a penny more in the Pierce & Whyte escrow account that had been established for him. They were almost halfway there. Who the fuck is bidding against me, he thought angrily. He raised his paddle emphatically.

Spence hit the mute button on his phone and loudly complained, "I wish I could look the son of a bitch who's bidding against us in the face. Who in hell would pay that kind of money for something that looks like an old census book?"

"Maybe someone else who knows what it is," Will said ominously.

"Not very likely," Spence sniffed, "unless . . . Alf, what do you think?"

Kenyon shrugged, "It's possible, Henry, it's always possible."

"What are you talking about?" Will asked.

"The watchers. The goons from Area 51 could have gotten wind of it, I suppose. I hope not." Then he declared, "I'm going to take this up a notch."

"Just how much money does he have?" Will asked Kenyon.

"A lot."

"And you can't take it with you," Spence said. He unmuted the phone. "Stein, you go ahead and bid £100,000 for me. I don't have the patience for this."

"Can I just confirm that you said £100,000?" Stein asked, his voice brittle.

"That's correct."

Stein shook his head, and announced loudly, "The telephone bid is now £100,000!"

Frazier saw that Toby's demeanor had turned from excitement to suspicion. He thought, this guy must have just figured out there's more to the book than he bargained for.

"Well, then," Toby said evenly, looking straight into Frazier's pugnacious face. "I wonder if sir would like to go to £125,000?"

Frazier nodded, opened his mouth for the first time all morning, and simply said, "Yes."

He was nearly maxed out. The last time he had experienced anything close to panic was in his early twenties, a young commando on a SEAL Boat team off the eastern coast of Africa on a mission that had gone bad. Pinned down, outmanned thirty to one, taking RPG fire from some rebel assholes. This felt worse.

He pulled out his cell phone and speed-dialed the Secretary of the Navy, who, at that moment, was playing an early-morning game of squash in Arlington. His mobile phone rang in a locker, and Frazier heard, "This is Lester. Leave a message and I'll get back to you."

Stein presented the new bid of 125,000. Spence told him to hang on a second then muted the phone. "It's time to finish this," he growled to his companions. Will shrugged. It was his money. When he came back on the line with Stein he said, "I'm bidding £200,000."

When Stein announced the bid, Toby seemed to steady himself by placing both hands on the podium. The Managing Director of Pierce & Whyte, an unsmiling, white-haired patrician, was observing from the wings, tapping his fingers together nervously. Then Toby politely addressed Frazier, "Would sir care to go higher?"

Frazier stood and made his way to an unoccupied corner. "I've got to make a call," he said. His constricted voice, coming from this hulk of a man, was almost comically squeaky.

"I can give sir a brief moment," Toby offered.

Frazier called Lester's mobile again, then his Pentagon line, where he reached an assistant. He began pelting the hapless man with a torrent of urgent whispers.

Toby watched patiently for a while, then asked, "Would sir like to raise his bid?" he asked again.

"Hang on!" Frazier shouted.

There was a hubbub from the other bidders. This was decidedly unusual.

"Well, do we have it?" Spence asked over the phone.

"The other bidder is seeking consultation, I believe," Stein replied.

"Well, tell him to hurry it up," Spence wheezed.

Frazier was in a cold sweat. The mission was on the brink of collapse, and failure wasn't a contemplated option. He was used to solving problems with calculated force and violence but his usual bag of tricks was useless in a genteel hall in central London surrounded by pasty-faced bibliophiles.

Stein arched his eyebrows to signal Toby that his telephone bidder was complaining.

Toby, in turn, sought out the stern eyes of his Managing Director, and mutual nods sealed the decision. "I'm afraid, unless we hear a higher bid, I will have to close this lot at £200,000."

Frazier tried to ignore him. He was still whisper-shouting into his phone.

Toby melodramatically raised his gavel hand, higher than usual. He spoke these words slowly, clearly and proudly:

"Ladies and gentlemen, going once, twice, and *sold*, to the telephone bidder for £200,000!"

Toby rapped the board with his gavel and the satisfying, hollow sound resonated for a moment before Frazier wheeled, and shouted, "No!"

Frazier paced furiously back and forth, oblivious to the crowded sidewalk on Kensington High Street, forcing pedestrians to scurry out of his steamroller way. He frantically worked his phone, trying to get his superiors to come to grips with the situation and formulate a plan. When he was finally connected to Secretary Lester, he had to duck into a quiet Boots pharmacy since the rumbling of a number 27 bus was making it impossible to hear.

He emerged into the din and diesel of the thoroughfare, his hands glumly thrust into his coat pockets. It was a sunny Friday lunch hour, and everyone he passed was in a far better mood than he. His orders bordered on the pathetic, he thought. Improvise. And don't break any UK laws. He supposed the hidden message was, at least don't get *caught* breaking them.

He returned to Pierce & Whyte and loitered in the reception hall, ducking in and out of the auction room until the session was over. Toby caught sight of him and gave the impression he wanted to avoid the snarling bidder. Just before he could escape through the rear staff door, Frazier caught up with him.

"I'd like to talk to the guy who beat me out on Lot 113."

"Quite a duel!" Toby exclaimed, diplomatically. He deliberately paused, perhaps hoping that having been tackled, the man might explain his enthusiasm. But Frazier simply persisted.

"Can you give me his name and number?"

"I'm afraid we can't. It's against our confidentiality policy. However, if you authorize it, I can pass your particulars to the winning bidder should he wish to contact you."

Frazier tried again, then made Toby visibly uncomfortable by suggesting he would make it worth his while. When Martin Stein approached, Toby hastily excused himself and moved away. As the two auctioneers chatted, Frazier edged close enough to overhear Stein say, "He was insistent on having the book sent to New York by courier for delivery tonight. He offered first-class return seats and hotel accommodations to a member of staff! He's already holding a seat on BA 179 this evening."

"Well I'm not doing it!" Toby said.

"Nor I. I have dinner plans," Stein huffed.

Toby spotted his assistants across the room and waved them over. Nieve was giddy with excitement over the Cantwell book while Cottle was, as usual, a piece of wood. "I need someone to courier the 1527 book over to New York tonight."

Cottle was about to speak, but Nieve opened his mouth first. "Christ, I'd love to go, Toby, but my passport's not sorted out! Been meaning to do it."

"I'll go, Mr. Parfitt," Cottle quickly offered. "I've got nothing on for the weekend."

"Have you ever been to New York?"

"On a school trip once, yeah."

"Well, okay. You've got the job. The buyer is prepared to have the duty fully paid at Kennedy Airport and have it added to his account. He's providing you with a first-class

ticket and deluxe hotel accommodations, so you shall not
want. They're quite security-conscious, so you'll be picking
up a letter from the BA desk at arrivals with the delivery
address."

"First class!" Nieve moaned. "Bloody hell! You owe me,
Cottle. You really owe me."

Frazier skulked off to the lobby. The girl at the reception
desk was packing up the brochures and sign-in sheets. "I
want to send a thank-you note to that young guy who works
here. Cottle. He was very helpful. Can you give me his first
name and tell me how to spell Cottle?"

"Adam," she said, apparently surprised that anyone as in-
significant as young Cottle could be helpful to a patron. She
spelled out his last name. That was all he needed to know.

A few hours later, Frazier was in a taxi heading to Heathrow, wolfing down three Big Macs from the only High Street
restaurant he trusted. Adam Cottle was in another taxi a
hundred yards farther on, but Frazier wasn't worried about
losing him. He knew where the young man was going and
what he was carrying.

Earlier, Frazier had reached the night duty officer at Area
51 and requested a priority search for an Adam Cottle, ap-
proximate age twenty-five, an employee of Pierce & Whyte
Auctions, London, England.

The duty officer called him back within ten minutes. "I've
got your man. Adam Daniel Cottle, Alexandra Road, Reading, Berkshire. Date of birth: March 12, 1985."

"What's his DOD?" Frazier asked.

"Funny you should ask, chief. It's today. Your guy's going
down today."

Frazier wearily thought, Why am I not shocked?

Will passed the string beans to his father-in-law. Joseph speared a few and smiled. They were just the way he liked them, buttered and *al dente,* which was not unexpected since his wife was the one who had made them. Mary had prepared the whole meal, actually, even the bread, and she had unpacked, reheated, and plated the feast in the kitchenette while the others fussed over Phillip.

The Lipinskis, newly minted grandparents, couldn't get enough of their grandson, and they thought nothing of driving forty-five minutes from Westchester down to lower Manhattan on a Friday evening to get their fix. Mary wouldn't saddle her beleaguered daughter with the cooking, so she made a lasagna and all the trimmings. Joseph brought the wine. Phillip was awake and on form and for the visitors; it was a slice of heaven.

Even though it was a family night, Mary was smartly dressed and had gone to the beauty parlor to get her hair done. She danced around the tiny kitchen in a cloud of perfume and hair spray, a heavier, rounder version of her daughter, still surprisingly pretty and youthful. Joseph's wild and wavy white hair made him look like a mad scientist crawling on the floor in hot pursuit of the grinning baby.

Nancy and Will had been sitting next to each other on the sofa, a good foot apart, unsmiling, tightly clutching their wineglasses. It was spectacularly apparent to the Lipinskis that they had entered an argument hot zone, but they were doing their best to keep the evening light.

Joseph had sidled up to his wife, poured himself more wine, then tapped her between the shoulder blades to make sure she saw his raised eyebrows. She had clucked, and whispered, "It's not so easy, you know. Remember?"

"I only remember the good things," he had said, giving her a dry peck.

Over dinner, Mary watched Will's hand pumping over his plate. "Will, you're using salt before you even taste it!"

He shrugged. "I like salt."

"I have to fill the shaker every week," Nancy said in an accusatory way.

"I don't think that's healthy," Joseph observed. "How's your pressure?"

"I dunno," Will said sullenly. "Never been a problem." He wasn't in the mood for dinner-party chitchat, and he wasn't trying to hide it.

Nancy had not been pleased about the auction, and in retrospect, he wished he'd kept the details to himself. She'd fumed all day that Will was allowing himself to be sucked into something that was none of his business, and she redlined when he casually mentioned he'd offered up the apartment for a late-night meeting.

"You agreed to let these people come into my home while Philly is sleeping ten feet away?"

"They're harmless old men. They'll be in and out in a few minutes. I'll make sure they don't wake you guys."

"Have you lost your mind?"

It had gone downhill from there.

"So how's work, honey?" Joseph asked his daughter.

"They're treating me like I came back from brain surgery. My assignments are ridiculous. I had a baby, not a disease."

"I'm glad they're acting that way," her mother said. "You're a new mother."

"You must be channeling my boss," Nancy said bitterly.

Joseph tried to inject a dose of hope. "I'm sure you'll get back to where you want to be." When Nancy ignored him, he tried his luck on his son-in-law. "Retirement still treating you well, Will?"

"Oh yeah. It's a laugh a minute," Will answered sarcastically.

"Well, you're my hero. In a couple of years, Mary and I plan to join you, so we're watching and learning."

In his foul mood, Will turned the comment over in his mind a couple of times, trying to decide if there was a coded insult lurking. He let it pass.

When they were alone, Nancy fussed over Phillip's crib, then got herself ready for bed. She was giving Will the icy, silent treatment, trying to avoid contact. The problem with relegating him to the doghouse was that the whole apartment wasn't much bigger than a doghouse to begin with.

Finally, she emerged from the bathroom, pink and exposed in her short nightdress. She crossed her arms over her chest and glowered at him. He was watching TV. Her folded arms were plumping her ripe breasts. He thought she looked awfully good, but her curdling expression wiped away any hope. "Please do not bring these people into the apartment."

"They'll be in and out. You won't even know they're here,"

he said stubbornly. He wasn't going to back down. It wasn't the way he worked.

She shut the bedroom door crisply behind her. If the baby hadn't been sleeping, she probably would have slammed it. Will let his eyes drift from the TV to the cabinet underneath, where his last bottle of scotch was ceremonially stored. He opened the cabinet with his mind and poured himself an imaginary few fingers.

The cabin crew was buttoning down the first-class cabin of BA 179 for its descent to JFK. Young Cottle sat expressionless throughout the entire trip, his usual inanimate self, seemingly immune to the sublime charms of British Airways champagne, cabernet, duck in cherries, chocolate truffles, first-run movies, and a seat that turned into a bed, complete with down-filled duvet.

Two cabins back, Malcolm Frazier was standing in a lengthy queue to use the toilet. He was rigid as a plank and terminally irritable from six hours wedged into a narrow, middle seat. The entire operation had been a disaster, and his masters had made it clear that he alone was responsible for pulling the chestnuts from the fire.

And now his mission had gotten considerably more complicated. It had morphed from a straightforward enterprise to secure the book into a full-blown investigation of who had paid an exorbitant sum and why. He was tasked with following the book to find the answers and, as usual, covering up his trail by whatever means necessary. And typically, everything was highest priority, and his boss's mood was bordering on hysteria. Secretary Lester had demanded to be informed of every single piece of minutia.

All this made Frazier surly. Angry enough to kill.

At the boarding gate at Heathrow's Terminal 5, Frazier had approached Cottle as the young man queued in the first-class check-in line. He was afraid Cottle might spot him on board and wanted to eliminate any suspicions. He also wanted to ask him a few "innocent" questions.

"Hey!" Frazier said mock-cheerfully. "Look who's here! I was at the auction earlier."

Cottle squinted back, "Of, course, sir. I remember."

"That was something, wasn't it?"

"Yes, sir. Very dramatic it was."

"So, we're on the same flight! How about that?" He pointed to Cottle's carry-on bag. "I'll bet I know what's in there."

Cottle looked uncomfortable. "Yes, sir."

"Any chance I could find out who's getting it? I'd still like to buy it, maybe make a deal with the guy who beat me out."

"I'm afraid I'm not at liberty, sir. Company policy and all." There was an announcement for first-class boarding. Cottle waved his ticket at Frazier, and said, "Well, have a good flight then, sir," before he inched away.

Will jumped up from the sofa before the buzzer could ring a second time. It was almost eleven, and the boys from the bus were right on time. He waited for them in the apartment hallway to remind them to be quiet. When the elevator opened, he was taken aback at the sight of Spence hunched over on a fire-engine red, three-wheeled mobility scooter, his oxygen box strapped to the luggage rack. Kenyon was towering over him.

"That doesn't make noise, does it?" Will asked nervously.

"It's not a Harley," Spence said dismissively, smoothly whirring forward.

The three of them made awkward company in Will's small

living room. They spoke sparingly, in whispers, the eleven o'clock TV news on low. Kenyon had tracked BA 179 and confirmed its on-time arrival. Accounting for immigration and customs, and taxi time, the courier was due any time.

Frazier used his federal ID to breeze through customs, then blended into the gaggle of people in the arrivals hall awaiting the deplaning passengers. One of his men, DeCorso, was already there. DeCorso was an aggressive-looking character in a padded-leather coat with a rough beard and a noticeable limp. He wordlessly handed over a heavy leather clutch. Frazier instantly felt relieved once again to have the tools of his trade at hand. He slipped the weapon into his empty shoulder bag, right where the Library book should have been.

DeCorso stood by his side, a silent statue. Frazier knew his subordinate didn't require idle conversation. He'd worked with him long enough to know he wasn't a talker. And he knew when he issued an order, DeCorso would follow it to the letter. The man owed him. The only reason he was allowed back to Area 51 after medical leave was Frazier's intervention. After all, he hadn't exactly covered himself in glory.

Will Piper had lit DeCorso up. Four to one, close quarters, and a lousy FBI agent had put all of them down. DeCorso had only been back on the job for a few months, with a jumble of hardware in his femur, a missing spleen, and a lifetime of Pneumovax shots to prevent infection. The other three men were on full disability. One of them had a permanent feeding tube sticking out of his stomach. As team leader, DeCorso had presided over a giant cluster-fuck.

Frazier didn't have to take him back, but he did.

When Adam Cottle finally entered the hall with his roller case, looking like a dazed tourist, Frazier raised his chin, and said, "That's him," before tucking himself behind De-Corso's frame to stay out of sight. They watched Cottle approach the British Airways information desk, where he was handed an envelope, then made for the exits.

"My car's at the curb, behind the taxi stand. I've got a cop watching I don't get towed."

Frazier started walking. "Let's find the cocksucker who outbid me."

They followed the yellow cab onto the Van Wyck Expressway. The traffic was light, so they were able to keep their mark comfortably in sight, no tense moments. DeCorso announced they were heading toward the Midtown Tunnel— a Manhattan destination. Frazier shrugged, dog-tired, and muttered, "Whatever."

Cottle's taxi dropped him off in the middle of the block. The young man took his bag and asked the cabbie to wait. Apparently, the level of trust was insufficient. He was required to pay in full before the driver agreed to hold at the curb. Cottle stood on the sidewalk and double-checked a piece of paper before disappearing into the lobby of an apartment building.

"You want me to go in?" DeCorso asked. They were across the street a short distance away, idling in their car.

"No. His cab's waiting," Frazier growled. "Get me data on all the residents of the building."

DeCorso opened his laptop and established an encrypted connection with their servers. While he typed, Frazier closed his eyes, lulled by the soft clattering of thick fingers on the keyboard.

Until, "Jesus!"

"What?" Frazier asked, startled.

DeCorso was passing the laptop. Frazier took it and tried

to focus his bleary eyes on the line listings. He shrugged. "What?"

"Near the bottom. See it?"

Then he did. *Will Piper.* Apartment 6F.

Frazier started kneading his lower face as if he were molding a block of clay. Then, a torrent of epithets. "I can't fucking believe it. Fucking Will Piper! Did I tell those fucking idiots at the Pentagon they were crazy to let him go?" His mind filled with the infuriating image of Will sitting pretty in the plush cabin of Secretary Lester's private plane, smugly sipping scotch at forty thousand feet, practically dictating terms.

"You did. Yes you did."

"And now here he is, working us."

"Give me a shot at him, Malcolm." DeCorso was almost pleading. He rubbed his right thigh, which still throbbed at the spot Will's bullet had shattered the bone.

"He's BTH. Remember?"

"That doesn't mean I can't seriously fuck him up."

Frazier ignored him. He was working angles in his head, scenarios. He was going to have to make some calls, push this way up the food chain to higher pay grades. "A retired FBI agent living in this neighborhood doesn't have three hundred thousand bucks to lay down on an auction. He's fronting for someone. We've got to play this out. Carefully." He passed the laptop back to DeCorso. "Fucking Will Piper!"

Young Cottle was sitting stiffly in an apartment in a strange city trading whispered pleasantries with a fat, sickly man on a scooter, his equally geriatric friend, and another younger man who was looming large and menacing.

Will figured the kid was probably feeling more like a drug mule than an antiquarian book dealer.

Cottle unzipped his bag. The book was swathed in bubble wrap, a soft, fat cube. The man on the scooter did a juvenile gimme with his hands, and Cottle obliged. Spence struggled to control its weight and immediately had to lower it onto the expanse of his lap, where he gingerly started to unwind the plastic, letting it slip to the floor.

Will watched Spence peeling back the layers of the onion, getting closer and closer to calf hide. Despite the profundity of the moment, above all, he was worried that Kenyon might tread on the bubble wrap and wake Phillip in a volley of pops.

The last layer removed, Spence gently opened the cover. He dwelled on the first page, taking it in. Over his shoulder, Kenyon had stooped low. He whispered a faint, "Yes."

Across the room, to Will, the ink scrawl was so dense the page almost looked black. Seeing the names in someone's handwriting gave him a different perspective than reading them in modern sterile fonts on Shackleton's computer database. A human being had dipped a feathered quill into a pot of black ink tens of thousands of times to fill these pages. What on earth was going on inside the writer's mind? Who had he been? How was he able to accomplish this feat?

Cottle broke the spell. Despite his dull expression, he was well-spoken. "They had experts. Oxbridge types. No one had a clue what it was or where it was from beyond the obvious that it's a registry of births and deaths. We were wondering whether you have any knowledge of its origins?"

Spence and Kenyon looked up at the same time. Spence said nothing, so Kenyon had to answer, diplomatically, obliquely. "We're very interested in the period. A lot was going on in the early sixteenth century. It's a unique book, and we're going to do our research. If we find any answers, we'll be happy to let you know."

"That would be appreciated. Naturally, we're curious. A lot to lay out for a book of unknown significance." Cottle checked out the room with his eyes. "Is this your flat, sir?"

Will looked at Cottle suspiciously. Something about his comments struck him as over the line.

"Yeah. All mine."

"Are you from New York, as well, Mr. Spence?"

Spence was evasive. "We're from out West." He decided to change the subject. "Actually, you can help us."

"If I can."

"Tell us about the seller, this Cantwell fellow."

"I've only been with the company a short while, but I'm told he's typical of many of our clients, land rich but cash poor. My supervisor, Peter Nieve, visited Cantwell Hall to review the consignment. It's an old country house in Warwickshire that's been in the family for centuries. Lord Cantwell was there, but Nieve mostly dealt with his granddaughter."

"What did they say about this book?"

"Not much, I think. It's been in their possession as far back as Lord Cantwell remembered. He imagined his family has had it for generations, but there's no particular oral history associated with it. He thought it was some sort of city or town registry. Possibly Continental, given the assortment of languages. He wasn't all that attached to it. Apparently his granddaughter was."

"Why's that?" Spence asked.

"She told Peter she always felt an attachment to the book. She said she couldn't explain it, but she felt it was special and didn't want to see it go. Lord Cantwell felt otherwise."

Spence closed the cover. "And that's it? That's all these people knew about the book's history?"

"That's all I was told, yes."

"There was another bidder," Spence said.

"Another main bidder," Cottle answered.

"Who was he?"

"I'm not permitted to say."

"What nationality," Kenyon asked. "Can you at least tell us that?"

"He was American."

When Cottle left, Will said, "He was kind of curious about us, don't you think?"

Spence laughed. "It's killing them that someone knows more about it than they do. They're probably scared shitless they sold it cheap."

"They have," Kenyon said.

"An American was bidding against you," Will said.

Spence shook his head. "Hope to hell the son of a bitch doesn't work in Nevada. We've got to be careful, keep our guard up." He tapped the book's cover with his finger. "So Will, want to have a look?"

He picked it off Spence's lap and sat back on his sofa. There, he opened it to a random page and lost himself for a few minutes in a litany of lives, long gone, a book of souls.

Cottle hopped back into the waiting taxi and asked to be taken to the Grand Hyatt, where he had a reservation. He was planning to have a quick wash and a good tramp around the city. Perhaps he'd find a club or two before he surrendered to the fatigue of an unexpectedly long day. As the cab pulled away, he left a brief message for Toby Parfitt on his office voice mail, letting him know the delivery was successful. He had a second call to make but he'd wait until he was alone in his hotel room.

Frazier had to make a field decision: follow the courier and extract potentially important information or go straight for Piper and the book. He needed to know whether Piper was alone. What kind of situation would he be getting into if he did a forced entry? He'd be crucified if he wound up dealing with the police tonight.

He wished he had a second team in place, but he didn't. He went with his gut, the knowledge of Cottle's DOD, and decided to go with the courier first. When DeCorso pulled away from Will's building, Frazier looked up at the lit windows on the sixth floor and silently promised he'd be back later.

In midtown, the taxi deposited Cottle at the elevated Vanderbilt Avenue entrance of the Hyatt, where the young man took the escalator down to the cavernous lobby. While he checked in, Frazier and DeCorso watched him from the elevator bank. He'd have to come to them.

Frazier whispered to DeCorso, "Intimidate him, but you don't have to beat the crap out of him. He'll talk. He's just a courier. Find out what he knows about Piper and why he wanted the book. See if anyone else was in his apartment. You know the drill."

DeCorso grunted, and Frazier slipped into the corner lobby bar before Cottle could make him.

Frazier ordered a beer and found an unoccupied table to nurse it. He drank half of it before his phone rang.

One of his men at the Ops Center was on the line with an urgent press of words. "We just dug up some info on your mark, Adam Cottle."

It wasn't easy to surprise Frazier, but the news wrong-footed him. He ended the conversation with a simple and irritated, "All right," then stared at the BlackBerry, trying to decide whether to call DeCorso. He put the phone on the table and drank the other half of the beer in a couple of gulps. It was probably too late to abort. He'd let it ride. There might be hell to pay, but he'd have to let it ride. Fate's the damnedest thing, he thought, the damnedest thing in the world.

DeCorso followed Cottle onto the elevator and looked squarely up at the ceiling where he figured the security camera was affixed. If anything went wrong, the police would focus on him—one hundred percent—once they eliminated everyone else on the elevator. It didn't matter. He didn't exist. His face, his prints: nothing about him inhabited any database other than his Groom Lake personnel file—all the watchers were off the grid. They'd be looking for a ghost.

Cottle hit the button for his floor, and politely asked De-Corso, "Where to?" because he was the only one who hadn't pushed a button.

"Same as you," DeCorso said.

They both exited at twenty-one. DeCorso hung back, pretending to look for his room key while Cottle consulted the hallway sign and made a left. The corridor was long and deserted. He looked free and light as he pulled his bag behind him, a single bloke with an expense account and a night on the town. He was getting his second wind at just the right time.

He slid his room key into the slot, and the lights blinked green. His bag hadn't cleared the threshold when a sound made him look back. The man from the elevator was three feet away, closing fast.

Cottle saw him, and uttered, "Hey!"

DeCorso kicked the door shut behind them, and quickly said, "This isn't a robbery. I need to talk to you."

Inexplicably, Cottle didn't look frightened. "Oh yeah? Then get the fuck out of here and call me on the telephone. You deaf, mate? Get the fuck out."

DeCorso registered disbelief. Something didn't compute. The kid should have been a quivering mass, begging for his life, offering his wallet. Instead, he held his ground. De-Corso demanded, "Tell me what you know about Will Piper, the guy you just saw."

Cottle dropped his bag and clenched and unclenched his fists a few times as if he were limbering them for a dustup. "Look, I don't know who the fuck you are, but you're either going to leave on your own account, or I'm going break you in two and throw out each half."

DeCorso was dumbstruck at the kid's aggression, but he warned, "Don't make this harder than it has to be. You stepped into dogshit, pal. You're just going to have to go with the flow."

"Who do you work for?" Cottle demanded.

DeCorso shook his head in disbelief. "You're asking me questions? You've got to be kidding." It was time for escalation. He pulled a folding knife out of his coat pocket and flicked the blade out with the snap of his wrist. "The book. Why did Piper want it? Was anyone with him tonight? Tell me, and I'm gone. Play with me, and you'll regret it."

Cottle answered by making himself low and compact and suddenly charging at DeCorso, smashing him into the door. The force of impact made him drop the folding knife onto the carpet. Instinctively, DeCorso smashed his fists against the back of Cottle's neck and got some separation by throwing a knee up into his chin.

They were two feet apart; both men had only a moment to look at each other before colliding again. DeCorso saw Cottle assume the crouched posture of a trained fighter, a professional, and this only furthered his confusion. He glanced down at the knife, and Cottle used that instant to attack again, unleashing a flurry of punches and kicks, all of them aimed at the neck and the groin.

DeCorso used his superior body mass to fend Cottle off and move him away from the door. He scanned the room for another weapon. The guy wasn't going to let him get the knife back. And DeCorso wasn't going to neutralize him with his bare hands. This kid was too good for that.

DeCorso lunged forward, and Cottle had the misfortune to step backward onto his roller bag and lose his footing. His landed awkwardly on his back, his head near the night table. DeCorso threw all 250 pounds of his hard body on top of the smaller man and heard a whoosh as the air expelled from Cottle's compressed chest.

Before Cottle could land any counterkicks or punches, DeCorso reached for the digital clock radio on the night-stand and ripped its plug out of the wall. In a wild frenzy, he brought the chunky plastic box down hard on Cottle's cheek, then kept smashing him again and again like a pile-driver until the box had pulverized into plastic shards and circuit boards and Cottle's face was a mass of blood and broken bones. Through secretions, he heard Cottle groaning and swearing.

DeCorso fell to his knees and twisted his waist to look for the knife.

Where was it?

And then he saw it, slashing toward him from Cottle's fist. The blade cut through his overcoat and got hung up in fabric long enough for DeCorso to get both hands on Cottle's fore-arm and snap it down hard against his own knee.

Cottle's primal yell made DeCorso lose control. Years of training and discipline suddenly washed away like a bridge knocked off its piers by floodwaters. The knife was in *his* hand now, and without a second of conscious thought, he leaned over and sliced the right side of the man's already-bloody neck, cleanly severing the carotid artery, and col-lapsed backward to avoid the jets of blood.

DeCorso sat and watched, panting and fighting for air as Cottle bled out and died.

When he was able to compose himself, he took Cottle's wallet and passport, and for show, rifled through his suit-case, scattering the contents. He found the paperwork with Piper's address and pocketed it.

Then he left, still breathing hard.

The newspapers would carry the story for two days,

before the metro reporters would lose interest. A young foreign businessman was the unfortunate victim of a violent hotel robbery.

Tragic, but these things happened in the big city.

Will would never even notice the story. He was preoccupied.

Back in London, alarms started going off after the normally reliable Cottle failed to make his second phone call. The Duty Officer got concerned enough to call Cottle's mobile phone but got no response. It was the middle of the night, deep within the grand modern SIS building at Vauxhall Cross, where the lights perpetually burned brightly. Cottle's SIS section chief finally had an assistant ring the Grand Hyatt to see if he'd checked in.

A desk clerk was dispatched to Cottle's room, pounded on the door, and let himself into a hellish scene.

Kenyon had the book. He was turning the pages with his long fingers, curled over it in a reverential posture. In all his years at Area 51, he had never had the luxury of holding one of the books without the harsh stares of a watcher jangling his nerves.

The three men were not making any noise, but Will was still unpleasantly surprised when the bedroom door opened.

Nancy was squinting at them in her robe.

"I'm sorry," Will said. "I thought we were being quiet."

"I couldn't sleep."

She looked at Spence on his scooter and Kenyon on the sofa with the open book on his lap.

Spence spoke up. "Mrs. Piper, I apologize for intruding. We'll be leaving now."

She moodily shook her head and disappeared into the bathroom.

Will looked guilty, a husband in trouble. At least Phillip wasn't crying.

"Can you rewrap it, Alf? We should go," Spence said.

Kenyon ignored him. He was absorbed. He was comparing the endpapers on the front and back covers, pressing down on them with the fleshy pulp of his fingers.

"There's something wrong with the back cover," he whispered. "I've never seen one like this."

He carried it over to the scooter and put it on Spence's lap. "Show me," Spence demanded.

"It's too thick. And it's spongy. See?"

Spence pushed down on the back endpaper with his pointer finger. "You're right. Will, do you have a sharp knife?"

"You want to cut it?" Kenyon asked.

"I just paid $300,000 for the privilege."

Will had a beautiful little William Henry folding knife, sharp as a razor, a Christmas present from his daughter.

While he rummaged for it in the coffee-table drawer, Nancy came out of the bathroom and pierced him with a look as pointed as the knife blade before clicking the bedroom door shut.

Spence took the pocketknife and boldly cut an eight-inch slit through the edge of the endpaper. Then he inserted the blade, tented up the paper, and tried to get some light in. "I can't see well enough. Do you have tweezers?"

Will sighed and went to the bathroom to get Nancy's.

Spence stuck the tweezers through the slit, probing and clamping until something started to emerge. "There's something in here!" He slowly pulled it through.

A folded piece of parchment.

The creamy sheet was surprisingly fresh and pliable, long protected from the light and the elements. He unfolded it once, twice.

It was written in a flowing archaic script, perfectly centered on the page, executed with care. "Alf. I don't have my glasses. What is it?" He handed it to his friend.

Kenyon studied it, shaking his head in disbelief. He read it to himself, then muttered. "This is incredible. *Incredible.*"

"What?" Spence wheezed impatiently. "What!"

His friend's eyes were moist. "It's a poem, a sonnet actually. It's dated 1581. It's about the book, I'm sure of it."

"Hell you say!" Spence exclaimed, too loud, making Will wince. "Read it to me."

Kenyon read it out loud, his voice hushed but husky with emotion.

Fate's Puzzle

When God did choose to show man's fickle fate,
Throwing wide the doors to heaven and hell,
Wise souls did try to wipe and clean the slate,
Forsooth such secrets surely can't be well:
'Tis best to tuck away and privy hide,
The puzzle pieces numbering one through four,
Lest foolish men awash in willful pride,
Pretend to comprehend and soak up more;
The first one bears Prometheus's flickering flame,
The next does bless the gentle Flemish wind,
The third soars high above a prophet's name,
The last, close by a son who darkly sinned;
When time doth come for humbled man to know,
Let's pray God's grace shan't ebb but swiftly flow.

W. Sh.
1581

Kenyon was shaking with excitement. "W. Sh! Holy Christ!"

"This means something to you?" Will asked.

Kenyon could hardly speak. "Fellows, I think this was written by Shakespeare! William Shakespeare! Do either of you know what year he was born?"

They did not.

"Do you have a computer?"

Will found his laptop under a magazine.

Kenyon literally grabbed it from him to get online, then leapt onto a Googled Shakespeare site. His eyes danced over the first few paragraphs. "Born 1564. He'd be seventeen in 1581. Early life a mystery. Didn't surface in London till 1585 as an actor. Stratford-upon-Avon's in Warwickshire! That's where Cantwell Hall is." He returned to the parchment. "Forsooth such secrets surely can't be well. It's a pun! Can't be well—Cantwell. Shakespeare was a big punster, you know. This is a puzzle poem. He's writing about a series of clues, and I'm certain they're about the origin of this book! They were hidden in Cantwell Hall, I'm sure of it, Henry!"

Spence's jaw was slack. He turned up his oxygen flow a notch for fortification. "Goddamn it! I was right about this book—it *is* special! We've got to go there immediately."

He said "we," but he was staring directly at Will.

When DeCorso met him at the car, Frazier didn't have to ask how it went. It was written all over his face in welts.

"What happened?"

"He was a pro."

"Is that right?"

DeCorso touched his swollen lip. "He was a pro!" he said defensively.

"Did you get anything out of him?"

"No."

"Why not?"

"He put up a fight. It was him or me."

Frazier shook his head. "For fuck's sake."

"I'm sorry." He handed Frazier DeCorso's papers.

Frazier examined the wallet. A license and credit card, some cash. His UK passport looked routine.

DeCorso was reliving the experience in his head. "The guy had commando training. I got lucky. It could've been me."

"He was SIS."

"When did you find that out?"

"A minute before you went in."

"Why didn't you tell me?"

"I knew you'd be okay."

DeCorso angrily folded his arms across his heaving chest and clammed up.

Frazier shook his head. Could a simple operation get more screwed up?

Frazier had been biding his time in the bar by composing a list. Now, he tossed it to DeCorso, who was looking shaky in the driver's seat, parked at a curb a few blocks from the hotel. "Look up these DODs for me."

"Who are they?"

"Will Piper's family. All his relatives."

DeCorso worked quietly, still seething and breathing hard.

In a few minutes, he said, "I just outputted it to your BlackBerry."

The device chimed as he spoke. Frazier opened the email and studied the dates of death for everyone in the world who mattered to Will.

"At least *this* is good," Frazier said. "This is very good."

Early the next morning, Will slipped out of bed to get in a run before his family awoke. The sun was already so bright and inviting it shone like a golden sword through the gap between the bedroom curtains.

He turned on the coffeemaker and hypnotically watched the liquid drip through the filter into the pot, so lost in his thoughts that he didn't notice Nancy until she opened the fridge to get orange juice.

"I'm sorry about last night," he said quickly. "They got their book, and they left."

She ignored him. That's the way this was going to go.

He gamely pressed on. "The book was the real McCoy. It was incredible."

She didn't want to know about it.

"There was a poem hidden in the book. They think it was written by William Shakespeare."

He could tell she was struggling to look disinterested.

"If you want to see it, I scanned it on the printer and left a copy in the top drawer of the desk."

When she didn't respond to that, he changed his tack and gave her a hug, but she kept her body unyielding, her juice glass in her outstretched hand. He let go, and said, "You're not going to be happy about this either, but I'm going to England for a couple of days."

"Will!"

He had the speech rehearsed. "I already called Moonflower this morning. She can give us all the time we need. Henry Spence is paying for it, plus he's giving me a slug of cash, which we can definitely use. Besides, I've been itching for something to do. Be good for me, don't you think?"

She was furious, pupils constricted, nostrils flared. She came out of her corner, throwing big hooks and crosses. "Do you have any idea how this makes me feel?" she fumed. "You're putting us at risk! You're putting Philly at risk! Do you honestly think these people in Nevada aren't going to find out you're fooling around in their sandbox?"

"I'm not going to be doing anything that bumps up against my agreements with them. Just a little research, try to answer a few questions for a dying man."

"Who?"

"You saw him in his wheelie thing and oxygen. He knows his date. It's in a week. He'd do the trip himself if he were healthy."

She was unmoved. "I don't want you to go."

They stared at each other in a standoff. Then Philly started crying, and Nancy stomped away, literally stomping her feet on the kitchen tiles, leaving him alone with his black coffee and matching mood.

It infuriated Frazier that with the vast resources of the US government at their disposal, he had to double up in a hotel room because New York City hotel rates busted through their departmental per diems. It was a second-rate hotel, at that, with a grimy, squishy carpet harboring a lord-knows-what-brew of old emissions. Frazier was sprawled on his twin bed, drinking an awful cup of room-service coffee in his boxers. On the other bed, DeCorso was working away at his laptop, his head wrapped in a good pair of acoustic headphones.

His mobile phone rang and displayed Secretary Lester's private line at the Pentagon. He felt his small intestine clench in involuntary spasm.

"Frazier, you're not going to believe this," Lester said with the controlled anger of a lifelong bureaucrat. "That Cottle guy worked for the Firm! He was SIS!"

"That's what they get for spying on their friends," Frazier said.

"You don't sound surprised."

"That's because I knew."

"You knew? Before or after?"

"Before."

"And you still had him killed? Is that what you're telling me?"

"I didn't have him killed. He attacked my man. It was self-defense, and anyway, it was his day to die. If it weren't us, it would have been a steak sandwich or a fall in the shower. He was dead anyway."

Lester paused long enough for Frazier to wonder whether the call had dropped. "Jesus, Frazier, this stuff can make you crazy. You should have told me, anyway."

"It's on my head, not yours."

"I appreciate that, but still, we've got a problem. The Brits are pissed."

"Do we know what his mission was?"

"They're being cagey," Lester said. "They've always had a chip on their shoulder about Vectis, at least the old-timers."

"Do they knew the book was from the Library?"

"Sure. There's enough institutional memory within their

MOD and Military Intelligence services for them to whisper Vectis whenever we come up with some crazy-ass, forward-looking scenarios—and then they come true! We're getting it now on Helping Hand. They're sure we know more about Caracas then we're letting on, and, frankly, we're sick of their questions and their griping. You and I know damn well the Brits would take the Library back in a heartbeat."

"I'm sure they would."

"They were fools to give it to us in 1947, but that's ancient history."

"What was their plan?"

"They embedded their man at the auction house to keep an eye on the book. They probably found out about it the same way we did, through an Internet filter. Maybe they were going to do a snatch and grab on you and hold us hostage. Who knows. They've got to know you're from Groom Lake. When another buyer got it, they followed their noses to see where the trail led. They definitely wanted to get leverage on us, that much I'm sure."

"What do you want me to do?" Frazier asked.

"Get the book back. And find out what that son of a bitch, Will Piper, is up to. Then immunize us. The Caracas Event is right around the corner, and I don't need to tell you that anyone who's involved in screwing up Helping Hand is as good as buried. I want to hear from you every few hours."

Frazier hung up. Caracas was driving everyone into a frenzy. The whole point of data mining at Area 51 was using knowledge of future events to guide policy and preparation. But Helping Hand was taking their mission to an unprecedented level. Frazier wasn't a political animal, but he was pretty sure a leak right now would blow up the government. Blow it to hell.

He glumly looked over at DeCorso; the man was lost in

his headphones. His face looked like it belonged in a meat locker. He'd been feeding Frazier a steady stream of surveillance information all morning: Piper had called the nanny to arrange for extra hours. He was going away for a few days, didn't say where. Finally, another team of watchers had flown in. One of their men had followed Piper jogging along the river. He'd gone food shopping with his wife and baby. Typical Saturday stuff.

But now DeCorso had something bigger. He spent a few minutes online getting answers to the questions he knew Frazier would ask. When he was done, he removed his headphones. It wasn't just bigger, it was seismic. In their world, a mag-eight quake.

Frazier could see by his face he had something important. "What? What now?"

"You know Henry Spence, right?" DeCorso asked.

Frazier nodded. He knew all about the 2027 Club, a harmless bunch of old coots, as far as he was concerned. The watchers checked up on them from time to time, but the consensus was that Spence ran nothing more than a glorified retirement social club. No harm, no foul. Hell, he'd probably join when he hung up his spurs, if they'd have him—not likely!

"What about him?"

"He just called Piper, cell phone to landline, so they're clueless he's being tapped. Spence is in New York. He bought Piper a first-class ticket with an open return for London. He's leaving tonight."

Frazier rolled his eyes. "For Christ's sake! I knew Piper wasn't alone in this, but Henry Spence? Does he have that kind of cash, or is he fronting for someone else?"

"He's seriously loaded. Dead wife's money. There's more."

Frazier shook his head and told him to spit it out.

"He's been sick. His DOD's in eight days. Wonder if it's gonna be natural causes or us."

Frazier was shoving his legs into his trousers. "God only knows."

Will felt good to be out on the road, traveling light, like the old days. He'd had an excellent night's rest in a cushy first-class sleeper seat which, by a twist of fate he'd never know, was originally intended for young, dead Adam Cottle. He wasn't an experienced international traveler, but he'd been to the UK and Europe a few times on Bureau business. He'd even given a talk at New Scotland Yard a few years back, titled "Sex and the Serial Killer—The American Experience." It had been well attended, and, afterward, a bunch of ranking detectives had taken him out on a pub crawl that predictably ended in amnesia.

Now he was chugging through the flat English countryside in a Chiltern Rail first-class car an hour out of Marylebone Station on the Birmingham line. The gray sprawl of London had given way to the earth tones of cultivated land, a palette of greens and browns muted by the wash of a wet autumn day. At full throttle, the rainwater on the train's windows streaked horizontally. His eyelids grew heavy watching the tilled fields, rolls of hay, and drab, utilitarian farm buildings whizzing by. Small villages filled the window for seconds, then were gone. He had the compartment to himself. It was a Sunday, and this was low season for tourists.

Back home, he imagined that Nancy would be up soon,

and later in the morning she would take Phillip out in the stroller, that is, if it weren't pouring there too. He'd forgotten to check the forecast before he left but regardless, he was certain Nancy would have her head in a personal little rain cloud. When he got done with his treasure hunt, he planned to spend some time in Harrods figuring out how to buy his way out of his mess. Anyway, he could afford it. He was embarrassed to tell her, but Spence had made an off-the-scale offer. He'd never considered himself someone who could be seduced by money, but then again, no one had ever thrown cash his way before. As a new experience, it wasn't unpleasant.

The price tag for the assignment? A check for $50,000 and the title to the bus! As soon as Spence kicked it, the motor home was his. He didn't know how he'd afford to gas it up, but worst case, he'd plant the thing in an RV park in the Florida panhandle and make it their vacation getaway.

The bigger carrot was still on the stick. Spence wanted the DODs for his clan, but on that request, Will would not relent. The number Spence put on the table made him gasp for air, but there wasn't enough money on the planet. If he flagrantly violated his confidentiality agreements, then he was afraid Nancy's assessment would be correct. He'd be putting their heads on the chopping block.

Awakening from a doze, he heard the conductor over the loudspeaker and blinked at his watch. He'd been out for the better part of an hour, and the train was slowing as it approached the outskirts of the large market town.

Stratford-upon-Avon. Shakespeare country. The irony made him smile. He'd gotten into Harvard because he could clobber a running back who was trying to get a football past him, not because of his aptitude in literature. He'd never read a word of Shakespeare in his life. Both his ex-wives were theater nuts, but it wasn't contagious. Even Nancy tried to get him to see a crowd-pleaser, *Macbeth,* if he recalled, but he'd pouted so much, she dropped it. He couldn't imagine what all the fuss was about, and here he was, carrying perhaps the rarest of all Shakespearean artifacts, possibly the only known piece of work definitively written in Shakespeare's own hand.

The station was Sunday-quiet, with only a handful of cabs at the stand. A driver was standing next to his car, smoking a cigarette in the drizzle, his cap soaked through. He flicked away the butt and asked Will where he was heading.

"Going to Wroxall," Will said. "A place called Cantwell Hall."

"Didn't figure you for a Willie Wonka tourist," the cabbie said, looking him up and down. Will didn't get his meaning. "You know, Willie Shake Rattle and Roll, the great bard and all that."

Everyone's a profiler, these days, Will thought.

Wroxall was a small village about ten miles north of Stratford, deeper into the ancient Forest of Arden, now hardly that, the forest cleared centuries ago for agriculture. The Normans had called Arden the beautiful wild country. The best description it could muster today would be pleasant and tame.

The taxi sped along the secondary roads past dense hedgerows of field maple, hawthorn, and hazel, and plowed, stubbly fields.

"Lovely weather you brung with you," the cabbie said.

Will didn't want to do small talk.

"Most folks going to Wroxall go to the Abbey Estate conferencing center. Beautiful place, all done up 'bout ten years back, stately hotel and all. Christopher Wren's country digs."

"Not where I'm going."

"So you said. Never been up to Cantwell Hall, but I know where it is. What brings you here, if I may ask?"

What would this guy say if he told him the truth, Will thought? I'm here to solve the greatest mystery in the world, driver. Meaning of life and death. Beginning and end. Throw in the existence of God while you're at it. That's why I'm here. "Business," he said.

The village itself was a blip. A few dozen houses, a pub, post office, and general store.

"Entering and leaving Wroxall village," the cabbie said with a nod. "Just two miles on now."

The entrance to Cantwell House was unmarked, a couple of brick pillars on either side of a threadbare gravel lane with a central row of untamed grass. The lane plunged through an overgrown, wet meadow dotted with the fading hues of late-season wildflowers, limp, blue speedwells mostly, and the occasional clump of fleshy mushrooms. In the distance, around a sharp curve, he caught sight of gables peeking above a high hedge of hawthorn that obscured most of the building.

As they got closer, the sheer magnitude of the house jumped out at him. It was a hodgepodge of gables and chimneys, pale, weathered brick rendered over a visible Tudor exoskeleton of dark purplish timbers. Through the hedge, he could see that the central face of the house was completely clad in ivy cut away from white-framed leaded windows by someone who seemed to lack a facility for right angles and straight lines. The pitched and multiangled slate roof was slimy and moss green, more animate than inanimate. What he could see of the tangled front garden beds suggested they were, at best, lightly tended.

Passing through a generous, hedge-formed portico, the

lane turned into a circular drive. The cab crunched to a halt on gravel near a latticed, oak door. The front windows were dead and reflective. "Dark as a tomb in there," the driver said. "Want me to wait?"

Will got out and paid. There was a wisp of smoke coming from one of the chimneys. He cut the man loose. "I'm good," he said, shouldering his bag. He pressed the buzzer and heard a faint interior chime. The taxi disappeared through the second hedged portico, back to the lane.

The entrance was unprotected from the elements, and while he listened for signs of life, his hair was slicking with rain. After a good minute, he pressed the buzzer again, then used his knuckles for emphasis.

The woman who opened the door was wetter than he was. She'd obviously been caught in the shower and without time to towel off had thrown on a pair of jeans and a shirt.

She was tall and graceful, a cultured, expressive face with confident eyes, skin, young and fresh, the color of buttermilk. Her clavicle-length blond hair was dripping onto her cotton shirt, and the outline of her breasts showed through its wet translucency.

"I'm terribly sorry," she said. "It's Mr. Piper, isn't it?"

She's gorgeous, he thought, not what he needed right now. He nodded, and said, "Yes ma'am," like a polite Southern gentleman, and followed her inside.

he housekeeper's at church, Granddad's deaf as a post, and I was in the shower, so you, I'm afraid, were left standing out in this wretched weather."

The entrance hall was indeed dark, a two-story paneled vault with a staircase ascending to a gallery landing. Will felt that it was as inviting as a museum, and he started worrying he'd clumsily knock over a porcelain plate, a clock, or a vase. She flicked a switch, and a giant Waterford chandelier started glowing over their heads as if a bottle rocket had exploded.

She took his coat and hung it on a hatstand and parked his bag though he insisted on keeping his briefcase with him. "Let's get you to the fire, shall we?"

The centerpiece of the dimly lit Tudor Great Hall was a massive hearth, large enough to roast a pig. The fireplace frame was as dark as ebony, ornately carved, and shiny with antiquity. It had a chunky mantel and a straight-lined, medieval appearance, but at some point in its history someone had been stricken with a Continental bug and overlain the hardwood fascia with a double row of blue-and-white Delft tiles. There was a modest fire, which seemed small and disproportionate to the size of the vault, going. The chimney wasn't drawing well, and wisps of smoke were backing into the room and floating up to the high, walnut-beamed ceiling. Out of courtesy he tried not to clear his throat, but he couldn't suppress it.

"Sorry about the smoke. Got to do something about that." She pointed him to a soft, lumpy arm chair closest to the flames. When he sat on it, he detected a whiff of urine, astringent and acid. She bent over and placed another couple of logs on the fire and prodded the stack with a poker. "I'll just put a pot of coffee on and make myself a bit more presentable. I promise I won't be long."

"Take your time, I'm fine, ma'am."

"It's Isabelle."

He smiled at her. "Will."

Through watery, irritated eyes, Will took in the room. It was windowless, densely packed with furniture and centuries of bric-a-brac. The zone near the hearth seemed the place that was most functional and lived-in. The sofas and chairs were twentieth-century, designed for cushioned comfort, a few high-intensity reading lights, tables littered with newspapers and magazines, tea and coffee mugs scattered about, careless white rings from wet glasses imprinting the wood. The middle and borders of the Great Hall were more museumlike, and if Henry VIII had just arrived from a hunt, he would have felt at ease with its Tudor airs and splendor. The coffered, walnut walls were covered to the beams in tapestries, taxidermy, and paintings, dozens of dour-faced and bearded Cantwells peering down from their sooty canvases in their frilly collars, robes, and doublets, a gallery of men's high fashion throughout the ages. The mounted stags' heads, locked in surprise at their moment of death, were a reminder how these men had spent their leisure.

A majority of the furnishings stood on or around a massive, Persian rug, worn at the edges but pristine at the center, protected by an oak trestle banqueting table ringed by high chairs covered in red cloth. Each cushion back was adorned with a single embroidered Tudor rose. Atop both ends of the table was a pair of silver candlesticks, large as baseball bats, with thick white candles half again as tall.

After a while, Will got up and took a tour of the dark recesses of the room. There was a layer of dust everywhere, blanketing all surfaces and objets d'art. It would take an army of feather dusters to make a dent. Through a doorway, he looked into another darkened room, the library. He was about to wander in when Isabelle returned with a tray of coffee and biscuits. Her hair was drier, pulled back into a ponytail, and she had hastily applied some makeup and lip gloss.

"I should put more lights on. It's like a mausoleum in here. This room was built in the fifteenth century. They seemed to have no desire whatsoever to let any light in—I expect they thought it was healthier to seal themselves away."

Over coffee, she inquired about his trip and told him how surprised and intrigued they had been to receive a call from the buyer of their book. She was keen to hear more, but she put Will off until her grandfather awoke from his nap. He was something of an insomniac, and it wasn't unusual for him to fall asleep at dawn and awake at midday. They marked time by sharing their backgrounds, and each seemed intrigued by the other's life.

Isabelle seemed fascinated she was conversing with a living, breathing ex–FBI agent, the kind of person who, to her, existed only in films and novels. She gazed into his magnetically blue eyes as he regaled her in his soft drawl with stories about old cases.

When the conversation turned to her life, Will found her charming and winsome, with a selfless, admirable streak, a young woman so devoted to her grandfather she took a year off from university to care for him in this remote, drafty old house and help him adjust to life without his wife of fifty years. She'd been slated to start her last year at Edinburgh, reading European history, when Lady Cantwell suffered a fatal stroke. Isabelle's parents were in London and tried to get the old man to come down, but he vehemently objected. He was born at Cantwell Hall and, like a good Cantwell, would die there too. Eventually, something would have to give, but Isabelle volunteered a temporary solution.

She'd always loved the house and would reside there for a year, doing spadework for a future doctoral dissertation on the English Reformation and comforting the grieving old man. The Cantwells, she told Will, were a microcosm of the sixteenth-century Catholic-Protestant divide, and the house had born witness to some of that cataclysm. A fear of hers was when Lord Cantwell passed, the inheritance taxes would force the family to sell it to a developer, at worst, or the National Trust, at best. In either case, it would be the end of a family lineage that stretched back to the thirteenth century, when King John granted the first Cantwell, Robert of Wroxall, a baronial tract of land, upon which he built a square stone tower, on this very spot.

Finally, she opened up about the book. They were over the moon it had fetched an astronomical price at auction but she was desperately unhappy to see it pass out of family hands. Even as a girl, she'd been captivated by it, always finding it strange and mysterious, and she offered that its 1527 date had fueled her interest in that period of British history. She had hoped one day to discover what the book represented and how it came to rest at Cantwell Hall. Still, she admitted, the auction proceeds would keep the estate functioning for a while longer though it didn't solve some very expensive and pressing structural issues. There was rising damp, rotting timbers, the roof had to be redone, the electricals were a disaster, the plumbing a bloody mess. She joked they'd probably have to sell off every piece inside the house to afford to fix the house itself.

Will was taking guilty pleasure in the conversation. This woman was his daughter's age! Despite his spat with Nancy, he was a happily married man with a new son. His days as a rover and a cad were behind him, no? He almost wished that Isabelle weren't quite so stimulating. Her long, sensual body and rapier-sharp mind were a twin-barreled shotgun aimed at the mass of his chest. He feared he was a double-trigger pull from being blown away. At least he was sober. That helped.

He was itching to get on with business and wondered when Lord Cantwell would make his grand appearance. Provocatively, he asked a question that caught her off guard. "How much would it take to fix the place up and clear out your future tax problems?"

"What an odd question."

He pressed for an answer.

"Well, I'm not a builder or an accountant, but I'd imagine it's in the millions!"

Will smiled impishly. "I may have something in my bag that'll solve your problems."

She arched her eyebrows, suspiciously, and said dryly, "Wouldn't that be marvelous. Why don't I see what's keeping Granddad?"

Just as she rose to find him, the old man shuffled into the Great Hall, staring quizzically at Will.

"Who's that?" he called out.

She answered at a volume he could hear. "It's Mr. Piper from America."

"Oh, right. Forgot about that. Long way to come. Don't know why he didn't just use the telephone."

She ushered Lord Cantwell over for introductions.

He was well into his eighties, mostly bald except for an unruly fringe of silvery hair. His red, eczematous face was a weed garden of hairy tufts the razor missed. He was dressed for a Sunday afternoon, twill trousers, herringbone sports coat and an ancient university tie, shiny with wear. Will noticed his trousers were too large for him, and he was using a fresh belt hole. Recent weight loss, not a good sign in an older fellow. He was stiff with arthritis and had the gait of a man who hadn't loosened up yet. When Will shook his hand, he got a stronger whiff of urine and concluded he'd been sitting on the fellow's favorite chair.

Will ceded Cantwell his usual seat, a courtesy Isabelle approvingly noticed. She poured her grandfather a coffee, then improved the fire and offered Will her chair, pulling up a footstool for herself.

Cantwell was not given to subtlety. He took a loud slurp of coffee and boomed, "Why in hell did you want to spend 200,000 quid on my book? Obviously pleased you did, but for the life of me, I don't see the value."

Will spoke up to penetrate the man's hearing impediment. "I'm not the buyer, sir. Mr. Spence called you. He's the buyer. He's very interested in the book."

"Why?"

"He thinks it's a valuable historical document. He has some theories, and he asked me to come over here and see if I could find out more about it."

"Are you an historian like my Isabelle? You thought the book was worth something, didn't you, Isabelle?"

She nodded and smiled proudly at her grandfather.

Will said, "I'm not an historian. More like an investigator."

"Mr. Piper used to be with the American Federal Bureau of Investigation," Isabelle offered.

"J. Edgar Hoover's gang, eh? Never liked him."

"He's been gone for a while, sir."

"Well, I don't think I can help you. That book's been in our family as long as I can remember. My father didn't know its provenance, nor did my grandfather. Always considered it a one-off oddity, some sort of municipal registry, possibly Continental in origin."

It was time to play his cards. "I have something to tell you," Will said, looking each one of them in the eye, playing out a melodrama. "We found something hidden in the book, which may be of considerable value and might help answer questions about the book's origins."

"I went through every page!" Isabelle protested. "What was hidden? Where?"

"Under the back endpaper. There was a sheet of parchment."

"Bugger!" Isabelle cried. "Bugger! Bugger!"

"Such language," Cantwell scolded.

"It was a poem," Will continued, amused by the girl's florid exasperation. "There wasn't time to vet it, but one of Mr. Spence's colleagues thinks it's about the book." He was milking it now. "Guess who it's written by?"

"Who?" Isabelle demanded impatiently.

"You're not going to guess?"

"No!"

"How about William Shakespeare."

The old man and the girl first looked to each other for reaction, then turned back to the certifiable American.

"You're joking!" Cantwell huffed.

"I don't believe it!" Isabelle exclaimed.

"I'm going to show it to you," Will said, "and here's the

deal. If it's authentic, one of my associates says it's worth millions, maybe tens of millions. Apparently there isn't a single confirmed document that exists in Shakespeare's handwriting, and this puppy's signed, at least partially—W. Sh. Mr. Spence is going to keep the book, but he's willing to give the poem back to the Cantwell family if you'll help us with something."

"With what?" the girl asked suspiciously.

"The poem is a map. It refers to clues about the book, and the best guess is that they were hidden in Cantwell Hall. Maybe they're still here, maybe they're long gone. Help me with the Easter egg hunt, and, win or lose, the poem's yours."

"Why would this Spence give us back something he rightfully paid for?" Cantwell mused. "Don't think I would."

"Mr. Spence is already a wealthy man. And he's dying. He's willing to trade the poem for some answers, simple as that."

"Can we see it?" Isabelle asked.

He pulled the parchment from his briefcase. It was protected by a clear, plastic sleeve, and, with a flourish, he handed it to her.

After a few moments of study, her lips began to tremble in excitement. "Can't be well," she whispered. She'd found it immediately.

"What was that?" the old man asked, irritably.

"There's a reference to our family, Granddad. Let me read it to you."

She recited the sonnet in a clear voice, fit for a recording, with nuances of playfulness and drama as if she had read it before and rehearsed its delivery.

Cantwell furrowed his brow. "Fifteen eighty-one, you say?"

"Yes, Granddad."

He pressed down hard on the armrests and worked himself upright before Will or Isabelle could offer assistance, then started shuffling toward a dim corner of the room. They followed, as he muttered to himself. "Shakespeare's grandfather, Richard was from the village. Wroxall's Shakespeare country." He was scanning the far wall. "Where is he? Where's Edgar?"

"Which Edgar, Granddad? We've had several."

"You know, the Reformer. Not our blackest sheep, but not far off. He would have been lord of the manor in 1581. There he is. Second from the left, halfway up the wall. You see? The fellow in the ridiculously high collar. Not one of the most handsome Cantwells—we've had some genetic variation over the centuries."

Isabelle switched on a floor lamp, casting some light upon a portrait of a dour, pointy-chinned man with a reddish goatee standing in an arrogant, puffy-chested, three-quarter pose. He was dressed in a tight, black tunic with large gold buttons and had a conical Dutch-style hat with a saucer-shaped brim.

"Yes, that's him," Cantwell affirmed. "We had a chap in from the National Gallery a good while back who said it might have been painted by Robert Peake the Elder. Remind your father of that when I pop off, Isabelle. Could be worth a few quid if he needs to flog it."

From across the room, a woman's foghorn voice startled them. "Hallo! I'm back. Give me an hour, and I'll have lunch ready." The housekeeper, a short, sturdy woman, was still in her wet scarf, clutching her handbag, all business.

Isabelle called to her, "Our visitor is here, Louise."

"I can see that. Did you find the clean towels I put out?"

"We haven't been upstairs yet."

"Well, don't be rude!" she scolded. "Let the gentleman have a wash. He's come a long way. And send your grandfather to the kitchen for his pills."

"What's she going on about?"

"Louise says, take your pills."

Cantwell looked up at his ancestor and shrugged emphatically. "To be continued, Edgar. That woman strikes fear in my heart."

The upstairs guest wing was cool and dark, a long, paneled hall with brass valances and dim-watted bulbs every few yards, rooms on either side, hotel-style, long, worn runners. Will's room faced the rear. He gravitated toward the windows to watch the intensifying storm and absently brushed dead flies off the sills. There was a brick patio below and a wild expanse of garden beyond, fruit trees leaning in the stiff wind and sideways rain. In the foreground, off to his right, he could see the edge of what looked like a stables, and over its roof, the top of an outbuilding, some sort of spired structure, indistinct in the downpour.

After he splashed some water on his face he sat on the four-poster and stared at the single bar of service on his mobile phone, probably just enough for a call home. He imagined the awkward conversation. What would he say that wouldn't just get him into more trouble? Better to get this over with and start to thaw out his marriage in person. He settled for a text message: *Arrived safely. Home soon. Love U.*

The bedroom was old-ladyish, lots of dried flowers and frilly pillows, gossamer, lace curtains. He kicked off his shoes, laid out his heavy body on top of the floral bedspread, and dutifully napped for an hour until Isabelle's voice, chiming like a small bell, called him for lunch.

Will's appetite took everything that Louise could throw at him and more. The Sunday roast dinner sat well with his meat-and-potatoes predilection. He ate a small mountain of roast beef, roast potatoes, peas, carrots, and gravy but stopped himself from drinking a third glass of Burgundy.

Isabelle asked her grandfather, "Is there any history of Shakespeare visiting Cantwell Hall?"

The old man answered through a mouthful of peas. "Never heard of anything like that, but why not? This would have been his stomping ground in his youth. We were a prominent family that largely maintained its Catholicism throughout that dreadful period, and the Shakespeares were probably closeted Catholics as well. And even back then, we had a splendid library that would have interested the fellow. It's perfectly plausible."

"Any theories why Edgar Cantwell would have gone to the trouble of having a poem written, hiding clues, then stashing the poem in the book?" Will asked.

Cantwell swallowed his peas, then drank the rest of his wine. "Sounds to me like they had the inkling the book was dangerous. Those were trying times, easy to get killed for your beliefs. I suppose they couldn't bring themselves to destroy the book. Thought it better to hide its significance in a fanciful way. Probably a rubbish explanation, but that's what I think, anyway."

Isabelle was beaming. "I have visions of my dissertation taking a rather more interesting turn."

"So what do you say?" Will asked. "Do we have a deal?"

Isabelle and Lord Cantwell nodded. They had discussed the matter while Will had napped.

"Yes, we do," Isabelle answered. "Let's begin our little adventure after lunch."

They began in the library. It was a generous room, with bare, plank floors shiny with wear, a few good rugs, and one front-facing exterior wall that let gray, stormy light in through diamond-paned leaded windows. The other walls were lined with bookshelves except for the space above the fireplace, which had a soot-darkened canvas of a traditional English hunting party.

There were thousands of books, most of them premodern, but one section on the side wall had a smattering of contemporary hardcovers and even a few paperbacks. Will took it all in with heavy, postprandial eyes. Lord Cantwell had already announced his afternoon nap, and despite Will's anxiousness to get the job done and get home, the thought of flopping in one of the overstuffed library chairs in a darkened corner and shutting his eyes again was appealing.

"This was my magic place when I was a child," Isabelle told him as she drifted through the room, lightly touching book spines with her fingertips. "I love this room." She had a slow, dreaminess, a languid contrast to the reference set in his mind of flighty college kids. "I played in here for hours at a time. It's where I spend most of my time now." She pointed at a long table crowded with notebooks and pens, a laptop computer, and stacks of old books with slips of paper sticking out, marking passages of interest. "If your poem's authentic, I might have to start from scratch!"

"Sorry. You're not going to be able to use it. I'll explain later."

"You're joking! It would launch my career."

"What is it you want to do?"

"Teach, write. I want to be a proper academic historian, a stuffy old professor. This library's probably responsible for that odd ambition."

"I don't think it's odd. My daughter's a writer." He didn't know why, but he added, "She's not much older than you," which made her giggle nervously. He headed off the politely inevitable questions about Laura by abruptly saying, "Show me where the book was kept?"

She pointed at a gap in one of the eye-level shelves in the middle of the long wall.

"Was it always there?"

"As long as I remember."

"And the books next to it? Was there a lot of rearranging?"

"Not in my lifetime. We can ask Granddad, but I don't recall any shifting about. Books stayed in their place."

He inspected the books on either side of the gap. An eighteenth-century botany book and a seventeenth-century volume on monuments of the Holy Land.

"No, they're not contemporaneous," she observed. "I doubt there's an association."

"Let's start with the first clue," Will said, retrieving the poem from his case. "The first one bears Prometheus's flame."

"Right," she said. "Prometheus. Stole fire from Zeus and gave it to mortals. That's my sum total."

Will gestured around the room, "Anything come to mind?"

"Well, it's rather broad, isn't it? Books on Greek mythology? Hearths? Torches? The barbecue pit!"

He gave her a "very funny" look. "Let's start with the books. Is there a catalogue?"

"Needs to be one, but there isn't. Another problem, of course, is that Granddad has been rather vigorous in his selling."

"Nothing we can do about that," Will said. "Let's be systematic. I'll start on this end. Why don't you start over there?"

While they focused on the first clue, for the sake of efficiency, they kept the others in mind to prevent redoing the exercise if possible. They kept a lookout for any Flemish or Dutch-themed books and any text that seemed to refer to a prophet of any sort. They had no inkling how to tackle the "son who sinned" reference.

The process was laborious, and an hour into it, Will was growing discouraged by its needle-in-a-haystack quality. And often, it wasn't as easy as pulling a book out, opening the title page, and shoving it back. He needed Isabelle's help with every book in Latin or French. She would come over, give a quick peek, and hand it back with a light, "Nope!"

The afternoon light, as muted as it was, faded completely, and Isabelle responded by turning on every fixture and taking a match to the fireplace kindling. "Behold, I give you fire!" she said as the flames licked the logs.

By early evening, they were done. Despite a not-very-old volume of *Bullfinch's Mythology,* there wasn't a single book that sparked a modicum of interest. "Either the poem's not referring to a book, or it's not here anymore. Let's move on," Will said.

"All right," she said agreeably. "We'll have a look at all the old fireplaces. Hidden panels, false mantels, loose stones. I'm having fun! You?"

He checked his phone again for a text messages from Nancy. There were none. "Having a blast," he answered.

By Isabelle's reckoning, there were six fireplaces that pre-dated 1581. Three were on the ground level, the library, the Great Hall and the dining room, and three were on the first floor—in her grandfather's bedroom above the Great Hall and in a second and third bedroom.

They began their inspection in the library, standing before the roaring fire and wondering what to do. "Why don't I just knock on the panels for hollow bits?" she suggested. It sounded like a perfectly good idea to him.

The ancient walnut mantel sounded solid to her knuckles. They checked the bevels of the mantelpiece for hidden latches or hinges, but it appeared to be one immovable carpentered board. The stones of the hearth floor were solid and level, and all of the mortar looked similar. The fire was still going, so they wouldn't be checking the brickwork in the firebox for a while, but nothing stood out to cursory inspection.

The fire in the Great Hall had long died out. Lord Cantwell was half-reading, half-dozing in his chair, and he seemed nonplussed over their investigative work as they tapped and felt their way around the massive fireplace. "Really!" he snorted.

The surround was beautifully fluted and shiny with age, and the mantelpiece was a massive beveled slab, hewn from one huge timber. Isabelle hopefully tapped on the blue-and-white square tiles, which were inlaid on the surround, each one bearing a little decorative country scene, but they all had the same timbre. Will volunteered to hunch over and crab-walk into the huge firebox, where he tapped at the bricks with a poker. But for his efforts he was rewarded only with patches of soot on his shirt and trousers. Isabelle pointed the smudges out and watched in amusement as he tried to brush them away with his palm.

The three other fireplaces got the same treatment. If something were hidden in one of them, they'd need a wrecking crew to find it.

It had gotten dark. The rain had stopped, and a cold front was racing through the heart of the country, bringing frigid, howling winds. Cantwell Hall lacked central heating, and the drafty rooms were getting chilly. Louise loudly announced she would serve tea in the Great Hall. She had restarted the fire and switched on the electric heater by Lord Cantwell's chair, then made clear she was anxious to be off for home.

Will joined Isabelle and her grandfather in a light assortment of meat-and-pickle sandwiches, shortbread biscuits, and tea. Louise scurried around, doing some last-minute chores, then inquired if they intended to stay in the Great Hall for the evening. "For a while longer," Isabelle answered.

"I'll light the candles then," she offered, "as long as you're careful to blow them out before you turn in."

As they munched, Louise used a disposable plastic lighter to light a dozen candles throughout the room. With the wind whistling outside, the fireplace hissing, and the ancient room in its windowless gloom, the candles seemed reassuring points of light. Will and Isabelle watched Louise as she ignited the last candlestick and retreated from the room.

Suddenly, they looked at each other, and simultaneously exclaimed, "Candlesticks!"

Lord Cantwell asked if they'd gone mad, but Isabelle answered him with an urgent question. "Which of our candlesticks are sixteenth-century or earlier?"

He scratched at his fringe of hair and pointed toward the

center of the room, "The pair of silver-gilt ones on the table, I should think. Believe they're Venetian, fourteenth-century. Tell your father that if I pop off, they're worth a few quid."

They rushed to the candlesticks, blew them out, and removed the thick, waxy candles, placing them on a silver tray. They were pricket style, with big spikes on bowls spearing enormous five-inch-diameter candles. Each candlestick had an elaborately tooled, six-petaled base of gold-coated silver. From each base rose a central column that progressively widened out into a Romanesque tower resembling the peak-windowed spire of a church, each of the six windows rendered in blue enamel. Above each spire, the column extended into the cup and pricket of the candleholder.

"They're light enough, they could be hollow," Will said, "but the bases are solid."

He closely inspected the joined segments of the complicated column. She urged him on, "Go ahead, give it a twist," she whispered. "Turn your back to Granddad. I don't want to give him a heart attack."

Will wrapped his left hand around the windowed spire and tried to turn the base with his right hand, gently at first, then with more force, until his face reddened. He shook his head and put it down. "No joy." Then he tried hers with the same maneuver. It held firm as if it were forged from a single piece of metal. He relaxed his shoulder and arm muscles when a spasm of frustration made him try one more furious twist.

The column turned.

Half a rotation, but it turned.

She whispered, "Go on!"

He kept up the pressure until the column was spinning freely and the nongilded sleeve of a tube within a tube became visible. Finally, the base gave way completely. He had one half of a candlestick in each hand.

"What are you two up to?" Cantwell called out. "Can't hear a thing."

"Just a minute, Granddad!" Isabelle shouted. "Hang on!"

Will put the base down and peered into the hollow-tubed spire. "I need a light." He followed her over to one of the standing lamps, stuck his index finger inside the tube, and felt a firm, circular edge. "There's something in there!" He pulled his finger out and tried to have a look, but the incandescent bulb didn't help. "My finger's too big to get it. You try."

Hers was thin, and she slid in all the way and closed her eyes to heighten the tactile impressions. "It's something rolled, like paper or parchment. I'm in the middle of it. There! I've got it turning."

She slowly twisted the candlestick around her finger, applying firm, gentle pressure with the pulp of her fingertip.

A yellowed scroll began to emerge.

It was cylindrical, about eight inches long, multiple sheets of parchment tightly rolled. In shocked excitement, she started to hand it to him, but he said, "No, you."

She slowly unrolled the cylinder. The parchment was dry but not brittle, and it unspooled easily enough. She flattened the sheets with both hands and Will tilted the lamp shade for more light. "It's in Latin," she said.

"That makes me especially glad you're here."

She read the heading on the first page and translated it aloud: An Epistle from Felix, Abbot of Vectis Abbey, written in the year of our Lord, 1334.

He felt light-headed. "Jesus."

"What is it, Will?"

"Vectis."

"You know the place?"

"Yeah, I know it. I think we hit the mother lode."

1334
Isle of Wight

In the stillness of the night, an hour after Lauds and two hours before Prime, Felix, Abbot of Vectis Abbey, awoke with one of his terrible headaches. There was cricket song outside his window and the faint pulse of waves from the Solent cresting against the nearby shore. The sounds were soothing but gave him only a moment's pleasure before a spasm of nausea made him sit bolt upright. He fumbled in the dark for the chamber pot and dry-heaved.

He was sixty-nine years old and fiercely doubted he would see his next decade.

There was little food in his stomach. His last meal was beef broth prepared specially by the sisters, greasy with marrow and flecked with carrots. He had left the bowl half-uneaten on his writing table.

He threw off his covers, pushed himself from his straw mattress, and managed to stand with some swaying. The rhythmic pounding in his head felt like a blacksmith striking repeated blows on an anvil, each one threatening to upend him, but he was steady enough to retrieve his heavy fur-lined robe, draped over a high-backed chair. He slipped it on over his night smock and immediately felt its comforting warmth. Then he shakily lit a thick yellow candle and slumped on the chair to massage his temples. The candlelight played against the uneven polished stones of his bed-chamber floor and reflected off the gaily colored glass of the courtyard windows.

The richness of the abbot house had always disquieted him. When he entered Vectis as a novice, so very long ago, his head lowered in humility, his coarse habit bound with cord, his feet cold and bare, he felt close to God, and thus, close to bliss. His predecessor, Baldwin, a flinty cleric who took as much pleasure poring over granary accounts as conducting mass, had commissioned a fine timbered house to rival those he had seen at abbeys in London and Dorchester. Adjoining the bedchamber was a magnificent great room with an ornate fireplace, carved settle, horsehair chairs, and stained glass. On the walls were cloth hangings, finely woven tapestries of hunts and acts of the Apostles, from Flanders and Bruges. Above the hearth was an artisan-tooled silver cross, the length of a man's arm.

Upon Baldwin's death many years earlier, the Bishop of Dorchester had chosen Felix, the abbey's prior to ascend to be Abbot of Vectis. Felix prayed hard for guidance. Perhaps he should eschew the finery of the position and opt for a modest reign, sleep in a monk's cell with the brothers, continue to wear his simple habit, take his meals communally. But would that not besmirch the memory of his mentor, his confessor? Would it not brand Baldwin a profligate? He bowed to the power of Baldwin's memory, the way he had bowed to the power of the man during his life. Ever the faithful servant, he never failed to do Baldwin's bidding, even when he had misgivings. What would have happened if he had questioned Baldwin's decision to abolish the Order of the Names? Would things be different today had he not, with his own hand, lit the hay that consumed the Library almost forty years ago?

He felt too ill to kneel, so he lowered his throbbing head and softly prayed out loud, his Breton accent as coarse and pebbly as when he was a boy. The choice of prayer, from Psalm 42, came to him with spontaneity, almost taking him by surprise:

> *Introibo ad altare Dei. Ad Deum qui laetificat*
> *juventutem meatum.*
> I will go to the altar of God. To God,
> the joy of my youth.
> *Gloria Patri, et Filio, et Spiritui Sancto. Sicut erat*
> *in principio, et nunc, et semper, et in saecula*
> *saeculorum. Amen.*
> Glory be to the Father and to the Son, and to the
> Holy Spirit. As it was in the beginning, is now,
> and ever shall be, world without end. Amen

He pursed his lips at the irony of the prayer.

World without end.

Once, his beard had been as thick and black as a boar's cheek. He had been muscular and robust, able to handle the rigors of monastic life tirelessly, the meager rations, the cold sea winds that frosted the bones, the manual labors that broke the body but sustained the community, the brief periods of sleep between the canonical hours that punctuated night and day with communal prayer. Now his beard was patchy, the dirty white of a seagull's breast, and his cheeks were sunken. His fine muscles had withered and sagged, and his skin, drained of suppleness, was as dry as parchment and so itchy and scabbed it distracted him from prayer and meditation.

But the most alarming physical change affected his right eye, which had progressively begun to bulge and stare. It was a slow, creeping process. At first he only noticed a pink dryness, like a mote of grit that could not be lavaged. Then the mild throb behind the orbit became worse, and his vision became troublesome. Initially, there was some blurring, then blinding flashes of light, now a distressing doubling of images that made it difficult to read and write with both eyes open. In recent weeks, every man and woman within the abbey walls had anxiously noticed the bulging prominence of his eyeball. They whispered among themselves while they milked cows or tended crops, and at prayer they beseeched God to show their brother mercy.

Brother Girardus, the abbey infirmarer and a dear friend, visited with him every day and repeatedly offered to sleep on the floor of his great room should Felix need his assistance during the night. Girardus could only guess at the nature of the malady but supposed there was a growth within the fine man's head, pushing against his eye and causing his pain. If this were a boil under the skin, he could open it with a lance, but none but God could cure a growth within the skull. He plied his friend with bark teas and herbal poultices to ease pain and swelling, but mostly he prayed.

Felix spent several minutes in meditation, then shuffled to the rosewood chest that sat between his bed and his table. Bending at the hips caused too much eye pain, so he lowered himself to his knees to open the large wardrobe box. It was filled with vestments, old habits and sandals, a spare bed cloth. Underneath the cloth and softness was something hard and solid. It took a good bit of his small strength to drag it out and carry it to his writing table.

It was a heavy book, ancient, the color of dark honey, a labor of distant centuries. It was the last of its kind, he supposed, the lone survivor of a conflagration that he himself had ignited. And the reason he had hid it so carefully over these many years was that it bore a date almost two hundred years in the future—1527.

Who alive today would understand? Who among his brethren would see it for what it was and adore its divinity? Or would they mistake it for a specter of blasphemy and malevolence? All who were with him that icy January day in 1297, when hell visited earth, were dead and buried. He was the last to bear witness, and it had been a weight on his soul.

Felix lit smaller candles illuminating his desk in an arc of straw-colored dancing light. He opened the book and removed a sheaf of loose vellum pages that had been cut for him in the abbey Scriptorium to fit neatly inside the covers. He had been feverishly working on his manuscript, rushing against time, fearful his malady would claim him before he was done.

It was painstakingly difficult work to overcome double vision and splitting headaches to pour out his recollections. He was forced to keep his right eye closed to fix a single image on the page and to keep the movements of his quill on a straight line. He wrote at night, when all was quiet and no one would intrude on his secret. When he exhausted himself, he would return the book to its hiding place and fall onto his pallet for a sliver of sleep before the abbey bells rang for the next call to cathedral prayer.

He gently lifted the first of his pages and, with one eye closed, held it close to his face. It began, *An Epistle from Felix, Abbot of Vectis Abbey, written in the year of our Lord, 1334.*

Lord I am your servant. Praise to you glory to you. Vast are you, Lord, and vast should be your praise. My faith in you is your gift to me, which

you have breathed into me by the humanity
your Son assumed.

I am determined to bring back into memory
the things I know and the things I saw and the
things I did.

I am humbled by the memory of all who have
come before me, but there is none as precious
and exalted as Saint Josephus patron saint of
Vectis whose sacred bones are buried in the Cathedral. For it was Josephus who in his true and
complete love of God did establish the Order of
the Names to exalt the Lord and sanctify his
divinity. I am the last member of the Order, all
others gone to dust. Were I not to make record of
past deeds and occurrences, then mankind would
be bereft of the knowledge that I your mortal
sinner alone do possess. It is not for me to decide if this knowledge is fit for mankind. It is
for you, Lord, in your infinite wisdom, to render
judgment. I will humbly write this epistle, and
you, Lord, will decide its fate.

Felix put down the page and rested his good eye for
a moment. When he felt ready to continue, he thumbed
through the pages and began to read again.

The knowledge of that day has been passed from
the lips of brothers and sisters through the mists
of time. Josephus, then Prior of Vectis, attended
a birth on that portentous seventh day of the
seventh month of the Year of Our Lord 777. The
period was marked by the presence of Cometes
Luctus, a red and fiery comet that to this day
has never returned. The wife of a laborer was

with child, and if that child was male, he would
be the seventh son of a seventh son. A male
child was born, and in fear and lamentation,
his father smote him dead. To the wonder of
Josephus, the woman then delivered an eighth
son, and this twin was called Octavus.

Felix easily conjured a mental image of Octavus, for he
had seen many infants like him over the years, pale, uncry-
ing, with emerald green eyes and fine ginger-colored hair
sprouting from pink scalps. Would Josephus have suspected,
amidst the blood and amnion-soaked birthing bed and the
terrified murmurs of the women attending the labor that Octavus was the true seventh son?

Believing that the child Octavus required the
presence of the Lord, his father took him to Vec-
tis Abbey at a young age. The child would not
speak and would not make company with men,
and Josephus took mercy on him and accepted
him into the care of the abbey. It was then that
Josephus made a miraculous discovery. Absent
any tutelage, the boy was able to write letters and
numbers. And, Lord God, not any letters and
numbers but the names of Your mortal chil-
dren and their days of birth and death into the
future. Such foretelling infused Josephus with
wonder and fear. Was this a dark power born
of evil or a shaft of heavenly light? Josephus
in his wisdom convened a council of members
of his ministry to consider the child and thus
was founded the Order of the Names. These wise
ministers did conclude that there was no evil
hand at work, for if this were so, why would the

child have been delivered into their protective bosom? Surely it was providence at work and a sign embodied by the confluence of the holy number seven that the Lord had chosen this humble creature Octavus to be His true voice of divine revelation. And so the boy was protected and cloistered in the Scriptorium, where he was given quill and ink and parchment and allowed to spend his hours doing his true vocation.

His headache was unabating, so Felix rose from his table to prepare himself a vessel of bark tea. In the great room, he poked at the embers in the fireplace and added a fistful of twigs. Soon, the iron pot of water hanging from an arm began to hiss. He shuffled back to his bedchamber to continue his reading.

As the years passed the boy Octavus grew into a man whose singular purpose did not alter. Night and day he toiled, and there was produced a small but growing library of his books, which did all contain names and foretold of births and deaths. Throughout Octavus had no discourse or commerce with his fellowman, and all his bodily needs were attended by the Order of the Names, which protected his person and his vocation. One fateful day, Octavus was consumed with animal lust and did violate a poor novice girl, and the girl did carry and bear his child. It was a boy with the same strange countenance as its father. The boy was called Primus, and he had green eyes and ginger hair and, like Octavus, was as mute as the stump of a tree and in time he revealed himself to have the same powers as his father. Where there was one were now two sitting side by side, writing out the names of the living and the dead.

The bitter tea was easing his pain, allowing him to read faster and finish the passage he had written the previous night.

Days turned to years and years to decades and decades to centuries. Scribes were born and scribes died and their keepers from the Order of the Names did also come into the world and depart to the next world, all the while providing womanly vessels for their procreation. The library grew to a size beyond imagination and the Order did provide for the keeping of the holy books by excavating vast caverns to keep the library hidden and safe and the bones of dead scribes entombed in sacred catacombs.

For many years, Dear Lord, I was the humble Prior of Vectis and a loyal servant to the great Abbot Baldwin and a faithful member of the Order of the Names. I confess, Dear Lord, that it did not give me pleasure to deliver young sisters to be used for purposes as were required, but I fulfilled my mission with love for You and certainty that Your library must endure and Your future children should have their chronicle.

I have long lost count of all the mute infants brought into the world who would grow to assume their places in the Hall of the Writers with quill in hand, shoulder by shoulder with their brethren. But I cannot forget the one happenstance when as a young monk I witnessed one of the chosen sisters issue not a boy but a girl. I had heard of such a rare occurrence happening in the past but had never seen a girl-child born in my lifetime. I watched this mute green-eyed girl with ginger hair grow, but, unlike her kin, she failed to develop the gift of writing. At the age of twelve years, she was cast out and given to the grain merchant, Gassonet the Jew, who took her away from the island and did with her I know not what.

Satisfied, Felix was now ready to complete his memoir. He dipped his quill and took up the tale in his florid script and wrote the final pages as quickly as he was able until his work was completely done.

He put down his quill and allowed himself to listen to the crickets and the seagulls while the last few lines of ink dried. Through the windows, he saw the blackness of night giving way to a creep of gray. The cathedral bell would ring soon, and he would have to muster his strength to lead the congregation in Prime prayer. Perhaps he should lie down a moment. Despite his discomfort, he felt lighter, unburdened, and welcomed a chance to close his eyes and have a brief, dreamless respite.

As he stood, the bells began pealing. He sighed. His writing had taken longer than he imagined. He would prepare himself for mass.

There was a firm tapping at his door, and he called out, "Come!"

It was Brother Victor, the hostillar, a young man who

rarely came to the abbot house. "Father, I beg your pardon. I waited for the bells."

"What is it, my son?"

"A traveler came to the gate during the night."

"And you gave him shelter?"

"Yes, Father."

"Then why should I be informed?"

"His name is Luke. He implored me to bring this to you." Victor held out a rolled sheet of parchment tied with a ribbon. Felix took it, undid the bow, and flattened the sheet.

The blood drained from his face. Victor had to hold the old monk under the armpit to keep him upright.

The page had a single written line and the date: 9 February 2027.

It was late, and the Great Hall was quiet. Lord Cantwell had struggled to keep up with his granddaughter's methodical readings, but he finally succumbed to his hearing problems, his age, and his snifter of brandy, and he trundled off to bed with a request for an accounting in the morning, when he was fresh.

Late into the night, accompanied by the background music of the crackling and popping fire, Isabelle slowly translated the abbot's letter. Will listened impassively as missing pieces of the Library's story fell into place. Despite the fantastic content of the letter, he wasn't shocked. He knew that the Library existed—that much was a fact, and its very existence implied a fantastic explanation. Now he had one that was no more fanciful than any he'd contemplated since the day Mark Shackleton dropped the bomb on him.

As Isabelle spoke, he tried to form a mental image of Octavus and his spawn, pale, spindly savants who lived their lives hunched over parchments in a chamber hardly more illuminated than this Great Hall. He wondered, did they have any inkling what they were creating? Or why? He studied Isabelle's face as she read, imagining what she was thinking and what he would tell her when she was done. He steeled himself for the punch line: was he about to learn the significance of 2027?

She read the last sentence: *At the age of twelve years she was cast out and given to the grain merchant, Gassonet the Jew who took her away from the island and did with her I know not what.* She looked up at him, blinking her dry eyes.

"What?" he asked. "Why are you stopping?"

"That's it."

"What do you mean, that's it?"

She answered in frustration. "There is no more!"

He swore. "The other clues. They're making us work for it."

Then she said simply, "Our book. It's from that Library, isn't it?"

He thought about stonewalling her but what was the point? For better or worse she'd become an insider. So he answered by nodding.

She put the letter down and got up. "I need a drink." There was a liquor cabinet in a sideboard. He heard the tinkling of bottles bumping each other and watched the curve of her back arching gracefully like a musical clef. When she turned to him, there was a bottle of scotch in her hand. "Join me?"

It wasn't his brand, but still, he could almost taste the warm, mellow sting. He'd gone a long time without and was proud of that. He was a better person for it, no doubt, and his family was better for it too. The Great Hall was hazy with particulate matter from the balky fireplace. Windowless and cut off from the outside, it was a sensory isolation chamber. He was tired, jet-lagged and off-kilter in unfamiliar surroundings. From the shadows, a beautiful young woman was waving a bottle of scotch at him.

"Yeah. Why not?"

In half an hour the bottle was half-empty. They were both drinking it neat. Will loved every mouthful, every swallow and with each one, the pleasantly rising tide of disinhibition.

She leaned on him for answers. She was a good interrogator, he had to admit. But he wasn't going to just give it up. She'd have to work for it, ask the right questions, work past his balkiness. Plead. Cajole. Threaten. He was peppered: "Then what happened? There's got to be more to it than that. What were you thinking? Please, go on, you're holding back. If you don't tell me everything, Will, I won't help you with the rest of the poem."

He realized he was taking a risk by opening the tent flaps and letting her inside. It was dangerous for him and dangerous for her but, damn it, she already knew more about the origins of the Library than anyone in Nevada or Washington. So he swore her to secrecy, the kind of oath solemnly taken by those with full glasses in their hands. Then he told her about the postcards. The "murders." The Doomsday case. How the killings didn't fit together. The frustrations. His partner who would become his wife. The breakthrough, shining a light on a man he knew, his college roommate, a pathetic computer genius who worked deep underground in a secret government base at Area 51. The Library. Government data mining. Shackleton's financial scheme with Desert Life Insurance Company. The watchers. Becoming a fugitive. The final act, played out in a hotel suite in Los Angeles, which left Shackleton with a bullet in his brain. The hidden database. His deal with the feds. Henry Spence. Twenty twenty-seven.

He was done. He'd told her everything. The fire was dying, and the room had become even darker. After a long silence, she finally said, "Quite a lot to take in." Then she poured herself another half inch of scotch, and mumbled, "That's my limit. What's yours?"

He took the bottle from her and poured. "I don't recall." The room was moving; he felt like a piece of driftwood on a choppy lake. He was out of practice, but he could get used to serious drinking again, no problem. It felt good, and he wanted the feeling to last. He could think of worse times to be numb.

"When I was little," she said with a faraway lilt, "I used to take the book from the library and lie right here by the fire and play with it. I always knew there was something special about it. Something magic. All those names and dates and strange languages. It boggles the mind."

"Yes it does."

"Have you come to grips with it? I mean, after living with it for a time?"

"Maybe on an intellectual level. Beyond that, I don't know."

She paused, then said emphatically, almost defiantly, "I don't find it frightening."

He didn't have a chance to respond because she was in too much of a hurry to finish her thought.

"Knowing there's a predestined moment of dying. In some ways it's comforting. All the running around, worrying about the future. What should we eat, what should we drink, what kind of airbags should we have in our cars, everything, ad nauseam. Maybe it's best to just live our lives and stop worrying."

He smiled at her, and said, "How old did you say you were?"

She crinkled her forehead as if to say, please don't patronize me. "My parents were always cross with me because I never took religion seriously. The Cantwells are famous old

Catholics. I liked the Latin bits, but I always found the rituals and ceremonies painfully irrelevant. Perhaps, in the morning, I'll reconsider." She rubbed at her eyes. "I'm knackered, so you must be absolutely paralytic."

"I could sleep." He finished his drink. Then, given their newly forged bond he felt comfortable enough to ask, "Do you mind if I bring the bottle with me?"

In New York, it was the Phillip's bedtime. After his bath, Nancy lay on the bed with her infant beside her. He was powdered and diapered on a soft fluffy towel. He was placidly playing with a plush toy, clutching at it, putting the bear's snout in his mouth. She opened her cell phone and reread Will's last message. *Arrived safely. Home soon. Love U.* She sighed and typed a reply. Then she stroked Phillip's soft, round belly making him giggle, and kissed him on both cheeks.

To Will, the long, upstairs hallway was swaying like a suspension bridge in a canopy jungle. It was a pleasant, free sensation, and he felt light on his feet, as if the law of gravity was about to be suspended. He carefully followed Isabelle as she tiptoed as not to wake the old man. He wasn't sure, but she seemed to be under the demon's influence too—she was weaving around invisible obstacles and midway down the corridor she brushed the wall with her shoulder. She opened his bedroom door with a whispered flourish. "Here you are."

"Here I am."

It was dark and the quarter moon shining through the lace curtains turned the furniture into black-and-gray shapes. "You'll never find the light," she said.

He followed her in, watching her slender silhouette against a window. Dormant circuits in his brain started tripping, the ones dealing with booze and women. He heard himself saying, "You don't have to turn the light on."

He knew that was all it would take. He sensed that her pump was primed by the drink, the excitement of discovery, the isolation of the country.

They were on the bed. Clothes were being shed in the once-in-a-lifetime way that marked first times. Cool, dry flesh became warm and damp. The heavy bed frame creaked at its joints, and the high-pitched squeals of wood on wood played counterpoint to their low grunts. He wasn't sure how long they were taking or if he was doing well. He only knew that it felt good.

When they were done the room was completely quiet until she said, "Wasn't expecting that." Then, "Did you bring the bottle?"

It was safely standing on the floor by the bed. "I don't have a glass."

"Doesn't matter." She took a swig, gave it back to him, and he did the same.

His head was swimming. "Look, I . . ."

She was already off the bed, reaching in the dark for her things, saying a quick sorry, when she brushed her hands against his privates, fishing for her knickers. "What time should I wake you?" she asked.

He was taken aback, unused to being on the receiving end of casual sex. "Whatever works for you," he said. "Not too late."

"We'll have a cooked breakfast, then we'll get on with it. I can't find my other sock—*now* can I turn the light on?"

He closed his eyes protectively at the flare and felt a peck on the lips, then squinted at her naked retreat, her clothes bundled under one arm. The door closed, and he was alone.

When he retrieved his cell phone from his pants pocket,

the little red light was flashing. He opened it and read a text message. *Not mad at you anymore. Miss U. Philly misses U 2. I read the poem. Amazing. Call me soon.*

He realized he'd been holding his breath for an uncomfortably long time, and his audible exhale sounded like a low woof. There was something unspeakable about texting her back while naked and wet from another woman. He thought about it for a while, then tossed the phone on the bed and took another hit from the bottle instead.

Outside, the tail end of the cold front was sending chilly, rolling winds through the back garden. A night-vision monocular scope was poking through the dripping branches of a lush stand of rhododendrons. Through the scope, Will's window glowed uncomfortably bright.

When Will rose to go to the bathroom, DeCorso saw his naked torso pass by. It was the first time he'd made him in hours; he was certain he was in the house, but still it reassured him to confirm his man was present and accounted for. A minute earlier, when the room was dark, he'd gotten a fleeting look of a woman's bare ass, goddess green in the scope's optics. Piper was having a better night than he.

It was going to be a long, cold stretch of time until morning, but he was steadfastly resigned to doing what watchers do.

1334
Isle of Wight

Felix led the congregation in the Prime prayers. Mercifully, it was the shortest office of the day because he was desperately fatigued, and his head was pounding again. The cathedral was filled with his brothers and sisters, dutifully responding, lifting their voices in prayer song that was surely as sweet as the songbirds perched on the rooftops of the church calling to their number in the nearby oaks. It was the rarest time of year, when the atmosphere within the cathedral was, in a word, heavenly—neither too cold nor too warm. It would be a shame, he thought, to depart this earth in the glory of summertime.

Through his good eye, he saw the monks sneaking furtive glances from the pews. He was their father, and they were worried about him and, indeed, worried about themselves. The death of an abbot was always a time of worldly concern. A new abbot inevitably changed things and altered the rhythms of abbey life. After all these years, they were used to him. Perhaps, he thought, they even loved him. Adding to the uncertainty, the chain of succession was cloudy. His prior, Paul, was far too young for the bishop to elevate, and there was no other candidate within their walls. That meant an outsider. For their sakes, he would try to live as long as he could, but he knew better than most that God's plan was set and inalterable.

From the high, carved pulpit, he searched the length of the cathedral for his visitor, but Luke was not to be found. He was not terribly surprised.

As Psalm 116, a Prime standard, was drawing to a close, he was suffused with a sudden joyful realization: that at the moment he had completed his confessional letter, Luke had arrived. Surely, this was providential. The Lord had heard his prayers and was providing an answer. In praise, he decided to insert one of his favorite old Prime hymns into the service, the ancient *Iam Lucis Orto Sidere*, Star of Light Now Having Risen, a poem dating back centuries, as far back as the lifetime of the blessed spiritual founder of their Order, Benedict of Nursia.

> *Iam lucis orto sidere,*
> *Deum precemur supplices,*
> *ut in diurnis actibus*
> *nos servet a nocentibus.*

> Now in the sun's new dawning ray,
> lowly of heart, our God we pray
> that He from harm may keep us free
> in all the deeds this day shall see.

The congregation seemed uplifted by the hymn. The high, soprano voices of the young nuns sounded lovely within the hollow, echo chamber of the great cathedral.

> *Ut cum dies abscesserit,*
> *noctemque sors reduxerit,*

*mundi per abstinentiam
ipsi canamus gloriam.*

That when the light of day is gone,
and night in course shall follow on,
we, free from cares the world affords,
may chant the praises that is our Lord's.

At the conclusion of the service, Felix felt rejuvenated, and if his vision was doubled and his eye was painful, he hardly noticed it. As he left the church, he motioned to Brother Victor and asked the hostillar to bring the night visitor to his rooms.

Sister Maria was waiting for him at the abbot house and immediately began to ply him with tea and coarse oatmeal drizzled with honey. He took a few mouthfuls to assuage her but gestured to have it cleared away when Brother Victor came knocking.

When he saw Luke enter, he instantly remembered the day some forty years earlier when he had first laid eyes on him. Felix had been prior when the strapping young man, who more resembled a soldier than a bookmaker's apprentice, arrived at the gate seeking entrance into the brotherhood. He had traveled from London, seeking out the island refuge because he had heard of the piety of the community and the simple majestic beauty of the monastery. Felix was quick to warm to the sincerity and intelligence of the lad and let him enter as an oblate. And Luke had repaid him by earnestly throwing himself into study, prayer, and work with a gleeful intensity and warmth of spirit that gladdened the hearts of all the members of the order.

Now he was looking at an old soul in his fifties, still tall and sturdy but thick around the middle. His face, which had been taut and beautiful, had been tugged at by time and was sagging and deeply inscribed. The glowing child-like smile was gone, replaced by the downward droop of scabbed lips. He was dressed in the simple, worn clothes of a tradesman, his streaked hair pulled tightly back into a knot.

"Come in, my son, and sit by me," Felix said. "I can see that it is you, dear Luke, disguised as an old man."

"I can see that it is also you, Father," Luke replied, staring at the abbot's bulging eye and the familiar but aged face.

"You notice my malady," Felix observed. "It is well you came to visit today. Perhaps tomorrow you would have been visiting my tomb. Sit. Sit."

Luke rested himself on a soft, horsehair chair. "I am sorry to hear this news, Father."

"I am in God's hands, as is every man. Have you been fed?"

"Yes, Father."

"Tell me, why did you not come to the cathedral for Prime? I sought you out."

Luke glanced uncomfortably at the finery of the abbot's great room, and said simply, "I could not."

Felix gently and sadly nodded. He understood, of course, and he was grateful the man had returned after all these years to close the long arc of two lives that had crossed for a while, then diverged on one terrible day.

There was no need for Luke to remind the abbot of the particulars of that day. Felix remembered them as if the events had unfolded minutes ago, not decades.

"Where did you go when you left us?" the abbot suddenly asked.

"London. We went to London."

"We?"

"The girl, Elizabeth, came with me."

"I see. And what became of her?"

"She is my wife."

The news shook Felix, but he chose not to pass judgment. "Have you children?"

"No, Father, she was barren."

In the mist and rain of a long-past October morning, Luke watched in horror as Elizabeth, a frightened, young novice, was dragged by Sister Sabeline inside the small chapel that stood in isolation in a far corner of the abbey grounds. During his four years at Vectis, he had heard whispered stories about the crypts, a subterranean world, strange beings underground, and strange doings. The other novices spoke of rituals, perversions. A secret society, the Order of the Names. He believed none of this—idle rumors emanating from simple minds. Yes, there was a secret chapel, but it was not for him to know all the inner workings of the abbey. He had a vocation to concentrate upon: loving and serving God.

Elizabeth became a test of his faith and commitment. From the first day he saw her close by, behind the Sisters' dormitory, where he helped her retrieve a shirt blown from a clothesline, her face began to crowd out prayer and contemplation in his thoughts. Her long sweet hair, not yet shorn for Sisterhood, her perfect chin, high cheeks, green-blue eyes, moist lips, and gracile body drove him to a fiery madness. But he knew that if he conquered his urges and refused to stray from his path, then he would be stronger for it and a better servant of God.

He could not know at the time that his last night as a

monk would be spent in a stable. Elizabeth had begged him to come. She was distraught. In the morning, she was to be taken to the crypts beneath the secret chapel. She told Luke she would be forced to lie with a man. She spun a tale of birth mothers, suffering and insanity. She begged Luke to take her virginity, then and there in the hay, to spare her from her fate. Instead, he fled, the sound of her soft wailing mixing with the restless neighing of the horses.

The next morning he hid behind a tree and kept watch over the path to the secret chapel. The sea was spraying, and the briny air braced him. Then, at dawn, he saw the desiccated, old nun, Sister Sabeline, dragging the sobbing young girl inside the wooden building. He fought with himself for several minutes before taking the step that would forever change the path of his life.

He entered the chapel.

What he saw was an empty room with a bluestone floor, adorned only with a simple gilded wooden cross on one wall. There was a heavy oak door. When he pushed it open he could see a tight spiral of stone stairs plunging into the earth. Hesitantly, he descended torchlit stones until he reached the bottom, a small, cool chamber where an ancient door with a large key in its iron lock stood ajar. The door swung heavily on its hinges, and he was inside the Hall of the Writers.

It took Luke a few seconds for his eyes to accommodate to the sparse candlelight of the hall. He had no comprehension of what he saw: dozens of pale-skinned, ginger-haired men and boys, seated shoulder by shoulder at rows of long tables, each one grasping a quill, dipping into inkpots, and writing furiously on sheets of parchment. Some were old, some were mere boys, but despite their ages, they all looked remarkably similar to one another. Every face was as blank as the next. Their only animation came from their green eyes, which seemed to drill into their sheets of white parchment with intensity.

The chamber had a domed ceiling that was plastered and whitewashed, the better to reflect the candlelight. There were up to ten writers at each of fifteen tables stretching to the rear of the chamber. The circumference of the chamber was lined with cotlike beds, some of which were occupied by sleeping ginger-haired men.

The writers paid Luke no attention; he felt he had entered a magical realm where, perhaps, he was invisible. But before he had time to try to make sense of the sights before him, he heard a plaintive cry, the voice of Elizabeth.

The cries were coming from his right, from a void at the side of the chamber. Protectively, he ran toward the black archway and promptly smelled the suffocating odors of death. He was in a catacomb. He fumbled in the dark through one room, brushing against yellow skeletons with rotting flesh, which piled like cords of wood in the recesses of the walls.

Her cries grew louder and in a second room he saw Sister Sabeline holding a candle. He crept closer. The candle illuminated the colorless skin of one of the ginger-haired men. He was naked, and Luke could see the caved-in cheeks of his emaciated buttocks, his spindly arms hanging limp by his side. Sabeline was goading him, calling in frustration, "I have brought this girl for you!" When nothing happened, the nun demanded, "Touch her!"

Then he spotted Elizabeth, cowering on the floor, covering her eyes, bracing herself for the touch of a living skeleton.

Luke acted automatically, without the fear of consequences. He leapt forward and grabbed the man by the bony shoulders and threw him to the ground. It was easy to do, like tossing a child. He heard Sister Sabeline shrieking, "What are you doing here? What are you doing?" He ignored her and reached out for Elizabeth, who seemed to recognize she was being touched not by evil but by the hand of deliverance. She opened her eyes and stared gratefully at his face. The pale man was on the ground, trying to pick himself up from the spot where Luke had roughly shoved him. "Brother Luke, leave us!" Sabeline screamed. "You have violated a sacred place!"

Luke screamed back. "I will not leave without this girl. How can this be sacred? All I see is evil."

He took Elizabeth by the hand and pulled her up.

Sabeline shrieked at him. "You do not understand!"

From the chamber, Luke began to hear sounds of chaos and turmoil—crashing, thuds, thrashing, and wet, flopping noises like large fish being hauled onto a ship's deck, writhing and suffocating.

The naked ginger-haired man turned away and walked toward the noise.

"What is happening?" Luke asked.

Sabeline took her candle and rushed toward the hall, leaving them alone in the dark.

"Are you safe?" Luke asked her.

"You came for me," she whispered.

He helped her find her way from the darkness into the light and into the hall.

The memory of what he saw must have been seared onto the back of his eyes because every time he shut them, every day of his long life, he could still see Sister Sabeline, walking numbly through that terrible place muttering, "My God, My God, My God," over and over, as if she were chanting.

He did not want Elizabeth to suffer what he saw and begged her to close her eyes and let him guide her. As they threaded their way toward the door, he suddenly had an uncontrollable urge to snatch up one of the parchments that lay on the wooden desks, and he chose one that was not soaked in blood.

They ran up the steep, spiral stairs, through the chapel, and out into the mist and rain. He made her keep running until they were far from the abbey gate. The cathedral bells were pealing in alarm. They had to make their way to the shore. He had to get her off the island.

"Tell me why you came back to Vectis?" Felix asked.

"I have been troubled the whole of my life by what I saw that day, and I did not want to go to my grave without seeking understanding. I have long thought of coming back. I was finally able."

"It is a shame you left the Church. I remember your great piety and generosity of spirit."

"All gone," Luke said bitterly. "Taken."

"I am saddened, my son. You surely have the opinion that Vectis Abbey was a place of sin and evil, but it is not so. Our great enterprise had a holy and sacred purpose."

"And what was that purpose, Father?"

"We were serving the needs of God by serving the needs of these frail, mute scribes. Through divine intervention, their labors spanned centuries. They were making a record, Luke, a record of the arrivals and passings of all God's children, then and into the future."

"How was this possible?"

Felix shrugged. "From the hand of God to the hands of these men. They had a strange, singular purpose. Otherwise, they were like children, completely dependent on us for their care."

Luke spat out, "Not only that."

"Yes, they had a need to reproduce. Their task was enormous. It required thousands of them laboring for hundreds of years. We had to give them the means."

"I am sorry, Father, but that is an abomination. You forced your sisters into whoredom."

"Not whoredom!" Felix cried. His emotion raised the pressure inside his head and made his eye throb ferociously. "It was service! Service toward a higher purpose! It was beyond outsiders to understand!" He clutched the side of his head in pain.

Luke worried that the old man would die in front of him, so he eased off. "What became of their labors?"

"There was a vast Library, Luke, surely the largest in all of Christendom. You were close to it that day but never saw it. After you fled, Abbot Baldwin, blessed be his memory, had the Library sealed and the chapel razed by fire. It is my belief the Library was consumed."

"Why was that done, Father?"

"Baldwin believed that man was not ready for the revelations of the Library. And I daresay he feared you, Luke."

"Me?"

"He feared you would reveal the secrets, that others would come, that outsiders would hold us in judgment, that evil men would exploit the Library for dark purposes. He made a decision, and I carried it out. I lit the fires myself."

Luke saw his parchment on the abbot's table, rolled back in its ribbon. "The parchment I took that day, pray tell me its meaning, Father. It has vexed me."

"Luke, my son, I will tell you all I know. I will be dead soon. I feel a great burden upon me, as I am the last man alive who knows about the Library. I have written an account of my knowledge. Please allow me to unburden myself by giving you that account and also pressing something else upon you."

He went to his chest and retrieved the massive book. Luke rushed over to take it from him, as it appeared too heavy for him to manage.

"It is the only surviving one," Felix said. "You and I have another connection, Luke. You knew not why you took that parchment that day, and I know not why I saved one book from the fire. Perhaps, we were both guided by an unseen hand. Will you take back your parchment and also take this book, which has within it a letter I have written? Will you allow this old man to pass the burden to you?"

"When I was young, you were kind to me and took me in, Father. I will."

"Thank you."

"What am I to do with them?"

Felix lifted his eyes toward the ceiling of his fine room. "That is for God to decide."

1344
London

Baron Cantwell of Wroxall woke up scratching and thinking about boots. He inspected his arms and abdomen and found small raised bumps, the telltale signs he had shared his mattress with bedbugs. Really! It was a privilege, to be sure, to be at Court, a guest at the Palace at Westminster, but surely the king would not wish his nobles to be eaten alive while they slept. He would have a stern word with the steward.

His room was small but otherwise comfortable. A bed, a chair, a chest, a commode, candles, and a rug to take the chill off the floor. It was lacking a hearth, so he would not have wanted to spend a midwinter night there, but in the pleasant blush of spring, it was satisfactory. In his youth, before he had curried royal favor, when Charles would visit London, he would stay at inns, where even at the more salubrious ones, he would have to share a bed with a stranger. Still, in those days, he would rarely retire in a state more conscious than blind drunk, so it hardly mattered. He was older now, with higher rank, and he assiduously favored his creature comforts.

He relieved himself in the chamber pot and inspected his member for sores, a precaution he always took after a night of whoring. Relieved, he had a long look out of one of the leaded windows. Through the greenish panes, he could see to the north the magnificent sweep of the River Thames. A high-sided cogge was passing by, setting its sails and making way for the estuary, heavy with goods. Beneath the royal apartments, at water's edge, a marsh harrier swooped for mice, and upstream, a rag and bones man was tipping a rubbish cart into the river, impudently close to Westminster Hall, where the Royal Council would meet in a day. Momentarily distracted by the sights of the great city, his thoughts drifted back to his feet, which looked particularly coarse and raw. Today he would get his new boots.

He smoothed out his pointy beard, flowing moustache, and shoulder-length hair with his tortoiseshell comb, then dressed quickly, slipping on breeches and linen shirt and selecting his best green woolen hose, which he stretched to his thighs and tied to his breech belt. His jacket was a gift from a French cousin, a style they called a cotehardie, tight-fitting, tufted, and blue, with ivory buttons. Despite being over forty years old, his body was still fit and manly, and he did not hesitate to accentuate it. Because he was at Court, he completed his outfitting with a particularly nice kirtle, a rakishly thigh-length cloak made of a fine brocade. Then, with disdain, he pulled on his old boots wincing at their shabbiness and lack of shape.

Charles had attained his station through a combination of good breeding and good sense. The Cantwells could reliably trace their bloodlines back to the time of King John, and they had played a minor role in negotiations with the Crown on the Magna Carta. However, the family languished as marginal nobility until fortune smiled on them with the ascension of Edward III.

Charles's father, Edmund, had fought besides Edward II

in the English king's ill-conceived campaign against Robert the Bruce in Scotland and was wounded in the disastrous battle at Bannockburn. Had the battle gone better for the English, the Cantwells might have prospered in the years that followed, but Edmund had certainly not discredited the family in the eyes of the Crown.

Edward II was, by no means, a popular monarch, and his subjects, for all intents and purposes, permitted him to be deposed by Edward's French wife and her traitorous consort, Roger Mortimer. The king's son, Edward, was only fourteen at the time of the coup. Though crowned Edward III, he became a puppet of the Regent, Mortimer, who wanted the old king to be more than imprisoned—he wanted him dead. Edward's murder at Berkeley Castle in Gloucestershire was a foul affair. He was accosted in his bed by Mortimer's assassins, who pressed a heavy mattress against him to hold him down, then shoved a copper tube up his rectum and thrust a red-hot iron poker through it to burn his intestines without leaving a mark. Thus, murder could not be proven, and the death would be ascribed to natural causes. But more slyly, Mortimer was delivering fitting punishment since the king was said to be a buggerer.

As Edward approached his eighteenth birthday, cognizant of his father's ghastly demise, he plotted a son's revenge. The word was spread by his father's loyalists that the young king was in need of conspirators. Charles Cantwell was contacted by agents and readily agreed to an intrigue because he was a Royalist, but also because, as an adventurer plagued by unsuccessful business dealings, he had few good prospects. In October of 1330, he joined a small brave party who audaciously snuck through a secret entrance into Mortimer's own fortress at Nottingham Castle, arrested the toad in his bedchamber, and in the name of the king, spirited him away to the Tower of London to meet his own grim fate.

Edward III, in gratitude, made Charles a baron and granted him a fat royal stipend and further tracts of land at Wroxall, where Charles immediately began improving his estate by building a fine timber house grand enough for the name, Cantwell Hall.

The stable master had Charles's horse ready and saddled. He set off at a trot, following the northern bank of the river, enjoying the fair breezes as long as he could before he had to turn his horse and plunge into the fetid, narrow lanes of the industrial city. In half an hour or so, he was on Thames Street, a comparatively broad and open thoroughfare, hard by the river, to the west of St. Paul's, where he easily maneuvered his beast through a gaggle of pushcarts, horse-and-riders, and pedestrians.

At the foot of Garrick Hill, he spurred the horse's belly to coax it north, into a snaking, claustrophobic lane, whereupon he promptly felt the need to press his nose into a cloth. Open sewer ditches ran along both sides of Cordwainers Street, but the human effluent was not the greatest offense to Charles's senses. Unlike the cobblers who made cheap shoes from used leather and cked out a living doing repairs, their more esteemed brethren, the cordwainers, needed fresh leather for new boots. So these city environs were also home to slaughterhouses and tanneries, the enterprises causing the greatest stench with their rank, boiling pots of leather, wool, and sheepskin.

All the good cheer of the morning had drained from him by the time he dismounted at his destination, a small shop marked with a hanging sign of black iron in the shape of a boot. He tied his horse to a post and sloshed his way through a mud puddle at the front of the two-story workshop, which was crammed cheek by jowl against other similar structures forming a long row of guild buildings.

Immediately, he suspected a problem. While the cobblers and other cordwainers on both sides of the street had their doors and windows open amidst signs of thriving commerce, this shop was shuttered tight. He muttered under his breath and banged upon the door with the heel of his hand. When there was no response, he banged again, even louder and was about to kick the bloody thing when the door slowly opened, and a woman stuck out her kerchiefed head.

"Why are you shut?" Charles demanded.

The woman was thin as a child but haggard and elderly. Charles had seen her at the shop before, and though aged, he had thought she must have been a great beauty in her youth. That impression was faded now, washed away by strong measures of worry and toil.

"My husband is ill, sir."

"'Tis a pity, I am sure, madam, but I am here to collect my new boots."

She looked at him blankly and said nothing.

"Did you not hear me, woman. I'm here for my boots!"

"There are no boots, sir."

"Whatever do you mean! Do you know who I am?"

Her lip was trembling. "You are the Baron Wroxall, sir."

"Fine. Then you know I was here six weeks ago. Your husband, Luke the Cordwainer, made wooden lasts of my feet. I made half payment, woman!"

"He has been ill."

"Let me inside!" Charles pushed his way through the front door and looked around the small room. It served as a workshop, a kitchen, and a living space. On one side, a cooking hearth with utensils, a table, and chairs, the other side a craftsman's bench, laden with tools and a paltry collection of cured sheepskins. A rack above the bench had dozens of wooden molds. Charles fixed his gaze on a mold that was inscribed "Wroxal" and exclaimed: "Those are my feet! Now where are my boots!"

From the higher floor a weak voice called out, "Elizabeth? Who is there?"

"He never began them, sir," she insisted. "He became ill."

"He's upstairs?" Charles asked, alarmed. "There's no plague in this house, is there madam?"

"Oh no, sir. He has the consumption."

"Then I will go and speak to the man."

"Please, no, sir. He is too frail. It might kill him."

In recent years, Charles had become wholly unused to not getting his way. Barons were treated like—barons, and serfs and gentry alike acceded to their every whim. He stood there with his fists thrust truculently into his waist, his jaw jutting. "No boots," he finally said.

"No, sir." She was trying not to cry.

"I paid you a Half Noble in advance," he said icily. "Give me my money back. With interest. I will take four shillings."

Now the tears flowed. "We have no money, sir. He has not been able to work. I have begun trading his leather stock to other guild members for food."

"So, you have no boots, and you have no money! What would you have me do, woman?"

"I do not know, sir."

"It seems that your husband will be spending his last days in prison at his majesty's pleasure, and you too will see the inside of a debtor's cell. When you see me next, I will have the sheriff."

Elizabeth fell to her knees and wrapped herself around his

stockinged calves. "Please, no, sir. There must be another way," she sobbed. "Take his tools as payment, take what you like."

"Elizabeth?" Luke weakly called out again.

"Everything is fine, husband," she shouted back.

While seeing these thieves to prison would give him satisfaction, he knew he would rather spend the rest of his morning at a new cordwainer than tramping around the foul city looking for the sheriff. Without answering, he went to the worktable and began to inspect the array of pincers, awls, needles, mallets, and knives. He snorted at them. What use to him, he wondered? He picked up a semicircular bladed instrument, and asked, "What is this?"

She was still on her knees. "It's a trenket, a shoemaker's knife."

"What would I do with this in my belt," he said derisively. "Cut off someone's nose?" He poked around the table some more, and concluded, "This is rubbish to me. Have you anything of value in here?"

"We are poor, sir. Please, take the tools and leave in peace."

He began to pace back and forth, looking around the small room for something that would satisfy him enough to abandon his threat to have them arrested. Their possessions were indeed meager, the kinds of goods his servants had in their peasant houses.

His eyes fell on a chest near the hearth. Without asking permission, he opened it. There were winter cloaks, dresses, and the like. He stuck his hands in and felt underneath and touched something hard and flat. When he parted the clothes, he saw the cover of a book.

"Do you have a Bible?" he exclaimed. Books were rare

commodities, and valuable. He had never seen a peasant or tradesman possessing one.

Elizabeth quickly crossed herself and seemed to say a silent prayer. "No, sir. It is not a Bible."

He lifted the heavy book from the chest and inspected it. He puzzled at the date on the spine, "1527" and opened it. A sheaf of loose parchments fell onto the floor. He picked them up, glancing quickly at the Latin. He saw the name Felix on the top page and put the sheets aside. Then he inspected the pages of the book and cast his eyes on the seemingly endless lists of names and dates. "What is this book, madam?"

The fear dried Elizabeth's tears. "It is from a monastery, sir. The abbot gave it to my husband. I know not what it is."

In truth, Luke had never spoken to her about the book. When he returned to London from Vectis years earlier, he had wordlessly placed it in the chest, and there it had remained. He knew better than to remind her of Vectis. Indeed, the very name was never uttered in their house. She had a sense, however, that the book was wicked, and she crossed herself every time she had to use the chest.

Charles turned page after page, each one awash in the year 1527. "Is this some kind of witchcraft?" Charles demanded.

"No, sir!" She struggled to sound like she believed her next words. "It is a holy book from the good monks of Vectis Abbey. It was a gift to my husband, who knew the abbot in his youth."

Charles shrugged. The book was bound to be worth something, possibly more than four shillings. His brother, who was more skilled with a pen than a sword, would know the value better. When he returned to Cantwell Hall, he would seek his views. "I will take the book as payment, but I am most displeased by this venture, madam. I wanted my boots for the Royal Council. All I have is my disappointment."

She said nothing and watched the baron put the loose parchments back into the book and stride out of the shop and onto the street. He dropped the book into his saddlebag and rode off in search of another bootmaker.

Elizabeth climbed the stairs and entered the cubby, where Luke lay in a feverish, wasted state. Her hale, strapping man, the savior of her life, was gone, replaced by this old, shriveled shell. He was slipping away. The tiny room smelled like death. The front of his shirt was smeared with old brown blood and sputum and a few fresh streaks, bright red. She lifted his head and gave him a sip of ale.

"Who was here?" he asked.

"The Baron Wroxall."

His watery eyes widened. "I never made his boots." He was seized by a paroxysm of coughs, and she had to wait for his chest to quiet.

"He has left. All is well."

"How did you satisfy him? He gave me payment."

"All is well."

"My tools?" he asked sadly.

"No. Something else."

"What then?"

She took his limp hand in hers and tenderly looked him in the eyes. For a moment, they were young again, two innocents, on their own up against the large, cruel forces of a world gone mad. Those many years past, he had rushed in and saved her, as chivalrous as a knight, plucking her from that stinking crypt and a horrible fate. She had tried her whole life to repay him and had woefully failed to produce a child. Perhaps, in a small way, she had saved him today by tossing a bone to the wolf at the door. Her beloved Luke would be able to die in his own bed.

"The book," she said. "I gave him the book."

He blinked in disbelief, then slowly turned his head to the wall and began to sob.

The instant Will awoke, he recognized the old unhappy syndrome, his head filled with lead weights, his mouth sponged dry, his body wracked by flulike myalgias.

He had a whopper of a hangover.

He cursed at his failings, and when he saw the quarter-full bottle next to him on the bed, lying there like a streetwalker, he angrily asked it, "What the hell are you doing here?" He had an urge to spill the contents down the sink, but it wasn't his property, was it? He covered it with a pillow so he wouldn't have to look at it.

He remembered everything, of course—he couldn't use the pathetic excuse he'd blacked out. He'd cheated on ex-wives, he'd cheated on girlfriends, he'd cheated on women he was cheating with, but he'd never cheated on Nancy. He was glad he felt like crap: he deserved it.

Nancy's text message was still there, unanswered on his cell phone. After he got out of the bathroom, full of minty toothpaste to mask his hangover mouth, he used the one available bar to call her. It was early there, but he knew she'd be up, feeding Phillip, getting ready for work.

"Hi," she answered. "You're calling me."

"You sound surprised."

"You didn't text me back. Out of sight, out of mind, I figured."

"Hardly. How're you doing?"

"We're okay. Philly's got an appetite."

"That's good."

His voice sounded off beam. "Are you all right?" she asked.

"Yeah, I'm fine."

She didn't sound convinced. "How're you getting on?"

"I'm in a big old country house. Feels like I'm in an Agatha Christie book. But the people here are being—very nice, very helpful. It's been worth it. There's been a breakthrough, but you probably don't want to hear about it."

She was quiet, then said, "I wasn't happy, but I'm over it. I realized something."

"What?"

"All this domestication. It's hard on you. You're too penned up. An adventure comes along, of course you're going to jump at it."

His eyes began to sting. "I'm listening."

"And there's something else. Let's look to move sooner rather than later. You need to get out of the city. I'll start talking to HR about possible transfers."

He felt unspeakably guilty. "I don't know what to say."

"Don't say anything. Tell me about your breakthrough."

"Maybe I shouldn't over the phone."

Concern crept back into her voice. "I thought you said you were safe."

"I'm sure I am, but old habits . . . I'll tell you in person soon."

"When are you coming home?"

"I'm not finished yet, maybe a day or two. As fast as I can. We found the first clue. Three to go."

"Prometheus's flame."

"Quite the puzzler, that Mr. Shakespeare. Big old candle-stick."

"Ha! Flemish wind next?"

"Yep."

"Any ideas?"

"Nope. You?"

"I'll think about it. Come home soon."

It was the middle of the night in Las Vegas, and Malcolm Frazier was sleeping beside his wife when his mobile phone vibrated and chimed him awake. One of his men was calling from the Ops Center at Area 51, offering a perfunctory apology for disturbing him.

"What've you got?" Frazier asked, swinging his feet onto the floor.

"We just intercepted cell-phone traffic between Piper and his wife."

"Play it for me," Frazier demanded. He shuffled out of the master bedroom, past his children's rooms, and he landed on the family room sofa as the file started playing.

He listened to the audio then asked to be patched through to DeCorso.

"Chief! What are you doing up at 2:00 A.M?"

"My job. Where are you?"

He was sitting in his rental car, by the side of the road within sight of the lane to Cantwell Hall. Nobody was coming or going without his noticing. He had just peeled the cellophane off a chicken sandwich and wound up greasing his cell phone with mayonnaise. "Doing my job too."

"Any sight of him?"

"Other than screwing the granddaughter last night, no."

"Moral turpitude," Frazier mumbled.

"Say again?"

Frazier ignored him. He wasn't a dictionary. "Funnily enough he just called his wife. Not to confess. He told her there'd been a 'breakthrough' and that he wasn't finished yet, another three clues to find, he said. Sounds like he's on a fucking scavenger hunt. Now you know."

"The food here sucks, but I'll survive."

Frazier had personal knowledge. "I know you will." Then he added, "Keep your head down. The CIA promised the SIS they'd find out what happened to Cottle, and our CIA liaison guys are asking us some halfhearted questions. Everyone on our side wants it to blow over. It's the other side I'm worried about."

Frazier had trouble getting back to sleep. He replayed the strategy in his head, trying not to second-guess himself to the point of madness. He had decided to let Spence run free for the time being to give Piper the rope he needed to do whatever the hell he was doing in England. So far, so good. It looked like Piper was onto something. Let him do the work, Frazier thought. Then we'll reel him in and reap the benefits. They could always pick up Spence and the book. He wouldn't be hard to find. Frazier had his house in Vegas under surveillance, and guessed he'd surface well before his DOD. Spence was a dead man walking. Time was not on his side.

When the housekeeper put a plate of fried bread on the table, Will looked at it suspiciously. Isabelle laughed and urged him to keep an open mind. He crunched down, then said, "I don't get it. Why would you ruin a good piece of toast?"

Fried eggs, mushrooms, and streaky bacon were served

up in short order, and out of politeness, Will forced himself to eat. His hangover was making everything arduous, even breathing.

Isabelle was fresh and chatty, like nothing had happened. That was fine with him. He'd go along with the game or delusion or whatever it was. For all he knew, maybe this was how kids hooked up these days. If it felt good, do it, then forget about it—no big deal. It seemed like a reasonable way to handle things. Maybe he'd been born a generation too early.

They were alone. Lord Cantwell hadn't surfaced yet.

"This morning I researched Flemish windmills," she said.

"That was industrious of you."

"Well, as you were going to sleep half the day, someone had to start in," she said saucily.

"So where's the next clue?"

"Haven't got one."

"One what?"

"A clue! Your brain's not up yet, Mr. Piper!"

"I had a rough night."

"Did you?"

He didn't want to go there. "Windmills?" he asked.

She had some pages printed off an Internet site. "Did you know that the first windmill was built in Flanders in the thirteenth century? And that at peak, in the eighteenth century there might well have been thousands of them? And that there are currently fewer than two hundred in all of Belgium and only sixty-five in Flanders? And that the last working Flemish windmill ceased operation in 1914?" She looked up and smiled sweetly at him.

"None of that's helpful," he said, gulping more coffee.

"No, it isn't," she agreed, "but it's gotten my mind cranking. We need to have a thorough look around for any objet d'art, image, painting, anything whatsoever with a windmill motif. We know there aren't any books of interest."

"Good. You're going full throttle. I'm glad one of us is."

She was enthused, a young filly straining at her bit for a morning run. "Yesterday was one of the most stimulating days I've ever had, Will. It was incredible."

He looked at her through his bilious haze.

"Mentally stimulating!" she said, exasperated, but then at a whisper, under the washing-up noises of the housekeeper added, "And physically stimulating too."

"Remember," he said with as much gravitas as he could muster, "you can't disclose any of this. They're some very serious people who will shut you down if you do."

"Don't you think the rest of the world should know? Isn't it a universal right to know?" She curled her mouth into a bright smile, "And, parenthetically, it would launch my academic career in a spectacular way."

"For your sake and mine, I'm begging you not to go there. If you don't promise me, I'll leave this morning and I'll take the poem with me and this'll be unfinished." He wasn't smiling.

"All right," she pouted. "What shall I tell Granddad?"

"Tell him the letter was interesting but didn't shed any light on the book. Make something up. I've got a feeling you've got a good imagination."

They began the day with a walk through the house, looking for anything remotely interesting. Will brought along another cup of coffee for the road, which Isabelle thought was very American of him.

The ground floor of Cantwell Hall was fairly complicated. The kitchen wing in the rear of the house had a series of pantries and disused servants' quarters. The dining room, a well-proportioned front-facing room, was located between the kitchen area and the entrance hall. Will had spent all his time the previous day in the Great Hall and the library and this morning he was shown another large, formal room facing the rear garden, the drawing room, which they also called the French room, holding a starchy collection of eighteenth-century French furniture and decorative pieces, which looked unlived-in and unvisited. Will also discovered that the reason the Great Hall was windowless was because its front-facing wall was no longer the outer wall of the house. A long gallery had been constructed in the seventeenth century, connecting the house and a stables area which had long ago been converted to a banqueting hall.

The gallery originated through an unnoticed entryway in the hall. It was a high-ceilinged, darkly paneled corridor lined with paintings and the odd piece of stone or bronze statuary. At its other end, it emptied into a vast, cold hall that hadn't hosted a banquet or a ball in a good half century. Will's heart sank when he entered. It was filled with packing crates and piles of furniture and bric-a-brac covered in sheets. "Granddad calls this his bank account," Isabelle told him. "These are things he's decided to part with to pay the bills for the next few years."

"Could any of this stuff date back to the fifteen hundreds?"

"Possibly."

Will shook his throbbing head and swore.

The banqueting hall was connected via a short corridor to the chapel, a small stone sanctuary, the Cantwells' private house of worship, five rows of pews and a small limestone altar. It was simple and quiet, Christ crucified looking down on empty pews splashed by morning sunlight that filtered through stained glass. "Not used much," Isabelle said, "though Granddad wants the family to do a private mass for him here when his time comes."

He pointed over his head. "Is this the spire I can see from my bedroom?" Will asked.

"Yes, come and look."

She led him outside. The grass was thick and wet, the sun made everything glisten. They stepped into the garden, just far enough to get a glimpse at the stone chapel, and the sight of it almost made him laugh. It was a curious little building, a novelty with a distinctive Gothic architecture, two rectangular towers at the front facade and at its center over a rectangular nave and transept, a steep pointy spire that looked like a lance thrust into the air.

"Recognize it?" she asked.

He shrugged.

"It's a miniature version of the Cathedral of Notre Dame in Paris. Edgar Cantwell had it built in the sixteenth century. I think the real thing made an impression."

"You've got an interesting family," Will said. "My guess is the Pipers probably cleaned the shit off of the Cantwells' shoes."

To Will, the only good thing about the long hours that followed was that his hangover slowly resolved. They spent the morning rummaging through the banqueting hall, focused on Flanders and the wind, but cognizant of the remaining clues as well—a prophet's name, a son who sinned—as vague as they were. By lunchtime he had a fair appetite.

The old man was up and about and joined them for sandwiches. His memory wasn't all there, so it was easy for Isabelle to deflect him from the Vectis letter. However, he did remain fixed on the purported Shakespeare poem because it seemed that financial worries were foremost on his mind.

He inquired again about Will's intentions and was reassured that if the research went well, the letter would be his. He encouraged his granddaughter to be as helpful as possible, then rambled on about auction houses and how he'd have to let Pierce & Whyte take a crack at the business owing to their success with the last auction, but that Sotheby's or Christie's made more sense for something of this importance. Then he excused himself to do his correspondence.

Before returning to the banqueting hall, they took advantage of Lord Cantwell puttering around the ground floor to sneak upstairs and have a poke through his bedroom. Isabelle couldn't recall whether there was anything of interest up there as she hadn't entered in years. But it was among the oldest rooms in the house so it couldn't be ignored. The bed was not yet made and smelled strongly of an old man's incontinence, which neither of them commented on. The few paintings were portraits, and the vases, clocks, and small tapestries were devoid of windmill motifs. They beat a hasty retreat back to the banqueting hall, where they toiled for the remainder of the early afternoon, prying open crates and examining dozens of paintings and decorative items.

By late afternoon, they had gone through the dining room and the French room and were sweeping back through the library and the Great Hall, becoming increasingly discouraged.

Finally, Isabelle begged to stop for tea. The housekeeper was off doing shopping so Isabelle decamped to the kitchen, leaving Will in charge of starting a fire. The task got him into Boy Scout mode, and he diligently started rearranging fireplace bricks and building a platform of kindling that would optimize airflow and prevent smoke kickback. When he was done, he carefully placed the logs, lit his structure with a wooden match, sat back, and admired his work.

The fire caught quickly and began to send flames high into the vault. Fewer wisps escaped. Will's old scoutmaster in Panama City would have been proud of him, prouder than his frozen-hearted father, who had verbally beat him up about most of his early accomplishments or lack thereof.

A melancholy was descending. He was tired, he was disappointed that he was getting his old cravings back. The bottle of scotch was still up in his room. As his mind wandered, so did his eyes. One of the blue-and-white Delft tiles lining the fireplace caught his eye. It was a charming scene of a mother walking through a field with a bundle of twigs under one arm and her toddler son on the other. She looked perfectly happy. She probably wasn't married to a bastard like him, he thought.

Then his gaze drifted to the tile below it. He froze for a second, then sprang up, and when Isabelle came back in with a platter of tea, she found him standing by the fireplace, staring.

"Look," he said.

She put the platter down and drew closer. "Oh my God," she exclaimed. "Right in front of our eyes. I tapped on it yesterday."

On the bank of a meandering country river was a small windmill, delicately painted in blue and white. The tile artist was skillful enough to make one imagine that the mill blades were about to be turned by a breeze rushing down the river valley, for in the distance, birds were dipping their wings in an unseen gust.

The tea went cold.

After Isabelle made sure her grandfather was upstairs napping, she fetched the toolbox from the hall closet and let Will choose his implements. "Please don't break it," she pleaded.

He promised to be careful but gave no guarantees. He

selected the smallest, thinnest flat-edged screwdriver and a light hammer. Then, holding his breath, he began gently tapping the chiseled end into the smooth, hard grout.

It was slow, painstaking work, but the grout was softer than the tile, so it gradually yielded to the steel. When a vertical line was cleared, he started on the top horizontal one. In half an hour, both horizontal rows were grout-free. Because he was working so closely to his exuberant fire, he was slathered in sweat, and his shirt was damp. He thought he might be able to tap under the tile and pry it loose without removing the last row of grout. She was almost pressing against his back, watching every move. She gave nervous approval.

It took only three light, oblique taps of the screwdriver to make the tile lift from the fascia a satisfying eighth of an inch. Blessedly, it was in one piece. Will put the tools down and used his hands, raising and lowering the tile fractionally, then wiggling it laterally.

It came free in his hands, intact.

Immediately, they saw a round plug of wood in the center of the exposed square.

"That's why it sounded the same as the others when I tapped on it yesterday," she said.

Will used the edge of the screwdriver to lever out the plug. It was covering a one-inch hole bored deeply into the wood.

"I need a flashlight," Will said urgently.

There was a penlight in the toolbox. He shined it in the hole and grabbed a pair of needle-nosed pliers.

"What do you see?" she pressed.

He closed the pliers on something, then pulled them out. "This."

There was a single sheet of parchment, rolled into a cylinder.

"Let me see!" she almost screamed.

He let her unroll it and stood over her as she dropped to a chair. "It's in French," she said.

"Are we screwed?"

"Of course not," she sniffed. "I read French quite well, thank you."

"Like I said, I'm glad you're here."

"It's a bit hard to make out, atrocious penmanship. It's addressed to Edgar Cantwell. It's dated 1530! Good Land, Will, look who's written it! It's signed, Jean Cauvin."

"Who's that?"

"John Calvin! The father of Calvinism, predestination and all that. Only the greatest ecclesiastical mind of the sixteenth century!" She scanned the page with wild eyes. "And Will, he's writing about our book!"

1527
WROXALL

A midwinter snowfall that blanketed the forest and the
fields surrounding Cantwell Hall made for a satisfying
day of hunting. The boar that Thomas Cantwell's party had
been following all morning was a fast, healthy creature but
he was trapped and soon to be roasted because his tracks
were easy to follow in the white crust, and the hounds were
not distracted by the usual smells of the soil.

The moment of the kill provided enough drama to be
retold by the fire for the rest of the season. When the sun was
at its highest, the glare off the snow stinging the riders' eyes,
the greyhounds finally cornered the boar against a thicket of
impenetrable briars. The beast lashed out and gored one of
the hounds and, in turn, was bitten in its hindquarter by another. It stood its ground, grunting and panting, with blood
dripping from its haunches. All this was in full view of the
hunting party, who had pulled their horses into a semicircle
a safe distance away.

The baron turned in his saddle to his son, Edgar, a scrawny,
hatchet-faced seventeen-year-old, and said, "Take it, Edgar.
Make me proud."

"Me?"

"Yes, you!" the baron said with irritation.

His brother William advanced his horse till he was saddle

by saddle with his father and complained. "Why not me, Father?"

William was a year younger than Edgar but in many ways seemed older. He was more powerfully built, had a squarer chin and a hunter's blood-filled eyes.

"Because I say so!" the baron growled. William's face contorted in anger, but he held his tongue.

Edgar looked around at his cousins and uncles, who shouted encouragement and a few good-natured jests. His chest swelled as he dismounted and was handed the tokke by one of the servants. It was a long spear, specially constructed for the boar hunt, with a crossbar beneath the point to prevent overpenetration. Properly wielded, it would pierce the heart and easily be withdrawn through the tough hide.

Edgar tightly gripped the tokke with both hands, advancing slowly through the snow. The frightened boar saw him coming and started to grunt and squeal, which in turn stirred the dogs to loud and feverish baying. Edgar felt his heart in his throat as he slowly drew within a few feet of the mass of animals. He had never been given this honor before. He was desperate to get it right and not show fear. When he saw his opening, he would charge and use his height to strike over the backs of the hounds. He hesitated for a few moments and looked over his shoulder. His father angrily motioned him to get on with it.

At the instant he plucked up the courage to strike, the boar decided to break for it by running headlong through the dogs. A hound reared up in panic just as Edgar was about to thrust his spear, forcing him to hold back. The boar engaged the greyhound in a furious skirmish that lasted only seconds before the dog's belly was torn asunder. Then, with the other dogs snapping at the boar's hind legs, the enraged creature leapt forward into the air, its tusks aimed squarely at Edgar's groin.

Edgar instinctively took a step in retreat but his boot stayed buried in the snow. He immediately lost his balance and started to fall backward, and when he did, the butt of the spear wedged into the ground. Providentially, the snarling, leaping boar literally impaled its own thorax upon the blade of the tokke less than a foot away from where it would have turned young Edgar into a eunuch. With an horrific shriek and a gush of blood, the boar died right between the boy's supine legs.

Edgar was still shivering from cold and mental trauma when the hunting party reassembled by the blazing fire in the Great Hall. The men were talking loudly and laughing themselves silly as they consumed large wedges of cake washed down by jugs of wine. Young William was merrily partaking in the banter, elated at his brother's travails. Only Edgar and his father were quiet. The baron sat in his large fireside chair, moodily drinking, Edgar off in a corner pouring sweet wine down his throat.

"Are we going to eat that boar?" one of Edgar's cousins asked.

"Why should we not?" another wanted to know.

"Because I have never before eaten a beast who took its own life!"

The men laughed so hard they cried, which only made the baron more taciturn. His oldest son was a source of worry and vexation. He seemed to excel at nothing of importance. He was an unenthusiastic scholar whom his tutors tolerated rather than praised, his piety and attention to prayer were suspect, and his ability at the hunt was debatable. Today had confirmed his father's doubts. It was a miracle the boy had not been killed. As the baron was painfully aware, the only skills Edgar had firmly mastered were wenching and drinking.

During the Twelve Days of Christmas, the baron had prayed in the family chapel, searched his soul, and reached a decision about the boy's fate. Now he was more certain than ever of its wisdom.

Edgar emptied his goblet and called the manservant for a refill. He caught the sour expression on his father's face and started shivering again.

In the evening, Edgar awoke from a nap in his cold, dark room on the upper floor of Cantwell Hall. He used the only active candle to light some others and tossed a few small logs onto the embers of his shallow fireplace. He pulled a heavy cloak over his nightshirt and poked his head out from the door. At the far end of the hall, Molly, the chambermaid, was sitting on a bench at her station outside Lady Cantwell's room, waiting at her beck and call. She was a small, buxom girl, a year or so younger than Edgar, her black hair stuffed into a linen bonnet. She had been watching out for him, and she shyly smiled.

He beckoned her with a finger and she cautiously rose and crept in his direction. Without exchanging a word, she followed him inside his room in a well-practiced routine. Just as the door was about to close behind her, William Cantwell emerged from his room and spied Molly slipping into his brother's chamber. He gleefully scuttled off down the stairs, ready to do his own brand of mischief.

Edgar flopped onto his bed and grinned at the chambermaid. "Hello, Molly!"

"Hello, my lord."

"Did you miss me?"

"I saw you yesterday?" she said sweetly.

"That was such a long time ago," he sulked. Then he pounded the bed with the flat of his palms. "Will you come see me again?"

"We need to hurry." She giggled. "My lady might call at any time."

"It will take precisely as long as it takes. One cannot interfere with the immutable laws of nature."

When she climbed onto the foot of the bed, he grabbed her and pulled her on top. They proceeded to roll from one side of the bed to the other, groping and tickling each other until she let out a loud, "Ow!" She was frowning and rubbing the top of her head. "What do you have under your pillow?" she asked.

She pulled the cushion away and underneath it was a large, heavy book marked on its spine: 1527.

"Leave that be!" he said.

"What is it?"

"It is just a book, and it is of no concern to you, Missy."

"Then why is it hidden?"

Her curiosity, so keenly aroused, was going to have to be addressed before he could get on with the business at hand. "My father does not know I took it from his library. He is protective of his books."

"Why does it interest you?" she asked.

"You see the date on it—1527? When I was a child, I would wonder about a book that possessed a future date. It held a fascination. My father always told me the book contained a great secret, and when I was twenty-one, he would show me an ancient letter he keeps in his strongbox that would reveal all. I used to dream about what I would be like in 1527, the year in which I would become eighteen. Well, that year has come. It is 1527, if you did not know. The book has come of age, and so have I."

"Is it magic, my lord?"

He threw the pillow on top of it again and grabbed her. "If little Molly is so interested in magic, perhaps she would like to see my wand."

Edgar was too involved with his amorous activities to hear his name repeatedly being called for supper. At a perfectly wrong moment, his father flung open the door to find his son's pink bottom nestled in a jumble of pulled-up chemises, his face buried in a generous bosom.

"What the Devil!" the baron shouted. "Stop that at once!"

He stood there, slack-jawed, as the young lovers rushed to pull themselves together.

"Father . . ."

"Do not speak! Only I will speak. You, girl, will leave this house."

She began to cry. "Please, your lordship, I have no place to go."

"That is not my concern. If you are still at Cantwell Hall in one hour, I will have you flogged. Now get out!"

She ran from the room, her clothes askew.

"As for you," the baron said to his cowering son, "I will see you at the supper table, where you will be informed of your fate."

The long trestle table in the Great Hall was set up for the evening feast, and the extended Cantwell clan was noisily tucking into the first courses of supper. The roaring fire and the press of bodies had taken the chill off the winter night. Thomas Cantwell sat at the center, with his wife beside him. He was troubled by his son's escapade but his appetite raged nonetheless, stoked by the exertions of hunting. He had greedily spooned down his meaty capon brewet and was starting in on his ham and leeks porray. Roasted boar, his favorite, was on the way, so room would have to be left.

All chatter ceased when Edgar came in, his eyes fixed on the floorboards rather than the faces of his family or the servants. He supposed everyone knew; he would have to bear it. His sniggering young cousins, and for that matter his uncles, were surely as guilty as he in these matters, but tonight he was the one ignominiously caught out.

He took his seat by his father and started in on an earthenware jug of wine. "You missed the blessing of the meal, Edgar," his mother said quietly.

His brother William, who was seated at his mother's side, grinned and wickedly whispered, "He had his own blessing, methinks."

"Quiet!" the baron raged. "We will not speak of this at my table."

As the feast progressed, the conversation was meager and subdued. One of the men had recently been to Court and asked the others what they thought of the king's petition to the Pope that his marriage to Queen Catherine be annulled. The Cantwells much admired the piety of the queen and had no use for the whore Boleyn, but even among family, this kind of banter was dangerous. Henry's influence bored into every parish. There would be an accommodation, Thomas assured his kin. The prospect of a schism with the Pope over this matter was unthinkable.

The carved and jointed boar was presented on a giant wooden platter, and it was hungrily devoured with slabs of dark bread. At the conclusion of the meal, frumenty custard was served, along with dried figs, nuts, and spiced wine. Finally, the baron wiped his hands and mouth on the cloth overhanging the dining table, cleared his throat, and once he was sure he had the full attention of his son, began his planned proclamation. "As my brothers and good wife know, I have been unsatisfied with your education, Edgar." The raspy sternness of his voice caused the members of the dining party to lower their eyes.

"Have you, Father?"

"I had hoped for greater results. Your uncle, Walter, benefited greatly from his education at Oxford and he is now, as you know, an esteemed lawyer in that city. However, the standards at Merton College have surely become lax."

Edgar's lower lip began to twitch. "How so, Father?"

"Well, look at you!" the baron bellowed. "What more evidence do I require! You are more schooled in wine, wenches, and song than Greek, Latin, and the Bible! You will not be returning to Oxford, Edgar. Your education will be elsewhere."

Edgar thought of his friends and his comfortable rooms at Merton. There was a cozy tavern near the college that would be the poorer. "And where is that, Father?"

"You will be going to the College of Montaigu at the University of Paris."

Edgar looked up in fright and sought out the dour face of his cousin Archibald. This joyless monster had spent six years there and had long regaled Edgar with stories of its austerity and strictness.

His father rose from his seat and as he stalked out of the Great Hall he declared, "This college will tame you, by God, and it will make of you a proper God-fearing Cantwell! You are bound for Paris, boy! That wretched city will be your home."

Archibald smirked and piled onto the miserable young

man. "There are only three things you need to know about Montaigu, cuz: bad food, hard beds, and harsh blows. I advise you to finish your wine, for what little you will get there is mostly water."

Edgar pushed himself to his feet. He would not let his damnable relations see him cry.

"A toast to my departing brother," William said, his head happily swimming in supper wine. "May the good ladies of Paris respect and honor his newly found purity and piety."

1527
PARIS

Edgar Cantwell awoke shortly before four in the morning in a miserable state. It was just as well that the incessantly clanging college bells were rousing him from his fitful sleep. He had never been so cold in all his life. His window had ice on the inside, and he could see his own breath when he emerged from under his thin coverlet to light a candle. He had retired wearing all his clothes, even his cloak and his soft leather shoes, but he was still frigid as an icicle. In self-pity, he looked around his tiny room, as basic as a monk's cell, and wondered what his friends at Merton would think if they could see his wretched circumstances.

Montaigu was living up to its reputation as hell on earth. Better if he were in prison, he thought. At least then he would not have to read Aristotle in Latin and suffer the whip if he failed to memorize a passage.

It was a bleak existence, and he was only weeks into it. The term would run until July, which seemed a lifetime away.

The mission of Montaigu College was to prepare young men to become priests or ordained lawyers. Under the absolute rule of Principal Tempête, a conservative Parisian theologian of the most venomous ilk, Montaigu strictly controlled its pupils' moral lives. They were forced to search their consciences in regular public confessions of their sins and to denounce the behavior of fellow students. To keep them in the proper repentant state of mind, Tempête kept them in a perpetual fast, with coarse food and small portions, and in the winter made them suffer the cold without succor. Then there were the merciless beatings at the hands of ruthless tutors and, at his pleasure, Tempête himself.

Edgar had to be up at four o'clock to attend the morning office in the chapel before stumbling off to his first lecture in a near-dark classroom. The lectures were in French, which Edgar had learned at Oxford, but now, painfully, he was forced to use it as his primary language. Mass was at six o'clock, followed by communal breakfast, its brevity assured by the fact that all they were served was a slice of bread with a dot of butter. Then came the *grande classe* on the topic of the day—philosophy, arithmetic, the scriptures, done in a format that Edgar dreaded.

The *quaestio* was a one-man disputation a member of his class had to endure each day. Tutors with whipping rods ready posed questions based on a passage of reading. The student would answer, eliciting in turn, another question et cetera, back and forth, back and forth, until the underlying meaning of the text was thoroughly explored. For the keen student, the process meant a continually stimulating creative involvement. For Edgar, it meant blistering beatings on the shoulders and back, insults and belittlement.

· Dinner followed, accompanied by readings from the Bible or the life of a saint. Edgar had the advantage over some of his less fortunate classmates of being one of the rich *pensionnaires,* who were fed at a common table where there was a minimum standard of daily rations. *Les pauvres* had to fend for themselves in their rooms, and some were close to starvation. As it was, Edgar's daily fare barely kept him going—bread, a little boiled fruit, a herring, an egg, and a piece of cheese, washed down with a jar of the cheapest wine, a third of a pint topped off with water.

At twelve o'clock, the students had an assembly, where they were questioned about their morning's work. This was followed by a rest period or a public reading, depending on the day. From three to five o'clock, they were back in the classroom for afternoon classes, then off to the chapel for Vespers, immediately followed by a discussion of their afternoon work. Supper consisted of some more bread, another egg or a chunk of cheese, and perhaps a piece of fruit eaten to the accompaniment of droning Bible readings. The tutors had one more opportunity to interrogate their charges before final chapel, and at eight o'clock it was bedtime.

Two days a week there was time in their schedules for an interlude of recreation or a walk. Despite the temptation for escape, albeit brief, the environs around the College were such that students mainly stuck to the Pré aux clercs, the college recreation ground. The other side of rue Saint Symphorien was a stinking nest of thieves and vermin who would gladly cut the throat of a student for a cloak pin or a pair of gloves. And to make matters even more unsavory, the sewers of Montaigu discharged directly onto the street, making for unhealthy and unwholesome circumstances.

Still hungry after breakfast, Edgar made his way to the *grande classe* with mounting feelings of dread. The discussion today would concern indulgences and the *Exurge Domine,* the discourse written by Pope Leo X condemning the errors of Martin Luther. It was a topic that was hot with controversy and thus, ripe for disputation. Edgar fretted that the tutor, Bedier, would call upon him as he had been spared the past week. The students, all twenty of them, took their seats at two rows of low benches, huddled shoulder against shoulder for warmth. Dawn was breaking, and a thin light seeped through the tall narrow windows of the dusty lecture hall. Bedier, fat and pompous, paced the floorboards, gripping his whipping rod like a cat about to pounce on a rat. As Edgar feared, the first words to drip from his thick lips were, "Monsieur Cantwell, rise."

He stood at the bench and swallowed hard.

"Tell me the three ways in which we may be granted penance?"

He was relieved he knew the answer. "Confession, priestly absolution, and satisfaction, Master."

"And how may satisfaction be achieved?"

"Good works, Master, such as visiting relics, pilgrimage to holy places, praying the rosary, and purchasing indulgences."

"Explain the meaning of *per modum suffragii.*"

Edgar's eyes widened. He had no idea. It was useless to guess as it would make matters worse for him. "I do not know, Master."

The fat tutor demanded he come forward and kneel. Edgar approached like a fellow walking to the gallows and knelt before the cleric, who whipped him four times on the back with all his might. "Now stand beside me, Monsieur, as I suspect this bee will need to sting you again. Who knows the answer?"

A pale young man stood up from his place in the first row. Jean Cauvin was tall and skeletal, a hollow-cheeked eighteen-year-old with an aquiline nose and the wispy beginnings of a beard. He was the finest student at Montaigu, bar none, his intellect often dwarfing the tutors'. In preparation for university study and a career in the priesthood, he had been sent to Paris by his father from their home in Noyon at age fourteen to attend the College de Marche.

After excelling in grammar, logic, rhetoric, astronomy, and mathematics he transferred to Montaigu for religious preparation. Edgar had had scant dealings with him so far. The boy seemed as cold and imperious as the masters.

Bedier acknowledged him, "Yes, Cauvin."

"If it pleases, Master," he said haughtily, "I have taken to Latinizing my name to Calvinus."

Bedier looked heavenward. "Very well then. Calvinus."

"It is an act of intercession, Master. Since the Church has no jurisdiction over the dead in purgatory, it is taught that indulgences can be gained for them only by an act of intercession."

Bedier wondered about the boy's use of language—"is taught" being different from "I believe," but he let it pass as his attention was on the English boy. He bade to Jean sit down. "Tell me, Cantwell, what did Pope Leo X say in his *Exurge Domine,* concerning the souls in purgatory?"

Edgar could not remember. He had repeatedly dozed off while reading the tract, and all he could do was desperately brace himself for another beating. "I do not know, Master."

This time Bedier went for bare skin, landing blows on his neck and cheek, drawing blood. "What did they teach you at Oxford, boy? Are the English not God-fearing? You will have no dinner on this day but will, instead reread and memorize the *Exurge Domine.* Who will answer me?"

Jean stood again and began to respond while Edgar cowered and tasted blood, which flowed from his cheek to his lips.

"Pope Leo wrote that the souls in purgatory are not certain of their salvation, and he further claimed that nothing in the Scriptures proves that they are beyond the state of meriting from indulgences."

There was something in Jean's tone, a note of skepticism, that unsettled the cleric. "Is this not what you, yourself believe, Cauvin—I mean Calvinus?"

Jean lifted his chin and answered defiantly. "I believe the Pope is the only one who does excellently when he grants remissions to the souls in purgatory on account of intercessions made on their behalf. For I believe, as others do, that there is no divine authority for preaching that the soul flies out of purgatory the moment the indulgence money clinks in the bottom of the chest!"

"Come here!" Bedier raged. "I will not tolerate Lutheran heresy in my classroom!"

"Do you intend to beat me?" Jean asked, provocatively. None of his fellow students could recall him ever receiving the whip, and they exchanged excited glances.

"I do, monsieur!"

"Well then, I shall make it easy for you." Jean strode forward, stripping off his cloak and his shirt, and knelt beside Edgar. "You may proceed, Master Bedier."

As the rod landed on his flesh, Edgar saw Jean looking over at him, and he swore he saw the boy wink.

Martin Luther had never been to Paris but his influence was surely felt in that city as it was throughout the Continent. The monk from Wittenberg had exploded onto the religious scene on the day in 1517 he nailed his *95 Theses* onto the door of Wittenberg Cathedral and began railing against the corrupt state of the Papacy and the abusive power of indulgences.

In the modern era of the printing press, certificates of indulgence had become a lucrative business for the Church. Indulgence salesmen would come into a town, set up their wares in a local church, suspending all regular prayer and service. Their certificates were mass-produced, with blank spaces for names, dates, and prices, and all good Christians were obligated, for the sake of their dead friends and relatives and for their own souls, to purchase this afterlife insurance to speed the sinner's exit from purgatory to heaven. Luther found the practice vile and replete with ecclesiastical errors and feared for the fate of people who believed that salvation could be bought. The priests in Wittenberg had a loathsome saying that sickened him, "As soon as a coin in the coffer rings, another soul from purgatory springs."

After all, Luther proclaimed, Paul had written in Romans that it was God who would save us: "For in the Gospel, a righteousness from God is revealed, a righteousness that is by faith from first to last, just as it is written the righteous shall live by faith." Surely, Luther argued, men did not need the Pope and priests and all the trappings and finery of the Church for salvation. All they required was a personal relationship with God.

Luther's Wittenberg thesis was quickly translated from Latin to German and widely published. Devout men had already been quietly grumbling about the decadence of the Church and the abuses of the Papacy. Now, it was as if a match had been tossed on the dry kindling of discontent. The fire that began to burn, the Reformation, was sweeping Europe, and even within a conservative bastion like Montaigu, smoke from the Reformist fires was wafting in. Students with open and brilliant minds, like Jean, were beginning to feel the heat.

Edgar was in his room struggling to memorize the tract of Pope Leo by the light of a small candle. He held the pamphlet with one hand and rubbed the welt on his cheek with the other. He was cold, tired, hungry, and sad. If suffering were a requirement for salvation, then surely he would be saved. This was the only positive thought he could muster. Then a knock startled him.

He opened the door and looked up at the placid face of Jean.

"Good evening, Edgar. I thought I would see how you were doing."

Edgar sputtered in surprise, then asked Jean to come in. He offered his chair, and said, "Thank you for visiting."

"I was only down the hall."

"I know, but it is still unexpected. It is the first time."

Jean smiled. "We have more in common today than yesterday. We have both been branded by Bedier."

"Perhaps," Edgar said glumly, "but yours was for brilliance, mine for stupidity."

"You are burdened by the language. If I had to conduct myself in English, I would not be so brilliant."

"You are kind to say that."

Jean rose. "Well, old Tempête will be patrolling the yard soon, looking for candlelight. We had better to bed. Here." He handed Edgar a piece of bread secreted in a handkerchief.

Edgar teared up and thanked him profusely. "Please, stay a short while," he begged. "I would like to ask you something."

Jean obliged and folded his hands on his lap, a benign and patient gesture. He waited for Edgar to wolf down the bread and finish swallowing.

"I am having great difficulties," Edgar said. "I am no scholar. I find the curriculum at Montaigu difficult, and I dread each day. Yet I cannot leave, for my father would suffer me worse than the masters."

"I am sorry for you, Edgar. Your soul is being tested. What can I do?"

"Help me with my studies. Be my tutor."

Jean shook his head. "I cannot."

"Why?"

"I do not have the time. There are not the hours in the day, for I am determined to read everything I can on the great issues of our time."

"The Reformation," Edgar grunted.

"We are fortunate to live in this exciting era."

"My family is wealthy," Edgar said suddenly, "I will find a way to pay you."

"I have no need for money. I only thirst for knowledge. Now, I must be gone."

"No!" Edgar said this so forcefully he surprised himself. He had to persuade Jean to help; he was at his wit's end. He thought quickly—perhaps there was a way. It would violate an oath he had given himself, but what choice did he have? He blurted this out: "If you will help me, I will show you something that will, no doubt, fascinate you and greatly stimulate your mind."

Jean raised his eyebrows. "You have stirred my interest, Edgar. What do you have?"

"A book. I have a book."

"What book?"

He had crossed the Rubicon. He fell to the floor, opened his clothes chest, and pulled out his father's large book. "This one."

"Let me see!"

Edgar placed it on the desk and let Jean inspect it, watching as the serious young man leafed through the pages with increasing amazement. "The year of our Lord 1527. Yet, most of these dates are in the future, in the months to come. How can this be?"

"I have pondered this since I could first read," Edgar said.

"This book has been in my family for generations, passed from father to son. What was the future has become the present."

Jean came across a sheath of loose parchments stuck into the pages. "And this? This letter?"

"I have not yet read it! I hastily took the pages from my father's collection when I left England last month. I have long been told it bears on the matter. I had hoped to have the opportunity to study it in Paris, but I have not had the time or strength to do so. It is no favor to me it is in Latin. My head spins!"

Jean regarded him disapprovingly. "Your father does not know you have these?"

"It is not a theft! I borrowed the book and the letter and intend to return them. I have confessed to myself a minor sin."

Jean was already reading the first page of the abbot's letter, breezing through the Latin as if it were his native French. He devoured the first page and was on to the second without uttering a word. Edgar left him to his task, studying his face for a reaction, resisting the urge to plead, "What? What does it say?"

As Jean turned pages, his expression was indecipherable although Edgar felt he was watching an older, wiser man, not a fellow student. He read on without interruption for a full fifteen minutes and when the last page was returned to the bottom of the stack, a page marked with the date 9 February, 2027, he simply said, "Incredible."

"Tell me, please."

"You truly have not read this?"

"Truly. I beg you—enlighten me!"

"I fear it is a tale of madness or wicked fancy, Edgar. Your treasure undoubtedly belongs on the fire."

"You are wrong, sir, I am sure. My father has told me the book is a true prophecy."

"Let me tell you about the nonsense written by this Abbot Felix, then you can judge yourself. I will be brief because if Tempête catches us up so late, we will surely glimpse the gates of hell."

The next morning, Edgar did not feel as cold and miserable as usual. He sprang out of bed warmed by the spirit of excitement and camaraderie. While Jean had remained derisive and skeptical, Edgar completely believed everything that was contained in the abbot's letter.

Finally, he felt he understood the Cantwell family secret and the significance of his strange book. But perhaps more importantly—for a scared, lonely boy adrift in a foreign city, he now had a friend. Jean was kind and attentive and, above all, not scornful. Edgar was sick of scorn being heaped on him like manure. From his father. His brother. His tutors. This French lad was treating him with dignity, like a fellow human being.

Before he departed for the night, Edgar had beseeched Jean to keep his mind open to the possibility that the letter could be a true and factual account rather than the ravings of a lunatic monk. Edgar proposed a plan he had been harboring for some time, and, to his relief, Jean had not summarily dismissed it.

In the chapel, Edgar made eye contact with Jean across the pew and received the precious gift of another small wink. Throughout the morning, the two boys exchanged furtive glances at prayer, in the classroom and at breakfast until in the early afternoon they were finally permitted to speak to each other privately at the start of one of their infrequent recreation periods.

There were flurries of snow in the air, and a crisp wind blew through the school's courtyard. "You'd better fetch your cloak," Jean told him. "But be quick."

They had only two hours for their adventure, and they would not have another opportunity for several days. Though Jean was serious and scholarly, Edgar could sense that he was enjoying the prospect of an escapade even if he thought it was folly. The two boys left the college gate and crossed the bustling and slippery rue Saint Symphorien, dodging horses and carts and piles of animal dung. They walked quickly with a determination and purpose, which they hoped would make them somehow less visible to the thieves and cutthroats who populated the neighborhood.

They passed through a warren of small slick streets populated with cart merchants, money changers, and blacksmiths. With the sounds of clomping horses and banging hammers ringing in their ears, they headed to the rue Danton, a short distance to the west. It was a moderately wide thoroughfare lacking the grandeur of boulevard Saint-Germain, but it was still a prosperous commercial street. Three- and four-story houses and shops crowded one another, their corbeled upper floors shouldering the road. The facades were brightly painted in red and blue, faced with ornamental tiles and paneling. Colorfully evocative signposts identified the buildings as taverns or trade shops. The shops opened onto the street, their lowered fronts doubling as display counters for all manners of goods.

They found number 15 rue Danton three-quarters of the way toward the river, the grand Seine a gray slash in the distance. Rising up from the Île de la Cité, the spire of the Cathedrale Notre Dame de Paris dominated the skyline like a spike drilled into heaven. Edgar had visited the cathedral on his first day in Paris and marveled that man could build something so magnificent. Its position on a plump little island in the middle of the Seine added to the wonder. He vowed to return as often as he was able.

Number 15 was a house over a pot and pan maker, the only building in its row that was plain black and white, simple white plaster and exposed black beams. "Monsieur Naudin said his apartment was on the second floor," Jean said, pointing at some windows.

They climbed the cold, narrow stairs to the second floor and banged on a green shiny door. When there was no answer they banged again, louder and more insistently. "Hello!" Jean shouted through the door. "Madame Naudin, are you there?"

From above their heads they heard footsteps, and a middle-aged woman came scraping down the stairs. She accosted the boys irritably. "Why are you making so much noise? Madame is not home."

"May I ask where she is?" Jean inquired politely. "We are from the College. Monsieur Naudin told us we could pay her a visit this afternoon."

"She was called out."

"Where?"

"Not far. Number 8 rue Suger. That's what she said."

The boys looked at each other and ran off. They could be there in under ten minutes but they had to hurry. Monsieur Naudin was the gatekeeper at the College de Marche, a coarse man with a scruffy beard who detested most of the young students who passed through his portal, with the notable exception of Jean Cauvin. During Monsieur Naudin's years at the College, Jean was the only student who treated Naudin with respect, engaging him with "pleases" and "thank-yous" and even finding a way to pass him a sou or two at holidays. He knew from their chats that Naudin's wife had an occupation that until today held little interest for him: she was a midwife.

Rue Suger was a street where weavers and those in the textile trade lived and worked. Number 8 was a shop that sold bolts of cloth and blankets. On the street outside, a gaggle of women were chatting and milling about. Jean approached, bowed slightly, and inquired whether the midwife Naudin was inside. They were informed she was on the top floor attending the birth of the wife of the weaver du Bois. No one stopped the young men as they ascended the stairs and they made their way all the way up to the apartment of Lorette du Bois but a woman accosted them at the door, and shouted, "There are no men allowed in the lying-in chamber! Who are you?"

"We wish to see the midwife," Jean said.

"She's busy, sonny." The woman laughed. "You can wait with all the other men at the tavern." The woman opened the apartment door and went inside, but Jean inserted his foot just enough to prevent it from closing. Through the crack they could see into the front room, which was crowded with relatives of the mother. They had a straight view into the bedchamber, where they could just make out the broad back and thick waist of the midwife tending her charge. There was an urgent duet being played out, Madame du Bois's moans and groans against the counterpoint of Midwife Naudin's insistent instructions. "Breathe now. Push. Push, push! Now breathe, please, madame. If you don't breathe, your child will not breathe!"

"Have you ever seen a baby born?" Jean whispered to Edgar.

"Never, but it seems a loud affair," Edgar replied. "How long will it take?"

"I have no idea, but I understand it can be hours!"

The piercing cry of a baby startled them. The midwife, apparently pleased, began to sing a lullaby, which was immediately drowned out by the newborn's wailing. Edgar and Jean could only see snippets of what Madame Naudin was doing: tying and cutting the umbilical cord, washing the baby and rubbing it with salt, applying honey to its gums to stimulate appetite, then wrapping it in linens so tightly that it looked like a tiny corpse by the time she handed the bundle to the mother. When she was done, she collected the stack of coins on the table and, wiping her bloody hands on her apron, flew out of the apartment, muttering about the need to start supper for her husband. She almost bowled over the two boys and exclaimed in her hoarse voice, "What are you lads doing here?"

"I know your husband, Madame. My name is Jean Cauvin."

"Oh, the student. He spoke of you. You're one of the nice ones! Why are you here, Jean?"

"This baby, does it have a name yet?"

She stood red-faced, hands on hips. "It does, but why is it your concern?"

"Please, Madame, its name."

"He is to be called Fremin du Bois. Now please, I have to pluck and cook a poulet for my husband's supper."

The two boys beat a hasty retreat to get back in time for their next class. The snow was falling steadily now, and their soft-soled leather boots were slip-sliding on the frozen mud and slushy roads. "I hope we have time to check the book," Edgar said, puffing for breath. "I cannot wait until tonight."

Jean laughed at him. "If you believe the name Fremin

du Bois is in your precious book, you will also believe this snow tastes like custard and berries! Have some." With that, Jean playfully scooped up a handful and tossed it at Edgar's chest. Edgar reciprocated, and the two of them spent the next few minutes being carefree boys.

Within a short distance of Montaigu on the rue de la Harpe, their mood turned darker when they encountered a somber funeral procession, a ghostly entourage in the blowing snow. The procession was just forming in front of a door to a residence draped in black serge. A coffin was on a bier, hoisted by a cortege of mourners, all clad in black. At the front of the cortege were two priests from the Church of Saint-Julien-le-Pauvre, the oldest parish in Paris. The widow, supported by her sons, was loudly lamenting her loss and from the character of the procession the boys presumed a wealthy man had died. A long line of mourners was organizing itself at the rear, paupers clutching candles, all of them expecting alms at the graveyard for their service. Edgar and Jean slowed to a respectful walk but Edgar suddenly stopped and addressed one of the paupers. "Who has died?" he demanded.

The man smelled rank, probably worse than the corpse. "Monsieur Jacques Vizet, sir. A pious man, a shipowner."

"When did he die?"

"When? In the night." The man was anxious to change the topic. "Would you care to give alms to a poor man?" His toothless, leering smile disgusted Edgar, but he nevertheless reached for his purse and gave the wretch his smallest coin.

"What purpose was that?" Jean asked him.

"Another name for my precious book," Edgar said gleefully. "Come, let us run the last!"

When they arrived, panting and sweating at the Pré-aux-clerc, their fellow students were filing back into their classroom for the prescribed session of liturgical study. Principal Tempête, himself, was patrolling the yard in his long brown cloak, plunging his cane into the snow as if he were stabbing the earth. Plumes of hot breath indicated he was muttering to himself. "Cantwell! Cauvin! Come here!"

The boys gulped and dutifully approached the bearded tyrant. Jean decided this was not an ideal time to correct the cleric's non-Latinate fashioning of his name.

"Where were you?"

"We left the College grounds, Principal," Jean answered.

"I know that."

"Was that not permitted?" Jean asked innocently.

"I asked where you went!"

"To the Cathedral de Notre Dame, Principal," Edgar said suddenly.

"Oh yes? Why?"

"To pray, Principal."

"Is that so?"

Jean chimed in, seemingly willing to lie for his new friend. "Is it not better, Principal, to exercise the soul than the poor body? The Cathedral is a wondrous place to praise God, and we were much benefited by the interlude."

Tempête pumped his hand on the cane handle, frustrated that he could find no excuse to wield it like a club. He grumbled something unintelligible and trod off.

It was all Edgar could do to keep himself focused enough to avoid the whip for the rest of the day. His mind was elsewhere. He desperately wanted to get his hands on his book and find out if the snow did indeed taste like custard.

The snow had stopped falling in the evening, and as the students made their way back to their dormitory after final chapel, the bright moonlight was making the surface of the courtyard snow appear like it was studded with millions of diamonds. Edgar looked over his shoulder and saw that Jean was making a beeline to follow him. For a skeptical soul, he was certainly overcome with a zestful enthusiasm.

Jean was on his heels when Edgar entered his room, and once the candles were lit, he hovered as Edgar retrieved the book from his chest.

"Find the date," Jean urged him. "Twenty-one February, come on!"

"Why so are you so excited, Jean? You do not believe in the book."

"I am anxious to expose this fraud, so I can return without distraction to my more productive studies."

Edgar snorted. "We shall see."

He sat down on his bed and tilted the book to catch the light. He flipped the pages furiously until he found the first entry for the twenty-first of the month. He stuck his finger at the spot and flipped forward until he saw the first notation of the twenty-second. "My goodness," he whispered, "there are names aplenty for a single day."

"Be systematic, my friend. Start from the first and read to the last. Otherwise, you will waste our time."

In ten minutes, Edgar's eyes were red and dry and the fatigue of a long day was catching up with him. "I am more than halfway through, but I fear I will miss something. Can you finish the task, Jean?"

The two boys traded places, and Jean slowly moved his finger down the page from row to row, name to name. He turned a page, then another, blinking rapidly and silently mouthing all the names, some of them difficult or impossible to decipher owing to the multiplicity of languages and scripts.

Then his finger stopped.

"Mon Dieu!"

"What is it, Jean?"

"I see it, but I can scarcely believe it! Look, Edgar, here—21 February 1537 Fremin du Bois Natus!"

"I told you! I told you! Now what do you say my doubting French friend?"

And then, a quarter page below he spied this: 21 February 1537 Jacques Vizet Mors.

He tapped the entry with his finger and bade the amazed Jean to read it also.

The spasm began in his diaphragm and rose through his chest into his throat and mouth. Jean's sobs alarmed Edgar until he realized his friend was shedding tears of joy.

"Edgar," he exclaimed, "this is the happiest moment of my life. I now see, in one instant and with absolute clarity, that God foresees all! No amount of good works or prayer can force God to change His holy mind. All is set. All is predestined. We are truly in His hands, Edgar. Come, kneel with me. Let us pray to His Almighty Glory!"

The two boys knelt beside each other and prayed for a long time until Edgar slowly lowered his head against his bed and began snoring. Jean gently helped him onto his mattress and covered him with his blanket. Then he reverentially returned the large book to the chest, snuffed out the candles, and silently left the room.

sabelle worked for an hour making a careful translation onto a lined pad. Calvin's handwriting was no better than a chicken scrawl, and the old French constructions and spellings challenged all her linguistic skills. At one point she paused and asked Will whether he'd care for a "little drinkie." He was sorely tempted, but he resolutely declined. Maybe he'd give in, maybe he wouldn't. At least it wasn't going to be a snap decision.

Instead, he decided to text a message to Spence. He assumed the fellow must be crawling out of his skin, wondering how he was getting on. He wasn't inclined to deliver blow-by-blow progress reports—it wasn't his style. For years at the Bureau, he drove his superiors to distraction by holding his investigations close to the vest, offering up information only when he needed a warrant or a subpoena, or better yet, when he had the case all wrapped up in ribbons and bows.

His thumbs were absurdly large on the cell-phone buttons, and the mechanics of texting never came to him naturally. It took an inordinate amount of time to send the simple message: *Making considerable progress. 2 down 2 to go. No guarantees but hopeful. 1 thing certain. We now know a lot more than we did before. U won't be disappointed. Tell*

*Kenyon that John Calvin is involved! Hope to be back in NY
in a couple of days. Piper.*

He hit SEND and smiled. It hit him: all this sleuthing
around the old house, the intellectual thrill of the chase: he
was enjoying himself—maybe he'd have to rethink his no-
tions of retirement, after all.

Fifteen minutes later, the message was forwarded from the
Operations Center at Area 51 to Frazier's BlackBerry. His
Learjet was taxiing to a halt on the Groom Lake runway. He
was due for a morning briefing with the base commander
and Secretary Lester, who'd be patched in via videocon. At
least he'd have something new to report. He read the message a second time, forwarded it to DeCorso in the field, and
thought, who the hell is this John Calvin guy? He e-mailed
one of his analysts to get a rundown on all the John Calvins
in their database.

His analyst had the diplomatic good sense to baldly reply
with a link to a Wikipedia page. Frazier scanned it before
stepping into the briefing room in the Truman Building deep
underground at the Vault level. For Christ's sake, he moaned
to himself. A sixteenth-century religious scholar? What was
his job turning into?

Isabelle put her pen down and announced she was done.
"Okay, a little background. Calvin was born in 1509 in a
village called Noyon and was sent to study in Paris round
about 1520. He went to a couple of schools affiliated with
the University of Paris, first the College de Marche for general studies, then Montaigu College for theology. You sure
you don't want a drink?"

Will frowned. "Thinking about it, but no."

She poured herself a gin. "In 1528 he went to the University of Orleans to study civil law. His father's doing—more money in law than the clergy, then as now! Now mind you, he's a Roman Catholic up to this point, very strict and doctrinaire but somewhere around this time he has his great conversion. Martin Luther's been stirring the pot, to be sure, but Calvin jumps in with both feet, rejects Catholicism and becomes a Protestant, basically founds a new branch that takes the religion in a radical direction. Until now, no one knows what caused his change of heart."

"Until now?" Will asked.

"Until now. Have a listen." She picked up her pad and began to read.

My Dearest Edgar,

I can scarce believe that two years have passed since I left Montaigu for Orleans to pursue the career of law. I sorely miss our discourse and camaraderie, and I trust, my friend, that your remaining time in Paris will be deservedly free of Bedier's cane. I know you long to return to your precious Cantwell Hall, and I can only hope you do so before the plague returns to Montaigu. I hear it has claimed Tempête, may he rest with the Lord.

You know, dear Edgar, that God drew me from obscure and lowly beginnings and bestowed on me that most honorable office of herald and minister of the Gospel. My father had intended me for theology from early childhood. But when he reflected that the career of the law proved everywhere very lucrative for its practitioners, the prospect suddenly made him change his mind. And so it happened that I was called away from the study of philosophy and set to learning law. I tried my best to work hard, but God at last turned my course in another direction by the secret rein of his providence. You know full well what I speak of, for you were there at the moment of my true conversion although it has taken a full measure of reflection to convince me of the course my life must take.

Your miraculous book of souls, your precious jewel from the Isle of Vectis, demonstrated that God is fully in control of our destinies. That we proved on that splendid winter's day in Paris when we found the book did foretell a precious birth and a grievous death.

We learned that God alone chooses the moment of our birth and our death, and by logic, all that transpires during our days on earth. We must, indeed, ascribe both prescience and predestination to God. When we attribute prescience to God, we mean that all things always were, and ever continue, under his eye; that to his knowledge there is no past or future, but all things are present, and indeed so present that it is not merely the idea of them that is before him, but that he truly sees and contemplates them as actually under his immediate inspection.

This prescience extends to the whole circuit of the world, and to all creatures. And it follows that God alone chooses whom to elect to bring to himself, not based on merit or faith or corrupt indulgences but on his mercy alone.

*The superstitions of the Papacy matter not.
The greed and conceit of degenerate forms of
Christianity matter not. All that matters is
the gift of true godliness that I received that
day, which set me on fire with a desire to progress to a purer doctrine founded on the absolute power and glory of God. I must count you
as the man who caused me to be imbued with
a singular and godly pursuit of all that is pure
and sacred, and for that I remain your obedient friend and servant,*

*Ioannis Calvinus
Orleans, 1530*

Isabelle put her pad down and simply delivered a breath-
less, "Wow."

"This is a big deal, isn't it?" Will asked.

"Yes, Mr. Piper, it's a big deal."

"How much is this puppy worth?"

"Don't be such a capitalist! This has the highest academic
value imaginable. It's a revelation of one of the underpin-
nings of the Protestant revolution. Calvin's philosophy of
predestination was based on knowledge of our book! Can
you imagine?"

"Sounds like big money."

"Millions," she gushed.

"Before we finish, you'll be able to add a new wing onto
the house."

"No thank you. Plumbing, wiring, and a new roof will do
nicely. Surely you'll join me in a drink now."

"Is there any more scotch lying around?"

*   *   *

After dinner, Will kept drinking, steadily enough to begin to feel his brain starting to vibrate harmonically. The notion of two down, two to go, reverberated in his mind. He was two clues away from finishing the job and heading home. The isolation of this drafty old house, this beautiful girl, this free-flowing whiskey, all of them were demonizing him, sapping his strength and resolve. This isn't my fault, he thought numbly, it's not. They were by the fire in the Great Hall again. He forced himself to ask, "Prophets, what about prophets?"

"Do you really have the energy to tackle the next one?" she answered. "I'm so tired." She was slurring her speech too. She reached over and touched his knee. They were heading for a repeat performance.

"Name me some prophets."

She scrunched her face. "Oh gosh. Isaiah, Ezekiel, Muhammad. I don't know."

"Any connections to the house?"

"None that come to mind, but I'm knackered, Will. Let's get a fresh start in the morning."

"I've got to get home soon."

"We'll start early. I promise."

He didn't invite her into his room—he had the willpower not to do that.

Instead, he sat on a lumpy bedside chair and clumsily texted Nancy: *Clue #2 was behind a windmill tile. Another revelation. The plot thickens. On to clue #3. Know any prophets??? Wish U were here.*

Twenty minutes later, as he was falling asleep, he didn't have the willpower to prevent Isabelle from slinking in. As she slid under the sheets he grumbled, "Look, I'm sorry. My wife."

She moaned and asked him like a child, "Can I just sleep here?"

"Sure. I'll try anything once."

She fell asleep spooning him, and when the morning came, she hadn't moved an inch.

It was pleasantly and unseasonably warm that morning. After breakfast, Will and Isabelle planned to take advantage of the fine, sunny day to walk in the fresh air and formulate their plan of attack.

As Will was fetching his sweater, Nancy called him on his mobile.

"Hey you," he answered. "Up early."

"I couldn't sleep. I was rereading your poem."

"That's good. How come?"

"You asked for my help, remember? I want you home, so I'm motivated. The second clue was important?"

"In an historical way. I'm going to have lots to tell you. A prophet's name. What do you think old Willie was referring to? You're a Shakespeare nut."

"That's what I was thinking about. Shakespeare would have known about all the Biblical prophets—Elijah, Ezekiel, Isaiah, Jeremiah, and also about Muhammad, of course."

"She thought of those."

"Who?"

He hesitated a moment. "Isabelle, Lord Cantwell's grand-daughter."

"Will . . ." she said sternly.

He responded quickly, "She's just a student." Then, "Nothing about any of those guys rang any bells."

"What about Nostradamus?" she asked.

"Isabelle didn't mention him."

"I don't think Shakespeare ever referred to Nostradamus in any of his plays, but he would have been popular throughout Europe in Shakespeare's day. His *Prophecies* were best sellers. I looked them up in the wee hours."

"Worth a thought," Will said. "What did Nostradamus look like?"

"Bearded guy in a robe."

"Lots of those around here." Will sighed.

The garden at the back of the house was wild and unruly, the grasses, high and unsown and beginning their autumn wilt. It had once been a fine garden, a prizewinner spanning five acres with wide, open views over native hedges to fields and woodlands. At its peak, Isabelle's grandfather had employed a full-time gardener and an assistant, and he had taken an active hand himself. No aspect of Cantwell Hall had suffered more than the garden from the old lord's advancing age and shrinking bank account. A local boy cut the grass from time to time and pulled weeds, but the elaborate plantings and immaculate beds had literally gone to seed.

Near the house there was a disused kitchen garden, and just beyond that, two generous triangular beds on either side of a central, gravel axis leading to an orchard. The beds were edged with low evergreens, and in their day had brimmed with tall ornamental grasses and sweeping schemes of perennials. Now they looked more like sad jungle thickets. Past the orchard was a large, overgrown and weedy wildflower meadow that Isabelle used to adore as a freewheeling young girl, especially in the summertime, when the meadow dazzled with a spectacular show of white oxeye daisies.

"Two for joy," she suddenly said, pointing.

Will looked up confused and squinted at the blue sky.

"There, on the chapel roof, two magpies. One for sorrow, two for joy, three for a girl, four for a boy."

The grass was wet and soon soaked their shoes. They trudged through an overgrown verge toward the chapel, its spire beckoning them in the sunlight.

Isabelle was well used to the oddity of the stone building, but Will was as taken aback as the first time he had seen it. The closer they got, the more jarring the perspective. "It really looks like someone's idea of a joke," he said. It had the identical iconic look of the Cathedral of Notre Dame in Paris, the Gothic exterior and flying buttresses, the two broad towers topped with open arches, the nave and transept crowned with a filigreed spike of a tower. But it was a miniature version, almost a child's toy. The great cathedral could comfortably accommodate six thousand worshippers, but the garden chapel held twenty at most. The spire in Paris soared 225 feet into the air, whereas the Cantwell spire was a scant 40 feet.

"I'm not very good at maths," Isabelle said, "but it's some precise fractional size of the real thing. Edgar Cantwell was apparently obsessed with it."

"This is the Edgar Cantwell in the Calvin letter?"

"The same. He returned to England after studying in Paris, and sometime later commissioned the chapel to honor his father. It's a unique piece of architecture. We sometimes get tourists wandering by from the walking path down the bottom, but we don't publicize it in the least. It's strictly word of mouth."

He held up his hand to block the sun. "Is that a bell in the tower closest to us?"

"I should ring it for you. It's a bronze miniature of the one that Quasimodo rang in the *Hunchback of Notre Dame*."

"You're better-looking than him."

"The flattery of the man!"

They began walking onward toward the meadow. Isabelle was about to say something when she noticed he had stopped and was staring skyward at the bell tower.

"What?"

"Notre Dame," he said. Then he raised his voice, "Notre Dame. That's pretty damned close to Nostradamus. Do you think . . . ?"

"Nostradamus!" she shouted. "Our prophet! Soars o'er the prophet's name! Nostradamus's name was Michel de Nostredame! Will, you're a genius."

"Or married to one," he muttered.

She grabbed him by the hand and almost pulled him up the path to the chapel.

"Can we get up there?" he asked.

"Yes! I spent a lot of my childhood in that tower."

There was a heavy wooden door at the base of the tower facade, which Isabelle pushed open with a shoulder shove, the swollen wood harshly scraping the stone threshold. She dashed toward the pulpit and pointed at the small Alice-in-Wonderland door off to the corner. "Up here!"

She squeezed through almost as easily as she had done as a child. It was more of a labor for Will. His large shoulders got hung up, and he had to throw off his jacket so it wouldn't be ripped. He followed her up a claustrophobic wooden staircase that was little more than a glorified ladder up to the bell landing, a wooden scaffolding that surrounded the weathered hanging bell.

"Are you scared of bats?" she said, too late.

Hanging above their heads was a colony of white-bellied Natterer's bats. A few took to flight, soaring through the arches, and darted crazily around the tower.

"I don't love them."

"I do," she cried. "They're adorable creatures!"

Inside the tower, he could barely stand without hitting his head. There was a view through the stone arches to neatly plowed fields and, farther away, the village church. Will hardly noticed the landscape. He was searching for something, anything, a hiding place. There was wood and masonry, nothing else.

He pushed at mortared blocks of stone with the heel of his hand, but everything within reach was solid and firm. Isabelle was already on the floor, on hands and knees, doing an inspection of the guano-covered planks. Suddenly, she stood up and started scraping at a spot with the heel of her boot, kicking up a small cloud of dried droppings. "I think there's a carving on this plank, Will, look!"

He dropped down and had to agree there appeared to be a small, curved etching of sorts on one of the planks. He reached for his wallet and plucked out his VISA card, which he used like a trowel to scrape the plank clean. Clear as day, there was a round, five-petaled carving, an inch in length, inscribed into the wood.

"It's a Tudor rose!" she said. "I can't believe I never noticed it before."

He gestured over his head. "It's their fault." He stomped hard on the plank, but it didn't budge.

"What do you think?" he asked.

"I'll get the toolbox." In a flash, she was down the stairs and he was alone with a few hundred bats. He warily looked up at them, hanging like Christmas ornaments, and prayed no one rang the bell.

When she returned with the toolbox, he hammered a thin, long screwdriver into the space between two boards and repeated the maneuver up and down the length of the inscribed plank, each time gazing upward to see if he was bothering the dormant mammals.

When he created enough separation, he drove the screwdriver all the way through and used it as a pry bar to jerkily raise the board a quarter inch. He slid a second, thicker screwdriver into the space and pushed down hard with his full weight. The plank creaked and popped up, coming away clean in his hand.

There was a space underneath, a foot deep, between the floor and the ceiling planking. He hated sticking his hand into a black space, especially with all the bats around, but he grimaced and plunged it in.

Right away, he felt glass against his fingertips.

He grabbed on to something smooth and cold and brought it into the light.

An old bottle.

The vessel was handblown into an onion shape, made of thick, dark green glass with a flat bottom and a rolled string lip. The mouth was sealed with wax. He held the glass up to the sun, but it was too opaque. He shook it. There was a faint knocking sound.

"There's something inside it."

"Go on," she urged.

He sat down and wedged the bottle between his shoes and began lightly chipping away at the wax with one of the screwdrivers until he saw the top of a cork. He switched to a Phillips head and gently tapped the cork into the bottle with the hammer. It plopped to the bottom.

He turned the bottle over and shook it hard.

A roll of parchment, two sheets thick, fell onto his lap. The sheets were crisp and pristine.

"Here we go again," he said, shaking his head. "This is where you come in."

She unrolled the pages with trembling fingers and scanned the pages. One was handwritten, the other printed.

"It's another letter to Edgar Cantwell," she whispered. "And the title page from a very old and very famous book."

"Which one?"

"The *Prophecies of Nostradamus*!"

1532
PARIS

Edgar Cantwell began to feel unwell while taking his evening meal at Madame Pucell's boardinghouse. He had been vaguely aware of a soreness in his groin for a day or two but had thought nothing of it, a strain of the muscle, perhaps. He was eating a lamb chop and a plate of leeks when the chill hit him, flying through his body like a swarm of winged insects. His colleague, Richard Dudley, another English student, noticed the unpleasant look on his friend's face and remarked on it.

"A chill, nothing more," Edgar said, excusing himself from the table. He made it only to the parlor, where he was seized with an overwhelming nausea and threw up a copious amount of undigested food onto Madame's chaise longue.

When the doctor visited him later that night in his bedroom at the top of the stairs, Edgar was doing poorly. He was pale and sweaty, and his pulse raced. The ache in his groin had progressed to exquisite pain, and his armpits too were sore. His nausea was unabated and he began to have paroxysms of dry coughing. The doctor lifted his sheet and directed his bony fingers straight for his groin folds where he palpated a cluster of firm lumps the size of hen's eggs. When he pressed down on them, Edgar howled in pain.

He needed to see nothing more.

In the parlor, Dudley seized the doctor's arm, and asked, "What is the matter with my friend?"

"You must leave this house," the doctor barked. His eyes were wild and fearful. "All must leave this house."

"Leave my house? Why?" the landlady exclaimed.

"It is the plague."

Edgar was only scant months away from completing his studies and returning to England for good. He had grown to be a confident young man who compensated for his rodent-like looks with a quiet air of nobility and superiority. He had survived Montaigu, so he reckoned he could tackle anything in life. Three years earlier, he had transferred to the College de Sorbonne, and he had acquitted himself well there. His final examinations were looming, and if all went according to plan, he would return to his country with a prestigious baccalaureate in canon law. His father would be proud, his life would be set on a glittering course.

Now, he was alone and most probably dying in a fetid room in a small boardinghouse in this wretched, plague-infested city. He was too weak to drag himself off his soiled bed, and he barely had the strength to sip at a jug of bitter tea the doctor had left at his fleeting last visit. In his feverish and desperate state, he saw images running through his mind: a snarling boar that turned into the snarling face of a cane-wielding Bedier, a funeral procession of somber, black-robed men, his precious book, flung open with the name Edgar Cantwell, Mors, floating above the page, then the long, animated face of a reddish-haired young man with a long, reddish beard and crimson cheeks, so close, so real.

"Can you hear me, Monsieur Cantwell?"

He heard a voice, saw a full pair of lips moving.

"Squeeze my hand if you can hear me."

He felt a strong hand underneath his palm and exerted all his will to grasp it.

"Good."

Edgar blinked in confusion into the man's gentle, gray-green eyes.

"I met your doctor at the house of another victim. He told me he had an English student. I am fond of the English, and I am especially fond of students as I was one myself not so long ago. All the study and hard work, a pity to have it snuffed out by the plague, wouldn't you agree? Also, I hear your father is a baron."

The man moved away from the bedside and flung open Edgar's window, muttering something about foul vapors. He was wearing the red robe of a doctor of medicine but to Edgar, he seemed a red angel, flying around the room, delivering a measure of hope.

"Your doctor is old and superstitious, the kind who is no use in the plague. I have discharged him and will personally assume your care, Monsieur. If you survive, you will find it in your heart to pay me, I am sure. If you do not, you will be added to my account in heaven. Now, let us get to work. This chamber is squalid and will not do!"

Edgar drifted in and out of consciousness. This red angel was a talker, and every time Edgar became sensate, he heard a torrent of words and exposition.

The only way to defeat the plague, the man was explaining, was to remove filth and effluents and administer apothecary medicaments. When the plague struck, he said, the streets had to be emptied of bodies and washed with fresh water, the corpses buried deep in quicklime, the trash burned, the houses of the victims cleaned with vinegar and boiled wine, the sheets kept clean and laundered, the servants to the dead and dying made to wear leather gloves and masks. He had no need to fear for himself, he chattered, as he had survived a mild case of the plague in Toulouse and was thus protected from future affliction.

But he insisted that nothing was as important as his medicines, and Edgar, scrubbed and clean, felt pleasant-tasting lozenges being pushed into his mouth followed by small mouthfuls of fresh, diluted wine. He heard the man telling him he'd return later with soup and bread, and Edgar was finally able to form some words and speak just above a whisper, "What is your name, sir?"

"I am Michel de Nostredame, Apothecary and Physician, and I am at your service, Monsieur."

True to his word, the physician later returned to Edgar's bedside and for that, the sick man was grateful. More lozenges were administered and small chunks of bread soaked in a potage of vegetables. Edgar remained feverish and in pain, his body wracked by paroxysms of coughing, but the sight of his red angel soothed him and gave him a respite from despair. The bread stayed down in his stomach, and before long he felt his eyes growing heavy, and he let the blackness come.

When he awoke, it was night, and the room was dark except for a single candle burning on his table. His red angel was sitting in a chair staring down with a glazed look in his eyes. There was a copper bowl on the table, filled to the brim with water. It was this bowl that commanded the man's full attention and every so often, he made the water move by wiggling a wooden stick into it. The candlelight played on the water's surface and cast a fractured yellow glow up onto the man's dark face. There was a soft humming emanating from his mouth, a low chant? He seemed fully absorbed, unaware he was being watched. Edgar thought he should ask what he was doing but before he could, fatigue overcame him again, and he drifted back to sleep.

* * *

In the morning, the light poured through his open window, and a refreshingly cool breeze wafted in. By the bed, there was a plate of salted cod carefully broken into little pieces, a chunk of bread, and a vessel of light ale. He had just the strength to take a few bites, then lift the chamber pot into service. He listened for any sounds in the house and, hearing none, found himself able to call out. There was no reply.

He lay awake waiting for the hopeful sound of footsteps on the stairs. Before the morning had fully passed, he was elated finally to hear them.

The red angel was back, with more lozenges and cloves of garlic. He seemed pleased with Edgar's progress, and cheerfully told him that it was a good sign he was not yet dead. He quickly inspected the hen's eggs in his armpits and groin but agreed to Edgar's panicky pleas not to put pressure on them as they were fiery hot and agonizing. He made it apparent he intended it to be a flying visit because he kept his cloak on and moved about the room quickly, cleaning and freshening.

"Please do not leave so soon, Doctor," Edgar said weakly.

"I have other patients, monsieur."

"Please. Just a little company, I pray."

The doctor sat and folded his hands on his lap.

"Was I dreaming?"

"When?"

"The night I saw you staring into a bowl of water."

"Perhaps, perhaps not. It is not for me to say."

"Are you using witchcraft to heal me?"

The doctor laughed heartily. "No. I only use science. The critical elements are cleanliness and my plague lozenges. Would you like to know what they contain?"

Edgar nodded.

"They are my own formulation, one I have been refining since my doctoral years in Montpelier. I pluck three hundred roses at dawn and pulverize them with sawdust from the greenest cypress wood and mix in a precise blend of iris of Florence, cloves, and calamus root. I trust your mind will be too feverish to remember this list as it is a secret! I am counting on my lozenges to make me very rich and very famous!"

"You are ambitious," Edgar said, managing a smile for the first time.

"I have always been so. My maternal grandfather, Gassonet, was an ambitious fellow, and he had a profound influence on my thoughts."

Edgar tried to prop himself up. "Did you say, Gassonet?"

"Yes."

Edgar was jolted. "That is not a common name."

"Maybe so. He was a Jew. Lay yourself back down! You look flushed."

"Please continue!"

"He was a great scholar from Saint Remy. From a young age he taught me Latin, Hebrew, mathematics, and the celestial sciences."

"You are an astrologer?"

"I most certainly am. I still have the brass astrolabe that Grandsire bequeathed me. The stars have a present influence on all things on earth, including the diagnosis of the body's ailments. Give me your birth date, and I will draw your chart tonight."

"Tell me, can your stars tell me the date I will die?" Edgar asked.

Nostredame looked at his patient suspiciously. "They cannot, sir, but that is a very curious question, if I may say.

Now, I advise you to chew three more lozenges, then go ye to sleep. I will return in the afternoon. There is a woman sicker than you on the rue des Ecoles who told me in her pitiful state this morning that if I did not come back to her soon, she would have to sew up her own shroud."

For two more days, the doctor visited his patient and administered his prescriptions. Edgar was anxious to talk to the man and weakly pressed him to stay longer, but the doctor would protest and complain about the number of poor souls afflicted in the district. Then, one evening, when Nostredame flew in with lozenges and a pot of soup, he found Edgar sobbing uncontrollably.

"What troubles you, Monsieur?"

Edgar pointed to his groin, and cried, "Look."

The doctor lifted the sheets. Both his inguinal folds were covered in bloody pus. "Excellent!" the doctor shouted. "Your buboes have ruptured. You are saved! If we keep you clean, I promise you, you will make a full recovery. This is the sign I have sought."

He took his knife from his satchel and cut one of Edgar's good linen shirts into bandages and cleaned and dressed the suppurating abscesses. He fed the man some soup and sat down wearily on the chair.

"I confess, I am tired," Nostredame said. The setting sun was casting a golden glow into the room, which made the bearded, red-robed man look beatific.

"You are an angel to me, Doctor. You have delivered me from death."

"I am gratified, sir. If all goes as expected, you will be restored to health within a fortnight."

"I must find a way to pay you, Doctor."

Nostredame smiled. "That would be most appreciated."

"I have little money here, but I will write my father, tell him what you did, and ask him to deliver a purse."

"That is most kind."

Edgar bit his lip. He had rehearsed this moment for the past few days. "Perhaps, Doctor, I can give you another gift in shorter order."

Nostredame raised an eyebrow. "Ah. And what would that be, Monsieur?"

"In my chest. There is a book and some papers I pray you to see. I believe you will find them of the greatest interest."

"A book, you say?"

Nostredame retrieved the heavy book from under Edgar's clothes and returned to the chair. He noted its date of 1527 on the spine and opened a page at random. "This is most curious," he said. "What can you tell me about it?"

Edgar spilled out the entire tale, the long history of the book within the Cantwell family, his fascination with the tome, his "borrowing" of the book and the abbot's letter from his father, his demonstration with a fellow student that the book was a true predictor of human events. Then he urged the doctor to read the letter for himself.

He watched the young doctor as he nervously pulled on his long beard with one hand and, with the other, held the pages up, one by one, to the last of the sunlight. He watched the man's lip begin to tremble and his eyes well up. Then he heard him whisper the name, Gassonet. Edgar knew he was reading this passage from Felix's letter:

> *But I cannot forget the one happenstance when as a young monk I witnessed a chosen sister issue not a boy but a girl. I had heard of such a rare occurrence happening in the past but had*

never seen a girl-child born in my lifetime. I watched this mute green-eyed girl with ginger hair grow, but, unlike her kin, she failed to develop the gift of writing. At the age of twelve years, she was cast out and given to the grain merchant Gassonet the Jew, who took her away from the island and did with her I know not what.

He concentrated his gaze on the doctor's reddish hair and greenish eyes. Edgar was not a mind reader, but he was certain he knew what was in the man's thoughts at that moment.

When Nostredame finished, he tucked the pages back into the book and placed it upon the table. Then he sat heavily back down and quietly began to weep. "You have given me something far greater than money, Monsieur, you have given me my raison d'être."

"You have powers, do you not?" Edgar asked.

The doctor's hands trembled. "I see things."

"The bowl. It was not a dream."

Nostredame reached for his satchel and pulled out a beaten copper bowl. "My grandsire was a seer. And his too, it is said. He used this to see into the future, and he taught me his ways. My powers, Monsieur, are strong and weak at the same time. In the proper state I can see fragments of visions, dark and terrible things, but I have not the ability to see the future with the precision that this Felix describes. I cannot say when a child will be born or a man will die."

"You are a Gassonet," Edgar said. "You have the blood of Vectis."

"I fear it must be so."

"Please look into my future, I beg you."

"Now?"

"Yes, please! By your healing hand, I have escaped the plague. Now I want to see what lies ahead."

Nostredame nodded. He darkened the room by closing the curtains, then filled his bowl from a pitcher of water. He lit a candle, sat before the bowl and pulled up the hood of his robe, pulling it forward until his face was hidden under its tented fabric. He lowered his head over the bowl and began to move his wooden stick over the surface of the water. In a few minutes, Edgar heard the same low vibratory hum emanating from the man's throat he had heard the night of his feverish state. The humming became more urgent. While he could not see the doctor's eyes, he imagined they were wild and fluttering. The stick was moving furiously over the bowl. The throaty sounds were building to a crescendo, growing louder and more frequent. Edgar grew anxious at the grunting and panting and regretted sending him down this fearful path. And then, in an instant, it was over.

The room was silent.

Nostredame lowered his hood and looked at his patient with awe. "Edgar Cantwell," he said slowly. "You will be an important man, a wealthy man, and this will happen sooner than you think. Your father, Edgar, will meet a foul and terrible fate and your brother will be the instrument. That is all that I see."

"When? When will this happen?"

"I cannot say. This is the full extent of my powers."

"Thank you for that."

"No, it is I who should thank you, sir. You have given me a history of my origins, and now I know I must not fight my visions as if they were demons but use them for greater good. I know now I have a destiny to fulfill."

*   *   *

Edgar gradually recovered his strength and his health, and the plague soon burned itself out in the University district. He sat for his examinations and was passed from the Sorbonne as a baccalaureate. On his last full day in Paris, he spent the morning sitting in the Cathedral of Notre Dame, admiring its grandeur and majesty for the last time. When he returned to his boardinghouse, his friend, Dudley pressed him to go to the college tavern for a last drink but there, lying against his bedroom door was a letter, left by his landlady.

He sat on his bed, broke the seal and read with horror:

Dearest Son,

A mother should never be suffered to write such a letter, but I must inform you that your father and brother are dead. The tragic circumstances have overwhelmed me, and I pray you to return at the earliest to take charge of your father's estate as the next Baron of Wroxall. Your father and William argued over some matter, and there was a violent struggle whereupon your father fell into the fire in the Great Hall and was burned on his shoulder. The burn healed not and led to a fever from which he died. William was much grieved, and by his own knife he took his own life. I am stricken with woe and misery and beg you to speed yourself back to my bosom,

Elizabeth

Twenty-three years later, in 1555, the old plague doctor sat in his attic study composing a letter. It was after midnight, and the streets of Salon-de-Provence were quiet, allowing him full concentration. This was his special time, when his wife and six children were in bed and he could happily work as long as he liked or until sleep overtook him, sending him tottering over to his study cot.

He had long since Latinized his name to Nostradamus as he imagined it sounded weightier and indeed, he had a reputation to nurture. His *Almanacs* were selling in large numbers throughout France and neighboring countries, and his fortune was growing. He no longer practiced his apothecary skills or medicine, instead turning his full attention to the more profitable life of an astrologer and seer.

Now, he held in his hand a copy of his new work, one which he hoped would bring him more notoriety, more accolades, and more money. The book had been printed in Lyon and would soon go on sale. His publisher had delivered a crateful of copies, and he took one of them and with his sharpest knife, cut away the title page: *LES PROFITIES, DE M. MICHEL NOSTRADAMUS*.

He dipped his quill and continued his letter.

My dear Edgar,

M. Fenelon, the French ambassador to England, informs me you are well. He tells me he visited with you at Whitehall Palace and that you have a good wife, two daughters, and a fine and prospering estate. I have consulted my charts and my bowl and you will certainly be graced with sons before long.

I could not be happier as you remain my English cousin who holds an esteemed place in my heart. As you well know, your Vectis book and papers have had a profound effect on my life and my endeavors. Knowing my lineage has given me the confidence to accept my visions for what they are, true and bona fide prophecies of great utility for all mankind. I have since desired to serve the public by using my skills to warn and educate princes and the masses alike what will become of them.

My own life has been reborn of late. My first wife and two dear children perished most cruelly from the plague, and with all my skills, I was powerless to save them. I have since remarried and my wife has borne three sons and three daughters who are a joy to me. I have recently published the first of my Prophecies, a great undertaking in which I am endeavoring to set out my predictions for many centuries to come in the form of one hundred quatrains for the interest and instruction of all who read them. I enclose the face page from the book for your amusement and I trust you will purchase a copy when it comes on offer in London. I have kept your family secret as you have asked me, and I likewise ask you to keep mine. You alone know that I am a Gassonet, and you alone know that the strange blood of Vectis flows through my veins.

Michel Nostradamus, 1555

1581
WROXALL

Edgar Cantwell looked and felt like a very old man. At age seventy-two everything had turned gray, his hair, his beard, even his shriveling, silvery skin. He was bothered by painful ailments from his abscessed jaw all the way down to his gouty toe, and his disposition was chronically sour. His main pleasures were sleeping and drinking wine, and he spent the lion's share of his days in both pursuits.

His daughters Grace and Bess were solicitous to him, and their husbands were tolerable fellows, he supposed. His youngest boy Richard was a good, studious lad, already proficient in Greek and Latin at the age of thirteen but he could not look upon his fair head without thinking of the boy's mother, who died of puerperal fever when he was only two days old.

But it was his oldest son, John, who was the bane of his existence, a source of anger and irritation. The nineteen-year-old had progressed to be no more than a drunk and a braggart who seemed to treat everything Edgar held sacred with an air of contempt.

He dimly recalled that in his day he had been a rebellious lad with a streak of licentiousness, but he had always obeyed his father and acquiesced to his wishes, even toddling off like a dumb lamb to slaughter to attend that horrible Montaigu.

His son did not subscribe to this kind of filial respect and obligation. He was a child of the times, his head turned by the trappings of Elizabethan modernity—dandyish clothes, frivolous music, theater troupes, and a far-too-cavalier approach to the serious business of God and religion. As far as Edgar was concerned, his son had more respect for a jug of wine or a lass's rump than his father's desires. If only Richard were the eldest, he would not have so dreaded the state of his legacy.

His legacy, he felt, was especially worthy of protection because he had labored so assiduously his entire life for Crown, for country and for Cantwell, and he was not about to blithely hand over his hard-acquired influence to a drunken fool. Thrust into baronial responsibilities immediately upon the untimely death of his father, he had begun a career as a public man who was forced carefully to navigate the treacherous waters of state politics.

When he returned to England in 1532, King Henry had already, unbeknownst to Edgar and indeed most of his subjects, secretly married Anne Boleyn, and thus begun his great conflict with Rome, seeking an annulment of his first marriage to Catherine. These were busy days for Edgar, who committed himself to taking charge of his estate, building his private chapel, his miniature Notre Dame, as a tribute to his murdered father, assuming a position befitting his legal education on the Council of the Marches, and finding a suitable wife.

The breaking of the chains that bound England to Rome occurred little by little, a succession of political moves and countermoves that culminated in Edgar's first great crisis when, in 1534, Parliament passed the Act of Supremacy making it high treason to refuse to swear that Henry was the Supreme Head on Earth of the Church of England.

Edgar pledged his affirmation especially quickly because he was aware of rumblings at Court about the papist shrine he was erecting at Wroxall. He was a good Catholic, to be sure, but his years at Paris, his friendship with Jean Calvin, and his secret knowledge of the certainty of predestination made him sufficiently "protestant" to convince himself he was not condemning his soul to damnation and hellfire by siding with the king in his Great Matter.

King Henry prodded Cromwell, and Cromwell prodded Parliament, and link by link the chain between England and Rome was separated until it was done in 1536. The Act Against the Pope's Authority drove the last nail into the coffin. England was the Reformer's country now.

Edgar married Katherine Peake, a homely woman from a substantial family, but she died in stillborn childbirth and left him a childless widower. He threw himself into his work and became in succession a judge at the Quarter Sessions Court, then the Great Sessions Court, where he rose to chief judge. To a degree, his fortunes swelled and deflated with the rise and fall of King Henry's third wife, Jane Seymour, since the Seymour family had blood connections to the Cantwells. But when her son, Edward, ascended to the Crown in 1547 and Jane's brother, Edward Seymour, became Lord Protector, Edgar was blissfully elevated to the House of Lords and the Privy Council.

King Edward's Reformation was harsher than his father's, and all vestiges of the Papacy were purged from the countryside. The business of dismantling Catholic churches was completed in an orgy of shattered stained glass, broken statues, and burned vestments. The clergy were released from celibacy, processions were banned, ashes and palms were prohibited, stone altars were replaced by wooden communion tables. Edgar's friend Calvin, in far-off Geneva, was exerting a profound influence on the English Isles. Edgar's tiny Notre Dame chapel survived the tumult only because it was on private land, and he was a powerful and discreet noble.

For a time, the pendulum swung in the other direction when Queen Mary succeeded her brother and reigned for five brief years. Mary zealously sought to restore the Catholic faith. So it was Protestant men who were being seized and burned at the stake. Edgar deftly rediscovered his papist roots, marrying his second wife, Juliana, who hailed from a Stratford-upon-Avon family of closeted Catholics. Juliana, almost fifteen years his junior, began to bear him children, and his two daughters were ushered into the world as Catholics.

Then the pendulum moved once again. In 1558, Mary was dead, her sister, Elizabeth became queen and England once again became a Protestant reign. Edgar shrugged it off and became Protestant again, closing his ears to the entreaties of his wife, who nevertheless, continued to take secret mass in their chapel and educate her daughters with the Latin Bible. Though advanced in years, he finally sired a son whom his wife baptized, John, in a clandestine Catholic ceremony. Five years later, Richard was born, and Juliana's life was lost amidst Edgar's salty tears.

Now, in his old age, the exertions of living a life as a political and religious chameleon had taken their toll. He was hobbled by infirmities and rarely left Cantwell Hall. He hadn't been to Court in two years, and he supposed the queen had forgotten he existed. But most of all, he obsessed about his ne'er-do-well son.

It was a hot summer day, but Edgar was perpetually cold. He insisted on sitting by his small bedroom fire, his shoulders covered by a shawl, his legs wrapped in a blanket. His appetite was naught, and his bowels were persistently liquid, which he attributed to the remedies his dolt of a country apothecary was administering for the gout. If the old healer Nostradamus were still alive, he would have begged him to travel to England to attend to his maladies.

From the garden below his window, he heard a burst of male laughter and cavorting, and when he clenched his infected jaw in anger, the pain almost toppled him from his chair. He drank the rest of the wine from his flagon in quick, large gulps, staining his chin red. Better his brain be dulled than to suffer this mental and physical anguish. He wished he possessed the book from Vectis, which contained the date *he* would die so he could know how much longer he had to suffer. His son was laughing again, prattling on like a girl.

John was drunkenly enjoying a glorious high-summer day where the grass was thick and green, the sun hot and yellow, and the flowers in the garden a blazing inferno of color. He was playing at archery, the hay-stuffed targets safe from his misguided arrows. Each time he missed, his friend literally fell to the grass in hysterics.

"Bugger yourself, Will," John cried. "You can do no better!"

John, though young, already had the thick body of a commoner—a drinker and a brawler rather than a gentleman or scholar. Like some of the youths of the day, he was clean-shaven, which as far as his father was concerned, made his face look naked. The Cantwell chin looked better under a beard, and the young man was no beauty. The beaky Cantwell nose didn't sit well between his watery eyes and fleshy cheeks, and his lips were pursed in a perpetual leer. During his woeful two years at Oxford before he was expelled for rioting, the ladies at his brothel dreaded being chosen by the violent oaf.

His friend was a more genteel sort. He was seventeen, wiry and muscular with an intelligent face and the earnest beginnings of a moustache and goatee. His long black hair flowed over his collar and looked like ebony against the hue of his smooth skin. He had mischievous blue eyes and a winsome smile that never seemed to fade. His elocution was clear and precise, and he possessed a presence that demanded men take him seriously.

He had known John Cantwell since childhood, when both of them attended the King's New School in Stratford. Though Will was far and away the superior student, Will's father, a merchant, lacked the means to send him to university. When John was expelled from Oxford, he returned to his country seat and remade acquaintance with the lad. The two of them became fast friends again, reveling in each other's bawdy company.

Will squirted ale into his mouth from a skin and seized the bow from his drunken companion. "Indeed I can do better, sir."

He smoothly pulled the bowstring back, aimed, and let an arrow fly. It sailed true and straight and struck the target in its center.

John groaned loudly, "Damn you to Hades, Master Shakespeare."

Will grinned at him and threw down the bow in favor of more ale.

"Let us go inside," John said. "It is too hot for sport. To the library, your favorite spot!"

In truth, whenever Will entered the Cantwell library, he looked like a little boy who had stumbled upon a roomful of unguarded fruit pies. He made a straight line for one of his favorite books, Plutarch's *Lives,* pulling it off a shelf and sinking into a large chair by the window.

"You should let me take this home, John," he said. "I will make better use of it than you."

John called the hall servant for more ale then flopped onto a divan, and replied, "You should steal it. Hide it under your shirt. I do not care."

"Your father might."

"I think he will never know. He does not read any longer. He does much of nothing. The only time he comes in here is to hold The Book in his lap and pet it like an old dog." He said *The Book* with mock reverence. He pointed contemptuously at the book sitting in its pride of place on the first shelf, its spine engraved with the date, 1527.

Will laughed, "Ah, the magic book of Cantwell Hall." Will affected a child's voice, "Pray tell me, sir, when shall I meet my darkest fate?"

"Today if you do not shut your mouth."

"And who will be the instrument of my death, knave?"

John sloshed more ale down. "You are looking into his eyes."

"You?" Will laughed. "You and what legions?"

This was an invitation to wrestle, and both boys rose and circled, sniggered at each other. When Will charged to upend his friend, John reached for the first book his hand could grasp and flung it hard at the back of Will's head.

"Ow!" Will stopped his charge, rubbed his occiput, then picked up the book from the floorboards. The pages had violently separated from the cover. "Ye Gods! A tragedy!" he cried melodramatically. "You have torn asunder a Greek tragedy and have awoken the wrath of Sophocles!"

A voice from the door startled them. "You ruined one of Father's books!"

Young Richard was standing there, hands on hips, like an indignant lady. His lips were trembling with rage. None in the family was more attuned to the sentiments of his father, and he took personal umbrage with the behavior of his brother.

"Be gone, brat," John said.

"I will not. You must confess to Father what you have done."

"Leave us, little toad, or I will have more to confess than that."

"I will not leave!" he said stubbornly.

"Then I will make you."

John dashed for the door. The boy turned and fled but not fast enough. He was caught in the center of the Great Hall just before he was going to slip under the banqueting table.

John roughly laid him on his back and straddled him, knees on shoulders, hips on waist so the boy was powerless to move. All he could do was spit, which so enraged his older brother that he boxed him on the side of his head with a closed fist, his signet ring scraping flesh and opening a scalp vein. A gush of blood brought the proceedings to an abrupt halt. John released him with an oath and as the boy ran off, he shouted at him that he had caused the incident by his own insolence.

Minutes later, John was moodily drinking back in the library; Will had his nose buried in a book. Edgar Cantwell appeared in their midst, painfully shuffling on his bad foot, an unseasonably heavy cloak lying over his shoulders. He had a fearsome visage, a mixture of rage and disgust, and his rasping shout curdled his son's blood, "You have hurt the boy!"

John pouted drunkenly, "He hurt himself. It was an accident. Shakespeare will tell you."

"I saw it not, sir," Will said truthfully, trying to avoid the old man's stare.

"Well, young sirs, what *I* can see are drunken idiots good

for nothing but their inclination to idleness and sinful pursuit. You, Shakespeare, are your father's concern, but this wretch is mine!"

"He is to marry, Father," John snorted impudently. "He will be Anne Hathaway's concern soon!"

"Marriage and procreation are nobler than any of your aspirations! Drinking and whoring are your sole desires."

"Well, Father," John sneered, "at least we share one common bond. Would you like more wine?"

The old man exploded, his face sanguineous. "I am not only your father, I am a lawyer, you fool! One of the best in England. Do not rest your haunches on primogeniture. There is precedent for ultimogeniture, and I have the influence at the Court of Assize to declare you an invalid heir and elevate your brother! You carry on without reform, and we shall see what happens!"

Shaking with anger, Edgar withdrew, leaving the two young men speechless. Finally, John broke the silence, and dryly croaked with a forced cheerfulness to his voice, "What say I have a servant fetch us a bottle of mead from the cellar?"

It was late at night, and the household had gone to bed. The two friends had whiled away the hours in the library getting drunk, napping, becoming sober, then drunk again. They had slept through the family supper, and the servants had brought them a tray later on.

The waxing and waning inebriation had turned John dark and surly. While Will flitted from one book to another, John stared into space and brooded.

By the glow of candlelight, he suddenly asked a question he had been ruminating on all day, "Why should I aspire to more than wine and women? What's the point of reading and studying and working myself silly? All this is mine anyway. I'll be a baron soon, with land and money enough."

"And what if your father makes good on his other plan of succession? Would your bleeding brother keep your jug and purse full, I wonder?"

"Father was spouting words, nothing more."

"I would not be so sure."

John sighed. "You, young Willie, have not the burden of nobility."

Will mocked him. "A burden, you say!"

"I have no inclination to better myself as I have always trusted time to do the job. To your credit, you have had to set lofty goals."

"My goals are not so lofty."

"No?" John laughed. "To be among the great actors? To be a writer of plays? To have London worshipping at your feet?"

Will waved his hand as an actor might. "Mere trifles."

John uncorked yet another bottle of mead. "You know, I have an aspiration long held and never shared, and it plays with a certain advantage I hold over my dear little prig of a brother."

"Other than your size?"

"The book," John hissed. "I know the secret of the book. He does not and will not until he is older."

"Even I know it!"

"Only because you are my friend, and you have sworn an oath."

"Yes, yes, my oath," Will said wearily.

"Do not take it lightly."

"All right. I am utmost serious."

John retrieved the book of Vectis from the shelf and sat

down with it near Will. He dropped his voice to a low, con-
spiratorial tone. "I know you are not as staunch a believer as
I, but I have a notion."

Will raised his eyebrows with interest.

"You have seen the letter. You know what this old monk,
Felix, wrote. Perhaps the Library was not destroyed after all.
Perhaps it exists still? What if I could find it and take possession of these books? What would I care if I had meager
Wroxall then? If I had the keys to the future, I would be as
rich as any lord, more famous than father's friend, old Nostradamus who, as we know, lacked full powers."

Will watched him rant, fascinated by his crazy eyes.
"What would you do, go there?"

"Yes! Come with me."

"You're mad. I am to marry, not partake in adventure. I
will travel to London soon, to be sure, but no farther. Besides, I take this Abbot's letter to be a work of fancy. He
spins a good story, I'll give him his due, but monks with
ginger hair and green eyes! It is too much."

"Then I will go alone. I believe in the book with all my
heart," John said truculently.

"I wish you good speed."

"Listen, Will, I refuse to let my brother learn the secret.
I wish to hide the papers, all of them. Without the letters
from Felix and Calvin and Nostradamus, the book is useless. Even if my father were to tell my brother its origins,
there would be no basis for belief."

"Where would you hide them?"

John shrugged. "I do not know. In a hole in the ground.
Behind a wall. It is a large house."

Will's eyes began to sparkle, and he sat upright. "Why not
turn this into a game?"

"What sort of a game?"

"So, let us hide your precious letters, but let us make them clues in a hunt for hidden treasure! I will compose a puzzle poem with all the clues, then we will hide the poem too!"

John laughed heartily and poured both of them more mead. "I can always count on you to thoroughly amuse me, Shakespeare! Let us proceed with your game."

The two of them scampered around the house, giggling like children, looking for hiding places, shushing themselves so not to wake the servants. When they had a rudimentary plan, Will asked for sheets of parchment and writing implements.

John knew where his father kept the Vectis papers, inside a wooden box secreted behind other books on the top shelf. He used the library ladder to reach it, and when he hauled it down, he reread Felix's letter while Will bent over the writing table. After dipping the quill, he would quickly write a line or two, then tickle his cheek with the feathered end for inspiration.

When he was done, he waved the sheet above his head to dry and presented it to John for inspection. "I am best pleased with my effort and so should you be," he said. "I have chosen the sonnet form, which adds further amusement to the enterprise."

John began to read it, and as he did, he squirmed in his chair with impish pleasure. "Can't be well! Clever, very clever."

"I thank you," Will said proudly. "It is pleasing enough that I have signed it, though I doubt my vanity will ever be discovered!"

John slapped his thighs. "The clues are challenging but not insurmountable. The tone, playful but not frivolous. It serves its purpose most ably. I am indeed pleased! Now, let us bury our treasure like a pair of filthy pirates marooned on an island!"

They returned to the Great Hall and lit a few more candles to ease their task. Their first clue went inside one of the great candlesticks that adorned the banqueting table. John had wrenched one open and satisfied himself it would hold several rolled sheets. Will had argued that Felix's letter should be divided into a first clue and a last, since the end of the letter held the greatest revelation. John placed the pages and forced the candlestick back together, banging the base on the carpeted floor to make sure it would hold firm.

The next clue, the Calvin letter, required more effort. John scurried off to the barn to fetch a mallet, chisel, an auger, and grout, and a full hour later, drenched in sweat, they had succeeded in prying off one of the fireplace tiles and drilling a deep hole. After inserting the rolled letter, they plugged the hole and regrouted the tile. In celebration, they raided the pantry, had some bread and cold mutton and the rest of a good bottle of wine from an onion-shaped green-glass bottle.

It was the middle of the night, but there was still work to do. The Nostradamus letter and the page from his *Prophecies* book needed to find their way up to the bell tower of the chapel. As long as they didn't drunkenly ring the bell, there was little chance of being discovered so far away from the house. That task took longer than they had planned because the planking was devilishly hard to rip up, but when they were done, they had put their spent bottle of wine to good use as the repository of the pages. To finish, Will etched a small rose on the plank with his sheath knife.

They feared that dawn would come before they hid the last clue, so they proceeded with great speed to complete this task, one that they might not have been able to accomplish if sober.

When they returned to the house smudged and smelly

from their physical labors, they retired to the library as the
first rays of sunlight streaked the sky.

John gleefully approved Will's idea for the poem's hiding
place and applauded its perfection. Will cut a piece of parchment to size and made it into a false endpaper. Then the
exhausted boys made for the kitchen, relieved that the cooks
were still in bed. The bookish Will knew how to make a
bookbinder's paste from bread, flour, and water, and in a
short while they had the white glue they needed to seal the
poem into place inside the back cover of the Vectis book.

When they were done, they placed the heavy book back
onto its shelf. The library was getting bright from the rising
sun, and they could hear the house stirring with activity.
They sank into their chairs for a final laughing fit. When
they burned themselves out, they sat for a while, chests
heaving, close to nodding off.

"You know," Will said, "this has all been for naught. You,
yourself, will undoubtedly undo all this fine work and retrieve the papers on your own account."

"You are probably right," John smiled sleepily, "but it has
been excellent fun."

"One of these days I may write a play about this," Will
said, closing his reddened eyes. His friend was already snoring. "I will call it *Much Ado About Nothing.*"

It was autumn when John Cantwell finally set out on the quest that had consumed him ever since the night he drunkenly conceived it. Then, he was warm and dry in his father's library. Now, the crossing of the Solent was treacherous, and he was shivering and sea-splashed.

A stiff gale was blowing from the mainland toward the Isle of Wight, and the captain of the sailing ferry had to be persuaded with a few extra shillings to make the passage that day. John was not a seafaring man, and he spent the brief journey heaving over the gunwales. At Cowes harbor, he made straight for the roughest public house he could find to buy himself a drink, converse with the oldest men he could find, and hire a couple of locals with strong backs.

He did not bother to buy himself a bed for the night because he was planning on toiling while most men slept. During the course of the evening, he consumed a good many tankards of ale and a large bowl of cheap stew, and, thus fortified, he waited in the moonlight for his hired men to return with picks and shovels and coils of rope. At midnight, the entourage of John Cantwell and three burly islanders wielding oily torches left the tavern and headed down a footpath through the woods.

They were never more than a few hundred yards from the

pounded shore. Nearby, the gulls called, the waves rhythmically crashed on the beach, and the salty, fresh breezes off the Solent sobered John and cleared his head. It was a cool night, and for warmth he clasped his fur-collared cloak over his high-collared doublet and pulled his cap down over the tops of his ears. His laborers led the way, whispering among themselves, and he gave himself to his own thoughts, daydreaming of wealth and power.

The old-timers at the tavern had been suspicious and taciturn until he loosened their lips with drink and coin. The Vectis Abbey was a ruined shell of its former self, he was told, done in during King Henry's days by Cromwell's henchmen. Like almost every Holy Roman church in the land, it had been sacked and looted, and the villagers and townsfolk of the island given license to use its stones for building works. The population of monks had largely dispersed, but there were diehards who lingered, and to this day, a small group of Benedictines stubbornly tied themselves to the ruins.

The old men knew nothing about any ruins of an ancient library, and they shook their heads and scoffed at the rich mainlander's questions. Yet when pressed, one grizzled fisherman did recall that as a boy he had walked the abbey fields with his grandfather and had scampered into a grassy hollow, a large, depressed squarish plot. His grandfather had shouted at him to return to his side and had batted him with his walking stick, warning him to say away from the spot as legend had it, it was haunted ground, populated by the ghosts of hooded black-robed monks.

To John, this seemed a promising place to begin his quest, and he made it his nocturnal destination.

The footpath opened into a field, and, by the light of the moon, the Cathedral of Vectis came into view. Even in ruins, it was an imposing structure, grand in scale. As he drew closer, he could see that there was no longer a spire, and the walls were half-gone. The windows that remained had no glass, and long grass and weeds had crept into open door-frames. There were other low buildings, some in shambles, some intact. From one row of stone cottages, wisps of fire-place smoke rose from a chimney. They gave these dwell-ings a wide berth and circled around them toward a more distant field closer to the shore.

The laborers knew the whereabouts of the sunken ground, and they grumbled as they approached it. They had been un-aware the patch of land had a taint, but the words of the old fisherman carried some weight, and they were nervous.

John took one of the torches and inspected the area. In the dark, it was hard to appreciate its boundaries. The tall grass sloped down into a flat depression not more than two feet below the level of the rest of the field. There were no visible features, no reason to favor one spot above another. He shrugged his shoulders and at random chose the ground beneath his feet. He called the men and bade them dig.

When the laborers hesitated at the edge of the hollow, John had to begrudgingly offer more compensation. But when they commenced their work, they proceeded at a furi-ous pace, slicing through the sod into the rich, soft soil. Two of them had been grave diggers, and they were capable of shifting dirt prodigiously. In an hour, there was a good-sized hole; in two hours it was large and deep. John squatted on the edge watching, occasionally jumping down and having a closer look by torchlight. The soil was moist and brown with a fertile, earthy smell, but in time he took note of some lumps of charred wood and a layer of ash.

His heart raced. "There was a fire here," he exclaimed.

The men were disinterested. One of them asked how much

deeper he wanted them to go. He replied by telling them to quiet themselves and keep digging.

Over the sound of the gulls, John heard a *clink*.

A shovel had struck stone.

John jumped back into the hole and scraped at the ground with his boot, exposing a flat stone. He grabbed one of the shovels and scraped it clean then thrust the shovel into the dirt two feet away. He hit more stone. He picked another spot and dug—more stone. "Clear the whole bottom of the ditch!" he commanded excitedly.

Soon, a surface of flat, smooth stones was exposed, a carefully fitted floor, long buried. John exhorted the men to take a pick to the stones to see what lay beneath. The laborers engaged in a nervously whispered debate among themselves but complied, and within a half hour, three of the large, flat stones had been dug out.

John got down on his hands and knees to inspect the area. With growing eagerness, he saw that the stones had been resting on a large-timbered frame. He gingerly placed his hand through the hole where the stones had been, and it went straight through, his entire arm disappearing. He took a handful of dirt and dropped it through the hole. It took a full second or more to hear the dirt rattling against something hard.

"There is a chamber below!" John declared. "We must climb down at once!"

The men began to back away to the farthest corner of their trench. They huddled and spoke to each other in low, urgent voices, then declared they would not go down. They were too afraid.

John begged them, then tried to bribe them and finally, in a rage he threatened them, but it was to no avail. They swore at him and climbed out of the trench. The best he could do was to get them to sell him their rope and leave a torch. In short order, he was alone in the night.

His apprehension was tempered by the excitement of the moment. He tied the rope around one of the timber beams, dropped it into the hole, and heard the loose end hitting solid ground. Next he tossed the lit torch down the hole and listened to it clatter. The torch stayed lit, and, looking into the void, he could see a zone faintly illuminated, a stone floor and perhaps an irregular wall. He took a deep breath to steel himself for the task, swung his legs into the hole, grabbed the rope, and began to use his arms and clenched feet to work his way downward.

The air in the chamber was stale and lifeless. He descended by inches, fearful of the dark, so he concentrated on the more reassuring glow of the torch. When he had descended about twenty feet, there was still another ten to go. He looked down and squinted through the particulate smoke emanating from the torch head.

"Ayyyy!"

His scream echoed in his ears as he lost his grip and fell hard to the floor, landing in a pile of brittle human skeletons. His feet landed on leg bones and slid out from under him, which saved him from breaking his own legs. His right hip crashed down on a skull, which crumbled under his weight.

He lay on the stone floor, gasping in pain and shock, eye to eye with empty eye sockets.

"God save me!" he cried.

He swung his head around and saw yellow bones everywhere: on the floor and stacked high in stone shelves in the walls. He was in a crypt, of that there could be no doubt. A second wave of panic hit when he realized that if he were badly injured, he would be unable to climb back to the surface. He might wind up lying there for eternity, one more pile of bones. He pushed himself to a sitting position and took stock of his limbs.

His arms and legs could move well enough, but there was sharp pain in his right hip. The only way he could gauge the extent of the injury was to try to bear weight on it so he rocked himself to his knees then straightened himself to a standing position. He gradually put pressure on his right leg and mercifully it held and he was relieved to conclude that it was bruised but not fractured. He took a step forward and heard the sickening sound of cracking bones under his boots, but he successfully limped to the torch and picked it up.

John painfully shuffled through the crypt, stepping around bones, inuring himself to the presence of so much death. There were hundreds of corpses, thousands, perhaps, some bare skeletons, some desiccated and mummified with remnants of reddish hair and adherent brown cloth. He tried to remain focused on the prize. Did Felix's Library still exist? He had no idea whether he was heading deeper into the cryptorium or in a more productive direction, but he committed to a path and slowly made his way by the light of the torch.

The arc of light found an archway, and, wincing at his painful hip, John quickened his pace almost as if he were fleeing the skeletons. He moved through the archway and found himself in altogether different environs.

He was in a large room, the edges indistinct to his eyes. A few feet away was the edge of a wooden table. He approached it and saw that it was a long table with a low bench on one side of it. He followed it along, touching its cool smooth surface with wonder. There were objects on the table, and he handled the first one he encountered. It was an earthenware inkpot! He lifted the torch over his head to cast its light farther. There were other tables, in rows!

It was then he noticed the stone floor, stained in blotches everywhere. Rust brown. Ancient blood. There had been buckets of blood.

It is true, he thought with a rush of exhilaration. The Felix letter spoke the truth, and, more importantly, the monks' Scriptorium had survived the conflagration! If it survived, the Library might have survived too!

He followed the row of tables, touching each one as he passed. There were fifteen. Behind the last one, he was momentarily disappointed to see only a wall, but his heart sped again when he saw a wooden door with heavy iron fittings. He pulled the enormously heavy door open with all his might and shined his torch in.

He immediately fell to his knees and began to weep with joy.

The Library! It existed! It survived!

To his left was a great wooden case, filled with enormous leather-bound volumes. To his right was an identical stack and in between the two was a corridor just wide enough for him to pass.

He regained his feet and limped, awestruck, down the central corridor. On both sides were high bookcases that seemed to go on into the darkness forever.

He paused and pulled out one of the books. It was identical in every way to the Cantwell volume, though this one was dated 1043. He put it back and kept moving forward. How far did the chamber go?

He kept walking for what seemed an amazingly long while. Besides the great abbeys and palaces of London, he had never been in such an enormous structure. Finally, he saw another wall. There was another archway through it, and he kept on his straight path. As he crossed the threshold, he thought he heard a small rustling.

Rats?

He was in a second vault, seemingly identical to the first. Vast bookcases lined the corridor, plunging into the blackness. He checked the spines in the nearest case—1457. His mind raced. Now that he had found the Library, how would he reap its harvest? He needed to find the books for 1581 and beyond. That was where the profit lay. He would have to figure out how he might haul the precious booty out of the hole. He was completely unprepared for success, but he had confidence in his cleverness and was certain he would be able to fashion a plan once his heart stopped beating in his throat.

At each successive case he stopped to check dates. When he spied a book dated 1573, he turned to his right and headed deeply into the stacks.

There—1575, 1577, 1580, and, finally, 1581. The present! There were a dozen or more books engraved with the current year. He stood before them, shaking like a cornered rabbit.

Before him was the ultimate power in the world, the power to see the future. No one on the earth but John Cantwell had the power to say who would be born and who would die. His chest puffed out in pride. His father was wrong. He had, indeed, made something of himself. He reached slowly and deliberately for one of the books.

He never saw the blow coming, never felt pain, never felt anything again.

The rock caved in his skull and his brain filled instantly with a killing tide of blood. He crumpled on the spot like a child's rag-filled doll.

Brother Michael called to his companion a few paces behind in the dark. "It is done. He is dead."

"God forgive us," Brother Emmanuel said, standing over the body and picking up the torch before it could ignite the books on the lowest shelf. They both dropped to their knees and prayed.

The young monks had spied the diggers passing their quarters and had followed them through the night and watched from afar as they worked the earth. When the local men fled, they had stayed to follow the activities of the remaining gentleman. When he climbed down a rope into the earth, they crossed themselves and quiet as snakes, slithering through the grass, followed him down.

Brother Michael was angry that the monastery had been invaded and angrier still that he had been compelled to take a life. "What is this place?" he spat.

His companion was a few years older, less of a physical sort, more cerebral. "Surely an ancient, sacred library, created by the brothers who lie peacefully in the crypt. It was sealed for a purpose, what, I cannot fathom. It is not meant for us. It was most assuredly not meant for this vile intruder. Taking a life is a great sin, but God will forgive us."

"Let us take our leave," Michael said. "I say we seal the hole, fill in the ditch, and say nothing of this to the others. Will you keep the secret with me, Brother?"

"In the name of our Lord, I will."

They left John Cantwell's corpse to lie where it fell and used his torch to find their way back to the rope. The body began its long, slow desiccation, and it would not be seen again by human eyes for 366 years.

A month passed, then another and another. Every morning Edgar Cantwell asked whether anyone in the household had heard anything of his son, John.

The autumn turned to winter, the winter to spring, and the old man incrementally came to accept that his oldest son had disappeared from the face of the earth. No one knew his destination when he left Cantwell Hall in secrecy, no one knew what might have happened.

One day, Edgar prayed in his chapel for guidance, and in his frail and increasingly confused state, he thought he heard the Lord whisper to him to reveal the family secret to his younger son, Richard, as he would need to be the bearer of the knowledge of the Vectis book. After chapel, he had the servants take him to the library. They sat him on a chair and he commanded them to climb the ladder to retrieve a wooden box hidden on the top shelf.

His manservant climbed up and passed some books to another pair of hands then announced he had found the box. He carried it over to his master and placed it on his lap.

The old man had not held the box in his hands for a long time. He was looking forward to spending a few moments with these papers, these old friends which bore so many memories—the Felix letter, which had made him spellbound as a young man, the enigmatic page with a date long in the future, the Calvin letter, which he treasured above all others for the memory of his esteemed friend, the Nostradamus letter for the memory of the man who had saved him from certain death.

He slowly opened the lid.

The box was empty.

Edgar gasped and was about to order the servant up the ladder again when he felt his chest explode with the pain of a thousand blows.

He was as good as dead when his withered body fell off the chair and hit the floor, and his servants could do nothing but frantically call for his children. His son, young Richard, was first on the scene, forever unaware that the secret of Vectis had just died with his father.

Will and Isabelle sat in the library, the Nostradamus letter before them on a table. The enormity of their discoveries of the past two days had left them spent. Each seemed more momentous. They felt like they were two souls floating within the eye of a hurricane—everything around them peaceful and routine, but they knew they were dangerously close to a swirling, violent storm.

"Our book," Isabelle muttered. "It's had a profound effect on great men. When this is finished, I'm going to rush out to buy a copy of Nostradamus and read it with a newly found seriousness."

"Maybe it was your book that made Calvin and Nostradamus great," Will said, sipping his coffee. "Without it, they might have been historical also-rans."

"Perhaps it will make us great too."

"There you go again." Will laughed. "I know it's getting harder and harder for you to think about keeping this a secret but I'd rather you lived a long anonymous life than a short famous one."

She ignored him. "We must find the last clue though I can't imagine how it could top the first three. I mean, my God, the things we've found!"

He had an urge to call Nancy to thank her for her contribution. She'd be at work. "It's all about the son who sinned," he said.

Isabelle frowned. "I don't know where to start on that one." She heard her name being called from the Great Hall. "Granddad!" she shouted loudly. "We're in the library."

Lord Cantwell came in, clutching the newspaper under his arm. "Didn't know where you were this morning. Hello, Mr. Piper. Still here?"

"Yes, sir. I'm hoping today's my last full day."

"Is my granddaughter not being an adequate hostess?"

"No, sir. She's been terrific. I just need to get back home."

"Granddad," Isabelle asked suddenly, "do you consider any of the Cantwells as great sinners?"

"Other than me?"

"Yes, other than yourself," she replied playfully.

"Well, my great-grandfather lost quite a bit of the family fortune in a speculative arrangement with a shipbuilder. If it's a sin to be a fool, then he's one, I suppose."

"I was thinking earlier—sixteenth century thereabouts."

"Well, as I mentioned, old Edgar Cantwell was always considered a bit of a black sheep. The man flip-flopped from Catholic to Protestant with whippetlike speed. Rather expedient, I should think, but he avoided the Tower and kept his head."

"Any blacker marks than that?" she asked.

"Well . . ." By his expression, Isabelle thought he had come up with something.

"Yes?"

"There was Edgar Cantwell's brother, William, I suppose. There's a small portrait of him as a boy hanging somewhere or other. In the early fifteen hundreds he accidentally killed his father, Thomas Cantwell. He's the largish picture in the Great Hall on the south wall. The one on horseback."

"I know the one," Isabelle said with growing intrigue. "What happened to William?"

Lord Cantwell made a throat-cutting gesture. "Did himself in, supposedly. Don't know if any of that is true."

"When was that? What year?" she asked.

"Damned if I can tell you. Best way would be to check the date on his headstone."

Will and Isabelle looked at each other and sprang up. "You think he's in the family plot?" she exclaimed.

"Don't think so," Lord Cantwell sniffed. "Know so."

"Tell me there's a family burial ground here!" Will said loudly enough to make the old man grimace.

"Follow me," Isabelle cried, running out the door.

Lord Cantwell shook his head, sat himself down in one of the vacated chairs, and began to read the paper.

The Cantwell cemetery was in a wooded glade at the far end of the estate, not an oft-visited corner as it distressed the lord to visit his wife's plot and the vacant patch that awaited his remains. Isabelle came by occasionally but usually on a bright, summer morning, when the cheerfulness of the day counteracted the heavy gloom of the place. It had not been attended for several weeks, and the grasses were high. The weeds were wilting from the lateness of the season, and they drooped lazily against the stones.

There were eighty or more stones in the plot, small for a village cemetery, large for a private family ground. Not all the Cantwells had made it in. Over the years, many had fallen in battle in one war or another and were buried on English battlefields or in foreign lands. As they entered the glade, Isabelle explained how difficult it had been to get the local Council to give her grandfather a permit to bury his wife there. "Health and Safety regulations," she huffed indignantly. "What about traditions?"

"I like the idea of a family plot," Will said gently.

"I've got a bit chosen for me. Under that lovely old lime tree."

"It's a nice spot," Will said, "but don't be in a hurry."

"Out of my hands, isn't it? All predestined, remember? Okay, then, where's our sinner?"

William Cantwell's headstone was one of the smallest in the graveyard, almost completely overgrown, so it required a methodical search through the centuries to find his marker near the middle of the plot. It simply had his name and the date, 1527.

"Darkly near a son who sinned," Will said. "I guess we need a shovel."

Isabelle returned from the garden shed with two. They were isolated but they began their work guiltily, looking over their shoulders since they weren't engaging in the most socially acceptable of activities.

"I've never done dug up a grave." She giggled.

"I have," Will said. He wasn't kidding. Years ago he had a case in Indiana, but he wasn't going to go there, and she didn't press for details. "I wonder how deep they planted them in the old days?" He was doing the heavy work and was starting to sweat. There were two other ancestors close by, so there wasn't enough room for both of them to dig simultaneously.

He shed his jacket and sweater and kept the shovelfuls coming, producing a mound of dark, rich soil on top of a neighboring grave. An hour into the enterprise, both of them were getting discouraged; they wondered if William was there after all. Will climbed out of the hole and sat on the grass. The afternoon sunlight was autumn-hard, and there was a crisp chill. Isabelle's lime tree was noisily rustling overhead.

She took over and jumped in like a little girl diving into a swimming pool, both feet hitting the bottom at once. There was a curious dull *thunk* when she landed.

As one, they both asked, "What was that?"

Isabelle choked up on her shovel, dropped to all fours, and began scraping the ground with the blade exposing a rough metallic surface. "God, Will! I think we've found it!" she shouted.

She dug around the object and identified its edges. It was a rectangle about eighteen inches in length, ten inches in width. As Will watched, she pushed the shovel into the ground beside one of the long edges and pried it up.

It was a heavily tarnished copper box. Below it was the rotting, green-stained wood of a coffin lid. She handed the box up to Will.

It had a heavy patina of green and black but it was evident that it was a nicely etched piece of metalwork with little round feet. The edges of its lid were encrusted in a hard, red material. Will dug at it with his thumbnail, and pieces chipped away. "It's some kind of wax," he said. "Sealing wax or candle wax. They wanted it to be watertight."

She was at his side now. "I hope they were successful," she said expectantly.

They had the discipline to cover up the grave before addressing the box, but they raced through the task. When they were done with the backfilling, they ran to the house and made straight for the kitchen, where Isabelle found a sturdy little paring knife. She worked the hard wax from the whole perimeter and, like a child opening the first present of Christmas morning, ripped the lid off.

There were three parchment pages, stained copper green ,but they were dry and legible. She recognized them immediately for what they were. "Will," she whispered. "It's the last pages of Felix's letter!"

They sat at the kitchen table. Will watched her eyes dart and her lips make small movements, and he exhorted her to translate on the fly. She began to read it slowly, out loud.

On the ninth day of January of the year of our Lord 1297, the end came to the library and to the Order of the Names. The scribes who numbered greater than one hundred had been acting strangely, lacking their ordinary diligence of task. It was as if a pall had been cast over them. Indeed, it seemed a lassitude which we were unable to fathom as they did not and could not speak their minds. And prior to this day a harbinger occurred which foretold the coming events. One of the scribes did incredibly violate the rules of man and God by taking his own life, thrusting his quill through his eye into the substance of his brain.

Then on the Last Day, I was summoned to the library, whereupon I found a sight that to the present makes my blood run cold on its contemplation. Every last one of the scribes by which I mean every green-eyed man and boy did by his own hand pierce an eye with the tip of his quill and cause his own death. And on their writing desks each one had completed one last page of writing, many of these pages stained red with blood. And on each page were written the selfsame words—9 February 2027. Finis Dierum. Their work was done. They had no need to write more names. They had reached the End of Days.

The great Baldwin, in his supreme wisdom, did proclaim that the Library should be razed as mankind was not ready for the revelation it contained. I did oversee the placement of the slain writers in their crypts, and I was the last man to walk through the vastness of the Library chambers amidst the endless shelves of sacred books. But these, dear Lord are my great confessions. I did light with my own hand the stacks of hay placed around the Library. and I used as torches the pages upon which were writ Finis Dierum until all were burned. I watched the timbers consumed by fire and saw the building collapse upon itself. But I did not, as Baldwin had proclaimed, throw a torch down into the vaults. I could not bear to be the earthly cause of the destruction of the Library. I fervently believed then, as I do now, that this decision should rest solely in the hands of God Almighty. In truth I do not know if the vast Library underneath the building was destroyed by the conflagration. The ground did smolder for a very long time. My soul too has smoldered for a very long time, and when I walk over the charred ground, I know not whether ashes or pages lie beneath my feet.

But I confess, dear Lord, that out of blasphemous madness I did randomly pick one book from the Library before it was sealed and burned. To this day I know not why. Please, I beg Your forgiveness for my wickedness. It is

*the book that lies before me. This book and
this epistle are evidence and testimony for
what has occurred. If, dear Lord, you want me
to destroy this book and this letter I will gladly
do so. If You wish me to preserve them, then I
will gladly do so. I seek from You my Lord my
God and Savior a sign, and I will fulfill Your
wish. I will be Your obedient and most humble
servant to the end of my days.*

Felix

The third and last brittle and yellowed page was written in a different hand. It seemed a hasty scrawl. There were only two short lines:

*9 February 2027
Finis Dierum*

Isabelle began to cry, softly at first, then in a crescendo, louder and louder until she was sobbing, sucking at air and getting red-faced. Will looked at her with sorrow but he was thinking about his son. Phillip would be seventeen in 2027, young and full of promise. He was a hairbreadth from crying himself, but he got up and rested his hands on her heaving shoulders.

"We don't know if it's true," he said.

"What if it is?"

"I guess we're going to have to wait and see."

She stood up, an invitation to hug her. They held the clench for the longest time until he told her simply and baldly that it was time for him to leave.

"Must you?"

"If I get back to London tonight, I can catch a morning flight."

"Please stay one more night."

"I've got to go home," he said simply. "I miss my guys."

She sniffed her nose dry and nodded.

"I'm going to come back," he promised. "When Spence is done with these letters, I'm sure he'll give them back to the Cantwell family. They're yours. Maybe one day you'll be able to use them to write the greatest book in history."

"As opposed to the middling thesis I'll write otherwise?" Then she looked him in the eyes, "You'll leave the poem?"

"A deal's a deal. Go fix your roof."

"I'll never forget the past few days, Will."

"I won't either."

"You have a lucky wife."

He shook his head guiltily. "I'm a lot luckier than she is."

She called for a taxi. He went up to his room to pack. When he was done, he texted two messages.

> *To Spence:*
>
> *Mission accomplished. All 4 found. Bringing them back tomorrow. Prepare to be amazed.*

> *To Nancy:*
>
> *U'r brilliant. U nailed the prophet. Amazing stuff. Home tomorrow. Can't believe how much I miss U. Won't leave U again.*

That night, Cantwell Hall was quiet again, down to two residents, an old man asleep and his granddaughter, tossing and turning in her bed. Before she turned in, Isabelle had stopped in the guest room and sat on the bed. It still had Will's scent on it. She breathed it in and started to cry again until she heard herself saying, "Don't be stupid." She obeyed herself, dried her eyes and turned off the light.

DeCorso was watching from the bushes. The guest bedroom went dark, then Isabelle's bedroom lit up. He checked his luminescent dial. He hunkered down and typed Frazier an e-mail on his encrypted BlackBerry, its keyboard glowing in the night, his hard thumbs mashing the keys:

Finishing up at Wroxall. Have received Piper's hotel and flight details from Ops Center. He used his credit card! Still has no idea we're on him. Plan to intercept before he gets to Heathrow. Still awaiting your instructions re Cantwells.

Frazier read the e-mail and wearily massaged his own scalp. It was midafternoon in the desert, but, underground, time of day was an abstraction. He'd been at his desk nonstop for two days and didn't want to spend a third there. The operation was coming to a head, but there were final decisions to be rendered, and his boss had made it clear that in light of the unsavory options, they were going to be Frazier's calls, not his.

"These things are in *your* job description, not *mine*," Lester had growled over the line, and Frazier had wanted to reply, "So *your* hands stay clean and *your* nights are restful."

Frazier's decision on Piper was the easiest one.

DeCorso would intercept him at his Heathrow hotel, immobilize him by any means necessary, and retrieve all the items he'd found at Cantwell Hall. A CIA extraction team would do a pickup at the hotel and transport them up to the

US airbase at RAF Mildenhall, where Secretary Lester had a navy transport plane standing by. Piper was BTH, so there was no chance of DeCorso killing the bastard, but there was no guarantee he wouldn't seriously damage the goods. So be it, Frazier thought. As long as we get our hands on any material that could compromise the integrity of the mission at Area 51.

Then they'd round up Spence and any of his confederates and add the missing volume to the vault. He imagined there'd be some kind of on-site ceremony, but that was the kind of nonsense the base rear admiral could decide.

The decision on Cantwell Hall was trickier. Ultimately, Frazier did what he'd often done when faced with these kinds of situations. He let the Library help him make up his mind. When he reviewed the pertinent DODs he nodded knowingly. His mind turned to the specifics of the plan. He had no doubt DeCorso could accomplish the job effectively. His only concern was the Brits. The SIS was behaving like a swarm of angry hornets over the Cottle affair, and the last thing he needed to do was poke a stick into the nest and twist it around. He would warn DeCorso to be careful, exceptionally careful. But on a risk-reward basis, he was certain it was the right course. What good was neutralizing Piper if the girl and her grandfather could spill their guts about whatever the hell they'd found.

He typed an e-mail to DeCorso with his orders and a stern litany of admonitions.

This was probably going to be his last mission with DeCorso, he thought, without a trace of sentimentality.

When Isabelle switched off her light, DeCorso peered through his night-vision scope to make sure she wouldn't go roaming. He waited a good half hour to be on the safe side, then began his work. He had his favorite cocktail for this kind of a job—cheap, easily bought, possessing the perfect balance of speed and coverage. Kerosene, paint thinner, and camping stove fuel in just the right ratios. He lugged two five-gallon jerry cans up to the house and quietly began soaking the entire circumference of the building. The old Tudor frame would catch quickly enough but he didn't want there to be any gaps. He was after a ring of fire.

He worked his way back around to the rear garden. There was still a half a can left. With a small suction cup and a diamond cutter, he carved out a pane of glass in the French Room, directly below Isabelle's bedroom. He poured the remaining liquid directly inside. Then, with the insouciance of a factory worker ending his shift, he lit a match and flicked it through the window.

Isabelle was dreaming.

She was lying at the bottom of William Cantwell's grave. Will was heavy on her, making love, and the top of the wooden casket was creaking and groaning under their weight. She was startled, and in fact deeply upset, at the incongruous pleasure she was experiencing amidst the ghastliness of the surroundings. But suddenly she looked over Will's shoulder into the sky. The sunset was glowing orange, and her lime tree was heaving in the breeze. The soft rustling of its great green branches soothed her, and she was completely happy.

As she was succumbing to smoke inhalation, the ground floor of Cantwell Hall was a raging inferno. The fine paneling, the tapestries and carpets, the rooms crammed with old furniture were no more than kindling and tinder. In the

Great Hall, the oil paintings of Edgar Cantwell, his ancestors, and all who followed him bubbled and hissed before dropping off the burning walls one by one.

In Lord Cantwell's bedroom, the old man was dead of smoke inhalation before the flames arrived. When they did, creeping up the walls and spreading over the furniture onto his night table, they caught the corner of the last thing he had read before going to bed.

The Shakespeare poem curled into a hot yellow ball, then it was gone.

DeCorso pulled his car into the Hertz lot at Heathrow off the Northern Perimeter Road. It was 3:00 A.M., he was tired, and he wanted to get over to the Airport Marriott, wash the smell of accelerants off his body, and get a few hours of sleep before his rendezvous with Piper. Since it was the middle of the night, and there were no lot attendants, he carried his bag into the lobby. There was a single night clerk, a bored young Sikh in a turban and polo shirt, who mechanically checked him in and began to settle the bill.

The clerk's demeanor changed and he started to glance at his terminal.

"Any problems?" DeCorso asked.

"Keeps freezing up on me. Just need to check the server. Won't be a minute."

He disappeared through a door. DeCorso swung the terminal around to have a look but the screen was blank. He shifted his weight from leg to leg in frustration and fatigue and drummed the counter with his fingers.

The speed with which the police arrived impressed him purely from a professional point of view. Blue lights flashed into the lot and surrounded the office. DeCorso knew that run-of-the-mill British cops didn't pack, but these guys had assault weapons. Probably an airport antiterror unit. They meant business, and when they yelled for him to get down on the floor, he did, without hesitation, but that didn't stop him from angrily swearing out loud.

When he was cuffed with plastic wristbands and hauled to his feet, he looked the ranking officer in the face. He was Special Branch, a deputy inspector who was looking as smug as the cat who'd caught the canary. DeCorso demanded, "What's this about?"

"You ever been to Wroxall, in Warwickshire, sir?"

"Never heard of it."

"Funnily enough, the local constabulary had a report from a member of the public of a suspicious vehicle loitering about up there on a country lane. Your vehicle, sir."

"I can't help you."

"There was a fire with casualties a few hours ago at a house in Wroxall. The number plate of your Ford Mondeo matches the report. We've been waiting for you to turn up." The DI sniffed a few times. "Do I detect a smell of kerosene, sir?"

DeCorso sneered at the officer. "I've got only one thing to say to you."

"What would that be, sir?"

"I've got diplomatic immunity."

Will awoke early at the Heathrow Marriott, unaware of the fire and its aftermath. Unimpeded, he caught the shuttle bus to Terminal 5, boarded the 9:00 A.M. British Airways flight to JFK, and filled the first-class cabin with snores most of the way across the Atlantic.

Will landed in New York and cleared customs before noon, local time. He strode through the arrivals hall, pulled out his cell phone, then put it away without using it. He'd hop in a cab and surprise Nancy at work. That was the play.

It was just before noon in Nevada, and Frazier was at the Area 51 Ops Center in a panic. They were following local news feeds from the UK and had confirmation that the first part of DeCorso's mission had been successful. Cantwell Hall, a stately old home in Shakespeare Country, was a smoking crime scene. But where the hell was DeCorso? It wasn't like him to go dark on this kind of assignment. They tried raising him by phone and e-mail, but he was off the grid.

Frazier's line lit up, and he answered, hopeful it was his man, but the familiar voice of an attaché to the Secretary of the Navy was there instead, instructing him to hold for Secretary Lester. Frazier banged his fist against the desk in frustration. This was not a good time for Lester to be calling for an update.

"Frazier!" Lester boomed. "What the hell?"

Frazier was confused. What kind of way was that to start a conversation? "Sorry, sir?"

"I just got a call from the State Department, who got a call from the US embassy in London. One of your guys is in the slammer invoking diplomatic immunity!"

Will stepped from the terminal out into a drizzling, washed-out morning. He was beginning to head to the taxi stand, when he heard a deep honk and saw Spence's bus rolling toward the terminal. He frowned with indignation. He'd get to them in time, but first he wanted to make amends to his wife and grab Philly and kiss his chubby little face. The bus door opened, and he had to deal with Spence's fat, bearded face instead. Unexpectedly, Spence didn't look pleased to see him. He urgently waved him on board.

Kenyon was hovering and said fussily, "We've been circling. Thank God you're here, and thank God we found you."

Will sat as Spence pressed the gas pedal. "Why didn't you call my cell?"

"Didn't dare," Spence said. He looked gray. "They burned the house. It's all over the UK news."

Will's gyroscopes went haywire, his equilibrium helter-skelter; he felt seasick, like throwing up. "The girl? Her grandfather?"

"I'm sorry, Will," Kenyon said. "We don't have much time."

His eyes welled, and he started to shake. "Take me down-town to the Federal building. I've got to get my wife."

"Tell us what you found," Spence said emphatically.

"You drive, I'll talk. Then we're done. For good."

Frazier ran through the corridors of the Truman Building, with two of his men trotting after him. They rode the elevator to the ground level and jumped into a waiting Humvee to take them out to the runway. A Learjet was scrambled and waiting on the tarmac, and Frazier ordered an immediate wheels-up. The pilots asked their destination. "New York City," Frazier growled. "I don't care how long it usually takes. Get there faster."

Will condensed the previous days into a staccato military-style debrief. All the wonder of discovery, the exhilaration of the chase, the thrill of revelation were flattened by the crushing news. Had he caused their deaths by sticking his nose in? The notion flashed through his mind. Yes and no, he concluded bitterly, yes and no. Some goddamned, red-haired monk savant had written their names down on a piece of parchment a thousand years ago: Mors. Yesterday was their day. That's all there was to it. Nothing could have changed their fate.

It could drive you crazy, he thought.

It *should* drive you crazy.

When he was done with his robotic briefing, he handed Kenyon the originals of the Felix letter, the Calvin letter, the Nostradamus letter, and Isabelle's neatly handwritten translations. On the flight from London, he had split the Felix letter into two parts as he and Isabelle had found them, to recapture the drama of its discovery. Now, he didn't much care about the impact of storytelling.

Will closed his eyes while Kenyon read aloud the translations and Spence drove, his teeth clenched, his heavy chest rising and falling, his oxygen lines sibilating.

Kenyon provided running commentary and gasping asides. Although it would be hard to find a more mild-mannered, mild-tempered man, the Cantwell letters were electrifying his thin body, turning his eyes wild.

The Felix letter thrilled them. In one fell swoop, all their years of speculative debate on the origin of the Library was replaced by a contemporaneous account. Kenyon cried: "You see, you big oaf, I was right! From God's mind to a scribe's hand. This is absolute proof. Finally, man has its answer to the age-old question."

Spence shook his head. "Proof of what? Why God? Why not the supernatural or mystical with all this seventh-son business. Or extraterrestrials, for that matter? Why is it always God?"

"Oh, please, Henry! It's as plain as the nose on your face." Then, all of a sudden, he realized the letter wasn't finished. "Where's the end of this? Is there more?"

Will raised his lowered head to say, "Yeah, there's more. Keep going."

Kenyon tackled the Calvin letter next and he read the last of it with rising triumph in his voice.

"Maybe you're not convinced, Henry, but the greatest religious scholar of his day damn well was!"

"What else was he going to think?" Spence huffed. "He fit it into the context he was familiar with. No surprises there."

"You're impossible!"

"You're monolithic."

Kenyon offered, "Well, here's something we can agree on—this is proof positive where Calvin got his bedrock belief in predestination."

"I'll give you that," Spence said.

Kenyon jumped on him, "And if I choose to believe with total certainty, as Calvin did, that God knows everything that will happen because he has chosen what will happen and therefore brings it about, then you'll have to give me that too!"

"Believe what you like."

The two old friends batted their arguments back and forth, making no effort to draw Will in. They could see he wanted to be left alone.

The Nostradamus letter made Spence chuckle. "I always thought he was an old charlatan!"

"Looks like you were half-right," Kenyon exclaimed. "For some reason the full powers weren't passed down the female line. He inherited half a deck. That's why his stuff is so sketchy."

The traffic was heavy on the FDR Drive, but the bus was steadily approaching their lower Manhattan exit. "Okay, Alf," Spence said. "Time for clue number four. That's going to be the pièce de résistance, isn't it, Will?"

"Yeah," Will answered ruefully, "it's the big enchilada, all right."

Kenyon turned to the last pages in Will's folder. He read Isabelle's translation of the conclusion of Felix's letter in a hushed monotone, and when he was done, no one spoke. It had started raining again, and the wiper blades beat like a slow metronome.

Finally, Kenyon whispered, "Finis Dierum."

"That's what I always feared," Spence said. "Worst-case scenario. Shit."

"We don't know for sure," Kenyon sputtered.

"We know I'm going to be dead in three days," Spence snapped.

"Yes, old friend, we know that. But this is altogether different. There could be other explanations for their mass suicide. They could have gone on the fritz and lost their bearings. Mental illness. An infection. Who knows what?"

"Or they could have been spot on. At least admit it's possible!"

"Of course, it's possible. Happy?"

"You've satisfied a dying man's wish to have you agree with me. Keep it up for another few days, will you?"

Will broke in with the pedestrian instruction, "Turn here."

He was sick of these old farts, sick of the Library and everything associated with it. He'd been wrong to let himself get sucked back into their bizarre world. He wanted to see the back of Spence and Kenyon and forget all this happened. Twenty twenty-seven was tomorrow. He wanted his wife and son. He wanted today.

He guided Spence to the FBI headquarters at Liberty Plaza and waited for him to open the door of the idling bus.

"End of the road, fellows," Will said. "I'm sorry about

next week. What can I say? You're still letting me have the bus?"

"The title and keys will be sent to you. Someone will tell you where to pick it up."

"Thank you."

The passenger door was still closed.

Spence exhaled forcefully. "You've got to let me see the database! I've got to know about my family! I'm not dying without finding out whether they make it to 2027!"

Will exploded. "Forget it! I'm not doing another god-damned thing for you guys! You've put me and my family at risk! I've got a whole lot of trouble on my plate now thanks to you, and I don't have a fucking clue how I'm going to get out of this. Your watchers are no more than paid assassins with get-out-of-jail-free cards."

Spence tried to grab his arm, but Will recoiled. "Open the door."

Spence turned to Kenyon with a pleading look of desperation.

"Is there anything that we can do to persuade you otherwise, Will?" Kenyon asked.

"No there isn't."

Kenyon pursed his lips and handed him a plastic carrier bag, bulging with objects. "At least take these and think about it. Call us if you change your mind." He plucked a cell phone off his belt clip and waved it at Will. "They're preprogrammed with our number. Plenty of minutes. We're going to have to fly back to Las Vegas. I'll get someone to deliver the bus."

Will looked inside the bag. There were a half dozen AT&T prepaid mobile phones. He knew the drill well enough. The watchers were bugging and tapping everything in sight. Anonymous prepaids were the only communication systems they couldn't breach. The sight of the phones and all they implied nauseated him, but he took the bag with him when he climbed down and left the bus.

He didn't look back, and he didn't wave.

One of the uniformed security guards at the lobby desk recognized Will and called out, "Hey, look what the cat dragged in! How you doin', man? How's retirement?"

"Life goes on," Will answered. "Any chance I can go up and surprise my wife?"

"Sorry, man. Got to be signed in and escorted. Same ole same ole."

"I understand. Can you call her for me and tell her I'm down here?"

She flew off the elevator and flung her arms around his neck and when he straightened his back, her feet lifted off the floor. The lobby was crowded, but neither of them cared.

"I missed you," she said.

"Ditto. I'm sorry."

"Don't be. You're home. It's over."

He let go of her. She knew there was something very wrong when she looked up into his mournful face. "I'm sorry to tell you this, Nancy, but it's not over."

DeCorso sat on the hard bench of his detention cell in the basement of the Met's Heathrow Airport Police Station. They had his belt and shoelaces and had stripped him of his watch and papers. If he was nervous, he didn't show it. He looked more like an inconvenienced passenger than a murder suspect.

When three policemen came to collect him, he assumed they'd be escorting him all the way to the terminal, where he'd be bundled onto a flight stateside, but instead, he was deposited only yards away in a bare, harshly lit interview room.

Two middle-aged men in dark suits came in, sat down, and announced that their conversation would not be recorded.

"You going to tell me who you are?" DeCorso asked.

The man directly across the table from him looked over the top of his glasses. "It's not for you to ask."

"Did someone forget to tell you guys I invoked diplomatic immunity?"

The other man sneered. "We don't give a flying fuck about diplomatic immunity, Mr. DeCorso. You don't exist, and neither do we."

"If I don't exist, why are you interested in me?"

"Your lot killed one of our lads in New York," the fellow with glasses said. "Know anything about that?"

"My lot?"

"Here's what we're going to do," the other man said. "We're going to tell you what we know, so we can cut through all the bullshit, okay? You're Groom Lake. Malcolm Frazier's your boss. He was on our patch quite recently trying to buy an interesting old book. He was outbid by a telephone bidder in New York. Our man delivers it, and before he can report in, he's snuffed. Then you show up this morning reeking of accelerants fresh from a barbecue involving the book's original owner."

DeCorso kept his best poker face and said nothing.

The second man picked up the thread. "So here's the thing, Mr. DeCorso. You're a guppy, nothing more. You know it, and we know it. But we're going to turn you into a very large whale as far as your government is concerned if you don't play along with us. We want to know things. We want to know about the current operational capabilities of Area 51. We want to know why you're so keen on the missing book. We want to know the intel behind the Caracas Event. We want to know what's coming down the lane. In short, we want a window into your world, Mr. DeCorso."

DeCorso hardly reacted. All they got was, "I don't know what the hell you're talking about."

The man with the glasses took them off for a handkerchief polish. "We're prepared to fight your immunity claim. We're prepared to publicly leak your role in the arson attack, which will embarrass your government and inconvenience your career, I should think. On the other hand, if you come over the wall and work with us, you will find yourself greatly enriched, the proud owner of a Swiss bank account. We want to *buy* you, Mr. DeCorso."

DeCorso shook his head in disbelief and fell out of stony-faced character to exclaim, "You want me to work for MI6?"

"It's called the SIS now. This isn't a Bond movie."

DeCorso huffed out a laugh. "I'm going to say this one more time: I'm claiming diplomatic immunity."

There was a sharp metallic knock, and the door opened. One of the senior Met officers barged in and declared to the man with glasses, "Sorry to interrupt, sir, but there are gentlemen to see you."

"Tell them to wait."

"It's the US ambassador and the Foreign Secretary."

"You mean their people?"

"No, it's them. In person!"

DeCorso stood up, stretched his arms over his head, and smiled. "Can I have my shoelaces back?"

Will and Nancy sat in the back of a taxi heading up the Henry Hudson Parkway toward White Plains. Nancy clutched Phillip to her chest and didn't speak. He could tell she was still absorbing the details he'd laid on her back at their apartment when Moonflower handed over the baby and left them alone.

He had told her the bare-bones facts; there wasn't time for embellishments: he'd found clues to the origin of the library at Cantwell Hall. Monk savants. Calvin. Nostradamus. Shakespeare. Somehow the watchers had gotten onto him. They had torched the house, killed the Cantwells. He feared they'd come after them next. They had to leave New York immediately. He omitted the Finis Dierum revelation: now was not the time. And he omitted being a lying, cheating scumbag: there might never be a time for that.

Nancy's first reaction was been a return to anger. How could he compromise Philly's safety? If she could see these problems coming, why couldn't he? What were they supposed to do now? Go underground? Leave the grid? Hide out in Will's fancy new bus? The watchers were ruthless. So what if the three of them were BTH? That didn't mean there wasn't going to be a price to be paid.

Will absorbed the body blows without fighting back. She was right—he'd come to the same conclusion.

They frantically packed a couple of bags and threw in some of Phillip's favorite toys, their service pistols and a few boxes of cartridges.

But before they left, Nancy flew around the apartment, making sure things were turned off, the milk was thrown down the sink. She finished and looked at Will, who was sitting on the sofa, bouncing Philly on his knee, lost in his son's laughs and gurgles. Her demeanor shifted. Her face softened.

"Hey," she said to him softly.

He looked up. She had a small smile. "Hey."

"We're a family," she said. "We're got to fight to keep this."

The taxi ride to Westchester gave them an opportunity to work the angles and try to come up with the semblance of a plan. They'd spend the night at her parents' house. They'd tell them their apartment was being fumigated or some such BS. Will would call his old college roommate and lawyer, Jim Zeckendorf, to see if they could use his house up in New Hampshire for a few days. That's as far as they took it. Maybe the biting winds off the lake would bring them some inspiration on where to go from there.

Mary and Joseph Lipinski said they were happy to have Philly drop out of the sky into their home for the night but seemed concerned that something was up with the kids. Nancy helped her mother bake a pie while Will brooded in the living room, waiting for his new cell phone to ring.

Joseph was upstairs with the baby, listening to the radio and reading the papers.

Finally, Zeckendorf returned Will's call.

"Hey, buddy, I didn't recognize this number," he started, his usual upbeat self.

"New phone," Will said.

Zeckendorf was Will's oldest friend, one of his freshman roommates at Harvard in a quad that had included Mark Shackleton. Shackleton evoked nothing but contempt and pity. He'd ruined Will's life by sucking him into the Doomsday plot and linking him forever with Area 51.

But Zeckendorf was completely different. The man was a prince, and Will considered him to be something of a guardian angel. As Will's lawyer, he had watched Will's back his entire life. Every time Will had a lease, a mortgage, a personnel problem at work, a divorce, or, more lately, an FBI severance agreement, Zeck was there with unlimited free advice. As Phillip's godfather, he promptly set up a college account for the boy. He'd always admired Will's law-enforcement career and considered it a noble thing to be his benefactor.

More recently, he was also his lifeline. When Will escaped from the watchers with Shackleton's Area 51 database, Zeckendorf was the anointed recipient of a hastily written and sealed letter, with instructions to open it in the event Will ever disappeared.

It was Will's insurance policy.

Will had told the watchers he'd put a dead man's switch in place with the location of the stashed memory stick. They had no choice but to believe him. As it happened, Will's monthly check-in calls to Zeck were an excuse for the two old friends to keep in touch.

"Always delighted to speak with you, but didn't we just talk?" Zeck asked.

"Something's come up."

"What's the matter? You don't sound so good."

Will had never told Zeck any of the details. They both preferred it that way. The lawyer had pieced a few events together. He knew Will's sealed letter had something to do with Doomsday and what had happened to Mark Shackleton. He knew it played into Will's early retirement, but that was the extent of it. He understood Will was in some danger and that the letter was, in a way, protective.

He'd always been able to offer Will a perfect blend of lawyerly concern and an ex-roommate's ribbing. Will could imagine the worried expression of Zeck's smooth face, and knew he was probably compulsively straightening out his crazy-kinky hair with his hand, something he'd always done when he was nervous.

"I've done something stupid."

"So what else is new?"

"You know my secrecy agreement with the government?"

"Yeah?"

"I kind of stepped all over it."

Zeck cut him short, transitioning into professional mode. "Look, say no more. We should meet to talk about it."

"I was wondering if we could stay at your place in New Hampshire for a couple of days if you guys aren't using it."

"Of course you can." Then he paused. "Will, is this line safe?"

"It's a clean phone. I've got one for you too—I'll send it."

Zeck could hear the tension in Will's voice. "Okay. You keep Nancy and my godson safe, asshole."

"I will."

Will and Nancy had arrived in White Plains with little warning, so the Lipinskis insisted they go out to dinner rather than assembling a meal of leftovers. An apple pie was cooling by an open window and would be ready when they returned. Up in Nancy's old bedroom, which she and Will used as their guest room, Nancy brushed on makeup in the mirror of her childhood vanity table. In the reflection she saw Will sitting on the bed, tying his shoes, looking tired and miserable.

"You okay?"

"I feel like shit."

"I can see that."

"Were they nice people?"

"The Cantwells?" he asked sadly. "Yeah. The old guy was a character. English lord right out of central casting."

"And the granddaughter?"

"Beautiful girl. Smart." He almost choked up. "She had a lot to live for, but it wasn't in the cards."

Will wondered if he'd just spilled a confession, but if Nancy had any suspicions, she let it pass. "Did Jim call you back?"

"Yeah. He's letting us have his place up in Alton. They won't find us up there. I've got a prepaid phone to give your parents so you can stay in touch."

"At least Mom and Dad are happy. They've got Philly for the night."

Frazier hated the lack of autonomy. He felt like a peon having to call Secretary Lester every few hours, but if he wasn't regular as a clock, Lester's aide would call him instead. The DeCorso business had sealed his fate. The shit was flowing downhill.

Lester picked up. It sounded like he was at a party, with background chatter and clinking glasses. "Hang on," Lester said. "Let me find someplace quiet."

Frazier was alone in his car. He'd kicked his men out into the cool night air for privacy. They were sullen, milling outside his window, a couple of them smoking.

"All right. I'm here," Frazier said. "What's your status?"

"It's done. Now we wait."

"Probability of success?"

"High. It's high."

"I just can't have a screwup, Frazier. You have no idea how damaging it was letting your man get caught. This has gone all the way up. I heard that the Prime Minister got the President out of the crapper to scream down the phone at him. He went on and on about a breach of trust among allies, damage to the special relationship et cetera, et cetera. Then the Brits threatened to pull their naval support for Helping Hand which, I don't need to tell you, screws up my life on multiple levels. You have no idea of the logistics that've gone into this. It's almost as big as the Iraq invasion. The minute the Caracas Event is over, we've got to be ready to move. With the Brits or without."

"Yes, sir, I understand," Frazier said flatly.

"I wonder if you do. Well, your reward is coming. To keep the peace, the President's agreed to open the kimono for the first time. He's letting the Brits into Area 51. They're sending an SIS team next week, and you're going to be their host, on your goddamn best behavior. But I swear to you, Frazier, screw this operation up, and you'll be their hostess instead."

On the way back from dinner at an Applebee's, Joseph stopped at a late-night UPS store to let Will mail a cell phone to Zeckendorf. Phillip was peacefully asleep in his infant seat. When Will got back in the car, he remarked on how chilly it had become. There was a sleety, cold rain falling. Joseph, ever cost-conscious, clucked, "Since Philly's here, I'll turn the heat on tonight."

The family settled in for the evening, the oil furnace rumbling in the cellar like an old friend. They tucked Philly into his crib and Nancy went to bed with a magazine. The Lipinskis disappeared into their bedroom to watch a TV show, and Will was left to himself to brood in the living room, tired beyond belief but too restless to sleep.

Suddenly he was seized by a powerful urge for a drink, not a glass of Joseph's ubiquitous Merlot but a proper glass of scotch. He knew that the Lipinskis weren't spirits drinkers but he had a rummage around in case someone had bought them a house gift. Finding none, he helped himself to Joseph's car keys and stole out of the house, destination, a bar.

He drove over to Mamaroneck Avenue, the main commercial drag, and parked the car at a meter near Main Street. It was a bleak, wet, miserable night and the street wasn't busy. Ahead of him, he saw the only cheerfully lit-up building, the new Ritz-Carlton Hotel, and he headed for it, his collar up against the rain.

The bar was up at the top of the high-rise, on the forty-second floor, and Will settled into an armchair and took in the spaceship view. To the south, Manhattan was a finger of pinpoint lights floating in the darkness. The bar wasn't busy. He ordered a Johnnie Walker. He promised himself he wouldn't go overboard.

An hour and three drinks later, he wasn't drunk but he wasn't exactly sober either. He was vaguely aware that a group of three middle-aged women across the room were fixated on him and that the waitress was awfully attentive. Typical. He got it all the time, and he usually milked it, but tonight he was in no mood.

In a way, he had been hopelessly naïve to think he could have signed a secrecy agreement and walked away from the Library without being saddled by its knowledge and a slave to its fate. He had tried to ignore it, live his life without thinking about the ball and chain of predestination, and he had been successful for a while, until Spence and Kenyon rolled into town on their bus.

Now he was in it up to his eyeballs, suffocated by the realization that Isabelle and her grandfather had to die because he *had* to visit them. And Spence *had* to persuade him to go to England. And Will *had* to retire because of the Doomsday case. And Shackleton *had* to steal the database and perpetrate his crimes. And Will *had* to be his college roommate. And Will *had* to have the athletic skills and brains to get into Harvard. And Will's alcohol-wicked father *had* to get it up and be able to perform the night he was conceived. And so on, and so on.

It was enough to make you crazy, or at least make you drink.

He stopped at three and paid the bill. He was overcome by an urge to hurry back to the house, lumber into bed noisily enough to wake Nancy, hold her in his arms, tell her again how sorry he was and how much he cherished her and maybe, if she wanted, make love, make absolution. He trotted back to the car and ten minutes later he was creeping back into the warm and cozy Lipinski house.

He sat on the edge of the bed undressing, the raindrops pinging the roof. Philly was peaceful in his crib. He slid under the sheets and put his hand on Nancy's thigh. It was warm and smooth. His head was swimming. He ought to let her sleep, but he wanted her. "Nancy?" She didn't stir. "Honey?"

He gave her a little squeeze but she didn't respond. Then another squeeze. Then, a shake. Nothing!

Alarmed, he sat up and turned on the light. She was on her side and didn't wake up to the harsh glare of the overhead fixture. He rolled her over onto her back. She was breathing shallowly. Her cheeks were red. Cherry red.

That's when he noticed his own brain was operating slowly, not a drunkenness, a sluggishness, like gears that were clogged with gritty sludge. With all his might he yelled, "Gas!" and forced himself off the bed to open both windows wide.

He threw himself over the side of his son's crib and picked him up. He was limp, his skin like shiny red plastic. "Joseph!" he screamed. "Mary!"

He began to give Philly mouth-to-mouth while he ran down the stairs. In the front hall he grabbed a phone, threw open the front door then put the infant on the rough welcome mat. He fell to his knees. In between chest-expanding breaths into his son's little nose and mouth, he called 911.

Then, he made a desperate decision. He left the baby on the mat and ran back inside for Nancy, screaming for her at the top of his lungs, like a man who was trying to wake the dead.

Will heard his name. The voice was coming from far away. Or was it close but whispered? Either way, it caused him to snap from a disturbingly light sleep to the reality of the moment: a hospital room streaming with daylight.

At the instant of wakening he was uncertain whether he was patient or visitor, in the bed or beside it, having his hand held or holding someone's.

Then, with a blink, it came back.

He was holding Nancy's hand, and she was staring up into his bloodshot eyes and pitifully squeezing his thick fingers. "Will?"

"Hey." He wanted to cry.

He could see the confusion on her face. The flashing, beeping ICU machinery didn't make sense to her.

"You're in the hospital," he said. "You're going to be okay."

"What happened?" She was hoarse. The intubation tube had been removed only a few hours earlier.

"Carbon monoxide."

She looked wild. "Where's Philly?"

He squeezed her hand tightly. "He's okay. He came out of

it fast. He's a little fighter. He's in the pediatric wing. I've been shuttling back and forth."

Then, "Where's Mom and Dad?"

He squeezed her hand again, and said, "I'm sorry, honey. They didn't wake up."

The chief of police and the fire marshal personally peppered Will with questions all day, cornering him in the hospital corridors, pulling him out of Nancy's room, ambushing him in the coffee shop. An electrical wire to the furnace blower motor had been disconnected, causing a deadly buildup of carbon monoxide. The safety cutoff switch had also been disabled. Compounding it all, the Lipinskis didn't have CO_2 detectors. This was a deliberate act, no doubt, and Will could tell from their initial questioning that he was a "person of interest" until the discovery of a broken bulkhead lock led them to believe he was more likely a victim than suspect.

The fact that he was ex-FBI and Nancy was active-duty didn't escape them, and by midafternoon, the Manhattan office of the FBI had pretty much elbowed the locals out of the way and taken control of the investigation. Will's former colleagues circled him warily, waiting for the right moment to grill him.

They tagged him making one of his shuttles between his wife and his son. He was only mildly surprised to see Sue Sanchez approaching, her high heels hammering the floor. After all she was Nancy's supervisor. On the other hand, he was repulsed to see John Mueller with her.

Will and Sanchez always had a relationship based on mutual distrust and animus. Years earlier, he had been her supervisor. By self-admission, Will was a piss-poor boss, and Sue was always sure she could do a better job than he. She got the chance when he was busted down a grade for having an "inappropriate relationship" with another supervisor's admin.

On a Friday she reported to him, on a Monday the roles were reversed. Their new chain of command was nightmarish. He responded to her by being asinine and passive-aggressive. If it hadn't been for his need to stick it out for a couple of years to get his full pension, he would have metaphorically and perhaps literally kicked her officious Latina ass.

Sanchez was his superior during the Doomsday case, and she'd been the stooge dispatched to remove him when he got too close to Shackleton. A chain of puppet masters had used her as a tool, and she still resented not knowing why she'd been ordered to terminate him, why the Doomsday case had entered a deep freeze without resolution, and why Will had been given an absurdly attractive early-retirement package.

As fractured as Will's relationship was with Sue, it was worse with John Mueller. Mueller was priggish, by the book, an agent more concerned with process than results. He was a ladder-climber, anxious to get out of the field as early in his career as possible and rise in the bureaucracy. He resented Will's cavalier, insubordinate attitude and his moral transgressions, the drinking, the womanizing. And he was horrified that Nancy Lipinski, a young special agent with the potential to be a Mueller clone, had been turned to the dark side by Piper and had even married the scoundrel!

For Will's part, Mueller was a poster child for everything wrong with the FBI. Will had worked cases to put bad guys away. Mueller worked them to accelerate his career. He was a political creature, and Will had no time for politics.

Mueller was the original lead special agent on the Doomsday case, and had it not been for his sudden incapacitating illness, Will would never have been assigned to the case. He would have never worked with Nancy. He would have never hooked up with her. The Doomsday case might have been solved. An entire chain of events would have been avoided if Mueller hadn't had a little clot that shot into his brain.

Mueller had fully recovered and was now one of Sanchez's pet poodles. When the call came in that Nancy and her family had been deliberately targeted, her first move was to get Mueller to drive her to White Plains.

In an empty visitors' lounge, Sanchez asked Will how he was and offered condolences. Mueller waited for the brief, human exchange to conclude, then jumped in hard with an unpleasant edge.

"The police report says you were away from the house for an hour and a half."

"You read the report perfectly, John."

"Drinking at a bar."

"In my experience, bars are pretty good places to find a drink."

"You couldn't find a drink at the house?"

"My father-in-law was a great guy, but he only drank wine. I felt like a scotch."

"Pretty convenient time to be out and about, wouldn't you say?"

Will walked two paces, grabbed him by the lapels of his suit jacket, and pushed the smaller man against the wall with a thud. He was tempted to hold him with one hand and smash his face with a closed fist. When Mueller started to thrust his arms upward to break the hold, Sanchez shouted at both of them to stand down.

Will let go and backed off, his chest heaving, his pupils pinpointed in anger. Mueller smoothed his jacket and smugly shot Will a grin that seemed to say, this is so not over between us.

"Will, what do you think happened last night?" Sanchez asked evenly.

"Someone made a forced entry when we were at dinner. They rigged the furnace. If I hadn't gone out, three people would be in a coma right now."

"In a coma?" Mueller asked. "Why not dead?"

Will ignored him as if he weren't there.

"Who do you think was targeted? You? Nancy? Her parents?"

"Her parents were innocent bystanders."

"Okay," Sanchez said patiently, "you or Nancy?"

"Me."

"Who's responsible? What's the motive?"

Will was talking to Sanchez. "You're not going to want to hear this Sue, but this is still the Doomsday case."

Her eyes narrowed. "What are you saying, Will?"

"The case never ended."

"Are you telling me this is the Doomsday killer back at it?"

"I'm not saying that. I'm saying the case never ended."

"This is nonsense, it's bull!" Mueller protested. "What's your basis?"

"Sue," Will said, "you know the case wound up screwy. You know I was deep-sixed. You know I was retired out of the Bureau. You know you weren't supposed to ask any questions. Right?"

"Right," she agreed softly.

"There's stuff going on so many pay grades above your head it would make you spin like a top. The things I know are covered by a federal confidentiality agreement that would take a presidential order to waive. Let me just tell you that there are people out there who want certain things from me and are prepared to kill to get them. Your hands are tied. There's nothing you can do to help me."

"We're the FBI, Will!" she exclaimed.

"The people after me play on the same side of the field as the FBI. That's all I can say."

Mueller snorted. "This is the most conveniently self-serving crap I've ever heard. You're telling us we can't investigate you or this case because of some high-level clandestine bullshit. Come on!"

Will answered, "I'm going to see my son. You guys do whatever the hell you want. Good luck to you."

The nurses left Will alone by Phillip's intensive-care crib. The breathing tube was out, and Philly's color was returning to normal. He was sleeping, his little hand grasping for something in a dream.

Will was steaming like a pressure cooker. He forced himself to focus. There was no time for fatigue. There was no room for sorrow. And there was no chance he'd be hobbled by fear. He concentrated all his energy on the one emotion that he knew would be a reliable ally: anger.

He understood that Malcolm Frazier and his minions were out there, probably close by. The watchers had an edge—they had dates of death, but that was as far as their prescience extended. They knew they'd be able to kill his in-laws. They hoped they'd be able to send him and his family into comas. But they failed. He had the upper hand now. He didn't need the police or the FBI. He needed his own strength. He felt the Glock in his waistband, its barrel painfully digging into his thigh. He channeled the pain against a mental image of Frazier.

I'm coming for you, he thought. I'm coming.

* * *

At JFK, DeCorso opened the back door of Frazier's car and slid in beside his boss. Neither of them spoke. Frazier's truculent chin said it all—he was not pleased. His phone was hot from constant usage.

The diplomatic immunity card that DeCorso played had wreaked transatlantic havoc. The State Department didn't have a clue who DeCorso was or why the Department of Defense was insisting they honor his claim. SIS brass furiously tried to shake information about DeCorso out of their CIA counterparts. The political football kept getting punted higher up the chains of command until the US Secretary of State was reluctantly corralled into personally interceding with the UK Foreign Secretary.

DeCorso got his get-out-of-jail-free card. The British government reluctantly acquiesced and turned DeCorso over to a detail from the US embassy. He was sped to Stansted Airport to board a private Gulfstream V belonging to the Secretary of the US Navy, and the arson and murder investigation was functionally closed.

Finally, DeCorso broke down and offered an apology.

"How'd you get made?" Frazier growled.

"Somebody called in my rental's license plate."

"Should've swapped it out."

"You've got my resignation."

"No one resigns on me. When I decide to fire you, I'll let you know."

"Did you get Piper?"

"We tried last night. Carbon monoxide at the Lipinski house. We rigged it while they were at a restaurant."

"Yesterday was their DODs, right?"

"Yeah. We were causative. Piper left the house, came back, and raised the alarm. His wife and son are going to recover. We never had a chance to retrieve whatever he found in the UK. For all we know, he could've passed the material to Spence by now."

"Where's Spence?"

"Don't know. Probably on the way back to Vegas. We're looking for him."

DeCorso sucked in air through his teeth. "Shit."

"Yeah."

"What's the plan?"

"Piper's at the White Plains Hospital. The place is crawling with FBI. We're watching it, and when he leaves, we'll pick him up."

"You sure you don't want to shitcan me?"

Frazier knew something his man didn't. DeCorso would be dead day after tomorrow. There was no sense in taking on a mountain of termination paperwork. "There's no need for that."

DeCorso thanked him and was quiet the rest of the ride to White Plains.

It was late afternoon when Nancy awoke again. She was out of ICU, in a private room. Will wasn't at her bedside, and she got panicky. She rang her call button, and the nurse told her he was probably at the PICU with the baby. In a few minutes, he was back, swinging the door open.

Nancy was holding Kleenex, dabbing at her eyes.

"Where are they? Mom and Pop."

"They're at Ballard-Durand."

She nodded. Their prechosen funeral home. Joseph was a planner.

"It's all set for tomorrow, if you can go through with it. We can also push it a day."

"No, I'll be ready. I need a dress."

She looked so sad. Those wet, oval eyes. "Laura's got it covered. She and Greg went shopping."

"How's Philly?"

"They're moving him out to the ward. He's great. He's eating up a storm."

"When can I see him?"

"Sometime tonight, I'm sure."

The next question surprised him. "How are you doing?" Did she really care?

"I'm holding it together," he said grimly.

"I've been thinking about us," she said.

He waited for it, held his breath. She wanted him out of her life. He never should have blackened her door in the first place. She and Phillip would be better off without him. He was in a bar drinking while his family was getting gassed. He had already cheated on her once. Who could say he wasn't capable of doing it again?

"Mom and Pop loved each other." She choked on the words, her lower lip quivering involuntarily. "They went to sleep together like they'd done every night for forty-three years. They died peacefully in their bed. They never got frail. They never got sick. It was their time. It was always going to be their time. I want that to happen to me when it's my time. I want to go to sleep one night in your arms and never wake up."

He lowered himself over the bed rail and held her so tightly she gasped. He loosened his python grip and kissed her forehead gratefully.

"We have to do something, Will," she said.

"I know."

"We need to get those bastards. I want to bring them to their knees."

*   *   *

Will couldn't use his cell phone without getting chewed out by the nurses, so he went down to the lobby. The address book of the prepaid phone had one number in its memory. He called it.

A breathy voice answered. "Hello?"

"It's Will Piper."

"I'm glad you called. How are you, Will?"

"The watchers tried to kill us last night. They got my wife's parents."

After a moment of silence, "I'm very sorry. Were you harmed?"

"My wife and son were, but they're going to be fine."

"I'm relieved to hear that. Is there anything I can do to help you?"

"Possibly. And I've made a decision. I'm going to get you the database."

That night, Will slept in a chair in his son's hospital room. All the arrangements for the following day had been made, and there was nothing to do but allow himself to get some restorative sleep. Not even the nurses coming and going every few hours for vital signs disturbed him.

When the morning came, he awoke to the sounds of Phillip in his crib, happily cooing and playing with his stuffed toy, and he used that optimistic beginning to psyche himself for the travails of the coming day.

He tensed at the sound of another nurse coming into the room, but instead it was Laura and Greg. They had driven up from Washington and had been a magnificent help in working through all the logistics. The Lipinskis were popular, and their funeral service would be crowded with mourners. Given the leaked reports of furnace tampering, there was media interest too, and a good contingent from the New York City press corps was expected. There were details to work out between their priest, the funeral home, and the cemetery regarding the final arrangements. Laura was slowed down by her pregnancy, but Greg took it upon himself to be the family point man with the outside world, and for that, Will was grateful.

"Did you get any sleep?" his daughter asked.

"Some. Look how good he looks."

Greg looked down on Phillip like he was trying out the role of father. "Hey there, bud."

Will got up, stood beside his son-in-law and put his hand on his shoulder, the first time he'd ever made physical contact with the young man beyond a handshake. "You've been a real help. Thank you."

"No problem," Greg said, mildly embarrassed.

"I'm going to find a way to repay you."

Will took on the role security chief, and over breakfast in the cafeteria, he meticulously planned the choreography. They needed to keep themselves in public view, in the middle of crowds. Frazier could watch all he wanted, but he wouldn't be able to do a snatch with people around. The details were important. Everything had to go perfectly, or they'd wind up at the bottom of a very deep hole.

When he went to Nancy's room, she was already wearing her new black dress and standing in front of the mirror in the lavatory. She seemed determined to keep her face dry while she applied makeup. An old friend from the Bureau had stopped off at their apartment and picked up one of Will's dark suits. The two of them hadn't looked so smart since their wedding day. He put his hand on the small of her back.

"You look nice," she said.

"You too."

"I don't know if I can do this," she said, her voice quavering.

"I'll be by your side every step," he said.

A Ballard-Durand limo picked them up at the hospital entrance. By discharge protocol, Nancy was rolled on a wheelchair right up to the curb. She held Phillip close and stepped inside the Cadillac. Will was surveying the drive and the street as if he were on the job, protecting a witness. A small cadre of agents from the New York office flanked the limo like a Secret Service detail assigned to dignitaries.

When the limo drove off, Frazier put down his binoculars and grumbled to DeCorso that Piper was in a cocoon. They followed at a distance and in a short while they were parking their car on Maple Avenue, the white-pillared funeral home in view.

The Lipinskis had been informal easygoing people, and their friends from the community made sure the service matched the couple's sensibilities. After a heartfelt eulogy from their priest from Our Lady of Sorrows, an endless stream of coworkers, bridge partners, parishioners, even the mayor, stood and delivered touching and funny anecdotes about two caring, loving lives, cut short. From the front pew, Nancy wept a steady stream and when Phillip got too loud, Laura would walk him up the aisle to the lobby until he settled down. Will stayed tense and ready, craning his neck, searching the crowded hall. He doubted they'd be inside, among them, but you never knew.

Mt. Calvary Cemetery was in north White Plains, a few miles away from the Lipinski home, adjacent to the grounds of the Westchester Community College. Joseph always liked the peaceful area and in his methodical way he had purchased a family plot thirty years earlier. It was waiting for him now, the dark brown earth freshly backhoed into side-by-side graves. It was the kind of crisp, autumn morning where the sun was thin and flat, and leaves crackled under the feet of the mourners tramping across the lawn.

Frazier was watching the graveside communion through binoculars from a service road a quarter of a mile away. He had his plan. They'd follow the funeral procession back to the Lipinski house. They knew the wake would be held there because they had the Ops Center in Groom Lake hack the funeral home's server to grab the Lipinski funeral itinerary and the limo drop-off address. They would wait until the evening, when Will and Nancy were alone with their son, then enter and extract Will, using as much or as little force as was required. They'd do a sweep of the house, looking for anything he might have found at Cantwell Hall. Once they had Will tucked away at forty thousand feet they'd seek further instructions from the Pentagon. His men agreed that two hits on the same house on two successive nights carried the best element of surprise.

While the priest said a graveside mass, Frazier and his crew munched sandwiches. While Nancy threw a handful of dirt on her parents' coffins, the watchers were caffeinating themselves with cans of Mountain Dew.

When the service broke up, Frazier was still closely observing. There was a crush of mourners surrounding Will and Nancy, and Frazier lost them for a while in a sea of dark blue and black overcoats. He shifted his attention to their limo, which was parked at the front of the procession, and when he spied a man and woman with a baby in her arms climbing in, he had his driver move out.

The funeral procession snaked its way back to the Lipinski

house. Anthony Road was a short, heavily wooded dead-end street. It was impossible for Frazier to park there without being made, so they took up position on North Street, the main artery, and waited patiently in the fading afternoon light for the visitors to depart.

The Ballard-Durand hearse, a black Landau coach, glided up to the private aviation terminal at the Westchester County Airport. The black-suited driver hopped out and had a look around before opening the passenger door. "We're good," he said.

Will got out first, helped Nancy with Philly, then hustled them into the terminal. He came back outside to lay some cash on the driver and extract their bags. "You weren't here, you understand?"

The driver tipped his cap and drove off.

Inside the terminal, Will immediately spotted a medium-built, hard-bodied man with cropped gray hair, jeans, and a leather bomber jacket. The man unfolded his arms and reached inside a pocket flap. Will cautiously watched his hand as it emerged pinching a business card. He came forward and presented it.

DANE P. BENTLEY, 2027 CLUB.

"You must be Will. And you must be Nancy. And who's this little man?"

Nancy took to Dane's kind, gray-stubbled face. "His name is Phillip."

"My condolences, folks. Your plane's all gassed up and ready to go."

Frazier waited all afternoon until the cars pretty much stopped coming and going from the Lipinskis' block. In the late afternoon, he spotted Laura Piper and her husband leaving in a taxi. At dusk, he pulled down Anthony Road for a quick drive-by. The only car in the driveway was Joseph's. There were lights blazing on both levels. He decided to give it another hour, to make sure there were no late arrivals.

At the appointed time, he and his men pulled into the driveway and split into two, two-man teams. He sent De-Corso through the bulkhead and personally shouldered his way through the patio door. His safety was off, and the silencer tube made his pistol look long and menacing. It felt good to be off his butt, on task. He was prepared, even anxious to engage in some level of violence. He was anticipating the pleasure he'd get pistol-whipping Piper across his temple, knocking the bastard onto the floor.

What he was unprepared for and what made him swear out loud was a completely empty house with a Phillip-sized doll lying on the living room sofa where Laura Piper had left it.

Dane Bentley piloted a twenty-year-old Beechcraft Baron 58, a sporty twin-engine with a top speed of two hundred knots and a range of almost fifteen hundred miles. There was hardly anywhere in the continental US where he hadn't touched down, and there was nothing he liked better than having an excuse to do some serious flying.

When his old friend Henry Spence called invoking the 2027 Club and told him he'd foot the gas bill, Dane was quickly behind the wheel of his '65 Mustang motoring to the hangar at Beverly Muni Airport on the rugged Massachusetts coast. On the way, he left a voice mail for his live-in lady friend informing her he was going to be away for a few days and a second voice mail to the younger woman he was seeing on the side. Dane was a young sixty.

In the distance, about fifteen nautical miles to the north, the late-afternoon sun was glinting over long, skinny Lake Winnipesaukee, a large deepwater body dotted with two hundred pine-bristling islands. Dane suppressed his tour-guide instinct to point it out. His three passengers were behind him, sound asleep in facing red-leather seats. Instead, he started chatting with the tower at Laconia Airport, and several minutes later, he was swooping over the lake and approaching the runway.

Jim Zeckendorf had left one of his cars for Will at the airport, its keys in an envelope at the general aviation desk. Will bundled his family into the SUV and took off for the house, leaving Dane behind to check the weather, file a flight plan, and catch a quick nap in the pilots' lounge.

It was a straight ten-mile shot east on Route 11 to Alton Bay, one of the small towns that ringed Winnipesaukee. Will had visited once a few years earlier for a weekend of fishing and drinking. He recalled he had a girlfriend in tow but for the life of him he couldn't remember which one. It had been a time when women were flying in and out of his life at speed, a bimbo blur. All Will could remember for sure was that Zeckendorf, who was wifeless that weekend, was more interested in his girlfriend than he was.

Zeckendorf's second house was befitting a big-time Boston law partner. It was a six-thousand–square-foot Adirondack, perched on a rocky ridge high over the choppy waters of Alton Bay. Nancy was too tired and numb to appreciate the rustic, airy, vaulted living room which flowed into an open-plan granite-topped kitchen. On a happier day, she would have been flitting from room to room like a honeybee in a field of clover, but she was impervious to the magnificence of the place.

It was dusk, and through a wall of lake-facing windows, stands of birch and pines were swaying in the wind and the gray-black waters were doing an imitation of the sea, methodically crashing against the stone breakwater. Nancy went straight for the master bedroom to change Philly and get out of her mourning dress.

Will zoomed around the house, checking things out. Zeck's wife had made a trip up from Boston and stocked the fridge and the pantry with provisions and baby food and boxes of diapers. There were fresh towels everywhere. The thermostats were adjusted. There was a car in the garage with keys. There was even a brand-new travel crib in the bedroom and a high chair, with a price tag still affixed, in the kitchen. The Zeckendorfs were unbelievable.

He unpacked Nancy's service weapon from its case, checked its clip and safety, then left it conspicuously on her bedside table next to a prepaid phone.

The baby was fresh and powdered, and Nancy was in comfortable jeans and a sweatshirt. Will tightly held Phillip to his chest and peered out the window while she rummaged in the kitchen. They exchanged banal domestic talk, a pretense the last two days hadn't happened, but it seemed all right to give each other a break. He waited until she was ready to start the baby's feeding, then placed Phillip, wiggling, into his chair.

Then he hugged her for a long time and only broke the clench to wipe away two streaks of tears on her red face, one with each thumb.

"I will call you every step of the way," he said.

"You'd better. I'm your partner, remember?"

"I remember. Just like the old days, back on a case."

"We've got a good plan. It should work," she said emphatically.

"Are you going to be okay?" he asked.

"Yes, and no." Then her confidence broke. "I'm scared."

"They won't find you here."

"Not for me, for you."

"I can take care of myself."

She gave him a squeeze. "You used to. You're an old retired guy now."

He shrugged. "Experience versus youth. You choose."

She kissed him full on the lips, then gently pushed him away. "I choose you."

* * *

It was semidark when Dane took off. He banked over the lake, then made a graceful turn westward. When his course was set and the plane was leveled off at a cruising altitude of eighteen thousand feet, he turned to Will, who was shoe-horned into the copilot seat, and he began to talk. It had taxed him to keep quiet for so long. They didn't come more talkative or gregarious than Dane Bentley, and for the next eighteen hours, he had a captive audience.

Their first leg was going to take them to Cleveland, a dis-tance of some 650 miles. By the time they landed about four and a half hours later to gas up, stretch their legs, get a bite from vending machines, and use the facilities, Will knew a great deal about his pilot.

Once Dane had decided in high school he was going mili-tary, it was a foregone conclusion he'd enlist in the navy. He grew up on the water in Gloucester, Massachusetts, where his family ran a charter fishing company, and his father and grandfather were ex-navy. Unlike most of his classmates, the Vietnam draft wasn't hanging over his head because he was a gung ho volunteer, itching to use his pent-up energy to steam up the Gulf of Tonkin and fire off some big ordnance.

On his second tour in 'Nam, he volunteered for naval in-telligence, got trained up in covert ops and communications, and spent that tour and one more motoring up and down the Mekong, tagging along with Swift-boat crews to scope out Viet Cong positions. When the war ended, he was persuaded to stay in with a plum assignment to the Office of Naval Intelligence in Maryland where he was made petty officer at the Maritime Operations Center.

He was a good-looking ladies' man, ill suited to a sub-urban military community that catered to married guys and their families. He toyed with throwing himself into a commissioning program to make the officer corps or chucking it in and going back to the family business. What he didn't know was that the Maritime Operations Center was ground zero for Area 51 recruiting. Over half the watchers at Groom Lake passed through Maryland at one point in their careers.

Like everyone who got corralled into Area 51, Dane was seduced by the mystery of an ultrasecret naval base landlocked in the Nevada desert. When he passed through final security clearance and the base mission was revealed, he thought it was about the coolest thing he'd ever heard. Still, he was an action, reaction guy. He'd never had a deep thought in his head, and he wasn't about to start contemplating his navel or the mysteries of the universe. The lush fringe benefits and a Vegas lifestyle were all he needed to convince himself he'd made the right choice.

Will was taken aback that the man who was helping him thwart the watchers had been one. He was initially suspicious, but he had to trust his own ability to read people, and Dane's earnestness and lack of guile satisfied him he was not a threat. What was he going to do anyway? Jump out without a parachute?

Dane provided an insight into the mind-set of the watchers. He'd done just about every job within their ranks during his three-decade career, from manning the metal detectors for the daily strip and scans to conducting field operations against employees who were suspected of obtaining unauthorized DODs for relatives or friends or otherwise compromising the integrity of the operation. They were a buttoned-down cadre, encouraged to be detached and humorless, interacting with staff in much the same menacing way that corrections officers deal with prisoners.

But Dane was too affable at the core to make management rank, and in his annual reviews, he was consistently advised to remain more aloof and warned not to fraternize. He and Henry Spence first met outside work when a chance Saturday encounter at a filling station led to a drink at the Sands Casino.

Dane knew all about Spence. The watchers were told he was a real hotshot, ex-CIA with a brain the size of a watermelon. The two men were polar opposites, brain versus brawn, but there was chemistry based on that kind of magnetism. Spence was a Princeton-educated country-clubber with a socialite wife. Dane was a beer-drinking Massachusetts townie who liked banging heads and dating showgirls.

But both shared a passion for flying. Spence owned a top-of-the-line Cessna while Dane rented shit-boxes by the hour. Once their friendship got going, Spence gave Dane liberal use of his plane, and, for that, the watcher was forever in his debt.

Dane told Will he had only retired a year earlier, just shy of the mandatory age cutoff of sixty. He kept his condo in Vegas for the winters and planned to use his inherited Massachusetts bungalow for summers on the water. He'd gotten a sweet deal on the Beechcraft. After a year, the plan was working, and he was a happy guy. Spence hadn't waited long to give Dane the distinction of being the only ex-watcher ever to be invited to join the 2027 Club, this to the consternation of other members, who had trouble getting comfortable with the idea.

In the distance Will could see the twinkling lights of Cleveland filling half the windshield and the blackness of Lake Erie filling the other half.

"You know Malcolm Frazier, right?" Will asked.

"Oh sure, he was my boss! From the second he got off the elevator on his first day, everyone thought he was going to become the top dog. Ruthless SOB. He'd give up his own mother. All the guys were scared of him. We'd be doing our jobs, and it was like, he'd be watching us. He'd rat out guys for stealing a paper clip. Anything to get ahead. You know, he made his bones on a hit. Some analyst who worked on the US desk smuggled out a little rolled-up note with DODs wrapped up in a piece of a baggie. Put it in between his cheek and his gum, like a wad of snuff. We're not sure what he was going to do with them, but they were all Las Vegas residents with dates coming up. The guy got drunk and blabbed to another guy at the lab. That's how we found out! Frazier took him out through a sniperscope at a thousand yards while the SOB was getting a drive-thru at Burger King. Maybe the guy was the Mark Shackleton of his day."

"What do you know about Shackleton?"

"Pretty much everything."

"What do you know about me?"

"Pretty much everything. Except for your recent antics. I want to hear about that after our next refueling stop."

Will gave Nancy a quick call from the airport lounge. She was okay, he was okay. Philly was asleep. He told her to get some rest. There wasn't more to say.

When they were ready to resume their trip, Dane did a visual inspection of the plane with a cup of black coffee in one hand and a flashlight in the other. On wheels-up, he declared brightly, "Next stop Omaha!"

Will wanted to sleep.

Dane wanted to talk.

A hundred miles to the south, at double their altitude and almost three times their speed, Malcolm Frazier's Learjet was passing them, heading for the same destination.

Frazier felt like a punching bag. Secretary Lester's reaction to the news that Piper had once again slipped the knot was the second coming of Vesuvius. Frazier promptly offered his resignation, and for a few hours it looked like Lester was either going to accept it or just fire him outright.

Then Lester reversed course after staring at his calendar. The Caracas Event was twenty days out. If he replaced Frazier with under three weeks to go to Helping Hand, it would sound alarms throughout the intel community. Instantly, he'd be elevating the hypothetical problem of a *potential* compromise of Area 51's security to an *actual* problem. He'd be obligated to brief the Secretary of Defense, who would probably haul Lester's ass to the Oval Office to take the heat directly from the President.

They still didn't know what Piper had discovered in the UK, they didn't know what Spence intended to do with the 1527 book, and they didn't know if anyone even remotely had the intention of blowing the lid off of Groom Lake. Medium term, Frazier had to go. Short term, he was better than a backup quarterback. Lester gritted his teeth and made his decision.

Frazier had already gotten used to the idea of being fired, and when Lester called to reverse course, he cycled through a panoply of emotions. On one level, he might have been relieved to walk away from the mess, to leave his Black-Berry on his desk and ride the elevators up to the desert floor one last time. Good luck to them and good riddance. But on another, more visceral level, he hated the idea of going out a loser. The capstone of his career: getting hosed by Will Piper? He didn't think so!

Piper always seemed a step or two ahead of him, and that scourged his self-esteem. Sure the fellow wasn't a run-of-the-mill target, sure he'd been an accomplished FBI agent, but please! He was solo, with limited resources at his disposal, and he was up against Frazier's machine. Based on the DODs he was carrying around in his pocket, he was pretty sure this was all going to end soon, he just didn't know how.

Lester had given him one last chance for redemption. Whenever a mission went off plan, Frazier had come to rely on one factor to get him back on track—his intellect. He had risen to head of Security because he was a thinker as well as a doer. Most of the watchers were glorified Military Police, order-followers who carried out other men's plans. He was a cut above, and in his own estimation, he could have been a high-level analyst like Spence or Kenyon if he could ever have tolerated being a deskbound paper-pusher.

So he committed himself to success, and a bit of lateral thinking came through for him. On a hunch, he had his men at the Area 51 Op Center put a filter on the landlines and mobile phones of all known members of the 2027 Club, every retiree in their files with more than a passing connection to Henry Spence. He guessed that Spence and Piper would be communicating on safe phones, but there was at least a chance they'd reach out more broadly.

The key phone intercept wasn't processed for the better part of a day because of the volume of material. When Frazier received it, he was floundering in White Plains trying to come up with his next move. The audio file was marked highest priority, and he played it on the BlackBerry's speaker.

Dane, this is Henry Spence, you got a minute?

For you, I got two minutes. I didn't recognize this number. How're you doing?

I'm hanging in there, at least for a few more days! I'm on one of those pay-in-advance phones. I think we're okay, but let me make this snappy.

All right.

You remember the Shackleton affair?

Of course.

Will Piper's been helping me with a 2027 matter. He went to England for us. He found it.

Found what?

The answers. We've got it all.

Tell me.

He'll tell you. I need you to gas up your Beechcraft—I'll pay—and fly him somewhere. Frazier and his boys are after him.

Fly him where?

Be at the general aviation terminal at Westchester County Airport in New York tomorrow at 2:00 P.M. He'll give you the details but pack a toothbrush. Are you in?

Is the Pope Catholic?

Frazier now had a new outlet for his pent-up rage: Dane Bentley. An ex-watcher, one of his own! The ultimate betrayal! He had always half liked and half disliked the guy. It was hard not to be drawn to Dane's affable side, but Frazier was always bitterly suspicious of his close ties with the worker bees. He'd never been able to pin any transgressions on him, but his suspicions kept Bentley out of his inner circle.

Immediately, he had one of his men check on Bentley's DOD and when he got it, he was disappointed with the result.

Via the FAA database, the Ops Center quickly looked up Bentley's plane registration and before long they had a filed flight plan: White Plains to Laconia, New Hampshire to Cleveland, Ohio, to Omaha, Nebraska, to Grand Junction, Colorado, to Burbank, California's Bob Hope Airport. They also now had the number of Spence's prepaid phone, and that might prove exceedingly useful.

"Los Angeles," Frazier growled when he got the news. "He's returning to the scene of the crime."

"He's going for the memory stick, isn't he?" DeCorso asked.

Frazier nodded. "Let's get our asses to L.A."

*   *   *

Will was amazed that Dane could be so energetic at that hour of the day. It was a good night for flying, with no significant weather on their route, so Dane was happy to concentrate much of his attention on Will's story, which he assured Will, Spence wanted him to hear.

Will walked him through it, his tongue thick with fatigue. Dane was not an educated man, but he was excited about the Shakespeare connection and thought the Nostradamus angle was fascinating. He'd never heard of John Calvin, but he wasn't sheepish about his lack of knowledge. He listened, spellbound by the account of the monk scribes and their mass suicide but was matter-of-fact about the Finis Dierum revelation.

"I don't think the world's gonna end just like that. I know Spence is into that kind of talk but, hell, I won't be around to see it."

Will looked at him sidelong.

"Yeah, I was a naughty boy. I got Spence to look me up before he retired. I'm outta here in 2025 at the not so ripe age of seventy-four. I've got to cram in a lot of hell-raising between now and then. You're BTH, right?"

"Is there anything about me you don't know?"

"Hey, the 2027 Club's a bunch of old guys who get together to shoot the shit! Your Doomsday case finally gave them something to talk about." He got distracted by some chatter on his headset. "I'm sorry about that girl and her grandfather. Sounds like you had a connection with her." The way he said connection sounded loaded. Dane was on his wavelength when it came to women.

"Is it that obvious?"

"Yes, sir."

"Not my proudest moment."

"Hey, a man's got to do what a man's got to do. That's my motto." He confirmed his altitude to an air traffic controller, then said to Will, "I want to thank you."

"For what?"

"For helping Henry. His ticket's punched for day after to-morrow. You're letting him go out scratching and clawing instead of watching the clock. Personally, I'd like to go out in the sack with a swimsuit model."

Will patted Dane on the shoulder. He was a good egg. "I hear you." He thought about it while Dane cut through the blackness of the plains. No, he was quite sure he'd make a different choice. He'd choose to go out with Nancy.

Dane clearly didn't like dead air, so he started moving his mouth again. "I'm going to tell you something that's off-the-charts classified, okay?"

"Okay. Why?"

"Cause it's burning a hole in my tongue. I think I know why they're putting the full-court press on to suppress you. You've opened up to me with a ton of intel tonight, my friend, and I'm going to reciprocate. We're both in deep shit anyway."

"Go ahead. I'm listening."

"Something really big's going to go down in about three weeks. Down in Caracas, Venezuela. They've known about it for a long time, but about two years ago, the CIA drafted up an action plan to exploit the situation and as of when I left Groom Lake, it was fully green-lighted."

"What's going to happen?"

"The mother of all Latin American earthquakes. Centered on Caracas. They'll have over two hundred thousand casualties in one day. At least the eggheads think it'll be an earthquake. Nothing else fits the probability profile."

Will shook his head. "That's a lot of people."

"I don't have to tell you that Venezuela's got two things that makes Uncle Sam sit up and pay it attention: oil and Commies. We're going to use the disaster to mix things up."

"An overthrow?"

"Basically. From what I heard, it'll go down as a humanitarian mission. There'll be a flotilla of tents, cots, food, and medical supplies ready to drop in the minute the dust settles. They figure it'll be total chaos. Their government's going to be overwhelmed. Their president survives, but a lot of his people don't. We'll have the pump primed with the opposition parties, who'll be ready to roll. The Colombians and Guyanese will do their parts by grabbing disputed border zones. The US, British, and French militaries are supposed to be ready to go in as peacekeepers. The bad guy is going out on his ass. One of our guys takes over and lets all the US and European oil companies back in. That's the plan as poor little old me understands it."

The drone of the Beechcraft engines drowned out Will's low whistle. It all made sense. Their insane interest in the missing book. Their coldly calculated decision to kill the Cantwells and his in-laws. Their determination to take Will Piper out of the equation. Frazier and his masters were fighting with a furious determination to keep a cover on the ultimate covert op: the overthrow of an unfriendly, oil-rich country using predictive data from the Area 51 Library. There was only one thing Will knew for sure: the full weight of the government would be used to crush him into dust.

As Dane started his descent toward the Nebraska plains, Will suddenly felt small. The twin-engine plane was only a speck against the vast night sky, and he was only one man going into battle against a very large machine.

They finished their journey the next day, the California sun dirty-yellow in the noontime smog. Will slept the entirety of the last leg and awoke only in time to see the endless expanse of L.A., dreamlike in the haze.

"End of the line," Dane said when he saw Will stirring.

"I don't know how you stayed awake."

"Maybe I was on autopilot!" Then, "Just kidding! I've been chatting with every female voice I could find on the radio. Like a flying trucker."

On the tarmac of the small airport, Will stretched in the sun like a dozy iguana as he waited for Dane to get his plane squared away. It was breezy, in the high seventies, and the air felt good on his skin, like a warm balm. He checked in with Nancy. She was doing all right, still anesthetized by grief, but all right. She had taken Philly down to the dock early in the morning, perched herself on a big flat breakwater stone, and rocked him back to sleep to the lapping of the waves.

The agenda was simple. Dane would rent a car. If Will used his own credit card, he'd be traceable. Then, while Will did his business, Dane would take a nap in a nearby motel. Later in the day, they'd meet up at the airport to make the quick jump to Las Vegas to see Spence and Kenyon. At least, that was the plan.

Will gave Dane a wave at the rent-a-car lot and turned south toward downtown L.A.'s Pershing Square.

Frazier was watching.

He was leaving nothing to chance. He'd flown in more men from Groom Lake to put three teams of three in play. One team led by DeCorso followed Will's rental, Frazier's command car backed up DeCorso, and a third team, led by an operative named Sullivan, stayed with Dane.

Frazier spat an order into his mouthpiece as soon as his car began to move. "Sullie, roll with the pilot and keep me in the loop. And when it's time, knee him in the nuts for me."

The midday traffic was light enough for Will to reach downtown in under half an hour. He parked in a municipal lot opposite the art deco Central Library and jaywalked across 5th Street with the assertiveness of a New Yorker.

The last time he'd been at the library was fifteen months earlier, but it seemed like no time had passed. He remembered the taste of fear in his mouth that day. He had just survived thirty seconds from hell in a close-quarter shoot-out at the Beverly Hills Hotel. He had left four watchers spilling blood onto the plush, pastel carpet of one of the bungalows. Shackleton's brains were bubbling from a wine-cork-sized head wound. Will had a memory stick in his hand with a copy of Shackleton's purloined database, all the DOBs and DODs of everyone in the US through the horizon. It was his insurance policy, his lifeline, and he needed a place to hide it. What better place than a library?

Will bounded up the library steps and pushed through the entrance doors, unaware that two young watchers were on his heels. Frazier kept DeCorso back, bestowing on him the indignity of being the wheelman. He wanted younger men doing the chase, and he knew that DeCorso's number was up. He didn't know how, he didn't know when precisely. But he didn't want any screwups.

Will fast-walked past the information desk and the elevator bank to the main stairs, and he began to descend to the third sublevel. In the sickly raw fluorescence of the basement, he plunged into the stacks, heading for a particular case in the center of the room. The watchers timed their descent perfectly, concealing themselves but keeping Will fleetingly in view as they split up and zigzagged the stacks. Luckily for them, there were at least a dozen patrons using the sublevel, so it was relatively easy to blend in.

Will found the spot he remembered so well, then stood there in confusion. The last time he'd been there, the entire stack had been a sea of ragged tan-colored books, the complete collection of Los Angeles County Municipal Codes, spanning seven decades. He had picked the collection because it looked pathetically long neglected and untouched.

The 1947 volume, the chosen one, wasn't there.

None of them were there!

He urgently moved from row to row searching in vain. He swore under his breath. He started to trot through the stacks, growing increasingly upset.

There was an unmanned information desk with a telephone against one of the walls. Will picked up the phone and waited until a library assistant answered. "Yeah, I'm down in the third sublevel looking for the LA County Municipal Codes. They were down here before." One of the watchers was listening from behind a nearby stack. "I'll hold," Will said. In a minute he was speaking again. "You're kidding me, right? No, I can't wait six weeks! Can you give me the address so I can talk to them directly?

What'll it hurt to give me the address? Thank you. I appreciate it." He hung up, shaking his head in frustration, and pounded up the stairs.

Frazier got this whispered transmission in his ear. "He was looking for a copy of the LA County Municipal Codes. For some reason they're not at the library anymore. He was given an address. He may be going there."

Will ran back to his car and unfolded the rental-agency map. East Olympic Boulevard was only about three miles away, and he was relieved he wouldn't have to haul himself big distances. He pulled out of the lot and drove down 5th Street toward Alameda. In under ten minutes he had crossed the concrete-banked Los Angeles River and entered a bleak industrial terrain of single-story warehouses. Frazier and DeCorso followed at a safe distance.

He found the Olympic Industrial Center and pulled into a visitor's space. He did not have a good feeling. It was rotten luck that his book was in a cache of volumes sent out to be digitized, a joint program between the L.A. County library system and an Internet search company. Now he had to deal with this nonsense.

When Will disappeared into the reception lobby of one of the warehouses, Frazier began to panic. He needed complete control over the situation, and now he had no eyes or ears on Piper. Across the parking lot he saw a big brown UPS truck. His mind moved fast. He dispatched the two watchers with him and told them he wanted one of them inside the warehouse in under a minute. The eager young men sprang out of the car.

The warehouse lobby was depressingly drab. A single bored receptionist sat behind a long counter. There were some plaques on the wall celebrating corporate accomplishments, but that was it. Will waited patiently for the girl to get off the phone and when she did he launched into a florid explanation of why he had to have access to one of the books they had in for scanning. She listened with noncomprehending eyes and he wondered if she spoke English until she finally said, "This is like a warehouse and scanning facility. We don't lend out books here."

He tried again, slowly trying to charm her into helpfulness. Her desk plate said her name was Karen. He used her name liberally, silkily, to try to make a connection, but whatever he was selling, this girl wasn't buying.

A UPS deliveryman came in, wearing a brown shirt and shorts that seemed awfully tight. Will could see he was a muscular guy, a lifter, but after a moment's pause thought nothing more of it. The young man waited a respectful distance away. Inside the UPS truck the man who fit the uniform better was lying among his packages, unconscious from a sleeper hold to his neck.

Will was begging now. "Look, I came all the way from New York to get this book. I know it's not something you guys do, but I would be personally grateful."

She stared at him icily.

He took out his wallet. "Let me make it worth your while, okay?"

"This is a warehouse. I don't know why you're not understanding that?" She looked past Will to the UPS man. "Can I help you?"

"Yeah," the deliveryman said. "I've got a package for 2555 East Olympic. Is this it? I'm filling in on this route."

"This is 2559," she said, pointing. "It's over there."

A warehouse employee came in, waved to the receptionist, then pressed a white security card from his retractable belt clip against a black magnetic wall pad. The door clicked open. As the UPS man dawdled for a while before leaving,

Will noticed the same type of security card sitting on the counter next to the receptionist's keyboard with an AUTHO-RIZED VISITOR label. The girl looked up at Will with an ex-asperated are-you-still-here expression.

"Let me speak to the manager of the facility, all right?" Will demanded. Nice hadn't worked, so he got menacing. "I'm not leaving till I speak to him. Or her. You got my drift, Karen?" This time he made her name sound like an epi-thet.

She nervously complied with his demand, made a call, and asked a man named Marvin to come to the desk. Will stood and waited, his arms so tightly folded across his chest he felt like he was bound by a straightjacket.

From the back of the UPS van, Frazier's man changed his clothes, checked on his still-breathing victim, then briefed his boss via their communicators.

The receptionist was relieved to see her plant manager as if the slight, bespectacled man could protect her from the hulking menace standing at her desk. She got up to whis-per something to him, and when she did, Will reached over, snatched the security card, and palmed it.

Marvin allowed Will to repeat his pleas, but the man was adamant. This facility was not open to the public. There were no procedures for accommodating his request. They weren't authorized to locate individual books. And by the way, he added, sarcastically, wouldn't it be easier to find another copy of the 1947 LA Municipal Codes in another library? It wasn't like they had the only copy in existence.

Will ran out of string. The conversation was veering toward if you don't leave, we'll have to call the police terri-tory. He stormed out, pocketing the security card. There was another black magnetic pad on the outside entrance. He'd be back.

Frazier watched through binoculars as Will walked back to his car empty-handed. When Will drove off, he followed, wondering, where the hell he was going now.

Will hadn't planned on it, but he had time to kill, and when the idea came to him, it seemed right. It smacked of symmetry and closure. At a traffic light, he checked the road map again. It might take an hour to get there, but he couldn't return to the warehouse until the evening. And then he'd be praying the scanning shop didn't run a second shift or have a security guard. He'd let Dane sleep, but sometime in the afternoon, he'd need to call to let him know there was a delay.

Will hopped on Highway 710, with Frazier in slow pursuit, the traffic flowing like molasses. Will used the sluggardly journey to call Nancy and share his frustration. She sounded better, stronger, and that made him feel better and stronger. She had enough fortitude to egg him on.

When 710 became the Long Beach Freeway south of the 405, it dawned on Frazier where Piper was heading. He announced into everyone's radios: "I don't believe it. He's going to Long Beach. Guess who's in Long Beach, boys and girls?"

The Long Beach Chronic Care Hospital made a weak attempt at cheeriness by placing a few clay pots of colorful annuals by the entrance. Otherwise, the low, white-brick complex looked its part: an industrial depository for the hopeless and helpless. You checked in, but you never checked out.

Even in the lobby, there was a stale smell of illness and antisepsis. Shackleton, Will was told, was in the east wing, and Will walked the dingy lime-colored corridors past visitors and staff, everyone moving slowly, nothing worth the rush. No one seemed happy to be there. The ocean was only half a mile away, fresh and vital, a world apart,

Frazier was parked outside the hospital, contemplating his next move. Should he send someone in and risk being made? What was Piper up to? Was it possible he somehow needed Shackleton to retrieve the database? That didn't make sense. He knew from Piper's own postincident interview that after the shoot-out in Beverly Hills, he had purchased a memory stick at a Radio Shack and hid it somewhere in L.A. Now they knew he'd stashed it inside a book at the Central Library. Shackleton wasn't on the critical path. "This is just a social visit, a time killer," Frazier told his men. "I'm sure of it. We'll just wait."

He contacted his man, Sullivan, and asked about the pilot's status. Dane, he was told, had put up a pretty good fight at his motel before being injected and stuffed into a laundry cart. He was on a Learjet heading back to his old stomping ground at Area 51, where he'd be interrogated and held till they figured out what to do with him. Frazier relaxed and dispatched one of his men to find coffee.

The nurses' station was vacant, and Will tapped his fingers against the desk waiting for someone to appear. A plump young woman stuffed into a starched uniform finally emerged from the lounge area with a smudge of something red and sticky at the corner of her mouth.

"I'd like to see Mark Shackleton."

She looked surprised. Will could tell there wasn't much demand for him. "Are you a relative?"

"No. An old friend."

"It's relatives only."

"I'm from New York. I came a long way."

"It's the policy."

He sighed. The pattern of the day. "Can I speak to your supervisor, please?"

An older black woman was summoned, a tough, no-nonsense gal who looked like she probably had the rule book tattooed on her arm. She began explaining to Will the hospital's visitor policy when she suddenly stopped and gave him a closer look over her half-rimmed glasses. "You're the one in his photograph."

"Am I?"

"His only photo. He doesn't get visitors, you know. Occasionally someone from the government with a special pass who's in and out in a minute. You say you're a friend?"

"Yes."

"Come with me. I'm going to make an exception."

The sight of Shackleton in his bed was shocking because he had gotten so small and inconsequential. There had never been much in the way of meat on his bones, but a year of coma and subsistence nutrition had produced a living skeleton with waxy yellow skin and sharply protruding bones. Will could have lifted him as easily as he could his infant son.

He was on his side, staged in a daily rotation to prevent pressure sores. His eyes were open but clouded over by a film, and his mouth was fixed in a permanent oval gape, showing brownish teeth. A filthy Lakers cap was tight on his bald head, covering up the indentation from his devastating wound. He was covered by a sheet from the waist down. His chest and arms were concentration-camp-thin, his hands flexed into claws. His chest moved dramatically, each breath a sudden gasp. One plastic bag drained into his body: white liquid dripping into a gastric feeding tube. One plastic bag drained out: urine from a catheter.

On his bedside table there was a single framed photo. The four college roommates at their twenty-fifth Harvard reunion. Jim Zeckendorf beaming on one end, Alex Dinnerstein at the other. In the middle, Shackleton with a forced smile wearing the same Lakers cap, standing next to Will, who was a full head taller, photogenic, and easy.

The nurse said, "When they went to his house, that was the only photo he had, so they brought it here, which was nice. Who are the other men?"

"We were roommates at college."

"You can tell he was a smart man even though he doesn't talk."

"Does anyone think he's going to come out of this?" Will asked.

"Heavens, no!" the nurse exclaimed. "This is as good as

he'll ever be. The lights are on, but Lord knows that no-body's home."

She left Will at the bedside. He pulled up a chair and sat a foot away from the rails, staring into Shackleton's empty eyes. He wanted to hate him. This unhappy little man had snared him like a rabbit and drawn him down into his mad world. He had force-fed him knowledge of the Library and sent his life spinning off into a strange orbit. Maybe it was all predestined, meant to be, but this pathetic man had will-fully plotted to muck up Will's life, and he had succeeded spectacularly.

But now he couldn't muster hatred against this half-dead, creature, gasping like a fish out of water, whose face re-sembled the openmouthed, anguished character in Munch's painting, *The Scream*. He could only feel a dull sadness for a life wasted.

He didn't bother to speak to him, in the hopeful manner of the naïve bedside visitor to the comatose. He just sat there and used the time to think about his own life, the choices he'd made, the paths traveled and those not. All the times he'd made decisions that had consequences affecting the lives of others, had each decision been predetermined by an unseen hand? Was he responsible for his own actions or not? Did planning his next move matter? Whatever was going to happen was going to happen, right? Maybe he wouldn't go back to the warehouse and spend a miserable night look-ing for the memory stick. Maybe he'd just strip off his shirt and spend the night lying on the beach, watching the stars. Maybe that was the next move on the grand chessboard.

Will's brain wasn't wired to be overly philosophical. He was a practical man who operated by instinct and action. If he was hungry, he ate. If he was horny, he found a woman. If a marriage or a relationship made him unhappy, he left it. If he had a job, he did it. If there was a killer, he'd track him down.

Now he was a husband again. And a father again. He had a great wife and a son full of promise. He needed to dwell on them. Nancy and the baby had to guide his decision-making. If there were other forces at play, so be it. He shouldn't over-think things. His next move was getting the memory stick. Then he'd metaphorically ram it up Frazier's ass.

He felt better, more like the old Will.

And what about 2027?

End of days or not, it was years away. He had seventeen years to make up for five decades of selfishness. There was time to redeem himself.

It was a pretty good deal.

"Thanks, asshole," he said to Shackleton.

On the way back to the warehouse, Will made one good phone call and two bad ones.

Nancy wasn't alone any longer. Will's daughter and son-in-law had just arrived to keep her company at the lake and stay until Will returned. She sounded happily distracted, and Will could hear the pleasant sounds of cooking in the background.

The other calls were troubling. Dane didn't answer his cell phone. A second call to the motel rang through, but no one picked up in the room. The clerk confirmed he had checked in. Will figured him for a heavy sleeper but was queasy, nonetheless.

At Area 51, Dane's cell phone registered the missed-call number of Will's prepaid mobile. A tech at the Ops Center picked up that number's beacon just north of Long Beach, heading north. He called Frazier with the news.

Frazier grunted. It was good to know Piper's mobile number, but hopefully he wouldn't need it. He had Will under direct visual, and if all went well, he'd be in custody soon enough, and Frazier would have the database.

Then he'd swoop down on Henry Spence and pick up whatever it was that Piper had found in England.

He looked forward to getting Lester off his ass. He wanted

to report that he'd done his job, the threat was over, their targets neutralized. He wanted to hear the bureaucrat fawn over him for a change. Then he'd take a few days off, maybe stain his deck or do something else pleasantly ordinary. At the one-week point from the Caracas Event, the base would be on lockdown, and he'd be living there twenty-four/seven.

It was still too early to make his move, so Will stopped for dinner a couple of miles from the warehouse. In the parking lot of the Chinese restaurant, he tried unsuccessfully to reach Dane again. This time he left a message on his voice mail: "It's Will. It's five thirty. Been trying to reach you. This is taking longer than expected. Call me as soon as you get this message."

An hour later, he was still there, full of moo-shu pork and up to his gills in green tea. The restaurant had a nice bar, and there was plenty of alcohol to be had, but he kept pouring himself the wretched tea instead.

Before leaving, he cracked open his fortune cookie: The smart thing is to prepare for the unexpected. Thanks for that, he thought.

As he turned the corner into the warehouse parking lot, Will held his breath. It was empty. Blessedly, no second shift. It was a half hour past sunset and the rapidly diminishing light gave him comfort though he would have preferred pitch blackness. He drove around the building twice to make sure he was going to be okay, then parked around the side and made for the front door. The purloined security badge turned the little red light on the magnetic pad green, and the door clicked open. He was in.

He steeled himself for a security guard, but the lobby and reception desk were empty, lit only by a single lamp. The card worked a second time, and he was inside the main warehouse.

It wasn't completely dark. A handful of ceiling fluorescents were on, illuminating the vast space in a highly dilutive glow.

The first thing that caught his eyes were the robots, a row of them at the front of the room. They were like giant TV sets without screens. Each one had an open box-shaped compartment with a V-shaped wooden support designed to securely hold a book by elasticized cover straps.

At the machine closest to him, a robotic arm was frozen in action, shut down for the night, grasping a page in a delicate pincer grip. The optical wand was poised to begin scanning when the robot powered up, and the page was laid down flat.

Behind the robots was a large open warehouse floor that was the industrial doppelganger of a library, row after row of black-metal bookcases that were low enough for a person to reach the top shelves comfortably. The perimeter of the warehouse was lined by darkened staff offices.

Will sighed at the task before him. There were surely tens of thousands of books. While there had to be some kind of catalogue-and-location system around, he imagined he'd spend as much time rummaging through offices and files as taking a shoe-leather approach. So he picked a row at one end of the warehouse and just began to walk.

Half an hour later, his mind was numbed by the sea of book spines, with their pressed-on warehouse bar codes. He had to be meticulous. He couldn't be sure all the L.A. Municipal Code books were grouped together. To his dismay, he noticed that some collections were scattered like birdseed. At the end of one of the rows, at the rear of the building, he stopped to call Dane again but got voice mail once more. Something was definitely wrong.

His eyes leapt to a glowing image. Inside the office nearest to where he stood, there was a black-and-white monitor, a security-cam view of the dim lobby. The nameplate on the door said MARVIN HEMPEL, GENERAL MANAGER. He could imagine the weedy plant manager sitting at his desk, slurping soup, voyeuristically watching the receptionist for his lunchtime activity. He shook his head and started on the next row.

He picked up the pace and forced himself to concentrate. If he weren't careful, he'd spend hours at it, complete the job empty-handed, and have to do it all over again. He began to touch each spine with his fingertip to make sure it registered before moving on, but stray thoughts kept entering his mind.

Where was Dane?

How was Nancy doing?

How was the endgame going to play out?

Frazier had the warehouse encircled, but he fretted that he was light on the ground for a building of this size. Only six men to cover the front, the rear loading dock, and an emergency exit on each of the long sides. He had DeCorso and two others at the front. Piper had gone in that way, he'd most likely exit that way. He dispersed his own team of three, sending one man to each side exit. He covered the loading dock himself and kept imagining Piper slowly opening the door and opening his mouth as Frazier fired a round into his body. Piper wouldn't die, but hopefully there'd be pain.

DeCorso, of course, was taking his last breaths. Frazier mentally bade him farewell. The next time they met, he'd probably be a corpse. Something was going to kill him within the next few hours. Piper? Friendly fire? A heart attack? The night wasn't going to end quietly.

Another hour passed, and Will marked his spot by pulling a book out halfway. He went to the men's room to let Chinese tea out of his system and splash cold water on his face.

At the same time, Frazier and DeCorso were having an urgent debate over their radios. What was taking Piper so long? Was there an exit they could have missed? Was it possible there was a tunnel system connecting warehouses in the park?

Frazier decided to send DeCorso's team into the lobby as an intermediate move. It was a good point of control if Piper came out that way, and it was closer to the mark if they opted to enter and take him down. One of DeCorso's men had a piece of standard hardware that quickly hacked magnetic security card readers. They entered the lobby and took up defensive positions.

Will was approaching the rear of the building again and in the last bookcase of his current row he got a shock, as if he'd brushed against a live wire.

There they were! A row of them, L.A. County Municipal Codes for the 1980s. Getting there, he thought, getting there.

He pivoted 180 degrees to inspect the first case in the next row, and his heart began to race with excitement. The entire case was filled with the tan books. They weren't in order, but his eye flitted over volumes covering all decades.

The 1947 volume had to be there. Somewhere.

He touched each spine and said the year out loud. He got to the bottom shelf. There, bent over, he touched it and quickly pulled it out—1947.

He sat down on the warehouse floor with the book on his

lap and opened it wide, bowing the spine wide and tapping the heavy volume against the floor. The gun in his waistband bit into his leg, but he ignored the discomfort. There was a small, pleasant clatter as the plastic memory stick fell out onto the concrete. He closed his eyes and said a silent thanks.

When he got up, he saw that he was opposite the plant manager's office again and instinctively he glanced at the TV monitor.

He froze.

There was movement on the screen.

Two men. No three. Weapons in their hands.

Watchers.

He pocketed the memory stick, drew out his Glock, and flicked the safety. There were seventeen in the mag and one in the chamber. That was it, no spares. Eighteen rounds wouldn't last long in a firefight. There had to be a better way.

They'd have all the exits covered. At least he had a small edge on them. He could *see* them. Was there a way onto the roof? The warehouse was probably on a slab, but if there was a sublevel, he'd better find out.

He ran around the building, looking for escape routes, figuring the angles, returning to the office with each circuit to check on the lobby crew.

There weren't any attractive options. He thought quickly and steeled himself for violence. He was BTH, but for all he knew, the next time Nancy saw him, he'd look like Shackleton. Fear left a coppery taste in his mouth.

DeCorso heard Frazier in his earpiece demanding a status report. He started to whisper back, "It's quiet, no signs of . . ." when all hell broke loose.

The office lights went blazing on and an ear-piercing siren

started blaring, almost too loud to stand without clamping hands over ears.

"The fire alarm!" DeCorso shouted, loud enough for Frazier to hear above the din.

"It's got to be central-alarmed!" Frazier screamed back. "The fire department'll be here any minute! Go in now! Take him! My team—maintain your positions at the exits."

"I copy!" DeCorso shouted. "We're going in!"

DeCorso ordered his man to unlock the door, and the three of them flew into the warehouse and immediately spread out.

They almost stopped dead at the sight before them.

The entire row of robots was dancing in a conga line of animation. Robot arms were turning pages. Flashes of blinding light illuminated pages. Digitized images of text appeared on computer displays.

DeCorso saw something. Through the scanning box of one of the middle robots he thought he picked up a glimpse of black steel. He shouted over the pulsating blare of the fire alarms, "Gun!" and raised his own to fire.

Will was in firing position behind a robot. He squeezed off two shots and placed both of them in the center of DeCorso's chest. The man blinked once, fell straight to his knees, then pitched forward hard. The two other watchers were very good, probably ex–special ops guys, and in the next few seconds, Will was conscious of their coolness under fire.

Neither was distracted by their team leader going down. The man on Will's left dove behind a metal cart and began spraying fire at all the middle robots. It was clear he didn't know exactly where Will was. Paper shredded, glass shattered, but the robot arms kept looking for pages to turn.

Will concentrated on the man to his right, who was in

a low crouch, searching for a target, more exposed. He aimed for central mass and let loose a three-shot volley. The man grunted and slumped, blood spreading from under his jacket.

Will's muzzle flash was an unavoidable beacon, and the third man fired into his robot. Will ducked behind the machine and felt a searing pain in his inner left thigh, as if someone had laid a red-hot branding iron across his flesh. His pant leg quickly soaked with blood. He couldn't deal with it now. If his femoral artery were hit, it was over. He'd know soon enough. Things would go gray, then black.

The robots were closely enough spaced to form almost a solid wall. Will dragged himself to his left until he was behind the farthest one. He no longer knew where the last watcher was positioned. His leg was bleeding heavily, but his senses were all operating. If it were arterial, he'd be struggling by now.

Then the last watcher mistakenly obeyed an order.

Frazier was shouting into his earpiece like a lunatic. "What's your status! Give me your goddamn status! Now!"

The man shouted back. "Two men down! Under fire! Front of the building!"

Will put his weight on his good leg and popped up through the robot's scanning box like a whack-a-mole at a fairground. He aimed at the direction of the voice and put six rounds into the metal cart. The last watcher tried to rise but fell over, leaking blood from his abdomen.

Will quickly pulled his own belt from its loops and wrapped it around his thigh, cinching it as tightly as he could stand. He could just about bear weight. He made a mad dash over the bleeding men, limped through the lobby, and emerged into the moonless night.

There were fire-engine sirens in the distance, getting louder.

He didn't know how many more watchers were out there, but he knew they'd have to cover the other exits at least for a while.

His car was only yards away.

He was going to make it.

The blood oozed from Will's thigh onto the car seat. He was buffeted by ripples of light-headedness, then slammed by a wave of nausea that forced him to pull over. He leaned out the open driver's door and vomited onto the side of the road.

He had to deal with his wound quickly. He needed his mind to keep working crisply. Without that, he was lost.

Frazier knelt over DeCorso's body, checking for the carotid pulse he knew would be absent. Piper two—DeCorso zero, Frazier thought. Shot twice by the same guy, the second time fatal. Guess who was the better man? DeCorso's wife was friendly with his. She'd get a good payout for a death in action, so it wasn't a complete loss.

He'd have to get Piper himself.

The other two men were alive but not by a lot. He had his team call for an ambulance. There wasn't anything they could do for them. He knew one of them was going to die. He knew the DODs for all his men, an operational imperative as far as he was concerned.

He didn't know his own.

He could have broken the rules and found out, but he was

always by the book. And besides, in his marrow, he was sure he was BTH.

The fire sirens were almost on top of them. On his way out, he noticed a blood trail back through the lobby. Good, he thought. I hope it hurts.

He drove away with his two able-bodied men before the fire department arrived. Piper could be anywhere.

At a red light, Will readjusted his tourniquet and kept driving. He was on Vernon Avenue, heading east, looking for open stores. He needed a drugstore. He needed a new pair of pants. He needed a computer. He needed to find Dane. He needed to ditch his car. He needed to talk to Nancy. He needed more bullets; he only had seven left in the mag. He needed a lot of things in a little time.

He called Dane's cell phone again and got voice mail one more time. There was no pickup at his motel room, and when Will pushed the front desk, someone ran over to pound on his door and open it with a pass key. It was empty. Finally, he called the general aviation terminal and was told that Dane's plane hadn't been touched since midday. The pilot hadn't been back.

That's that, Will thought. The watchers got to him. He was on his own. He looked at the phone in his hand and swore at himself in disgust.

If they had Dane, they had his phone, and they had his prepaid phone number. If they had that, they had him. He opened his window, dropped the phone onto the street, and said good-bye to his lifeline.

Frazier was in constant contact with the Area 51 Ops Center. He was driving east on Vernon, being guided by the location of Piper's mobile signal. The tech shouted into Frazier's earpiece, "The signal's gone!"

"What do you mean, gone?"

"It's gone dead. He must've turned it off or pulled the battery."

Frazier banged the dashboard in frustration. "We were less than a mile behind him!"

His driver asked, "What do you want me to do?"

"Keep driving. Let me think."

Will was on Crenshaw, aimlessly driving north through the dark urban sprawl. The pain was making him crazy, and the dizziness was getting hazardous. In the distance, there was a sign for Baldwin Hills Crenshaw Plaza, and he pressed on until he got there. When he saw there was a Wal-Mart, he pulled into the covered parking garage and grabbed a space as close to the entrance as he could find.

He painfully pulled himself out of the car and clamped his hands onto the first shopping cart he could find, to give him support and to hide his bloody trousers leg as much as possible. Grimacing, he hobbled into the store, passed an elderly man in a smock, the Wal-Mart greeter, who immediately saw his red-stained pants and red footprints but minded his own business, something you did in that neighborhood.

Will wheeled his cart straight to the pharmacy section and dropped sterile gauze, bandages, tweezers, and antiseptic into the cart plus a bottle of acetaminophen, as if that were going to make a dent in his pain. He needed narcotics, but that wasn't in the cards.

Then he headed to men's wear and picked up a pair of thirty-four-waist dark slacks and a fresh pack of underwear and socks. In the dressing room, he went to the back stall and peeled off his bloody pants. Standing shakily in front of the mirror he inspected his wound. There was a quarter-inch purplish hole in the inner thigh, about five inches from his groin fold, steadily oozing dark red blood. He'd attended enough autopsies to know he was lucky. The adductor muscle was a good distance from the femoral artery. But he wasn't completely lucky. There was no exit wound. The robot must have decelerated the bullet enough to make it lose some of its energy. The bullet was lodged. Within a day or so, his leg would be infected. Without surgery and antibiotics, he'd be septic.

He unwrapped the three-pack of undershorts, rolled one of them into a tight cylinder, and bit down on it to keep himself quiet. He bathed the wound in a dark brown iodine solution, then got down to the painful business. With the tweezers, he pushed a ribbon of gauze into the bullet hole. He clamped down on the cloth, and his eyes watered in torment. He had no choice. The wound had to be packed to staunch the flow. If he didn't clot, he'd bleed out. He subjected himself to repeated thrusts of the tweezers and pushed gauze through the skin and subcutaneous tissues, deep into the pulpy muscle.

When he had done as much as he could bear, he drenched the gauze in iodine and wrapped a bandage tightly over the wad. Then he spat out the cloth and sank to the floor, breathing heavily. In a minute, he was ready to put on fresh clothes. On the way out of the dressing room he trash-canned his bloody garments.

The pain was blinding but he had to suck it up to ask a clerk at the electronics department for help. "What's your cheapest laptop with a USB port and a wireless card?"

The kid replied, "They all have USB ports and wireless cards."

"Then what's your cheapest laptop?"

"We've got an Acer for 498."

"I'll take it. And give me a shoulder bag too. Will the battery have any charge?"

"Should have. Why?"

"Because I want to use it out of the box."

There was a taxi stand near the Wal-Mart. Will had all his provisions stuffed into his new shoulder bag and folded himself stiffly into the backseat of a cab. He touched his new pants and was relieved they were still dry.

"Where to?" the cabbie asked.

"Greyhound station. But stop at a liquor store first."

Frazier got tired of driving around looking for a needle in a haystack. He had his man pull over into a diner. They had Piper's info circulated to LAPD, including his rental-car tag number. He was suspected of murdering federal agents. He was armed and dangerous, possibly wounded. The police would take this seriously. The hospitals were on alert. All Frazier could do now was outthink him. What was he going to do with the database, assuming he had it? Where was he going to go? He wasn't going to be able to fly back to New York without getting picked up. Then it hit him.

Spence. Tomorrow was Spence's DOD.

He lived in Las Vegas. It only made sense that Will was going to meet Spence there to hand off the database. That was probably going to be Bentley's next stop.

He didn't have to chase after Piper. All he had to do was go to Las Vegas and wait for him to arrive.

The Ops Center was in his ear. "Piper used his VISA card twenty minutes ago at a Wal-Mart on Crenshaw."

"What did he buy?" Frazier asked.

"A computer, a bag, some clothes and a shitload of gauze and bandages."

"All right. We're heading back to Nevada. I know where he's going."

Will purchased his one-way ticket to Las Vegas at the Greyhound station and paid cash. He had a few hours until the departure time but didn't feel comfortable waiting around the terminal. There was a donut shop across the street. He limped into a booth, with a coffee and an extra paper cup. Under the table he poured himself a half a glass of Johnnie Walker, put six acetaminophens into his mouth, and drank them down in a series of fiery gulps.

The alcohol helped dull the pain or at least distracted him enough to get the new computer out of the box and booted up. There were no wireless networks detected.

"You got WiFi?" he called over to the dull Mexican girl behind the counter, but he might as well have asked her to explain quantum mechanics to him. She stared through him and shrugged.

He plugged in the memory stick and downloaded Shackleton's database. In a minute, he was prompted for the password and he instantly recalled it: Pythagoras. It had significance to Shackleton, he imagined, but he'd never know what it was.

The searchable database was ready for his queries. There was a God-like feeling to be able to type a name, some identifying information, and find out, in an instant, that person's date of death. He began with Joe and Mary Lipinski, just to pay them a moment of respect. There they were. October 20.

Then he did a double check on Henry Spence. It was confirmed: October 23rd. Tomorrow.

He typed in a couple of more names and stared at the screen.

He had some idea of what was going to happen tomorrow.

It was after midnight in New Hampshire, but he had to talk to Nancy, even if it meant waking her up and worrying her to distraction. He had no choice. For all he knew, it would be their last conversation.

There were pay phones by the bathrooms. He got a bunch of quarters from the girl and dialed Zeckendorf's Alton landline. The watchers probably had a complete log of all the prepaids he'd called and would be tapping them all. They wouldn't have this number. Yet. As the phone rang, he noticed fresh blood seeping through his new pants.

Nancy answered, surprisingly alert.

"It's me," he said.

"Will! How are you? Where are you?"

"I'm in L.A."

She sounded concerned. "And?"

"I've got the memory stick, but there've been some problems."

"What happened?"

"They got Dane. There was a bit of a dustup."

"Will, are you hurt?"

"I'm shot. Left thigh. Missed my nuts."

"Jesus, Will! You've got to get to a hospital!"

"Can't do that. I'm getting on a bus. I've got to get to Spence."

He could tell she was trying to think. He heard the baby stirring. "Let me call the L.A. office," she said. "The FBI can pick you up."

"God, don't! Frazier'll be all over that. He'll be monitoring the local chatter. I'm on my own. I'll make it."

"You don't sound good."

"I've got a confession to make."

"What?"

"I bought a bottle of scotch. Nancy?"

"Yes?"

"Are you mad at me?"

"I'm always mad at you."

"I mean really mad."

"Will, I love you."

"I've been nothing but trouble."

"Don't say that."

"I want to be able to take care of you and Philly in 2027."

"You will, honey. I know you will."

I f the alternator on the L.A. to Las Vegas Greyhound bus
hadn't given out, the next day might have ended differ-
ently. Such was the nature of predestination and fate. One
variable influencing another, influencing another in an in-
finitely complex daisy chain. Instead of leaving L.A. at ten
thirty the night before, the bus didn't pull out of the terminal
until four hours later.

Will suckled at his bottle for comfort for most of the six-
hour trip through the desert night, dozing when he got numb
enough. He had half the rear to himself. Most of his fellow
passengers had bailed out for a later bus. There were only
a few diehards who had hung in and waited for the repairs,
and people who took the bus to Las Vegas in the middle of
the night tended to leave each other alone.

Periodically, he visited the restroom to stuff more gauze
into the wound and douse it with iodine. But he was still
bleeding and getting weaker by the hour.

He awoke in the tinted glare of the morning, in pain, with
a dull headache and a dry mouth. He was shivering, and he
clutched his jacket to his neck for warmth. The terrain outside the window was flat, brown, and scrubby. He wished the
air-conditioning would fail and the temperature would equil-
ibrate to the desert heat. Infection was probably setting in.

The last hour of the journey was an ordeal. He endured nausea and pain and spasms of teeth-chattering chills, which he fought by stiffening his joints in anger. It was going to take sheer determination to finish the job. If he gave in to the advancing infirmity, Frazier would win. He refused to let that happen. He concentrated on Nancy and his son. An image of Philly breast-feeding while she dreamily looked out their apartment window settled into his mind. Then he found himself laughing when the image was replaced by an image of Spence's huge RV.

"I want that bus," he cackled out loud.

Through the green-tinted windows, Las Vegas appeared in the distance, rising out of the flat plain, crystalline, like the Emerald City. He pulled himself up for one more bandage change. The fellow who cleaned the restroom bin was going to think there'd been one heck of a situation on board.

Finally, the bus pulled into the Greyhound terminal near the Golden Nugget Casino just off the Strip. Will was last off, the driver watching him suspiciously as he struggled to make his way down the aisle and down the stairs. "You okay there, fellow?"

"Feeling good," Will mumbled to him. "Feeling lucky."

He hobbled straight for a taxi. The hot sun made him feel more comfortable. He slowly pulled himself into the back of a cab. "Take me to Henderson. St Croix Street."

"Fancy neighborhood," the driver said, giving him the eyeball.

"I'm sure it is. Get me there fast and there's an extra fifty for you."

"Sure you wouldn't rather go to a hospital?"

"I feel better than I look. Turn off the AC, will you?"

His previous time in Las Vegas he'd made a mental note to make it his last. It was more than a year earlier, when he flew out to interview the CEO of Desert Life Insurance Company as part of the Doomsday investigation. It had been one of those right-church, wrong-pew deals. Nelson Elder, the head of the company, had been involved in the case, just not in the way Will ever expected. And his social call to his old roommate, Mark Shackleton, had also been far from a what-you-see-is-what-you-get kind of experience. The trip had left him queasy about Vegas and, frankly, he'd never been a fan anyway. One way or another, this really was going to be his last time, he swore.

The rush-hour traffic was heading north into Vegas, but going in the opposite direction, they made pretty good time to Henderson. The chocolate mountains of the McCullough Range occupied the windshield as they got closer to Mac-Donald Highlands, Spence's exclusive country club community. As Will pressed himself to stay conscious, defiantly balling up his fists, the driver kept checking him out in the rearview mirror.

It was a gated community on the verdant grounds of the Dragon Ridge Country Club, an enclave of ultra-high-end homes, nestled in the hills overlooking the fairways. At the gatehouse, Will lowered his window and told the guard that Will Piper was there to see Henry Spence. Will could hear Spence's voice through the guard's phone. The cab was waved through.

At the curb, Will was looking at the biggest house he'd ever seen, a huge Mediterranean-style affair the color of sandstone. He could see Spence at the open front door, sitting on his scooter. Kenyon came bounding down to the curb, waving and calling, then stopped with a start at the sight of Will staggering out of the taxi. He ran forward and circled him with an arm to help him up the path.

"Good Lord! What happened to you?" Kenyon gasped.

Will gritted his teeth. "The watchers. I think they got Dane."

"We were worried sick," Kenyon said. "We heard nothing. Come. Come inside."

Spence backed his scooter up to let the men past. "Alf, put him on the couch in the family room! Christ, he's bleeding! Will, were you followed?"

"Don't think so," he rasped.

The house was nine thousand square feet of opulence, a Vegas-style Taj Mahal built for Spence's socialite wife. Kenyon dragged Will through the horseshoe-shaped interior to a room with a fireplace, a computer desk, and a large brown sectional facing the backyard pool. Will slumped onto the sofa, and Kenyon carefully lifted his legs to get him recumbent. He was pale and sweaty, breathing rapidly. His pant leg was soaked through with sticky blood, and there was a sickly, ripe aroma in the air. "You need a doctor," Kenyon said quietly.

"No. Not yet."

"Henry, do you have a scissors handy?"

Spence wheeled up next to them, his oxygen lines hissing. "In the desk."

Kenyon found the pair and cut a big square out of Will's trousers, exposing the bloody bandage. He sliced through it, laid the gauze back and took a look at the wound. During his stint in the Nicaraguan jungle, he had learned rudimentary first aid. "You packed this yourself?"

Will nodded.

"Without painkillers?"

"Afraid so."

The thigh was beefy and swollen. The gauze had a fruity, fetid odor. "It's infected."

Spence said, "I've got a whole drugstore in my medicine chest. What do you need?"

Kenyon answered, "Get me some pain pills, codeine, Vicodin, whatever you've got, and any antibiotics you have lying around. Is there a first-aid kit somewhere?"

"Trunk of my Mercedes. Germans think of everything."

Will tried to prop himself up. "I've got it," he said. "It's in my bag."

Spence closed his eyes. "Thank God."

"Let's sort you out first," Kenyon insisted.

Kenyon worked quickly, pumping Will full of Percocet and Cipro, then asked him to forgive him as he pulled out the old gauze pack and painfully replaced it with fresh packing. Will groaned and gritted his teeth, and when it was done, he asked for a scotch.

Kenyon didn't think it was a good idea, but Will persuaded him to pour a stiff one anyway. When he handed back the empty glass, he said, "I'm quitting tomorrow."

Kenyon sat down beside him, and Spence drew his scooter near. It was then that Will noticed that Spence was all dolled-up, looking his best. His hair and beard were carefully combed. He had on a nice shirt and a tie. "Why're you dressed up?" Will asked.

Spence smiled. "I don't have any more birthdays to celebrate. We thought we'd celebrate my death day. Alf's been a peach. Made me pancakes. Planned the whole day, not that I'm guaranteed to participate in all the activities. Pizza and beer for lunch. We're going to watch *Citizen Kane* in the media room in the afternoon. Steaks on the grill for supper. Then I'm going to unhook the oxygen and have a cigar on the patio."

"That's probably what'll kill him," Kenyon said sadly.

"Sorry to interrupt your plans," Will said. "Hand me my bag."

He took out his laptop, and while it was booting up, he told them about the retrieval of the memory stick and the deadly encounter with the watchers. He hadn't seen Frazier, but he sensed his presence. "Let's finish our business before we watch any movies, okay?" he urged.

"I couldn't agree more," Spence said. "Besides, I already know all about Rosebud."

Will opened Shackleton's database and unlocked it with the password. He announced he was ready.

Spence took a deep breath and wet his dry lips with his tongue. He wanted to know but the process was going to be agonizing. He spoke the first name. "William Avery Spence. Baltimore, Maryland. He's my oldest son."

Will started typing, then, "He's BTH."

Spence exhaled and coughed a few times. "Thomas Douglas Spence, New York City."

BTH.

"Susan Spence Pearson, Wilmington, Delaware, my daughter."

BTH.

"Good," he said calmly. "Let's move on to the grandchildren. I've got lots of them."

All BTH.

There was a list of daughters-in-law and sons-in-law next, his younger brother, a few close cousins.

One of the cousins had a DOD, in seven years' time. Spence nodded at the news.

He was nearly done now, relaxed and satisfied, his tension melted away.

Then finally, Spence said, "Alf, I want to know about you too."

"Well I don't!" Kenyon protested.

"Then leave us alone for a minute. You don't have to hear it, but you've got to grant a dying man's wish."

"Christ, Henry, that's all I've been doing for the past two weeks!"

"Your burden is coming to an end. Now get out of here." The two men gave each other brotherly smiles.

A couple of minutes later, Kenyon came back in with a tray of coffee mugs. He looked at both men and clucked. "I'm not asking, and you're not telling. I don't want you messing up my nice, organized relationship with God. I want the Lord to surprise me. The natural way."

"Suit yourself, Alf," Spence said. "I'll take one of those coffees. I'm all done now. Will's given me a great gift. I can die in peace."

The narcotics were kicking in, and Will felt himself wanting to sleep. "I need to get online."

"There's a wireless network," Spence said. "It's called HenryNet."

Will clicked on it. "It's looking for a password."

"Can you guess it?" Spence asked with a twinkle.

"No, I can't." He didn't feel up for games.

"I'll bet you can."

Glass shattered.

A mass of hot air rolled off the hillside and blasted through the broken sliding doors.

There were two more men in the room.

Then, from the hall, a third.

Will was looking at a couple of Heckler & Koch machine pistols resting in the hands of heavily breathing, fit young men. Frazier was sporting something lighter, a Glock, like his.

Will didn't have the strength or the speed to pull his gun

from his waistband. One of the watchers plucked it away from him and threw it through the broken glass, splashing it into the swimming pool.

Frazier ordered his man, "Get the computer."

It was pulled from Will's weak grasp.

"Where's the memory stick?"

Will reached into his pants pocket and tossed it onto the floor. There was no point being cute. He'd lost.

"You could've knocked, Frazier," Spence said.

"Yeah, next time. You don't look so good, Henry."

"Emphysema."

"I'm not surprised. You were always a big smoker. You used to break the rules and smoke in the lab, remember?"

"I remember."

"You're still breaking the rules."

"I'm just a retiree who runs a little social club. You might want to join one day. We don't charge dues."

Frazier sat down wearily on a chair across from them. "You need to give me the 1527 book and all the materials you recovered from Cantwell Hall. Every piece of it."

"Why don't you just leave us alone?" Kenyon protested. "We're just a couple of old men, and he's hurt. He needs medical attention."

"I'm not surprised you're involved with this, Kenyon. Always palling around with Henry." He waved his gun toward Will. "He killed two of my men," Frazier said evenly. "You think I'm going to get him to a doctor? Who do you think you're talking to? You think I'm going to turn the other cheek?"

"Greater men than you have done it."

Frazier laughed. "Save it, Alf. You were always one of the weak ones. At least Henry had balls." He turned his attention back to Spence and Will. "Give me the book and tell me what you found in England. I'll get it one way or the other."

"Don't give him anything, Henry," Kenyon said indignantly.

Frazier raised an eyebrow, and one of his men swatted the side of Kenyon's face with the back of his hand. He fell to the floor onto his knees.

"Leave him alone!" Will shouted.

"What are you going to do about it?" Frazier spat. "Squirt blood at me?"

"Go to hell."

Frazier ignored him and spoke to Spence. "You know what's gone into keeping the Library a secret all these years, Henry. Do you think we're not going to pull out all the stops to find out everything there is to know about the missing book? This is more important than any of us. We're just little pawns. Haven't you figured that out yet?"

"I'm not telling you anything," Spence said defiantly.

Frazier shook his head and turned his gun toward Kenyon, who was still on the floor, kneeling in pain and shock, or maybe in prayer. He fired once into his knee.

Blood sprayed into the air, and the man shrieked in agony. Will tried to rise, but the watcher closest to him shoved him back down with a hand to his chest. Will swung his arms wildly, but the man subdued him with a sharp, cruel punch to his thigh, right over the bullet wound. He howled in pain.

"Alf!" Spence screamed.

"Put a tourniquet on it," Frazier told the other man. "Don't let him bleed out."

The young man looked around, then hurried over to Spence to pull his tie from around his neck. He rushed back to Kenyon and began to cinch it tight, just above the knee.

"Now, listen to me, Henry," Frazier said. "If you don't give me what I need, I'm going to take that tourniquet off, and he'll be gone in a minute. Your call."

Spence was purple with rage and gasping for air. "You bastard!" he shouted.

Then he full-throttled his scooter, aiming it straight for Frazier.

It wasn't much of a ramming wagon, a red three-wheeled scooter, barreling down at six miles per hour. Frazier probably could have just lifted up his legs to avoid contact, but he was tired, and he wasn't wired to underrespond. Instead, he put two rounds into Spence's face, one in the mouth, one through the left eye.

The forward momentum carried the scooter into Frazier's shin, and Spence's body dropped heavily off onto the carpet. Frazier sprang up hurt and swearing, and in anger put another two rounds into Spence's lifeless side.

Kenyon began to wail, and Will bit his lip in anger. He looked around for something he could use as a weapon.

Frazier was standing over Will, pointing his gun at his head. "Alf, tell me where he's got the material, or I'll shoot Piper too."

"I'm not dying today," Will seethed.

"I can't argue with that," Frazier growled. "But I'm going to give you the next best thing." He changed his aim to Will's groin.

"Don't tell him anything," Will shouted to Kenyon.

Frazier countered, "Don't be stupid."

Will saw something. Frazier was unnerved by his sudden smile.

"I'm not dying today," Will repeated.

"You already said that."

"You are."

As Frazier opened his mouth in a sneer, his head exploded in an eruption of red-and-gray foam.

By the time his body hit the floor, Nancy had already gotten off a second shot, narrowly missing the watcher closest to Kenyon. She was firing through the shattered sliders, flanked by John Mueller and Sue Sanchez, all of them fighting to get a handle on the chaos in the room.

Will rolled off the sofa and locked his arms around the lower legs of the closest watcher. As the man struggled to free himself, he released a burst of automatic fire, which streaked across Mueller's abdomen like the tail of a comet. Staggering backward, Mueller managed to fire a half dozen rounds before collapsing into the pool. The watcher fell back onto Will, gasping, with a sucking lung wound.

The other watcher spun around to help his partner and when he saw he was down, he pointed his machine pistol at Will, ready to squeeze the trigger.

Sue and Nancy fired simultaneously.

The watcher crashed through the coffee table, a deadweight.

Nancy ran to Will while Sanchez made sure the scene was secure, kicking away weapons, prodding each man with her shoe.

"Will! Are you okay?" Nancy cried.

"Jesus, Nancy. You came!"

Sanchez was calling her. She needed help getting Mueller out of the bloodstained water. The two women struggled to pull him onto the pool deck, but it was too late.

Sanchez pulled out her cell phone and called 911. She screamed she was FBI. She yelled for them to send every ambulance they had.

Will dragged himself over to the communications headset lying next to the closest watcher, lured by the tinny chatter just audible. He put the headset on. There was a voice, hollering away, asking for their status.

"Who is this?" Will asked into the mic.

"Who's on this frequency?" the voice asked.

"Frazier's dead. The other ones don't look so hot."

"Who is this!"

"How's the weather at Area 51?" Will asked.

There was silence.

"Okay, now that I've got your attention. This is Will Piper. You tell the Secretary of the Navy, you tell the Secretary of Defense, you tell the goddamned President that this is over. And you tell them right now!"

He ripped off the headset and stamped on it with his good leg.

Nancy rushed back to him. They held each other for a moment, but this wasn't the time or the place for a long embrace.

"I can't believe you're here," he said.

"I called Sue. I told her you were in trouble, that we couldn't bring in outsiders."

Sanchez had the postadrenaline shakes. She was trying to comfort Alf Kenyon and keep him from going into shock.

Will knelt and squeezed Kenyon's hand. "You're not going to die, Alf. Not for a good long time."

Kenyon grimaced in pain and nodded.

Will turned to Sanchez. "Thank you." That was all he needed to say.

Her jaw was quivering. "Nobody tries to kill my people. We protect our own. I scrambled a jet from Teterboro. We picked Nancy up in New Hampshire and flew all night. We just got here this second. Will, Mueller's dead."

"I'm sorry," Will said. He truly was.

Then it hit him that if his bus hadn't been delayed in LA,

he would have gotten to the house too early to be saved. It was meant to be, he thought.

Nancy was standing over Frazier's body. "Is this the man who killed my parents?"

"Yes."

"Good."

Will asked, "Where's Philly?"

"Laura and Greg have him up at the lake. I need to call them."

With Nancy's help, Will dragged himself back onto the sofa. "All hell's going to break loose here. Another wave of watchers is going to come. We've got to move fast."

"What do you want me to do?" she asked.

Will squeezed Kenyon's hand again. "Alf, where did Henry put the Cantwell papers?"

Weakly, "Lower desk drawer. Over there."

Nancy ran over to the desk. The parchments were in a plain folder lying on top of the 1527 book. The letters from Felix, Calvin, Nostradamus, and that simple page with the scrawl: 9 February 2027. Finis Dierum.

"Does that printer scan?" Will asked her, pointing to the printer beside the desktop computer.

It did. It was a fast, expensive one, and the pages flew out of the feeder. He had Nancy scan the Vectis letter and the others to the memory stick they recovered from Frazier's pocket.

Will opened his laptop computer, plugged in the memory stick, and clicked on HenryNet. There were sirens echoing off the hills. He needed the password. "Alf, what's Henry's network password?"

Sanchez shook the man. "He's passed out."

Will rubbed his eyes and thought for a moment.

Then he typed *2027*.

He was in.

With the wail of sirens getting closer, Will banged out a quick e-mail, attached some files, and hit SEND.

Greg, old boy, your life's never going to be the same, he thought. No one's is.

Nancy helped him to his feet and got on her tiptoes to kiss him, the only way she could reach his mouth.

He told her, "Go get the book and the papers. I want to go to the hospital, and I want to go home with you. In that order."

The only thing moving slowly in Will's life was the drip, drip, drip of the antibiotics flowing into his veins.

Lying in his bed at the New York Presbyterian Hospital on that Monday evening, he savored a rare period of solitude. From the moment the ambulances and police had arrived at Spence's house in Henderson, he'd been inundated with doctors, nurses, cops, FBI agents, and an Air Ambulance crew of EMTs that talked his ear off all the way from Vegas to New York.

His hospital room had a killer view of the East River. If it were a condo, it would have been insanely pricey. But for the first time ever, he missed his one-bedroom shoebox because that was where his wife and son were.

This was a relative calm before the storm kicked up again. He'd had his sponge bath, administered by a tough little nurse at car-wash speed. He'd picked at his dinner tray and watched a few minutes of ESPN for normalcy. Nancy would be in shortly with a shirt and a sweater to put on for the TV cameras.

Outside his door, a cordon of FBI agents protected his room and secured access to his floor. Agents from the Department of Defense and the CIA were trying to get to him, and the Attorney General was engaged in internecine warfare with his angry counterparts at the Pentagon and Homeland Security. For the moment, the FBI wall was holding firm.

The world hadn't been expecting the news that hit the streets, mailboxes, doorsteps and the Internet on a sleepy Sunday morning just before Halloween.

The headline in *The Washington Post* trumpeted a story that at first blush made people think the venerable newspaper was perpetrating a hoax:

US GOVERNMENT HAS VAST LIBRARY OF MEDIEVAL BOOKS WHICH PREDICT FUTURE BIRTHS AND DEATHS UP TO 2027; SECRET INSTALLATION AT AREA 51, NEVADA ESTABLISHED BY HARRY TRUMAN TO MINE DATA; SOURCE OF LIBRARY: A BRITISH MONASTERY; CONNECTIONS SEEN TO DOOMSDAY KILLER CASE.

by Greg Davis, Staff Reporter,
Washington Post Exclusive

The five-thousand-word story was not a hoax. It was rich in documentation and extensively quoted Will Piper, former FBI Special Agent in charge of the Doomsday case, who described the circumstances of one Mark Shackleton, computer scientist, Area 51 researcher, and the architect of a fictitious serial-killing spree in New York, and the violent government cover-up orchestrated to protect a secret desert installation hidden for six decades. The *Post* had in its possession a copy of the library database that covered the United States through the year 2027, and they had been able to successfully correlate database predictions for hundreds of individuals across the country against actual contemporaneous birth and death data.

They also had a group of letters from the fourteenth and sixteenth centuries that purported to explain the origin of the books and place them in some historical context. The article made reference to a mysterious order of monk savants on the Isle of Wight but stressed the lack of corroborating proof. Future *Post* articles would talk about the influence of the Library on famous historical figures such as John Calvin and Nostradamus.

Finally, there was the matter of 2027. In a fourteenth-century letter, there was a notation about some kind of apocalyptic end-of-days event, but the only certainty was that the books did not have entries beyond February 9, 2027.

Piper had been a target of violence that had claimed the lives of his in-laws, and he had been wounded in an action against covert government agents. His whereabouts were unknown, but his condition was reported to be stable.

On Sunday morning, the White House, the Pentagon, and the State Department all issued official no comments, but senior sources close to the administration, namely the White House Chief of Staff and the Vice President, without attribution, told the paper they had no idea what the *Post* reporter was talking about—and in retrospect they were, in fact, telling the truth. They hadn't been in the Area 51 loop.

By Monday, the official Washington language was shifting by degrees from "no comment" to "stand by for an announcement from the White House," to "the President will address the nation at 9:00 P.M. EST."

The newspaper story sparked a fire that spread across the globe at the speed of electrons. The revelations hijacked nearly every conversation on the planet. By that first evening virtually all sentient adults in the world had heard about the Library and had an opinion. People were consumed by curiosity and gripped by apprehension.

All across America, constituents called their elected representatives, and congressmen and senators called the White House.

Across the globe, worshippers flocked to their priests, rabbis, imams, and ministers, who worriedly tried to match official dogma to the supposed reality.

Heads of state and ambassadors of virtually every nation barraged the State Department with demands for information.

TV, cable, and radio airwaves devoted themselves to wall-to-wall coverage. The problem became quite apparent several hours into the news cycle that there was no one to interview. No one had heard of the *Post*'s Greg Davis, and the paper wasn't making him available to the media.

Will Piper was nowhere to be found. The *Post*'s Publisher made the rounds, standing by the story, but could do no more than repeat the facts as they had been reported. The paper was refusing to make any of the data public, referring the matter to the *Post*'s attorney at Skadden Arps, who issued a statement that matters of ownership and privacy were under study.

So, for the moment, pundits could only interview each other, and they were whipping each other into a lather while their media bookers hotly pursued philosophers and theologians, people whose phones were normally quiet on weekends.

Finally at 6:00 P.M. EST on Monday, CBS News issued an urgent press release that *60 Minutes* would present a special live televised interview with Will Piper, the source of the story. The world had only two hours to wait.

The White House was outraged that the President was being preempted, and the White House Chief of Staff called the president of CBS News to inform him that issues of national security were at stake and remind him that the man they were going to put on camera had not been interviewed by the appropriate authorities. He hinted that there could be serious charges forthcoming against Piper and that he was a potentially unreliable rogue source. The network executive politely told the White House to go pound sand and sat back to wait for a federal court to issue an injunction.

At 7:45, Will was sitting up in his hospital bed, wearing a nice blue sweater. He was bathed in TV lights. Considering what he'd been through, he looked handsome and relaxed. Nancy was there, holding his hand, whispering encouragement out of earshot of the camera crew and producers.

The network's general counsel bounded off the elevator at Will's floor, waving the faxed injunction. The network president was huddling with the show's executive producer and Jim Zeckendorf, who was there advising Will as a friend and lawyer. The network president had just finished talking to Will and was still visibly moved.

He took the injunction, folded it, and put it in his coat pocket. He told his lawyer, "This is the biggest story in history about the biggest cover-up in history. I don't care if I spend the rest of my goddamn life in jail. We're going live in fifteen minutes."

Cassie Neville, the veteran *60 Minutes* anchor, sailed down the corridor with a pack of assistants in tow. Although well into her sixties, after an hour in hair and makeup, she looked youthfully radiant, branded by her trademark steely eyes and pursed lips. Yet that night, she was frazzled by the time lines and the subject matter, and she blurted out her main concern to the network president. "Bill, do you think it's wise to do this live? What if he's a dud? We'll be dead ducks."

He replied, "Cassie, I'd like you to meet Will Piper. I've

just spent some time with him, and I can assure you, he's not a dud."

Zeckendorf piped up, "I just want to remind you that I've instructed Will not to answer any questions about the murder of the Lipinskis and the circumstances of his being wounded. There's an active criminal investigation that can't be compromised."

Nancy stepped aside when Cassie entered the room. The anchor went straight to Will's bedside and stared into his eyes. "So, I'm told you're not a dud."

"I've been called a lot of things, ma'am, but that's not one of them."

"I haven't been called 'ma'am' in a great many years. Are you from the South, Mr. Piper?"

"Florida panhandle. Redneck Riviera."

"Well, I'm pleased to meet you under these extraordinary circumstances. We go live in about ten minutes, so let's get set up. I want you to relax and be yourself. I've been told this may be the most-watched interview in history. The world wants to hear this story. Are you ready, Mr. Piper?"

"Not until you call me Will."

"Okay, Will, let's do it."

The director finger-counted down to one and pointed to Cassie, who looked up and started reading off the tele-prompter. "Good evening ladies and gentlemen, I'm Cassie Neville and tonight *60 Minutes* is bringing you a ground-breaking, exclusive interview, live from New York City, from the hospital bed of the man everyone has been talking about, to get his perspective on, what I sincerely believe, is the most extraordinary news story of our time: the revelation that a mysterious Library exists which predicts the births and deaths of every man, woman, and child on the planet."

She ad-libbed the next line. "Just saying that sends shivers down my spine. And further, that the US government has kept the knowledge of this Library a deep secret since 1947, hidden in Area 51 Nevada, where it is used for classified research purposes. And the man who has revealed this is with me today, a former FBI agent, Will Piper, who is not here in any official capacity, in fact, he was on the run and in hiding, a target of a government cover-up of the story. Well, he *was* on the run, but no longer. He's here tonight, with me to tell you his incredible story. Good evening, Will."

Cassie's jitters began to fade a few minutes into the interview. Will was calm, articulate, and so plainly credible that she and the rest of the audience hung on every word. His blue eyes and big handsome face were utterly camera-ready. From her reaction shots, it was clear she was smitten.

The facts established, she wanted to see how he felt about the Library, as if he were an everyman, a surrogate for universal reaction.

"My brother, John, passed away last year very suddenly from an aneurysm," Cassie said, a tear welling. "Someone knew about it, or could have known about this in advance?"

Will replied, "That's my understanding, yes."

"That makes me angry," she said.

"I don't blame you."

"Do you think his family should have known, do you think *he* should have known?"

"That's not for me to say. I'm not any kind of authority on morality, but it seems to me that if someone in the government has that information, it ought to be given to a person if they want it."

"And what if they don't want to know?"

"I wouldn't force it on anyone."

"Did you look yourself up?"

"I did," he answered. "I'm good until at least 2027."

"And what if you had found out that it was next week, or next month or next year instead?"

"I'm sure everyone would have a different reaction, but I think I'd take it in stride and live every day I had to the fullest. Who knows, maybe they'd be the best days of my life."

She smiled at the answer, nodding in agreement, "Twenty twenty-seven. You said the books stop in 2027."

"That's correct. On February 9 of that year."

"Why do they stop?"

"I'm not sure anyone knows."

"There was some reference to an apocalyptic event."

"I'm sure people need to look at that," Will said evenly. "It's pretty sketchy stuff, so I don't think folks should get all bent out of shape."

"Hopefully not. And you say that little is known about the people who produced these books."

He shook his head. "They obviously possessed an extraordinary power. Beyond that, I couldn't speculate. There're going to be men and women a lot more qualified to give opinions than me. I'm just a retired federal agent."

Neville set her famous jaw. "Are you a religious man?"

"I was brought up a Baptist but I'm not really religious."

"Can I ask if you believe in God?"

"Some days more than others I guess."

"Does the Library change your views?"

"It tells me there are things about the world we don't understand. I guess that's not all that surprising."

"What was your personal reaction when you learned about the existence of the Library?"

"Probably the same as most people. I was shaken. I still am."

"Tell me about Mark Shackleton, the government employee who stole the database and was shot and seriously wounded."

"I knew him from college. I was there when he was shot. He seemed like a sad fellow, I'd say pathetic."

"What motivated him to perpetrate the hoax of the Doomsday case?"

"I think it was greed. He said he wanted a better life."

"Greed."

"Yes. He was a very smart man. He was in a position to pull it off."

"If you hadn't broken the case."

"I had help—my partner, Special Agent Nancy Lipinski." He sought her out with his eyes from behind one of the cameras and smiled at her. "She's my wife now."

"Fortunate woman," Cassie said coquettishly. "The US government doesn't want us to know about the Library."

"I think that's pretty obvious, yes."

"And people within the government were willing to kill to keep the secret."

"People have died."

"You were a target."

"I was."

"Is that why you went public, why you gave the story to the press?"

He leaned forward as much as he could. "Look, I'm a patriot. I was in the FBI. I believe in law and order and our system of justice. The government can't be judge, jury, and executioner even if they're protecting classified data. I have every reason to believe that they were going to silence me, my family, and my friends if I didn't act. They killed people trying to get at me. I'd rather my fate be in the hands of my fellow citizens."

"I'm told that you're not going to answer questions about Mr. and Mrs. Lipinski or about how you got wounded. You're recovering well, I trust?"

"Yeah. All of that will come out eventually, I guess. And thanks, I'm going to be fine."

"When you were briefing the press on the supposed Doomsday case, they called you the Pied Piper. Are you?"

"I can't play the flute, and I don't particularly like rats."

"You know what I mean."

"I'm sure as heck not a follower, but I've never thought of myself as a leader either."

"That may change tonight. Tell me, why did you choose to give this to a very young reporter at *The Washington Post* who broke the story yesterday in that remarkable front-page article?"

"He's my daughter's husband. I figured this might give his career a kick."

She laughed, "What honesty!" Then she got serious again. "So, Will, last words: what should be done? Is the Library going to be released to the public? Should it be released to the public?"

"Will it be? Maybe somebody ought to ask the President that tonight. Should it be? I'd say, put a lot of smart and good people from all over the world in a big room and sort it out. It's not for me to decide. It's for the people to decide."

When the tungsten lights were off, and Will's lapel mike was shed, Nancy came out of the shadows, embraced him, and held on for dear life. "We got them," she whispered. "We got the bastards. There's nothing they can do to us now. We're safe."

The President of the United States gave a brief speech, heavy on national-security themes about the dangers the country faced from foreign enemies and the vital importance of intelligence operations. He obliquely acknowledged the role of Area 51 in the grand scheme of intelligence assets and promised to consult with congressional and world leaders in the coming days and weeks.

At his flat in Islington, Toby Parfitt, read his home-delivered copy of *The Guardian* while a croissant warmed in the toaster oven. A journalist had found the old Internet auction listing from the Pierce & Whyte catalogue. On the front page was a picture of the 1527 book with a "no comment" comment from Toby, who had been rung by the reporter the evening before for his views.

In fact he had strong views, though none for public consumption. He had held the book in his hands! He had felt an emotional connection to it. It was undoubtedly one of the most valuable books on the planet! And now there were claims that a Shakespearean sonnet had been secreted in its endpapers!

Two hundred thousand pounds! He'd sold it for only two hundred thousand pounds!

His hand shook as he lifted his cup of breakfast tea to his lips.

In a few days, the *Post* announced that no one was getting access to its copy of the database until a federal lawsuit seeking its return wended its way through the system, presumably all the way to the Supreme Court. In the meantime, the paper's newest star reporter, Greg Davis, began doing interviews and proved to be good at them.

And the media circus and the public outcry did not abate, nor would they for a very long time. Life and death were very hot topics.

On Garden Street, north of Harvard Square, most of the staff at the Harvard-Smithsonian Center for Astrophysics were having lunch at the campus cafeteria or at their desks.

Neil Gershon, an associate professor of astrophysics at Harvard and the Assistant Director of the Minor Planet Center, was cleaning a gob of mayo off his keyboard which had squirted out the end of his roast beef wrap. One of his grad students came into his office cubicle and watched with amusement.

"I'm happy to entertain you, Govi. Can I help you with something?"

The young Indian researcher smiled and accommodated his boss's forgetfulness. "You told me I could see you lunchtime, remember?"

"Oh yeah. February ninth, 2027."

Astrophysicists were suddenly popular.

The *Post* article and the Piper interview had unleashed a torrent of academic and amateur speculation on humanity-eliminating events. To dampen down the hysteria, governments turned to scientists, and scientists turned to their computer models. While they worked on the problem the popular press blithely dived in.

That very morning, *USA Today* published a survey of three thousand Americans asking about their favorite hypotheses concerning that suddenly famous date. There were a lot of theories ranging from the plausible to the ridiculous; a quarter of Americans believed that an alien invasion was in the cards, *War of the Worlds*-style. Divine retribution and the Last Judgment scored fairly high too. Asteroids were also in the double digits.

A task force was immediately established at NASA's Jet Propulsion Laboratory in Pasadena comprehensively to explore some of the plausible extraplanetary scenarios. The Minor Planet Center at Harvard-Smithsonian was assigned to sift through their Near-Earth Asteroid Tracking database to eliminate collision threats.

That was quickly accomplished. Of the 962 Potentially Hazardous Asteroids, PHAs, in the database, only one was relevant to the 2027 time frame: 137108 (1999 AN_{10}), an Apollo-class near-earth asteroid discovered in 1999 at MIT's Lincoln Lab. It was a very large body, almost thirty kilometers in diameter, but only of casual interest. Its nearest pass to earth in the next one thousand years was going to take place on August 7, 2027 at a distance of 390,000 kilometers. On the ten-point Torino Impact Hazard Scale, the asteroid rated only an anemic score of one, hardly noticeable.

To be ultraconservative and thorough, Gershon had assigned his best student, Govind Naidu, to relook at the asteroid and update its orbital parameters. The NASA project had a priority designation, and Naidu was able to cut into the queue to task the forty-eight-inch telescopes at the Maui Space Surveillance Site and at the Palomar Observatory to reimage 137108. He was also given eight precious hours of time on the government's supercomputer at the National

Energy Research Scientific Computing Center at the Lawrence Berkeley National Laboratory.

"You've got the new MSSS and Palomar data?" Gershon asked.

"Yeah. You want to go over to my workstation?"

"Just log on from here."

"You've got mayo on your keypad."

"And this is against your religion?" Gershon got up and relinquished his chair. "I've got a telecon with JPL this afternoon, and I want this nailed."

Naidu sat down and logged on to the observatory databases. "Okay, here's the orbital plot for 137108 as of the last observation point in July 2008. Right now, it's past Jupiter heading inbound with an orbital period of 1.76 years. Here's the last simulation—let me fast-forward to August 2027. You see, there, it gets within 400,000 kilometers of us."

"I need the new data, Govi."

"I'm getting there." He clicked through and opened spreadsheets that were time-stamped to the previous night. "Okay, both telescopes got clean images. Let me merge the databases from Hawaii and Palomar. It'll just take a minute."

His fingers flew over the keyboard as he conformed the two sets of observations, and when he was done, Gershon said, "Let's see it."

Naidu clicked on the orbital plotting tool and fast-forwarded the simulation to 2027. "See? It's unchanged. The closest point is still in August at a distance of almost half a million kilometers. On February 9, it's not even close."

Gershon looked satisfied. "So that's it. We can scratch 137108 off the *oy vey* list."

Naidu didn't get up. He was accessing the Lawrence Berkeley database. "I thought you might get more questions, so I ran a series of scenarios on the NERSCC supercomputer."

"What kind of scenarios?"

"Asteroid-asteroid hits."

Gershon grunted his approval. The young man was right, he'd probably get the question. There were about five thousand asteroids in the main belt between Mars and Jupiter, and it wasn't unprecedented for them to slam into each other from time to time, changing their orbital characteristics. "How'd you model it?"

Naidu puffed out his chest and proudly described a sophisticated statistical model he'd constructed which exploited the massive computing power at the NERSCC to examine hundreds of thousands of hypothetical asteroid-to-asteroid strikes involving 137108.

"Lot of second-body variables," Gershon whistled. "Mass, speed, angle of contact, orbital dynamics at point of collision."

Naidu nodded. "Each potential hit can change every parameter of 137108. Sometimes not by a lot, but you can get meaningful differences to the aphelion, the perihelion, the orbital period, the ascending node longitude, the inclination, the argument of perihelion, you name it."

"So show me. What do you have?"

"Okay, since I had only eight hours of computing time, I limited the model to about five hundred higher-probability asteroids based on their orbital characteristics with respect to 137108. Only one simulation out of six hundred thousand produced something interesting."

Naidu launched a graphical-simulation program and provided running commentary. "This one assumes an asteroid-to-asteroid collision between 137108 and 4581 Asclepius, an

Apollo-class object that's just a little guy, about three hundred meters diameter. It passed within 700,000 kilometers of earth in 1989. If it had hit, it would have been no big deal," he snorted, "just the equivalent to one Hiroshima-sized explosion every second for fifty days! This simulation assumes 4581 gets tweaked by another rock, gets its own orbit perturbed, and hits 137108 near Jupiter in March 2016. Here's what goes down if that happens."

Naidu set the orbital simulator to run from the present. On the screen they watched a green dot representing 137108 move through the solar system in an eccentric elliptical orbit, approaching the earth approximately every two years, then sling-shotting past Jupiter before turning back again toward the sun.

When the simulation got within five years of 2027, he slowed it down so they could watch it more carefully. They stared at two independent orbits, the earth's and the asteroid's, a green dot and a red dot moving through the solar system. At a January 2026 time-point, Naidu slowed the simulation again to a snail's pace.

Gershon leaned in over his student's shoulder. "It's really hard to say visually whether its new orbital is going to make things better or worse."

Naidu said nothing.

The clock turned slowly and at mid-2026, asteroid 137108 turned toward the sun. The earth's orbit was slowly positioning the planet to get close to an intersection with the asteroid's track.

October 2026.

November 2026.

December 2026.

January 2027.

The red and green dots were getting close.

Then February 2027.

The simulation halted on February 9.

A pop-up box appeared on the screen:

Impact Probability – 100% ****Torino 10****
Torino 10****Torino 10****

Gershon gasped. "The asteroid's size. Does it change postimpact with 4581?"

Naidu scrolled down to a table, double-clicked on a cell, and pointed. "It's still huge, a game-ender." He logged off the terminal and stood up. "It's all hypothetical, but I thought you needed to see it. We're not talking about large probabilities."

Gershon looked out the window. It was a blustery fall day, and sharp gusts were separating the last leaves from their branches. He had an urge to feel the wind on his face and to crunch through the dry leaf piles on the lawn.

He gently touched his student's shoulder, and said, "I'm sure you're right, Govi. Listen, I'm going to go out for a little walk."

The earthquake struck at 11:05 A.M. The epicenter of the 7.8 mag event was twenty kilometers east of Caracas along the El Pilar Fault. At the moment the first tremor hit, the day was sunny and windy, the sky, hazy blue with wisps of fast-moving clouds. Forty seconds later, the sun was blotted out by plumes of concrete dust rising above pancaked apartment blocks, high-rise offices, municipal buildings, and schools. Then ruptured gas lines started fires, which were wind-whipped into conflagrations that roared through the historic Altamira district and the Parque Central Complex.

Eighty percent of the 220,000 casualties occurred within seconds of the first shock—men, women, and children mercilessly crushed to death by steel, glass, and masonry. Most of those trapped under the rubble would fall victim to slow dehydration. Others would be killed by the serious aftershocks and fires which plagued the city for the next seventy-two hours.

Incoming telemetry lit up the Global Seismographic Network like a Christmas tree. At the USGS monitoring site at the Albuquerque Seismological Lab, the Caracas quake was immediately classified as a Major Seismic Event, and, per protocol, hot-line calls went out to Homeland Security, the Pentagon, the State Department, and the White House.

In the C Ring of the Pentagon, deep within its inner core, the Secretary of the Navy got the news from a minor aide to the Deputy Secretary of Defense. Lester listened, grunted an acknowledgment, and hung up. He'd been consumed with the planning for this day for two years, and this was not the way it was supposed to go down.

The Mission Plan stipulated that at the moment the Caracas Event occurred, Lester would descend to a command bunker in a Pentagon subbasement and authorize the US Southern Command to signal the Fourth Fleet. The fleet would be positioned north of Aruba, engaged in a mock joint exercise with the British Royal Navy. They would be ordered to proceed to Venezuela as the spearhead of Operation Helping Hand. Key Venezuelan opposition leaders and senior dissident army officers would be standing by with their families in Valencia, out of harm's way. They'd be choppered into the capital city and under the protection of a US Marine expeditionary force, the government would be tilting toward Washington within twenty-four hours.

None of that happened.

Will Piper single-handedly blew up Operation Helping Hand.

After the *Post* story broke, the Vice President urgently convened a Task Force meeting and shut Helping Hand down: no adjustments, no modifications, just ash-canned. There was zero dissent. Anyone with a brain in their head would connect the dots between Area 51 and a military operation that looked in retrospect like it was preplanned to coincide with the disaster.

The humanitarian supplies would be airlifted, and the

prompt US response would be cordially received by the shell-shocked Venezuelan president, who vowed to rebuild Caracas and continue the country on its socialist path.

Two years of work, down the drain.

Lester sighed, checked his day planner, and told his secretary he was going out. His afternoon was wide open, and he decided he'd head over to his club and pick up a game of squash.

EPILOGUE
SIX MONTHS LATER
ISLE OF WIGHT

It was a sparkling, fresh spring afternoon, the sun impossibly yellow, the newly mown grass impossibly green. Across the meadows, the seagulls were soaring over the Solent, urgently calling to one another.

The redbrick tower of the abbey church rising into the clean blue sky gave the tourists an irresistible snapshot opportunity. Although Vectis Abbey had always been open to the public, the revelations about its ancient Library had turned it into a substantial point of interest, much to the consternation of the resident monks. On weekends, local women from the village of Fishbourne volunteered to conduct guided tours, mostly to encourage visitors into bunches as this was less disruptive to the routine of monastery life than having people aimlessly wandering through the church and the abbey grounds.

The baby in the stroller began to cry. The tourists, mostly seniors well past their infant-loving years, looked annoyed, but his parents were unfazed.

His mother checked his diaper. "I'm going to find a place to change him," Nancy said, peeling off toward the teahouse.

Will nodded and kept listening to the guide, a heavily

haunched middle-aged woman who was pointing at tender shoots sprouting up from behind a rabbit fence and expounding on the importance of vegetables to a fraternal order.

He'd been looking forward to the vacation to escape the hectic world he'd created for himself. There were still interviews to give, books to write, all the unwanted trappings of celebrity. Even now, paparazzi hung around 23rd Street. And he had newly found obligations. Alf Kenyon, who had largely recovered from his knee wound, was going to be going on a tour in a few months to promote his book on John Calvin, Nostradamus, and the Cantwell papers. Kenyon asked him to do some media with him, and he couldn't say no. And Dane Bentley had a bachelor party and a wedding coming up, although Will still wasn't sure which of his girlfriends he was marrying.

For the moment, Will was able to put the swirl of recent months out of his mind and concentrate on the here and now. He was fascinated with everything about their island visit—the chilly, wind-strafed car-ferry crossing from the mainland, the pub lunch in Fishbourne, where he wavered at the bar before ordering a Coke, the first glimpse of the monastery from the footpath, the sight of the robed monks, who, despite their habits and sandals, looked like ordinary men—until they filed into the church precisely at 2:20 for the None service. Inside the sanctuary, the monks were transformed into different sorts, all together. Their concentration at prayer and song, their intensity of purpose, the seriousness of their spiritual pleasure set them apart from the visitors, who sat at the rear of the vaulted church, curious observers, awkwardly voyeuristic.

The monks were now at afternoon work, some tending the garden and the chicken coops, others indoors in the kitchen, the pottery, or bookbinder's shop. There weren't many of

them, fewer than a dozen, mostly older men. The young in-
frequently sought the monk's life these days. The tour was
winding down, and Will hadn't yet seen what he came for. His
hand shot up along with the hands of others. They all wanted
the same thing, and the guide knew what was coming.

She called on him because he stood out from the crowd,
tall and handsome, his eyes shining with intelligence. "I'd
like to see the medieval monastery."

The group murmured. That's what everyone wanted.

"Yes, funny you should ask!" she joked. "I was going
to point you in the right direction. It's less than a quarter
mile up that lane. Everyone wants to go there lately, not that
there's much to see. Just some ruins. But seriously, ladies
and gentlemen, I understand the interest, and I encourage
you to visit the site for some quiet contemplation. The spot
has been marked with a small plaque."

As the guide was answering questions, she kept staring
at Will, and when she was done, she approached him and
unself-consciously inspected his face.

"Thanks for the tour," he told her.

"May I ask you something?"

He nodded.

"By any chance, are you Mr. Piper, the American who's
been in the news over all this?"

"Yes, ma'am."

She beamed. "I thought so! Would you mind if I told the
abbot you're here. I think he'll want to meet you."

Dom Trevor Hutchins, the Lord Abbot of Vectis Abbey was
a portly, white-haired man brimming with enthusiasm. He
led Will and Nancy up the gravel lane toward the crumbling
medieval walls of the ancient monastery and asked to push
the stroller to "give the young man a ride."

He insisted on repeating the history that Will and Nancy had just heard about the medieval abbey being shuttered and looted by King Henry's Reformation in 1536, the masonry dismantled stone by stone and shipped to Cowes and Yarmouth for castle-building and fortification. All that now remained were the ragged ghosts of the grand complex, low walls and foundations.

The modern abbey was built in the early twentieth century by French monks who used red bricks to revive the Benedictine tradition, choosing to build near the hallowed ground of the old abbey. The abbot himself was approaching his twenty-fifth year at Vectis, having joined as a young man fresh from a classics degree at Cambridge.

Around a bend, the rough, tumbledown walls came into view. The ruins were in a field overlooking the Solent, the south coast of England looming across the narrow stretch of sea. The pebbled walls that had survived the centuries were clipped-off facades with a few remaining cutouts where windows and arches had been. Sheep were grazing around the ruins.

"Behold ancient Vectis!" the abbot said. "Is it what you expected, Mr. Piper?"

"It's peaceful."

"Yes it is. We have bags of peace here." He pointed out the walls that had belonged to the cathedral, the chapter house, and the dormitories. Farther off were scattered low remains of the medieval abbey wall.

"Where was the Library?"

"Not here. Farther on. Unsurprisingly, they appear to have tucked it away in a far corner."

Will held Nancy's hand as they reached the depression in an adjacent grassy meadow, a large rectangular hollow dipping a meter below the level of the rest of the field. At the edge of the low-lying ground was a newly laid granite marker with a bronze plaque. The inscription was starkly simple: THE LIBRARY OF VECTIS—782–1297.

The abbot stood over the marker, and said, "This was your gift to the world, Mr. Piper. I've read all about what you did on the Internet."

Nancy laughed at the thought of monks online.

"Oh, yes, we have a high-speed connection!" the abbot boasted.

"Not everyone thinks what I did was a gift," he said.

"Well, it's certainly not a curse. The truth never is. I find everything about the Library very reassuring. I can feel God's unwavering hand at work. I feel a connection with Abbot Felix and all his predecessors who zealously protected and nurtured the great endeavor as if it were a delicate orchid that would perish if the temperature was one degree higher or lower. I've taken to coming here for meditation."

"Does 2027 concern you?" Nancy asked.

"We live in the present here. Our community concerns itself with working together to praise the Lord, to celebrate the mass and to pray the Holy Scriptures. In essence, our concern, is to know Christ Jesus. The year 2027, asteroids, and all those things are not our concern."

Will smiled at him. "If you ask me, all the fuss about the 2027 is probably for the good. The whole world's going to be too focused on space rocks and that kind of stuff to beat up on each other. For once, we've got a common goal. Win or lose, my guess is it's going to be the best seventeen years we've ever had."

The abbot turned the stroller over to Nancy. "He's a fine

young man, and he has good parents. He's got a bright future. I'm going to leave you now. Stay as long as you like."

When they were alone, Nancy asked him, "Are you glad you came?"

He looked down into the hollow and imagined the green-eyed, ginger-haired scribes who mutely labored there for centuries, the monks who guarded their secret as a sacred obligation, the final blood-spattered catastrophe that ended it all. He imagined what the library would have looked like, the vast assemblage of thick, heavy books in their cavernous vault. He was still hoping that one day, he'd be invited to Nevada to see what the Library looked like now. But he wasn't holding his breath.

"Yeah, I'm glad. And I'm glad you and Philly are here with me." He looked across the meadow toward the sea. "God, it's peaceful here."

They stayed for a while, until the sun started to set. They had a ferry to catch and a long drive. In a family cemetery in Shakespeare country, he had a grave under a lime tree he wanted to visit before they flew back to Miami. Nancy had a new Bureau job in Florida to settle into and a house to decorate.

And he had some fishing to do in the beckoning waters of the Gulf of Mexico.

ELECTRIFYING THRILLERS FROM INTERNATIONAL BESTSELLER

GLENN COOPER

ECRET OF THE SEVENTH SON

978-0-06-172179-3

ine people have been slain in New York City—
ne strangers with nothing in common—the
parent victims of a frighteningly elusive
rial killer. Only one thing links the dead:
ostcards they received, mailed from Las Vegas,
nouncing the day they would die.

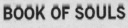

BOOK OF SOULS

978-0-06-172180-9

The Library: Only a handful of people know it
exists. It holds the world's most astonishing—
and terrifying—information. But the one
book that is the key to the greatest secret of
all time . . . is missing.